W9-BPK-927

PRAISE FOR

THE FORGOTTEN SOLDIER

"COMPARISONS TO VINCE FLYNN AND BRAD THOR ARE EXPECTED . . . BUT TAYLOR IS NOW IN A CLASS BY HIMSELF."
—*BOOKLIST* (STARRED REVIEW)

"THE LIGHTNING-FAST PLOT FILLED WITH TRADECRAFT AND INTRIGUING POLITICS WILL SATISFY SERIES FANS AND NEWCOMERS ALIKE."
—*LIBRARY JOURNAL*

"BRAD TAYLOR TAKES HIS CONSIDERABLE TALENTS TO A NEW LEVEL . . . [BRINGING] US INTO THE ACTUAL MIND-SET OF THE SPECIAL OPS WORLD HE KNOWS SO WELL."
—*PROVIDENCE JOURNAL*

"A REALISTIC PAGE-TURNER THAT FILLS A NEED FOR THRILLS WHILE QUESTIONING THE COMPLICATED PROCESS OF STATECRAFT."
—*KIRKUS REVIEWS*

Praise for the Novels of Brad Taylor

The Forgotten Soldier

"Taylor has become one of the very best writers of thrillers with a military and special-ops background. His consistency and his ability to mirror headline news with relevant, engrossing narratives are uncanny, and this exploration of the human side of war should quickly be recognized as one of Taylor's best efforts. Comparisons to Vince Flynn and Brad Thor are expected and not inaccurate, but Taylor is now in a class by himself."

—*Booklist* (starred review)

The Insider Threat

"The alternating first- and third-person viewpoints offer up a splendidly intense plot peeled back layer by layer in the best tradition of Jack Higgins and Frederick Forsyth." —*Providence Journal*

"Through well-defined characters and dialogue this novel is a page-turner that is a must read."

—*Military Press*

"Strongly recommended for the many fans of the 'Logan' series and those who enjoy a breakneck pace. . . . Taylor gives hope for a positive resolution to today's hostilities." —*Library Journal*

No Fortunate Son

"With his latest, Taylor firmly entrenches himself on the level of James Rollins, Vince Flynn, and Brad Thor as the modern master of the military thriller."

—*Providence Journal*

"Logan and Cahill are a dream team, and military-thriller fans who seek realistic scenarios should consider Taylor mandatory reading." —*Booklist*

"A chilling novel for our time, with a frighteningly realistic plot." —*The Huffington Post*

"Few authors write about espionage, terrorism, and clandestine hit squads as well as Taylor does, and with good reason. . . . His boots-on-the-ground insight into the situation in the Middle East and special skills in 'irregular warfare' and 'asymmetric threats' give his writing a realistic, graphic tone."   —*Houston Press*

"Taylor gets exponentially better with each book, and if someone is hunting for a literary franchise to turn into a film, they need to be looking at this series."—*Bookreporter*

All Necessary Force

"Fresh plot, great action, and Taylor clearly knows what he is writing about. . . . When it comes to tactics and hardware, he is spot-on."
   —#1 *New York Times* bestselling author Vince Flynn

"The first few pages alone . . . should come with a Surgeon General's warning if you have a weak heart."
                              —*Bookreporter*

"This fast-moving thriller poses the dilemma: Must he obey the law, or must he use all necessary force to thwart the enemy? Well written, edgy, and a damn good yarn."
                              —*Kirkus Reviews*

One Rough Man

"Taylor's debut flows like the best of Vince Flynn and Brad Thor. An intense and intriguing character, Logan is definitely an action hero to watch."   —*Booklist*

"Brad Taylor has created a feisty, devil-may-care hero in Pike Logan. . . . A coiling plot, crisp writing, and constant braids of suspense make *One Rough Man* one exciting read."   —*New York Times* bestselling author Steve Berry

"A fast and furious tale with a boots-on-the-ground realism that could only have been evoked by someone who intimately knows combat. . . . Pike Logan is a tough, appealing hero you're sure to root for."
         —*New York Times* bestselling author Joseph Finder

Also by Brad Taylor

One Rough Man
All Necessary Force
Enemy of Mine
The Widow's Strike
The Polaris Protocol
Days of Rage
No Fortunate Son
The Insider Threat
The Forgotten Soldier
Ghosts of War

Short Works

The Callsign
Gut Instinct
Black Flag
The Dig
The Recruit

THE
FORGOTTEN
SOLDIER

★★★★★★★★★★★★★★★★★★

BRAD TAYLOR

A Pike Logan Thriller

DUTTON

DUTTON

An imprint of Penguin Random House LLC
375 Hudson Street
New York, New York 10014

Previously published as a Dutton hardcover.

First premium mass market printing, January 2017

Copyright © 2016 by Brad Taylor
Excerpt from *Ring of Fire* copyright © 2016 by Brad Taylor
Penguin supports copyright. Copyright fuels creativity, encourages diverse
voices, promotes free speech, and creates a vibrant culture. Thank you for
buying an authorized edition of this book and for complying with copyright
laws by not reproducing, scanning, or distributing any part of it in any form
without permission. You are supporting writers and allowing Penguin to
continue to publish books for every reader.

DUTTON is a registered trademark and the D colophon is a
trademark of Penguin Random House LLC

ISBN 978-0-451-47719-4

Printed in the United States of America
1 3 5 7 9 10 8 6 4 2

For every soldier who has paid the ultimate price in the Graveyard of Empires. You are not forgotten.

For it's Tommy this, an' Tommy that, an'
"Chuck him out, the brute!"
But it's "Saviour of 'is country" when the
guns begin to shoot!

Rudyard Kipling, "Tommy"

★ THE FORGOTTEN SOLDIER ★

★ 1 ★

The box arrived at the front door like any other delivery. It had nothing on the outside detailing what it held. Nothing to show that what was inside was anything other than an online order. Just a FedEx label on brown cardboard. Maybe a fantasy kit inspired by *Fifty Shades of Grey*. Or maybe not. Treating this like every other delivery, the FedEx driver ringing the bell had no idea that what it contained were the final vestiges of a man who'd given his life fighting in a land far, far away. A land that most of America had forgotten, precisely because the sacrifices represented by the contents of the box allowed them to do so.

Putting on a plain oxford shirt, Guy George heard the bell and was surprised. He wasn't expecting anyone, and he was more worried about a meeting he had to attend in forty-five minutes. A meeting he knew would be crucial to his future. He didn't have time for someone selling Girl Scout cookies.

Tucking in his shirt, he padded to the front door in his socks, a little bewildered that someone would bother him here—in his condominium, behind the gate of security at the building's entrance. He put his eye to the peephole, expecting to see a mother who lived in his tower, a child in tow, exploiting her ability to penetrate security to sell raffle tickets or something else. What he saw was a FedEx man, and he felt his stomach clench.

He knew what the man held. It had arrived days earlier than he expected, but he knew.

Usually, FedEx deliveries were dropped off downstairs, but he'd told the management of the tower he lived in that this box was special and that he would sign for it personally. It wasn't outside of the ordinary, given his job. At least, given the job the management thought he held. There had been more than one box that came to his door, all having to be signed for personally. It came with the territory, so much so that he knew the FedEx man by name.

He opened the door and said, "Hey, Carl."

"Got another one for you. You must have some pull. You're the only apartment they let me up for."

Guy smiled, feeling ill, and said, "Not really. That's for me?"

"Yeah. I haven't had a delivery for your roommate in over a year. He must be on the shit list."

Carl grinned at his joke, and Guy felt like punching him for no reason whatsoever. It wasn't Carl's fault. He couldn't possibly understand the sore he was poking with that statement, especially today. Truthfully, Guy should have moved out a year ago, precisely to prevent such questions, because Guy's roommate was dead. Just like the man represented by the contents of the box Carl held.

Carl sensed a shift and said, "Welp, just sign here and it's yours. Not nearly as heavy as some other stuff I've delivered."

Guy thought about signing his brother's name. Just as a memory. But didn't.

Guy waved at Carl and shut the door, grasping the box in his hands as if it held a secret truth. He knew that was stupid. He'd done inventories for the very reasons this box held, more times than he wanted to remember. He just didn't know, in this case, that the box *did* hold a truth, and it was dark.

He went back into the living room, glancing at the other bedroom. The empty one. He remembered inventorying everything in it as if he'd done it yesterday. The pictures and notes. The flotsam and jetsam accumulated in life that seemed like trash but took on a special meaning when the person they were attached to never returned.

Putting them all in a box like the one in his hands.

He placed the package reverently on the floor, then glanced at his watch, one eye on the cardboard as if it would do something. He was running out of time, and the boss didn't take kindly to subordinates being late. But he might for this.

He pulled out an auto-opening knife from the inside of his waistband and flicked it, the black steel of the blade looking for something to bite, the weapon a stark contrast to his business-casual dress. He took a knee. He sliced the tape, the blade moving as easily as if it were touching air. He methodically went through every joint the tape touched, not pulling. Only slicing. Delaying the inevitable. Eventually, there was nothing left to cut.

He sat for a moment, then opened the box.

The first thing he saw was a sterile US Army bureaucratic inventory sheet detailing what was inside. He knew it wouldn't be accurate, because he'd made a call. He set it aside and saw the MultiCam uniform. He pulled it out and took in the damage. The ragged tears and burned edges. The blood.

Guy turned the phone on, surprised to see it had a charge. The screen appeared and he saw the Pandora app. He clicked on it, not wanting to, but wanting to. He found the channel his brother had talked about the night he died, telling him it was the perfect one for the warrior. Kidding him about how Guy's music tastes had shifted since he'd left the Special Mission Unit. Ribbing Guy for no longer being in the fight.

But his brother didn't know what Guy did now.

The app engaged and the music softly floated out. Guy shut it off, staring at the screen. Wondering if Pandora understood the significance of a music channel from beyond the grave, his brother working laboriously to thumbs-up and thumbs-down songs until he thought it was perfect.

He put the phone aside and pulled out an armband, not unlike what NFL quarterbacks wore detailing plays. About four inches long, with Velcro straps to cinch it to the forearm, it was the last target his brother had chased. A bit of history that nobody outside of Afghanistan should see.

Four pictures with Arabic names were under the plastic, followed by radio callsigns, medevac frequencies, and other coordination measures. Guy was surprised it had been included. He wanted the essence of his brother, but not what his brother was chasing. He understood operational security. Understood that his brother's target wasn't in the equation. Soldiers died all the time. Some valiantly, others because they happened to drive down the wrong road at the wrong time.

And then he found himself staring at the pictures on the armband. Thinking. Wondering.

Hating.

★ 2 ★

Even though he was late, Guy chose to walk the short distance to his office. Inside a building a block long, the only thing indicating what was within was a small brass plaque proclaiming Blaisdell Consulting. Behind those doors was anything but a consulting firm.

He could have driven, as his office building had an underground garage, but that would have taken just as long, if not longer, and he wanted the time to think.

He put in his earbuds and brought up his Pandora app, signing in as his brother. He'd managed to manipulate the login on his brother's phone and now could listen to the channel on his own device. The music came through, and he began rehearsing his speech. The one he was going to use on his boss.

The meeting was supposed to be for coordination about some ridiculous award he was getting for his actions on a target in Dubrovnik, Croatia, but the request had been a little odd. The boss didn't usually schedule premeetings for awardees in his office. Everyone knew the awards were bullshit anyway, given out to keep them competitive with their military peers. Men who weren't buried in an organization so secret it didn't even have a name.

Guy, like everyone he worked with, lived a dual life. While showing up at Blaisdell Consulting for his real work, he was also, ostensibly, one more military cog in one of Fort Myer's motor pools, just off Arlington Cemetery in Washington, DC. Which, given he hadn't served a day there, would be odd if you asked for a reference from the men and women who actually turned wrenches on Fort Myer. Stranger still, his rank was sergeant major. Not really cog material anymore, but he had to be sheep-dipped somewhere, and Fort Myer worked. To maintain the facade, his military records had to show progress, so every once in a while, he—like every other member of the Taskforce—was thrown the bone of an award.

None of the men gave a crap about them, and they understood that—while the Oversight Council presented them proudly—they were really used just to maintain the cover. But Colonel Kurt Hale, the commander of the Taskforce, understood this as well, which made the scheduled meeting odd.

Guy hit Arlington Boulevard in the shadow of the Iwo Jima memorial, the green carpet of Arlington directly behind, speckled with white dots. In the distance he saw a blip of brown against the green, upturned earth from a burial, and recognized it as Section 60, an area of Arlington he knew well. The Global War on Terrorism section. It was where his brother would earn his own pile of brown. The thought brought him up short.

He ignored the honking horns and speeding Washington lobbyists on Arlington Boulevard, all of whom drove by this national treasure every single day, completely oblivious to the sacrifices it held. He fixated on the piece of brown desecrating the expanse of green. He felt a darkness cloak him. A blackness blanketing his soul, and it was unsettling. He'd known many men who were killed in combat, but this was different. This was *his* blood.

He cranked the volume on his iPhone and began speed-walking down the sidewalk, rehearsing his speech.

★ 3 ★

Clearly irritated, Colonel Kurt Hale looked at his watch and said, "Where the hell is he?"

Johnny, Guy's team leader, said, "He's on the way. He just texted."

Kurt shook his head. "This isn't helping his case."

Johnny said, "Sir, he got the box today. Just now. Give him a break."

Kurt leaned back, taking in the words. "Bad timing. I don't think it's a discussion anymore. I no longer want to feel him out. I want him on ice, for at least a month. Get him involved in something operational, here in headquarters, but he's not deploying with you."

Axe, the second-in-command of the team, said, "Sir, wait a minute. We need him. We can't deploy without a teammate. We run bare bones as it is. Just take a look when he gets here."

Kurt said nothing. Johnny chimed in, "Sir, really, you can't give him an award and then tell him he's on ice. What signal is that sending?"

"Spare me. You and I both know how much this award means to him. Jack squat. I can't have a guy on the edge. Especially where you're going."

George Wolffe, Kurt's deputy commander and an old

CIA hand, said, "We all know the stakes, but a blanket statement is a little much. We've all lost someone along the way, and we kept fighting. We aren't talking about a Pike situation here. Let's feel him out before making a decision."

Johnny nodded in appreciation. Kurt scowled at his deputy and started to respond, when a shadow passed in the hallway. Guy leaned in, lightly knocking on the door-jamb.

He took in the audience and said, "Hey, sorry I'm late."

Kurt saw the emotions flit across his face, recognizing who was in the room, and knew Guy understood this was more than a coordination meeting. He said, "Come on in, Guy. Have a seat."

Guy did so, glancing at his team leader, then at his 2IC. "What's up? I know this isn't about some bullshit ceremony. If you thought I was going to embarrass the Taskforce, you wouldn't have sent me to Croatia to begin with."

Kurt said, "Yes. It isn't about the ceremony. You're due to deploy tomorrow with your team, but I'm not sure you should. Make no mistake, this is my call. The men in this room feel otherwise."

He saw Guy relax, realizing it wasn't an ambush.

Guy said, "I'm good. I can operate. I'm on my game."

Despite what he'd said earlier, George Wolffe went into attack mode. "Good? You took Decoy's death last year pretty damn hard. You hit the bottle. Don't tell me you didn't. You were on the edge then, and you barely pulled out. You've done solid work since then, but now you've had another sacrifice. There's no shame in taking a break. None at all."

Decoy was the name of Guy's roommate who'd been

killed in action on a mission in Istanbul. The death had been hard for everyone, but especially for Guy.

Guy said, "What do you want me to say? That my brother meant nothing? That I'm a robot? People die in combat all the time. Jesus. We'd have never left the Normandy beach if everyone who'd lost a friend was sidelined."

Kurt said, "This isn't Normandy, and you know it. We operate in a world without mistakes. Period. You fuck up, and you bring us all down. I need every man at one hundred percent."

He flicked his head toward Johnny and Axe. "They seem to think you're okay. I do not. I'm thinking you stay home for this one. Get your head on right. Axe said you weren't even going to the memorial in Montana, which raises a concern with me."

Guy said, "Sir, I can't go to the memorial. All I'll get is questions like 'Weren't you in the military?' and 'What do you do now?' I don't need to go back to respect my brother. That's for my family. It has nothing to do with how I feel. Shit, why are you even giving me an award?"

Kurt said, "Don't go there. You earned it, even if you don't want it. Don't make this into something else. This is Taskforce business, not Oversight Council."

Guy flared. "Those fat fucks have no idea of the sacrifice. *None*. Fuck them."

The words settled, the air now still. Guy shifted in his chair, but nobody else moved. Softly, Kurt said, "I think I could use you here in headquarters. Doing research. Our analysts are the best in the world, but they could use an Operator's touch. Show them what they're missing. Show them what to look for."

To Kurt's surprise, Guy leaned forward and said, "I could do that. If you let me research something specific."

Kurt looked at George, wondering where this was going. He said, "What?"

Guy pulled out the operational armband and held it up. "This. These are the fucks that killed my brother. And I want them. They're terrorists, and it *is* Taskforce business. Look, I know they aren't something that'll destroy democracy or cause the downfall of a country. They aren't high enough as a threat for the usual Taskforce envelope—but they killed my brother. Let me find them."

Axe leaned forward and took the armband, analyzing the targets on it.

Sensing buy-in of his stand-down order but wary of where it would lead, Kurt held up his hands and said, "Guy, come on. We don't do overt actions in a war zone. Yeah, you can research them, but we aren't going to hunt Taliban in Afghanistan."

Kurt saw Guy's eyes gleam and knew he'd lanced a boil, the heat coming out like a fervent missionary. Guy wanted to believe. "They aren't Taliban. Tim was hunting ISIS, and the fuckers in that target package aren't Pashtun or Uzbek or anything else in Afghanistan. They're Gulf Arabs, and they're funding the fight. It's right up our alley."

Kurt glanced again at George, his plan of sidelining Guy now taking a different turn. George said, "Guy, okay, you want to use our assets for research, that's fine. But understand we aren't going after them. A couple of Arabs in Afghanistan doesn't rise to our level. That's an Afghanistan problem. A NATO problem. Not a Taskforce problem."

Guy simply looked at him. George continued. "You understand that, right? Your brother was killed in combat, but we don't react to that. We execute actions based on the national threat. Period. We aren't in the vendetta business."

Guy said, "I got that loud and clear. I understand. I'll stand down for a spell and let these guys go have the fun." He pointed at a wide-screen television behind Kurt's head, tuned to cable news. "But that fat asshole had better be at my award ceremony."

Kurt turned and saw Jonathan Billings, the secretary of state, exiting a building, followed by a scrum of men dressed in traditional Gulf attire.

He rotated back around and grinned. "Yeah, that 'fat asshole' will be there. He's leaving Qatar tomorrow. He was doing something with investment in Greece. The ceremony isn't for a week. I'll make sure he's here."

Kurt should have reprimanded Guy for the slur, but Billings *was* an asshole. Out of the thirteen members in the Oversight Council—the only people read on to Taskforce activities in the entire US government—he was the single sticking point, constantly fighting any operation solely because he was afraid of the exposure. Afraid for his own skin, regardless of the deaths that were saved by Taskforce intervention.

In truth, Kurt understood the reticence. If Taskforce activities were exposed, it would make Watergate's revelations look like they'd detailed shoplifting at the local 7-Eleven, but Billings constantly erred on the side of caution, preferring that the terrorist attack occur to prevent his own political demise. Kurt lived in the same world, and held the same fear of exposure, but despised Billings for his willingness to sacrifice American lives. It was a fine line, and as far as Kurt was concerned, Billings was always on the wrong side.

Kurt said, "So we're good? You spend a spell here, and Johnny takes the team without you?"

Guy nodded and Axe said, "Holy shit. Look at the guy behind Billings."

They turned, seeing a well-manicured Arab wearing traditional Gulf dress, a Rolex on his wrist and a blazing smile. Kurt said, "What about him?"

Axe held up the armband and pointed at a picture. "It's this guy."

Guy became agitated, leaning into the TV. He said, "It *is* him. He's the one. I knew it wasn't some fleabag Taliban hit. That guy killed my brother!"

Kurt said, "Hold on. Jesus. Calm down. That *guy* is Haider al-Attiya. His father is a bigwig with the Qatar Investment Authority. They have nothing to do with any attacks in Afghanistan. Billings is working with them on the Greek euro crisis. The kid is a rich Gulf Arab, with a silver spoon shoved up his ass."

Guy said, "Look at him. Then look at the picture. It's him."

Kurt glanced at George, knowing he needed to stamp out wild conspiracy theories. George said, "Guy. Look at me. You're giving me worry about your control. The man on TV is a respected member of the Qatari government. Don't make this into something it's not from a damn CNN clip. Don't make me doubt you."

Guy said nothing, still staring at the screen. Kurt leaned over and took the armband away from Axe. He said, "This man's name is Abu Kamal."

A wolf smile spread across Guy's face. "Yeah, like he'd use his real name in Afghanistan. That's him. And that's his picture."

Kurt balled up the armband and said, "Don't go all Alex Jones on me here. Keep the conspiracies within the realm of the possible."

Guy leaned back and said, "All right. Okay. I'm good

with sitting out the deployment. I'll stay and do a little help on the analytical side."

Kurt said, "I think it would be better if you went home. For the memorial."

"No. I already told you. Too painful. I'll help out you guys here. Even if I can't deploy. I'm good."

Kurt sized him up, trying to see if Guy was really as even-keeled as he professed. He wasn't sure, but honestly, it wasn't like the man had threatened to go postal. And he *was* a Taskforce Operator. Handpicked by Kurt himself.

Kurt said, "Okay. Then it's settled. You help on the analytical side and take some time off. But you'll see the psychs here. No questions asked. You can tell them whatever you want, but you're seeing them."

He saw Guy bristle and leaned forward, speaking barely above a whisper. "Guy. Trust me. They can help. I've walked your path. Talk to them. I don't need to lose an Operator over something that can be helped."

Guy let the words settle, then nodded. Johnny exhaled, glad it was over. He clapped Guy on the back and said, "Hey, if there's anything to the Qatar thing, Pike will find it. He drew the card for the James Bond mission."

Guy looked confused, and Johnny snapped back in embarrassment, stealing a glance at Kurt. Speaking of compartmented missions was a nonstarter, and he just had. Kurt waved it off and said, "Pike's investigating some ties between Brazil and Qatar. Nothing to do with this."

Kurt saw a wicked grin slip out. Guy said, "Pike's on it? Oh yeah, if there's a connection, he'll find it. That guy's a trouble magnet."

★ 4 ★

I caught a flicker of movement in the corner of my eye and froze. *This* was the time. I was sure of it. Slowly, ever so slowly, I turned my head, looking at our kitchen counter. Sure enough, I saw the enemy, crouched and eating a crumb. The damn bane of my existence. A mouse that had been terrorizing my house with turds and torn-open bread loafs.

I slowly swiveled my head to the front door, listening. I heard nothing. Jennifer had an irrational soft spot for "innocent" foragers, but she was probably a good five minutes behind me on our run. Five minutes to crush the skeevy life out of that damn spawn of Satan, dispose of the carcass where she wouldn't find it, and then act like I was just doing postworkout stretching. Plenty of time.

My hands and arms rigidly held just as they had been when I heard the noise, I rotated my head back. Like I did on operations, I calculated the available options. The little bastard was on the left side of the sink. He could run right, in which case he'd fall into the stainless-steel basin. Good for me. He could run left, in which case he'd round a corner and hit the plethora of cookbooks

Jennifer had stacked on the counter, get behind them, and be gone. Bad. I needed to push him right.

I shuffled ever so slowly. The Satan-mouse continued crunching on his find. I got closer. I leaned over to a drawer and slowly pulled it open. I glanced inside, looking for a weapon. I saw a small mallet. Apparently used for some type of cooking, it had spikes on one side and a flat head on the other. The spikes would do. I pulled it out slowly, like I was playing that old game Operation and afraid to touch the sides of the drawer.

The mouse continued where he was, oblivious.

I inched forward and caught a flash of movement to my right. A blur that jumped to the countertop on the other side of the sink. It was Knuckles, our mange-ridden cat. The same one who for some reason didn't give a shit about mice, and another rescue by Jennifer when the cat was found digging in our trash can.

I stood with the mallet raised, not daring to breathe. The cat began licking her paws. Glancing at me with disdain. I thought very hard about using the mallet on her. I hated the beast, and the feeling was mutual. I was convinced that the only reason the mouse lived was precisely because that damn cat was spiting me. She brought all manner of dead things to my door, but now, with a mouse looking her in the eye five feet away, she does nothing?

I returned to my prey, inching forward ever so slowly. The mouse crept left, taking the bread with it. I analyzed again. It was moving into the corner and wouldn't escape unless it made the turn behind the cookbooks, although my strike would be exponentially lengthened. The corner was better than nothing.

I advanced, watching the little bastard nibbling away,

feeling triumph in my veins. No more would I be awakened worrying about a burglar because of a noise. No more would I find small turds in my shoes.

The front bell rang, and I could hear the door open. I froze, watching the mouse. He didn't move. I turned around and saw Knuckles, my second-in-command.

What the hell. He isn't supposed to arrive for three more hours.

He started to talk and I hissed. He shut up, giving me a look of confusion. I pointed the mallet. He grinned.

I crept closer and closer, getting within striking distance. I raised my weapon, about to close the deal, and heard, "Pike! Don't you dare!"

The damn spawn of Satan escaped behind the cookbooks and I turned, now trying to explain the mallet.

Breathing heavily, having just finished her run and entered the door my traitorous teammate had left open, Jennifer said, "Tell me you weren't going to bash that defenseless animal. Tell me your word means something."

I said, "My word is my bond. I would never do such a thing."

Okay, actually I said, "I . . . uhhh . . . I . . . wasn't going to hurt it."

She said, "Pike! Really? We got the live traps. We talked about this."

Yeah, we had. She'd made me buy these stupid traps that capture the mouse alive, so we could return it to the "wild"—read someone else's house—and they didn't work for shit. We might as well have put out strips of cardboard on the floor and wished for Peter Pan to show up. The damn mouse had been able to take out every bit of bait and had never been caught. And now it never would be.

Knuckles picked up our mangy cat and started cooing, "Hey, Knuckles, how ya been."

Yes, our beast was named after my teammate. It was supposed to embarrass him, but it backfired. The cat loved him and *still* hated me.

Jennifer stood in the kitchen doorway and glowered at me. Which, of course, made me feel like a heel. As she knew. I threw the mallet on the counter and said, "The mouse is a health hazard."

Jennifer, a hand on her hip, shook her head and said, "Really? That's the best you can come up with?"

Knuckles broke free, jumping down. Knuckles the cat, that is. Knuckles the man said, "I don't know what just happened here, but I'm pretty sure it falls in line with my proscription against teammates getting involved with each other."

Jennifer smiled, held out her arms, and said, "Sorry. It's Pike's fault. He's been trying to murder that poor thing forever."

Knuckles grinned and embraced her, saying, "I'd whack that little bugger in the head too."

Jennifer pulled out of the embrace and he backpedaled, "But it'd mean I don't get to be the date. Remember, I'm the sensitive one."

She smiled at him, then glared at me. I said, "I can be sensitive too. I can. But I don't look like a fashion-model hippie. That's why he's the date."

Which was true. Knuckles would fit in on a billboard for Abercrombie & Fitch. Flowing black hair, chiseled features, and chiseled abs. Whenever we went out, the number of women who threw themselves at him made me sick, because I knew, in his heart, he was a rodent-smashing knuckle dragger. But he was smart enough to play it off with Jennifer. And handsome enough to pull off our assigned mission.

Not that I'm saying I wasn't.

The mission itself wasn't dangerous, but it *was* going to be fun. We were detailed to check out a meeting between some Qatari interests and a shipping magnate from Brazil. Apparently, the Brazilian wanted to start mining a rare earth element called neodymium and was looking for investors, because a deposit had been found in his country. Neodymium was something that created very, very powerful magnets, which wouldn't be a concern, except that such magnets were used in every single bit of modern technology in existence, from wind turbines to cell phones to hybrid cars. Currently, the major producer was China, which caused its own problems when they shut down production on a whim, but now the United States was wondering where Qatar was going by investing in the endeavor. Especially since we didn't have a mine in our own country. We were dependent on foreign supply.

At the end of the day, it wasn't a traditional Taskforce problem. We primarily dealt with terrorism. We targeted groups on the State Department's official list of Foreign Terrorist Organizations, but our missions had been bleeding out into other areas for a couple of years because of our skill. And our ability to remain anonymous.

Two things made the beltway in Washington soil their pants when a paramilitary covert action was proposed: One—could they do it? And two—would it leak? On both counts, the traditional intelligence and military architecture had been beat up over the years. The CIA, focused primarily on intelligence collection, didn't have the in-house talent for the intricacies of kill or capture missions, and the DoD, focused primarily on overt combat operations with an enormous overhead bureaucracy, didn't have the ability to keep such missions secret. Put together, they had the expertise and the security if they'd quit fighting among themselves like schoolkids. Which is where my organization came in.

Created after the terrorist attacks on 9/11, off the books for anyone looking, we'd been given the charter to take it to the terrorists, but with strict left and right limits. Now folks in the know were broadening those limits. Using us to get things done that weren't exactly within our charter.

I didn't mind, because I'd argued for the blending of intel and direct action since forever, but I'd be lying if this mission didn't cause me concern. Not because of the mission but because of the ramifications. Like case law, this would start defining who we were, and who we were was only as strong as *who* we were.

Replace people like me with something less, and the damn thing would be out of control. I'd lived through enough scandals in Special Operations to know that we were all only one man away from disaster.

But that was someone else's concern. For me, I got to take Knuckles and Jennifer to the Cayman Islands to attend a party. Literally dressed in formal wear, just like James Bond.

Jennifer said, "Can I go pack? Or are you going to try and kill the mouse?"

"Damn it," I said, "I wasn't going to harm him. Get packed and cleaned up. The plane leaves in four hours."

She gave me her disapproving teacher stare, then disappeared into the bedroom. Knuckles moved to the fridge and popped a Coke. He said, "You really suck at this."

The cat came close to my legs and I tried to flick it

away. And missed. I said, "You'd better not suck on the mission. I'm not sending Jennifer in just to watch you get compromised."

He rolled his eyes and took a swig. He said, "Whatever. You're just pissed it's me doing the mission."

I grew indignant and said, "Don't give me that. You guys go into that place, and it's all you. She can't fight her way out by herself."

"Pike, I got it. I don't think you do. This is a cakewalk for her."

Which really aggravated me. We were going off on a tangent I hadn't expected, and I should have just shut up. I didn't. Any conversation about her always brought my back up. "What's that mean? I know what she can do. I'm the one who trained her. I'm the one who brought her in. I just want to make sure you understand."

"Understand what? That you don't trust her on her own? That's a switch."

I floundered for a moment, because that's not what I meant. I think. He said, "I saw the Decoy tape. I saw what she's capable of."

Decoy was a teammate who had been murdered on an operation right in front of Jennifer, shot by a Russian who was about six foot six. The bear of a man had then tried to kill her. And had failed. It had been caught on a surveillance camera and had become Taskforce lore, surreptitiously passed around the team rooms on a thumb drive. I'd seen it myself, right after it happened, and it was the human condition at the most basic level. Survival of the fittest. It wasn't pretty, but in the end, only one person had stood back up. Jennifer.

I'd never watched the tape again, precisely because of my connection to her. The damn thing gave me nightmares. Which was probably unfair, and exactly what

Knuckles was trying to tell me. Jennifer had earned her sleepless nights because of the action, tossing in the dark like a thousand other Operators from a thousand different hits. I had not, and was doing her a disservice by trying to protect her.

I said, "Just don't let her get in trouble. This sounds like fun, but it might be dangerous. Sometimes even *we* get in over our heads. Treat her like you would me."

Knuckles laughed and said, "So I should put a muzzle on her mouth?"

"No, damn it. You know what I mean."

Knuckles gave me a long stare. I heard Jennifer moving around in the bedroom, throwing things into a suitcase. He said, "Pike, she'll be fine."

I said nothing else, just nodding. The moment passed and he said, "Anyway, it's not going to matter. This is a boondoggle. What's a Brazilian billionaire got to do with terrorism? Who cares if he's talking to some guy from Qatar?"

★ 5 ★

Sharif al-Attiya watched the footage of the US secretary of state until he waved to the cameras and entered a car, Sharif's son, Haider al-Attiya, closing the door. He clicked off the wide-screen and said, "He did pretty well."

Sharif's assistant, Tarek al-Attiya, nodded and said, "He's learning."

Assistant was a little bit of a misnomer. Tarek was more a confidant. Twenty years Sharif's junior, he was not immediate family, but he was of the same tribe, and he was shrewd, in both the ways of money and the ways of politics. The latter skill was critical in the state of Qatar and had facilitated Sharif's rise despite the lack of a royal name.

Neither man was a member of the al-Thani tribe, and thus not automatically provided access to the inner circle of the ruling party—but also not placed in the line of fire from the multiple coups and machinations that name brought. No, Sharif was happy to remain safe as a trusted member of the business development sector of the extremely wealthy Qatar Investment Authority.

Since 2005, the emir of Qatar, through the QIA, had been aggressively investing in diverse portfolios throughout the world, touching everything from European football teams to pumping millions of dollars into Washington, DC, real estate. They invested in infrastructure in France, owned the venerable Harrods department store in London, had a majority stake in Miramax films in Hollywood, and were partners in energy production in Greece. They ran under the radar for most of it, with the world recognizing only the name Al Jazeera, the television network founded and owned by the Qatari government. They were everywhere, having a stake in just about every major bank in the world and many other financial institutions—including an almost 10 percent stake in the London stock exchange—and Sharif's job was to seek new investment opportunities.

A perfect cover for his true passion: defending Islam and spreading jihad.

Sharif stood, walking from behind his desk to the floor-to-ceiling window overlooking the city of Doha, the cranes and metal buildings blooming like weeds, changing the skyline almost daily.

He said, "He's learning, but not fast enough. That activity in Afghanistan was almost a debacle. He's still naïve. Still wants to carry the gun instead of work behind the scenes."

Tarek said, "Like his father used to be."

Sharif's face clouded. "Don't confuse my journey to fight the Soviets with his. What I did was out of duty. He did it craving a sense of adventure."

Soothingly, Tarek said, "Sharif. Sir. You are cut from the same cloth. He did what he did for the same reasons as you. *Both* reasons."

"He was supposed to just deliver the money. Create a conduit to fund the Islamic State in Afghanistan. Sow the seeds of chaos. Not go fighting."

"He had to get it out of his system. As did you."

"He almost got killed! And he killed American Special Forces."

"He showed the Islamic State he has mettle. They trust him now."

Sharif grunted, saying nothing.

Tarek said, "Is killing the Americans so bad?"

Sharif turned and said, "Only if they can connect it to us. They have long memories. When I fought there, I was a part of a group that killed Spetsnaz. We cheered for a day, and then were hunted for a year. They caught some of us."

His face grew distant, lost in an ugly memory.

Tarek said, "He's home now. They all are. Let the Americans hunt. They won't find anything."

Sharif waved his hand and said, "The landscape *here* is not the same. They don't need to kill us with an iron rod, like my men endured. They can kill us with a diplomatic démarche. Times change. The emir will throw us to the wolves if we are seen as helping the fighters."

Qatar was a Sunni state that adhered to Sharia law. They followed a competing agenda of integrating into the greater world system while actively funneling help to the very jihadists who had sworn vengeance on that system. Whether it was to curry favor to protect themselves from the jihadists or simply because of inherent desire was anyone's guess. Eventually, with the Syrian civil war and the rise of the Islamic State, the issue had come to a head, with the Sunni states of the Gulf Cooperation Council, headed by Saudi Arabia, breaking ranks with Qatar, and the United States and the European Union starting to rumble, no longer willing to look the other way.

Under pressure, at first Qatar eschewed governmental

backing, proclaiming their innocence while turning a blind eye to wealthy government members individually supporting various jihadist groups. Then, when evidence of the secret deals began to mount, they began taking overt action, the state system trumping jihadist fervor.

It was a fine line, and everyone on the world stage knew it. Qatar was still the closest state system that could penetrate into the world of the jihadi, having proven that by brokering the release of the captured US soldier Bowe Bergdahl for five Taliban terrorists held in Guantánamo Bay, along with numerous ransom negotiations from a plethora of European countries for members held by various groups, but the world couldn't abide a government that had such close ties to killers. At least overt ties. Because of it, Qatar had taken a strong and vocal hand against support.

Tarek glanced at his phone, reading a text message, and said, "He's in the building. On the way up."

Sharif nodded, caressing his neatly groomed beard. He said, "Should we continue?"

"Yes. You have the method. You send money all over the world, and Greece is the perfect place. Well, Istanbul would be better, but Greece is good enough. Stay out of Turkey. Too political. Greece is lying on the ground, bleeding. They need us, and we can use their banks."

Sharif nodded and the door opened, allowing in his son, Haider, and two others. Sharif turned, a smile on his face, which faded to a scowl when he saw the entourage. He said, "Please, wait outside."

Dressed in traditional Gulf attire, like Haider himself, both men nodded with downcast eyes and exited, closing the door behind them.

Sharif said, "What are they doing here?"

Haider, a tall, hawk-faced man with a neatly trimmed

beard, said, "What do you mean? They're with me. They're my security."

"You don't need *security* here." Sharif spat the word out with disdain.

Haider faltered and said, "They protected me in Afghanistan. They're my friends. You've met them before. What's wrong?"

Tarek glanced at Sharif and said, "Your father has concerns with them. They are bastards, yes? No father?"

Exasperated, Haider said, "Yes. Yes, you both know that. We've been friends for a long time. They have a father. He just chooses not to claim them. Sometimes I feel the same way."

Sharif took that in without a ripple and said, " 'Friends from school' does not get them into our business. Friends, you play football with after studies. You don't invite them into your world."

Haider said, "I trust them. Without them I would have died in Afghanistan. Father, you have Tarek. I have them."

Sharif bristled and Tarek stepped between them, breaking the tension. He said, "Yes. He does. Let's hope their counsel is as good as mine."

Sharif chuckled, and Tarek continued. "So what did you learn today? Is the United States willing to support our investment in Greece? Will we get pushback?"

Now happy to inflate his meeting, Haider said, "No, not at all. The crisis in Greece has reached a boiling point, and the EU isn't backing down. That leaves foreign investors to float them. The United States isn't going to step in in an official capacity, but they don't want to see the euro fall apart. They would love for us to invest, if only to stave off the inevitable."

Sharif said, "Good. Good. So we can start inflating

our accounts in Alpha Bank without fear of the United States protesting?"

"Yes, but that's not the best news."

Not hearing, Sharif said, "I want to start using those banks. I want to start transferring funds employing the usual mechanisms. Siphon off the same amount. Small enough to remain under the radar but large enough to do some good. As we did in London. As you're going to do in the Cayman Islands. We need to get you there as well."

Haider said, "Father, you didn't hear the best part."

Looking at a calendar, Sharif said, "We missed the visit to the Caymans because of the secretary of state's visit, but you can go the week after next. After you solidify your Greek contacts."

Haider said, "We didn't miss the Cayman trip. I sent Ahmed."

Sharif snapped back to Haider and said, "What?"

Haider ducked his head and said, "I sent Ahmed Mansoor. I told you I trust him."

★ 6 ★

Sharif was flabbergasted. "The friend of those idiots outside? You sent him on a fact-finding trip? What on earth does he know about Cayman banks? What do any of them know about that?"

"He's actually doing more than checking out the banks. Father, let me be my own man. I have learned much watching you. I've found an investment for the QIA. A real investment in Brazil. He's investigating it for me. It'll be worth it. An inroad into South America."

Sharif felt the rage grow, squeezing the head of Tutankhamun on his desk, a gift from the former president of Egypt Mohamed Morsi. A supporter of the Muslim Brotherhood. Now gone. Another failure.

Speaking slowly, he said, "You. Do. *Not* have the authority to do this. You have *no* authority."

Haider stammered for a moment, then drew up. His voice not nearly as strong as his stance, he said, "You gave me the mission to the Caymans. I've made it more than just dithering with the banks. I have created an opportunity for an investment in Brazil."

Sharif looked at Tarek, shaking his head, saying without words, *See what I mean?*

But he couldn't bring himself to chastise his firstborn.

He had five daughters, but only one son. Something he secretly cursed. What he wouldn't give to have a brood of men to choose from. But he had only one.

He said, "Tell me about it."

Haider did, and Sharif was mollified somewhat. He said, "Okay. Ahmed can continue, but he flies home immediately. No further contacts. He comes to me, personally. With you."

Haider shifted again, agitated. Sharif said, "What now?"

"I told Ahmed he could take one of our boats to America. To Key West. For a vacation."

The yachts owned by the QIA were legendary for their splendor, and they were all over the world, but they were restricted to those who had earned the right to use them. Sharif was astounded.

"You actually gave him access to one of our yachts? Even I can't use them without . . . without . . . ever."

Sharif tried to maintain control but was having difficulty. How to explain that slight? How to explain someone not of royal blood was taking a yacht to Key West from the Cayman Islands?

Haider said, "It was going to Miami anyway. He's just riding. I didn't order it to go. All I did was ask for a stop in Key West."

Tarek stepped in and said, "Haider, you mentioned that we hadn't heard the best part of your visit. Please, what was that?"

Sharif glared at his son, saying nothing. Haider, on shaky ground, hesitated. Tarek nodded. Haider said, "Jonathan Billings—the United States secretary of state—said they were holding peace talks with the Taliban. They're holding a secret meeting, hoping for a ccasefire."

Sharif heard the words, but didn't believe them. "Peace meeting? Something we don't know about? The Taliban have an office here, in Doha. The peace overtures happen here, in Doha."

"Not according to Billings. He said the government of Afghanistan has worked a separate front, away from Qatar and away from the world. The Taliban wants to talk, but can't do it on the world stage, with everyone looking at their every word."

The thought was disquieting, because it meant the Taliban was willing to capitulate. Move away from the reason they existed: a Sharia state. It meant an end to fighting in Afghanistan, an end to the influence of Salifist thought. A country that would become exactly what he despised: another secular state.

It was the very reason he had sent his son to open up discussions with the nascent Islamic State in Afghanistan. He'd feared the Taliban peace overtures in Qatar, the fear solidifying when they'd opened up an official office with the support of the Qatar government.

Peace would free up the hated United States to focus on areas they'd been woefully misguided about, precisely because of their fixation with Afghanistan. Iraq, Syria, and Yemen were all viewed under the optic of Afghanistan. A peace there would embolden future incursions. Future engagements. And future successes.

He had fought the Soviets, but had no illusions about the United States. They were a different animal altogether. Naïve for sure, but not dumb.

"Why would Billings tell you this? If it's to remain secret? He was supposed to be here solely for Greece."

"I think it was his back-channel way to inform the emir. I think he believes I have the ear of the government, which, given your position, we do."

"When is this happening?"

"I don't know for sure. I do know he'll tell me. He trusts me and wants to include Qatar behind the scenes."

"Did you promise anything?"

"No, no. I demurred, neither confirming nor denying his thoughts."

"And you now have contacts with ISIS in Afghanistan? You can infiltrate the meeting?"

Haider hesitated, then said, "Maybe. I don't know."

"You will. You're the man Billings trusts, and your actions in Afghanistan have given you leverage with the Islamic State."

Haider absorbed the newfound responsibility and looked as if he wished he hadn't spoken.

Sharif continued. "When is Ahmed Mansoor going to the Caymans?"

Confused at the intensity of his father, Haider said, "He's there now. The meeting is tonight. Why?"

"Because I can't let that imbecile affect what you've just told me. We need to stop that peace overture. In the most violent way possible."

★ 7 ★

The sea was fairly calm, but the boat was rolling enough to cause the view from my spotting scope to swing wildly due to the magnification level. I hit the stabilization feature, and the front patio and swimming pool of the "castle" came into crystal view, the setting sun backlighting it in a halo. I saw the security walking back and forth, then a glint of reflected light as one put some glass on us.

Satisfied with the angle, I flipped the switch sending the feed to a tablet I had mounted on a bench, right next to the dive package I wouldn't use. Beside it hung a tuxedo and formal dress. I turned to Jennifer and said, "Frogman done yet? The guys are looking now. They need to see him."

Jennifer smiled, dropped her swimsuit cover-up, and picked up a mask and snorkel. She said, "He's having fun. We don't need to bring him up. Let 'em see me instead."

I adjusted the focus and said, "Yeah, I'm sure they'd rather have that view."

She threw a towel at my head and left the cabin, going to the rear of the boat, where the dive platform was located. She made a show of prepping her mask, then slid into the water with a dive-marking buoy. Plying our cover for action.

We were currently anchored about four hundred meters off the eastern end of Grand Cayman, near Rum Point, and directly across from our target—a large stone house overlooking the ocean. It was rented for the party tonight by a ranking member of Grand Cayman's Barclays Bank Trust Company, and it was a pretty impressive structure. Built on an outcropping of rock, it was made to look like a turreted castle with three floors, each complete with balconies, and had an infinity pool and two sunbathing areas terraced into the rock flowing away from the house, the lower one sitting right by the ocean's edge.

Earlier, we'd done a reconnaissance from the road running by the house and I was surprised at the security that was in place for this party. The building was behind a fifteen-foot stone wall, with the gate manned by two goons. Inside, near the front door, was another checkpoint, and the landscaping consisted of a thick tangle of jungle-like growth. It was going to be damn near impossible to penetrate the place. At least from the landlubber side. The ocean was a different story, but in order to do anything from there, we had to lull the security into thinking we were innocuous. In this case, a charter boat out for a night dive.

The easiest way to accomplish the mission would have been for the Taskforce hacking cell to simply get us invitations, but they'd failed—which told me how invested this bank was in security. There were very few pieces of cyberspace that those guys couldn't own. But security was a double-edged sword, a facet I hoped to exploit.

Without an invitation, we were left with two courses of action: Penetrate the house covertly while the party was going on, or magic ourselves into the house in formalwear. After looking at the security and the terrain, I'd opted for scenario two. After all, nobody checks an invitation once you're inside the ball. Just ask the White House gate-crashers. With that decision made, we needed to work only on the magic component to get my team inside.

The hacking cell *had* managed to get us a floor plan and some historical data points on previous parties the bank had hosted—to include the interesting fact that Qatar had more than a 10 percent stake in Barclays International. All of the soirees had been at this location, habitually rented by the bank to entice foreign deposits in its system.

After studying the data, one tidbit stood out—a strange activity that occurred at every party: The host made guests give up their electronics. Cell phones, cameras, and anything else with a battery was confiscated, which was something the guests apparently preferred. Past events had included some high-profile celebrities, and I suppose selfies were verboten. Or maybe it was to prevent the digital existence of other shenanigans that went on.

It didn't interfere with our mission, but it did present an opportunity. Having all the cell phones located in one spot was something I couldn't pass up. Originally, I'd planned on simply getting Knuckles and Jennifer inside the party, with Knuckles wearing a recording device slaved to directional microphones built into the buttons on the sleeves and front of his tuxedo. Each mic was under his control, allowing him to turn one on and another off, depending on where the targets were located, thus preventing him from having to awkwardly rotate, trying to get audio.

Basically, he was a walking human bug.

With the cell phone confiscation information, I'd decided to expand the mission. While Knuckles wandered around gathering audio, I wanted to get Jennifer inside whatever area they used to store the electronics and have her copy the SIM cards of our target cell phones. It would be exponentially more information gleaned.

I heard a splash from the diving deck and saw Jennifer coming out of the water. I looked at the tablet, and sure enough, they were watching. I was also sure they weren't watching because they thought we were some nefarious secret intelligence organization about to cause them harm. Not that I blamed them. I'd have done the same thing.

Because I'm a misanthrope.

She came in, wringing out her hair, and said, "Knuckles was right below me, exploring some old rowboat that sank. I told him to come up."

I said, "I think we're good. If he climbs the ladder with a tank on his back, they'll fade away. Come here. Take a look."

The sun was sinking below the horizon, and the first guests were arriving. I tapped the tablet and said, "I've been watching the posture, and they're focused almost exclusively on the front, where the road is. There're only a couple of guys on the deck, and they're by the pool, up high."

"Anything on the phones?"

Immediately zeroing in on her part of the mission.

I said, "Yeah. They're taking the phones to a bedroom on the left. The one that's a stand-alone."

She leaned forward, looking at the screen but seeing nothing except a few early arrivers. She said, "The one with the sliding glass door? The bedroom that's separated from the rest of the house?"

"Yeah. *That* one. Any ideas on how to get in?"

The building had seven bedrooms. Six were inside the house. One, the seventh, was accessed only by a sliding glass door on the left side of the compound, right in front of the infinity pool. I wasn't too surprised, since it would be the single location they could store all the phones without worry of someone wandering in—especially with a man outside—but it did present a problem.

Jennifer tapped the screen, switching from the video feed and bringing up the 3-D floor plan the Taskforce had given us, rotating it until she found what she was looking for.

"Right there. If I can get to the top bedroom, I can scale down outside and enter through the bathroom. Nobody will expect that. No guards."

"But how will you get to that bedroom? It's the master at the top of a spiral staircase. I doubt it'll be in use for the party."

I heard a splash, then Knuckles shouted, "Give me a hand?"

I shouted back, "Screw you. Some of us are working. Glad you got a dive vacation."

Jennifer laughed and went to the platform, helping him up and pulling his tank off his back. She set it aside and Knuckles said, "Really? I'm preventing them from penetrating our elaborate cover, and you scoff?"

I said, "They smell the seaweed on you, and you can explain it. Jennifer told me you were just screwing off down there."

He rubbed his hands through his ridiculously thick hair and said, "Diving is never screwing off. Helps to get my mind right."

I said, "Okay, Frogman. Whatever."

Jennifer switched back to the video feed and said, "Target. Target's here."

Knuckles quit drying off and came forward. He tried to pop me with the towel and I wrapped my hand around it, jerking him off-balance. Jennifer hissed, "Stop it. Look at the screen. Is that him?"

We immediately quit, feeling a little foolish. We both leaned into the monitor, seeing a well-groomed older man of about seventy, flanked by two women half his age. Well, maybe a quarter his age. And both were stunners, their clothes leaving little to the imagination.

Knuckles said, "Yep. The Brazilian. Now just waiting on the guy from Qatar."

We watched security make them place their phones in a Faraday bag—a special pouch designed to prevent any electronic emissions either in or out—then seal it, tagging it with a number. Jennifer hit the image capture, and we had the number on the bag. The security man with the bag began to move outside of view, and Jennifer manipulated the tablet, panning the camera.

Knuckles said, "Wait. What are you doing? We know where they put the bags. Keep on the target."

He tapped the screen, moving the scope back to the Brazilian. And the stunners.

I said, "Yeah. That would be best."

Jennifer saw the reason for Knuckles's call and slapped my shoulder.

She said, "Really? That's what you want to see?"

I stepped back and said, "No, no. I was checking out the target. Knuckles, pan to the Faraday bag."

He grinned and did so. Jennifer crossed her arms and gave me a hip bump, glaring.

The security man came out of the glass doors next to the infinity pool and took the bag to the same bedroom. The disconnected one.

I said, "Looks like that's the target room. A little rough to get into."

Jennifer panned the spotting scope back and we saw an influx of people, the host greeting each one. Within five minutes, a man came in, wearing a tuxedo and a sissy-looking groomed beard, flanked by two men with the same facial hair. They were Arabs, no doubt about it. Jennifer split the screen and brought up our Qatar target package, the image given to us from the Taskforce on the left of the screen, and the live action on the right.

I said, "That's not him. No match."

We waited until the unknowns had finished their Faraday transfer, the security man running a wand over each to make sure they weren't hiding anything. He tagged the pouch, allowing us to get the number.

We continued, watching every guest who arrived, but our target from Qatar never entered. I now had a hard call. Abort? Or go ahead, with the other man the focus? In the no-fault world of the Taskforce, this was a definite abort. No way was the mission worth the risk. Nobody was going to die because of the meeting. No direct threats to the nation were involved. It was just a stupid expansion of our mission set by the Oversight Council.

On the other hand, when on earth would we get to do a movie-version James Bond mission? Never, that's when. No way was I flying all the way to the Caymans, renting a dive boat and formalwear, just to walk away. That was simply a nonstarter.

We watched the last guest enter, the crowd now at about seventy people, and Jennifer said, "Okay, no target. Let's contact the Taskforce and ask for guidance."

Like this was some super-secret sniper mission to assassinate a head of state.

I looked at Knuckles and read the same feeling I had. I said, "You good with this?"

He grinned. "Are you kidding?"

Jennifer looked back and forth between us and said, "We don't have our target. We've met abort criteria."

I said, "Nope. That sissy-boy in the beard is the target. You're going in. All we need to do is wait an hour or two to let them get juiced."

★ 8 ★

Three hours later, on the other side of our boat, shielded from the castle, I slowly lowered Jennifer into the small rubber Zodiac. Already in, Knuckles helped to keep her from falling overboard. Something necessary, given the dress she was wearing.

A black, formfitting top with long sleeves, the dress was actually a Lycra bodysuit. The long, flowing skirt was simply applied to her waist by Velcro, allowing her to remove the skirt and operate unencumbered. At the small of her back was a waterproof pouch, making the skirt look like it had a bustle. In her left hand was a pair of high heels.

Knuckles stabilized her waist and I let go of her hand, saying, "Looks like the Taskforce is going to get their money's worth from those shoes."

She sat on the bench in the middle of the small rubber craft and smiled, saying, "My favorite piece of Taskforce kit."

She'd had to dress up once before, on a mission in Kenya six months ago, and had gone hog wild buying an outfit on the Taskforce's dime, including a ridiculously expensive pair of high heels called Jimmy Choos. I couldn't believe how much they cost—and neither could the bean counters when we returned. But it was a successful mission, so the boss, Kurt Hale, had shushed them and allowed Jennifer to keep the shoes. Up until now, they'd held a special place in our closet, gathering dust.

I climbed down the ladder and took my position in the rear of the Zodiac. I was nothing but the infil-exfil platform for this mission. I said, "Comms check."

First Knuckles talked, then Jennifer answered. I couldn't hear either one, because they were wearing microscopic earbuds that slaved through Bluetooth to small transmitters hidden in their clothing.

Ordinarily, we communicated through a proprietary earpiece that worked encrypted through the cell network with our special Taskforce phones. Looking like an ordinary cell phone Bluetooth, they usually blended in fine, but since the host of this party confiscated all cell phones, running around with that in their ears would look a little silly. We'd opted for a covert communication system, which had far less power. It would allow Jennifer to talk to Knuckles, but I wouldn't be able to hear anything on the dive boat.

Satisfied, Knuckles looked at me and nodded. Dressed in his tuxedo, his hair in surf-boy disarray, he really *did* look like something from an Abercrombie & Fitch poster. I chuckled.

He said, "What's so funny?"

I glanced at Jennifer, her dirty-blond hair piled high on her head, wearing expensive-looking earrings and a faux emerald necklace, and said, "I can't believe we get paid for this shit."

Knuckles grinned and said, "Somebody's got to do it."

I said, "Okay. Primary mission is the audio for the Brazilian and the guy from Qatar. Specifically, any discus sion of investing in the mine and the reasons why Qatar would be interested. Secondary mission is the cell phones. Jennifer, if you can't get upstairs to the master bedroom, let it go."

She nodded, but said, "I think I can get up there. As a female."

"How?"

She grinned and said, "Let me worry about that."

I paused for a moment, then nodded. She was pretty good at solving problems, and I knew she was working some plan that wouldn't be finalized until she was in the lion's den, after she could take a look at the atmospherics.

I said, "Okay. Showtime. Knuckles, cast off." He did so and I turned around, starting the outboard by punching a single button. It was a fairly powerful motor, but was electric. All that came out was a small whine, like that of a remote-control car.

We broke the cover of the dive boat and circled to the left, toward a small beach and away from the rocky outcropping the house sat upon. We'd remain out of sight of the castle until we were beneath the level of the rock, then slide in parallel to the coast, out of view of the security by the pool.

Scooting along barely fast enough to cause a wake, I said, "Any changes to contingencies?"

Knuckles said, "Nope. This goes south, and we're running straight to the water. I'll activate the beacon in my phone once I get the chance, but the only early warning will be you with an eye on the scope. You see us getting thrown out, you start chugging forward in the Zodiac."

I nodded, then said, "What if you can't get out?"

"Then you'd better call in a Taskforce assault team."

Neither one of them had a weapon, because we'd decided it would be too much to try to hide. Well, the lack of weapons wasn't exactly true. They had their hands, and their fighting skills were positively lethal.

I grinned and said, "Not much of a plan."

Jennifer said, "We'll get out. That'll be the easy part. Getting in is going to be the issue. We might be in the water before you've made it back to the boat."

Knuckles glanced back at me, and I saw a smile in the moonlight. Jennifer clearly didn't like our plan. Knuckles had come up with it, and I thought it was downright devious.

We reached a point where we were below the line of sight of the men on the patio, and I slowed the boat to a crawl, lowering my night vision goggles. I cut closer to the shore, paralleling the rock and looking for the parapet of the lowest sunbathing deck. I saw it above me, about ten feet up the cliff, a primitive set of stairs cut out of the stone leading down from it to the water. Jennifer pulled out a thermal scope, checking for body heat along the top of the crest and around the deck.

I puttered closer, seeing the waves slap into the rock. I whispered, "Hey, the surf's worse than it was before. I'm going to get bounced into the cliff."

Crouching down, Knuckles said, "You call that surf? That's nothing. I should have known better than to let an Army guy drive the boat. Just get it close. I'll buffer while Jennifer gets out, then I'll go, pushing you away."

We crept toward the stairway and I slowed further still, letting Jennifer complete her sweep. She put the scope down and nodded at me, her eyes bright with excitement, making me grin involuntarily. A year ago, she would have been soiling her bodysuit. Now she looked like a kid about to take a roller-coaster ride. Eager for the prospect of some harmless thrills. Only this one might not be so harmless.

We bumped into the rock, the underside eaten away from years of surf, making a mushroomlike shape. Knuckles grabbed a plant growing out of the stone and pulled us forward until we were abreast of the primitive staircase. Shoes around her neck, Jennifer scrambled up, clambering with one hand while hoisting her skirt with the other. I waited until she was clear, then hissed at Knuckles.

Still holding the plant and starting to exit, he turned around. I said, "Remember what we talked about. She likes to push things. She wants those cell phones, but don't let her push too hard. You have the experience here."

He grinned and nodded, saying, "I'll bring her back in one piece. We might be wet, but she'll be fine."

He slipped out of sight, kicking the rubber of the Zodiac and pushing me away from the rocks. I did a tight turn and motored about fifty feet away, sweeping the crest of the sunbathing deck with my night vision. I caught a slash of movement, but nothing else. I turned around and began steaming back to our dive boat and my lonely vigil.

★ 9 ★

Clinging like a cat to the steps carved in the rock, Jennifer waited until Knuckles was behind her. He tapped her and she began to climb. She moved slowly, taking the steps one at a time, bent forward so far she could almost go up on all fours, listening for any sign of movement over the soft noise of the surf.

They reached the plateau of the sunbathing deck, and the lights from the house spilled out. Jennifer paused and surveyed, seeing five lounge chairs lined up, facing the ocean. At the back of the deck was a proper staircase made of crushed coral, leading to the next terraced deck, then a farther staircase going up to the infinity pool and patio.

The noise from the party spilled down the hill, tinkles of glass, conversation, and laughter. She rose up slightly, until she could pinpoint the security at the edge of the patio. She ducked back down and whispered, "They're still in place, on our side of the pool."

Knuckles grinned and said, "Should we use one of the chairs or just lie down on the deck?"

Jennifer scowled, inwardly cursing Pike for talking her into this plan. He routinely came up with some pretty outrageous ideas, but agreeing to Knuckles's suggestion was about the worst.

After spitballing various ways to get inside, they'd decided that they needed to play on the guard force's reason to exist. In other words, let the guard force find them, but do so in such a way that they'd be laughing instead of suspicious. Let the guard force discover them engaged in something embarrassing, then apologize in the face of the laughter and slink "back" into the party.

But what? What could the guards stumble upon that wouldn't get them thrown out? Knuckles had come up with the idea: sex on the beach. Or more appropriately, sex on the sunbathing deck.

Jennifer was mortified just thinking about it.

Knuckles said, "Well?"

Jennifer shook her head and said, "The lounge chair."

Knuckles said, "Me on the bottom or you?"

"Jesus. Seriously?"

"Well, it's got to look real."

"You on the damn bottom."

He crept to a chair and lay down. She straddled his waist, glaring at him. He said, "Put your shoes on."

"What?"

"Your damn Sammy Foos or whatever they're called. They're still around your neck. It'd look pretty silly when they find us."

She bent over and put on the high heels, muttering. She leaned back up and said, "Satisfied?"

"Oh yeah. This is every male's fantasy. High heels, formal dress . . ."

She tried to thump him in the head, but he blocked it, continuing, ". . . secret mission in the Cayman Islands. I'm with Pike. I can't believe I'm getting paid."

Exasperated, she said, "Are you done? Can we get on with the mission?"

He grinned and said, "Yeah. Final equipment check.

You can get to the Octopus? And your Third Lung if this goes south?"

She reached back and felt the butt pack, saying, "Yeah. It's good. All I need to do is ditch this skirt."

He said, "Stand up for a minute." She did, and he unbuckled his belt, dropping his pants to his mid-thigh, but not touching his underwear.

He patted his lap and said, "Okay then, lover. Let's get it on. Start moaning."

She did, embarrassingly trying to sound like she thought someone in the throes of passion would sound. She'd never really paid attention to what she truly did. It came out like a wounded kitten.

Knuckles said, "That's it?"

"Well, what the hell am I supposed to do?"

"Shit. I can barely hear that, and I'm underneath you. Get them over here."

She shook her head and took a breath, then let out a moan like a porno film. Knuckles whispered, "That a girl! Pretend like I'm Pike."

Her eyes flashed, and she let out another moan, which sounded dangerously close to a lion closing in on a gazelle. Knuckles said, "Uhhh . . . might want to tone that one down a bit. You sound a little like you want to hurt me."

She said, "Shouldn't you be helping?" And dug her hands into the soft flesh right above his hip, twisting. He involuntarily yelped, grabbing her hand, and they both saw the flashlight beam flick above their heads. He let go and said, "This is it. Get ready to act."

She moaned again, getting into it, and the flashlight came bouncing down the stairs. They jerked their heads up as if in surprise, then Jennifer sprang to her feet, pretending to adjust her dress. Knuckles leapt up, buckling his pants.

He squeezed his eyes shut, fighting for control, wondering if he'd made a mistake in his request.

His brother, Sergeant First Class Timothy George, had been killed in a mechanical ambush in Afghanistan. Hunting a new threat of the Islamic State infiltrating the area, he'd located the leader of the nascent movement and had gained a hard-fought concurrence for a unilateral US mission. Such things were no longer allowed in the Graveyard of Empires, but this threat had been deemed worthy. The Taliban was an Afghan Army mission, but this was something else.

And he'd died, along with most of his team.

When Guy heard of the casualties, he'd made some calls to friends in Special Operations. Telling them, first, not to mail the box to his parents. To mail it to him. And second, not to sterilize the contents. Give him everything.

Ordinarily, when a service member died, the inventory was conducted with one thing in mind: Protect the memory for a grieving family. Give the family everything they deserved, but remove anything that would be embarrassing. Porno magazines, unmailed letters of hatred, evidence of infidelity, or anything else that would cause the family grief was destroyed. First on the list was the uniform the deceased wore the night he died. That was usually burned.

But not this time. And Guy was regretting it.

He put the uniform aside and found his brother's cell phone. The one Tim had used Apple iMessage to text while he'd been deployed. The same one he'd used to send a last message, talking about his final mission. No specifics, just that he was doing good work and taking it to the enemy.

Only the enemy took it to him.

The guard said, "What the hell are you two doing down here?"

Jennifer ducked her head and moved behind Knuckles. Looking sheepish, he said, "Nothing. Nothing at all. Just looking at the view."

The guard tried to hide a grin, but could not. He said, "Sir, madame, I'm sorry, but the party is up at the house. Please, for my job, save this for after you leave."

Knuckles adjusted his tuxedo, gathered his feigned dignity, and said, "Sure. Sorry. Can you keep this between us, please?"

The guard nodded, obviously having no intention of doing so once the party was over, and the three marched up the stairs and entered the house. Nobody paid them a second glance.

Jennifer couldn't believe it had worked, whispering that into Knuckles's ear. He said, "It was the moaning."

She dug her hand into his kidney, twisting the flesh and making him jump. She said, "Now it's your turn. Find the target."

They passed across the patio, the separate bedroom off to the left, a man outside. Knuckles said, "Still no way in from the front." She nodded and they entered through the sliding glass door to the lower level. Knuckles looked around, seeing impossibly beautiful couples dripping wealth, but not his target.

They went up the wooden staircase to the main floor and Knuckles saw him sitting on a couch in the corner, next to the balcony, the Brazilian in a chair adjacent to him, both deep in conversation. Knuckles took stock of the area, seeing the acre-size kitchen island, the expanse of food, and servers darting in and out among the guests. He looked for a couple close enough to the targets to be worthwhile. He found one about their age and said,

"Let's go. You lead, I follow. Comment on the woman's dress or something."

He got no response and said, "Jennifer? You switched on?"

She was staring farther in, at the metal spiral staircase leading to the master bedroom. She refocused and said, "Yeah. I'm good."

He saw where her attention had been and said, "One step at a time. That may be a bridge too far."

She snatched a champagne glass from a passing waiter and said, "Let's get in the fight."

Walking toward the couple, she said, "I'll start the introductions, but I'm going to excuse myself. Check things out."

"Check things out how?"

"Just look around. You've got the magic microphones. It's your mission." They got closer and Jennifer took in the décolletage of the woman. She said, "Just remember to look her in the eye."

"What's that mean?"

She glanced sideways at him, but said nothing. He came within frontal view of the woman and said, "Okay, okay. I see."

Jennifer introduced herself, asking something innocuous about the woman's jewelry, then turned it over to Knuckles, rotating her body to let him enter the conversation closest to the targets. Knuckles shook the man's hand, then began spilling out his cover story as the CEO of a paint firm specializing in anticorrosive and low-visibility enamel, dedicated to the US military. Jennifer was actually amazed at how knowledgeable he sounded. Nothing like the man-child who'd demanded she moan for a thrill.

She asked the woman for the location to a bathroom,

then moved away, following her directions, sliding in between the groups of people and weaving her way to the back of the room. She reached a hallway and saw exactly what she wanted: a line of three women waiting outside a door.

She said, "Is this the only bathroom?"

"I doubt it, but it's the only one outside of a bedroom."

Perfect.

She went back to the great room, seeing Knuckles still engrossed in conversation and catching him surreptitiously stealing a glance at the woman's cleavage. *Damn Neanderthal.*

She pulled up next to him and caught his attention. He smiled and said, "That was quick." Appearing embarrassed, she said, "Honey, I really have to go to the bathroom, but there's a line outside."

Knuckles looked at her in confusion and said, "Yeah? Uhhh . . . I guess wait."

She bored into him with her eyes and said, "I *really* have to go. Something I ate."

She was beginning to wonder if he would make the connection, when it finally clicked. He said, "Let's see if we can find another one."

He pointed to the winding metal staircase and said, "You guys know if there's a bathroom up there?"

The man said, "I came early and got a tour. It's the master bedroom, and yeah, it has a bathroom, but I don't know if they want guests to use it."

Jennifer put on a pouting face, looking at Knuckles as if she were a dimwit wanting him to solve the problem. He said, "I'm sure they won't mind."

He flagged down one of the roving security and said, "My date really needs to use the bathroom, but the one in back has a line. Something she ate. Would you mind if she went upstairs?"

The guy hesitated, then spoke into his wrist. He waited for a response, touching his earpiece, then said, "That would be fine, but I'll have to take her up."

Jennifer smiled and said, "Thank you. I really have to go."

Knuckles squinted at her and said, "I'll be right here. Don't take too long."

She nodded and he flicked his eyes at the targets and said, "You do, and I might wander off, looking for another date."

Jennifer got his meaning, but the comment drew a scowl from the other woman. Jennifer pecked him on the cheek and said, "I'll be quick. I promise. Nobody else will have to moan for you."

She walked away, leaving Knuckles to respond to the couple now standing with their mouths open.

★ 10 ★

Jennifer followed the security man up the winding staircase, feeling the adrenaline build. She started to wipe a sheen of nervous sweat off her face, then realized it might help her story.

They broke into a large master suite dominated by floor-to-ceiling windows and glass doors facing the ocean. The man pointed across the bed to another door, one that slid into the wall. Jennifer grabbed her stomach and hurried through the room, saying, "Thank you. I might be a while."

She slid the door closed, made a show of noise by dropping the toilet seat, then focused on the window. It was large enough.

She kicked off her Jimmy Choos and began to pull the Velcro off her skirt, the noise sounding as if she was tearing a bedsheet. She stopped and listened. Nothing. She looked at the wall and saw three light switches, one down. She flicked it and was relieved to hear a fan crank up, the noise enough to cover her transformation.

She peeled off the skirt, leaving her in what looked like a black leotard. She piled the clothes and shoes in the walk-in shower, not really sure what hiding them would accomplish. She slid the window open and stood on the toilet, slithering through legs first and hanging by her fingers from the sill. She glanced left and saw two security men on the paved drive, one smoking. Neither looking her way. She looked right and saw her target window, at ground level and below the foliage. In between were two other windows she'd have to avoid. She surveyed the exterior, assessing what she had to work with. The building itself was constructed of stone, made to look like a real castle, with irregular bumps and ridges that were perfect for her skills.

A gymnast in a previous life, she'd worked a spell with Cirque du Soleil and found she had a talent for free climbing. Like a gecko, she could scramble up just about anything, and the Taskforce took full advantage of that skill. Here, she would need every bit of it, because going down a vertical surface was exponentially harder than going up. Instead of eyesight, she'd have to rely on feel.

She slid her toes to the right, searching for crevices and finding purchase. She followed with her hands, leaving the safety of the windowsill. She began the climb down, moving as fast as possible without slipping, curving around the castle toward her target.

Eventually, she was at the top of the foliage, and close enough to the ground. She pushed off and dropped, hitting softly in the mulch. She leaned against the rock wall underneath the bathroom window of her target room and did nothing but breathe deeply for a few seconds. She called on her tiny radio, "I'm down. Outside the bedroom."

She heard Knuckles say a sentence, followed by "Okay, that's good," using his ordinary conversation with another guest as a means to let her know he'd heard.

She stood up and found the bathroom was actually

sunk into the hillside a little bit, leaving the window a mere four feet off the ground. She rotated her butt pack around to the front and pulled out a red-lens penlight, shining it on the lock.

They knew the castle had a built-in security system, but also that it was disabled during the parties. What they didn't know was the type of window locks in use. Jennifer was hoping it was like the one she'd left upstairs, a simple sliding lever on the left and right.

It was. She fished in her pouch again and pulled out a flexible metal tool designed specifically for such breaches, and within two minutes, she was through the window and inside the bathroom.

She alerted Knuckles, then crept to the door and peeked out; the lights in the bedroom were off, but the illumination from the outside patio gave a soft glow. The room was empty, the drapes pulled closed across the sliding door. As her eyes adjusted, she saw a desk, a wide-screen television, and stacked neatly on the king-size bed, two dozen Faraday bags looking like Easter eggs waiting to be plucked.

She opened her pouch again, pulled out what Knuckles had called her Third Lung—a miniature scuba tank—and set it aside. She removed a device that had a round disk in the center, about two inches in diameter and one inch thick, with multiple cords extending from it.

Called an Octopus, its sole function was to access and copy the entire contents of a cell phone's SIM card. Contacts, call history, text messages, surfed web pages, all of it would be duplicated by the Octopus—even deleted information—and it had a dozen cords coming out, with adapters for every conceivable type of cell phone.

She placed it on the bed and picked out packets four

and seventeen—the ones from their surveillance earlier. She opened the Faraday bags and dumped out seven phones of various makes. She plugged them all in, punched a button on the center of the disk, then sat down to wait, knowing that some encryption protocols would take longer to break than others.

One minute in, proud of her work, she heard a call that caused a jolt of adrenaline.

"Koko, Koko, the host is getting antsy. He's seen the security at the top of the stairs, and he's asking questions."

Uh-oh.

"Knuckles, I'm not done. I need another minute here, and probably ten to get back inside. I have to climb the wall again."

"I don't think we have that sort of time. Abort. Get out."

Already moving, unplugging the phones that were complete and shoving them in their respective bags, she said, "Interdict him. Slow him down."

"I'm going to try. What's your ETA? What do I have to work with?"

"Best case? Seven minutes."

She unplugged the other phones, the last two still being drained, and placed the Faraday bags back where she found them. She scuttled back to the window, shoving everything into her pouch. She was outside in seconds, staring up at the wall.

She took a breath, found her first handhold, and hoisted herself off the loam of the ground. Starting the climb back.

★ 11 ★

Knuckles saw the host talking to security, but wasn't unduly concerned. They'd done nothing to spike, and nobody at all had paid them a second glance, with most buying his CEO story, hook, line, and sinker. His concern grew when the host pointed up the spiral staircase, clearly asking why one of the security men was in the master bedroom.

A diminutive man of about sixty, with close-cropped gray hair and skin the color of coffee, the host wouldn't appear to be a threat, but Knuckles saw how the security man kowtowed to him, nodding his head repeatedly, then talking into his sleeve. Clearly, the host held a power far exceeding his physical stature.

Knuckles excused himself from his conversation, not wanting to pull his directional microphones away from the targets still seated on the couch, but feeling something amiss. He called Jennifer, getting the readout on the length of time she had left. And felt the first bit of adrenaline begin to flow.

He watched the host carefully, checking for a change in demeanor. The man at the top of the stairs came down and talked to him, then pointed at Knuckles. Into the radio, he said, "It's reached a boiling point. Status?"

He heard a grunt, then, "Climbing. Can't talk."

He started moving toward the host, saying, "Give me a time."

"Five. Need five."

Shit. That ain't going to happen.

He walked up to the host and stuck out his hand, introducing himself and using his CEO title as he had previously. The host said, "I don't remember that company being invited."

Knuckles gave his most charming smile and said, "Well, here we are! And it's a great party. There's nothing like coming down to the Caymans on business. Hoping to get some diving in—"

The host cut him off. "Who is upstairs in the bedroom?"

"My date. We ate at a hole-in-the-wall in George Town, and I think some of the conch was bad. She's been on the toilet most of the afternoon."

The host nodded and said, "Would you mind showing me your invitation?"

Knuckles said, "Sure, sure," then made a show of searching the pockets of his tuxedo. He came up empty, extended his hands, and said, "I don't know. Maybe I left it with the man out front."

The host flicked his head at one of the guards, and he disappeared. The host said, "Let's go check on your date. I don't want any medical emergencies."

He started up the staircase and Knuckles said, "She'll be fine. It's just Montezuma's revenge."

The host ignored him. The security man who had come from the top of the stairs held out his hand, telling Knuckles to follow. Knuckles began to climb, keying his radio and saying, "We're coming up the stairs."

The host said, "What?"

Knuckles said, "Nothing," and heard Jennifer grunt, "I'm not there, I'm not there."

Shit.

They reached the master suite, walked around the bed to the sliding bathroom door. The host put his ear to the door, listening for a second, then knocked, saying, "Miss, miss, are you all right?"

No answer.

Knuckles pretended to be concerned, leaning forward and knocking on the door himself. He said, "Jennifer, is everything okay?"

No answer.

The host pulled the handle, finding it locked. He turned to the security man and said, "Open this. Right now."

The guard turned and scurried downstairs. Knuckles made a show of banging on the door, acting as if he was about to panic, shouting her name. Creating enough noise to cover her return—if she made it.

The guard came huffing back up the stairs, carrying a small crowbar. He pushed Knuckles out of the way, jammed it in between the crack of the door and the wall. He cranked back hard. The doorjamb split, and the snap of noise spiked Knuckles into the next zone. No longer concerned with the charade, he now went into combat mode, preparing for a controlled dose of violence.

In the split second between the man jamming in the crowbar and the door exploding open, Knuckles sized up the two men, determining positioning and his next actions. He knew he'd have to take out the security guy first but couldn't become so engaged that the host escaped back downstairs. He had to take them both out before an alarm was raised. Which meant some serious damage to the guy holding the crowbar. There was no time for a nice submission.

The security man pried the crowbar loose, then slammed the door into its sliding well, the wooden protection rolling back with a finality that only Knuckles understood. Knuckles stutter-stepped forward, winding up for a temple strike, and a shriek filled the air.

His arm cocked, the muscles a millisecond away from putting the guard out for the night, Knuckles caught a glimpse of Jennifer and a tangle of clothes.

She screamed, "Get out of here, asshole!"

They all stumbled back, the host looking mortified. Into the damaged doorway, he said, "I'm sorry, I'm sorry." He turned to Knuckles and said, "I apologize profusely."

Knuckles looked indignant, and Jennifer came through the door, holding her skirt and flashing her eyes.

She said, "What in the world is going on? I can't use the bathroom without you guys breaking in? Who's in charge of this damn event?"

The host bowed his head and said, "My sincerest apologies. We thought there was a medical emergency. We thought . . ." He let his comments dribble off, looking to Knuckles for support.

Jennifer glared at the host and said, "Tell that to the next woman you barge in on." She looked at Knuckles and gave an imperceptible nod, saying, "I've had enough of this party. Honey, let's go."

She stormed toward the stairs, and the men followed, the host saying, "Please, don't make a scene. I'm sorry. We only had your best interests at heart."

They reached the bottom and were met by the security man who'd left previously. He leaned in and whispered to the host. He nodded, his face hardening.

Knuckles took Jennifer's hand and headed to the stairwell leading to the bottom floor, and to their escape. He heard the host's voice float above the crowd.

"Wait. Could I have a word before you go?"

★ 12 ★

Knuckles held up, turning around and pulling Jennifer to a stop. The host said, "You aren't on the invitation list. There is no record of you coming through the front door."

Knuckles said, "I've had about enough of this buffoonery. Doesn't matter anyway. You got what you wanted. We're leaving."

One of the security men circled to the right and the host said, "I'm sorry, not until I know who you are."

"I told you."

The host looked at the security man who'd whispered in his ear earlier. The man said, "They do have a website. Based in Tampa, Florida. That checks out, but they sure aren't on the invitation list."

The host nodded, then looked at Knuckles. He said, "You can go, but not until we search you for electronics."

The security man understood what was required before the host could tell him. He spoke into his sleeve.

Knuckles said, "What are you talking about? We had to give all of that up when we came in here."

"Yes. I'm wondering why you haven't asked for your cell phones back before you leave."

Knuckles silently kicked himself and said, "We were searched when we came in, which I'm now regretting. We don't have any electronics. Come on, my date has a little stomachache and now you want to search us? Fuck you. We're leaving."

Even as the words left his mouth, Knuckles knew that it would do no good.

A guard from the front door approached, carrying a wand like those in airports. No way could Knuckles allow that thing to come near them. The conversation had reached a head.

It was time to leave.

He said, "Okay. Fine, fine. Run that thing over us, but after that, we're out of here." He turned to Jennifer and said, "You got your Third Lung handy?"

Ignoring the men, Jennifer said, "Yes, but we still need to get down to the first floor."

"Yeah. I know. That could be a little dicey."

Jennifer looked to the balcony, the guests moving about, enjoying the breeze and the view. She said, "Not really."

The host appeared confused at their conversation and Jennifer said, "These shoes are killing me." She bent down and took them off, holding them in her hand. She looked at Knuckles and said, "Try to keep up."

The guard with the wand motioned to Knuckles, telling him to hold out his arms.

All eyes focused on Knuckles, Jennifer took off running, exploding straight through the open sliding glass door, their original targets still on the couch, staring like everyone else. Before the men around Knuckles had even realized she was moving, she vaulted over the balcony and disappeared from view. The last Knuckles saw was her Velcro skirt floating away, caught in the ocean breeze.

Holy shit.

He turned to the open mouth of the host and said, "Great party. Gotta go."

He sprinted through the room, racing through the sliding glass door and following Jennifer over the balcony. His feet finding purchase on the inch shelf of concrete at the bottom of the balcony, his hands still holding the railing, he searched for Jennifer. He saw her scrambling down a pillar, holding her Jimmy Choos in her mouth.

She hit the patio, creating a stir, but she held her ground and looked up. He heard the host shout and saw the two security goons around the pool begin to react.

Jennifer saw it as well and began running to the ocean, threading her way through the crowd. Knuckles judged the drop, then scrambled until he was hanging from the bottom of the balcony. He took one more look, making sure he wasn't going to break a leg, and let go. He landed hard and rolled, slamming into a statuesque blonde in a red dress, knocking her drink into the air.

He leapt up, ignoring her shouts, disgusted that he didn't have a witty James Bond response. He sprinted around the infinity pool, reaching the stairs that led down to the sunbathing decks. Jennifer was right in front of him, skipping down the steps two at a time. A guard was to her front, both arms out wide, as if he was trying to capture a loose animal.

It was the man who'd "discovered" them doing hanky-panky.

Knuckles took the steps in leaping bounds, closing the gap. He saw Jennifer fling her high heels at the man's head, causing him to raise his arms to block the projectiles. She slid low at that exact moment, taking the guard's legs out from under him and springing back up. He continued to fight, trying to grab her from the ground. He got one ankle in his grasp, but Knuckles reached the scrum, punching him in the head with a rapid one-two strike, stunning him.

Jennifer jerked her leg free and Knuckles jumped over the body, shouting, "You got your lung?"

She held it up, and he dug into his own pouch at the small of his back, seeing a squad of security racing out of the house, all convinced they had their targets cornered against the ocean.

They reached the lower sunbathing deck and Knuckles ripped off his shoes, then tied his tuxedo jacket around his waist, not wanting to leave it behind for the host to find all of the hidden microphones. He glanced back, seeing the men bounding down the stairs.

He flicked out an eight-foot section of 550 cord, one end already tied to his wrist, the other with a loop for Jennifer. He tossed the end to her, speaking fast. "When we hit the surf, I'm going right, away from the lights. Just keep swimming. You feel the line go taut, swim back into the slack."

He held out his Third Lung and said, "Remember, we only have about twenty breaths with these things. We go under, and don't come up. I'm going until we're out of air. You run out first, give the line a tug."

The Third Lung was a modified scuba gadget based on the HEED—helicopter emergency egress device— used by aircrews flying over water. A quarter of the size, it had a quarter of the life.

She nodded and Knuckles moved to the cliff edge, Jennifer putting the loop around her left wrist and waiting on his command.

Knuckles looked back, saw the men running down the stairs, now past the first sunbathing deck, and said, "Hope Pike's watching. Time to go."

And jumped off the cliff.

They broke the water together, bobbed up long enough to emplace the small mouthpiece of the Third Lung, and Knuckles went under, stroking hard. He swam with fast, deep strokes to get away from the light, hoping to cause their pursuers to see nothing on the surface and wonder what the hell had just happened. The ocean became black, the light from the castle fading away. He kept swimming, one hand extended to his front to prevent him from slamming into a rock, using an internal compass and the experience from a bazillion night dives to dictate where he should go.

Three minutes later, he felt a tug on his line and stopped swimming. He drifted to the surface, breaking the water silently. He saw they were on the western side of the outcropping, nothing but tangled scrub between them and the house, vague shouting drifting over the surf.

Jennifer popped up next to him, just as quietly. She dropped the Lung and gasped, whispering, "Are you a fish? I ran out thirty seconds ago."

He said, "Why didn't you tug?"

She said, "I thought for sure you would run out too."

He chuckled and said, "We keep going west." He pulled out his phone—an innocuous replica of an iPhone 6 but definitely not original equipment, including the fact that it was waterproof—and initiated an internal beacon.

He said, "Hope Pike's on the ball."

Twenty minutes later, now swimming on the surface, the castle far behind them, Knuckles caught a glimpse of movement on the open water. He aimed his phone at the movement and took a picture, causing the camera to flash. The movement swerved his way, and he bobbed, waiting. The Zodiac pulled abreast of them, making no noise, Pike working the motor. He said, "I take it things didn't go as planned."

Knuckles tossed his waterproof pouch over the gunwale and said, "The microphones and earbuds are destroyed, but the digital recorder and Octopus are fine. They have no idea what our target was or what we were doing there. As far as I'm concerned, it was mission success."

Jennifer threw in her own pouch, grabbed the rope anchored to points around the Zodiac, and said, "Not really."

Knuckles said, "What? You didn't get the phone data?"

She hoisted herself over the side and said, "Yeah, I got it. But I lost my damn Jimmy Choos."

★ 13 ★

Murphy's pub was beginning to fill up with the happy hour crowd, the locals starting to push out the tourists by sheer numbers. Having worked plenty of hours up in Washington, DC, I knew the rhythm of Old Town Alexandria, and had managed to get a table in the back, facing the door. Even though it was a little touristy, I still loved it, and since I was the stationary element for this meeting, I got to pick the location. If it had been up to Knuckles, it would have been at some hipster coffee shop where he could hit on a coed, using his sensitive lines.

We'd been back a week from the Caymans, and for some reason, Kurt Hale wanted a face-to-face meeting. It wasn't unusual, really, but it didn't happen that often, especially since I'd left active duty and started working with Jennifer.

We were partners in a company called Grolier Recovery Services, a unique—or, as Jennifer liked to call it, "boutique"—business that specialized in archeological work around the world. We didn't actually do the digging. We facilitated it by coordinating everything from getting the proper permits from the host nation to providing security on the site. Since we'd formed in 2011, we'd been contracted by everyone from private millionaires who fancied themselves to be Indiana Jones to accredited universities, but by far our primary work was for the US government. As in the Taskforce.

Created with support from Kurt Hale, our true mission was as a cover organization conducting counterterrorism missions around the world. Because it *was* under deep cover as a functioning, for-profit corporation, we didn't want to be associated with the umbrella cover of Blaisdell Consulting the Taskforce used over in Clarendon, and thus did these little face-to-face meetings at innocuous places around DC.

Jennifer came over carrying a couple of drinks, sat down, and said, "Quicker service from the bar." I saw that there wasn't a lime attached to the glass and said, "Is that just a Coke?"

Indignant, she said, "It's only four thirty. And we're on the clock."

I started to mutter something about Kurt paying for the drinks, when I saw Knuckles come through the door, by himself.

I waved and he walked over, taking a chair. I said, "Where's Kurt?"

"Held up doing something with personnel. Some sort of crisis. He'll be here shortly. He told me to go ahead."

I said, "Okay, then, what's this all about? I know it's not that castle mission. Nothing in it that was life-or-death. Unless he's going to make me pay for the waterlogged electronics."

He laughed and said, "Well, it's not the castle mission per se. But it *is* because of that. Remember Guy George?"

"Yeah, of course. His brother was just KIA, right?"

Guy had served in the same troop as me in a Special Mission Unit on Fort Bragg, before I'd been recruited to the Taskforce by Kurt. We knew each other well enough, and had been in more than one scrape overseas together, back in the bad days of Iraq. Well, back in the *US* bad days of Iraq. I didn't think Iraq would see any good days during my lifetime.

Guy had come over to the Taskforce a few years after me, along with a SEAL called Decoy. The one Jennifer had seen killed in front of her. They'd done Assessment and Selection together, then he'd gone to Johnny's team, and Decoy had come to mine. Well, that's not exactly true. Decoy had gone to my old team. Knuckles, as my second-in-command, had taken over as team leader after I left active duty—under a cloud. Since then, I'd come back and had become team leader again, as a civilian in Grolier Recovery Services.

As Facebook would say, it's complicated.

Knuckles said, "Yeah. That's right. Guy's brother was KIA in Afghanistan working with seventh group. You know the Oversight Council update is tomorrow, right?"

"No. I don't keep track of that shit. That's what Kurt gets paid for."

"Yeah, I'm with you. Well, it was also our biannual monkey show for the Oversight Council, where they anoint some poor fuck with an award. Guy was the chosen one this time for that hit in Croatia. The one that gave us the intel on the vice president's son."

"Good for him. Better him than me. What's that got to do with this meeting?"

"He was adamant about not going to his brother's memorial in Montana, saying he would wait until the burial at Arlington, so he was good to go for the ceremony. The memorial is either tomorrow or the next day, I can't remember. Anyway, after our data from the Caymans was fed into the system, he had some meltdown. I don't know why. Long and the short of it is, he decided he needed to go. Needed a break."

"So? That's a good thing. If I were Kurt, I'd have ordered him to leave. Better he's doing it voluntarily."

I had a little personal experience on losing someone close to you. Losing blood kin. I too had been ordered to stand down after, and had ignored it until it became a blister of pus, which was the reason I left active duty—and the Taskforce—under a cloud. I was glad Guy was taking the time off.

Knuckles grinned and said, "The 'so what' is that Kurt needs a new awardee. Someone to prance in front of the Council. And that Cayman mission fits the bill."

I immediately snapped back, "Bullshit! I'm not doing that. I'm a damn civilian. This is supposed to help out guys on active duty. Guys like you. I am *not* going in front of the Council and getting some bullshit award. No way."

Jennifer understood my tolerance for such dog and pony shows, which was nonexistent, but also saw the bigger picture. She said, "Hey, hey. Come on. It's not all gunfighting. You want to play in the game, you also have to play by the rules. All they want to do is thank you. Look at it this way: It's your chance to show them you're a thinking, erudite man instead of a muscle with a trigger finger."

She looked at Knuckles and said, "It might help alleviate all of the fear those guys have about Grolier Recovery Services. Pike can be the smartest guy in the room when he's forced to act like a human. I think it's a good idea."

Knuckles grinned and leaned forward conspiratorially. He said, "I'm glad you feel that way, Koko, because they don't give a shit about Pike. The award's for you."

★ 14 ★

I heard his words, and, embarrassingly, my first thought was *What the hell?* I'm *not good enough?* Like a guy who said he'd never go to a party, then found out he wasn't invited.

Jennifer said, "Me? What for? The whole purpose of those awards is to help the guys still on active duty. I've never even been in the military."

Knuckles said, "Yeah, I know, but we're in a whole new world. Kurt wants to showcase you. No offense, but you're the only female Operator in the Taskforce. It'll sell well on the political front."

I said, "That's absolute bullshit. No way is GRS going to be leveraged for some sort of political horse-trading. They can use our company for killing terrorists, but we're not playing those games. Kurt can't just bang the drum and ask us to start dancing."

Knuckles laughed and held up his hands. "Calm down. I told Kurt this would happen. Nobody's being hurt. Guy will still get his award; he just won't have a ceremony. Kurt's got something he wants to say tomorrow at the Council meeting, and the only time he can guarantee they all attend is one of these award ceremonies. He wasn't going to tell them it was off."

Jennifer said, "I don't like being a showpiece. I didn't come to the Taskforce because I have some mission for women's rights. It's hard enough just getting any of the males to trust me. This ceremony will set that back to the beginning."

The words hung for a bit, then Knuckles said, "Remember what you just told Pike? About showing the Council what he's really like? And how that would do some good? This will do some good. The Taskforce knows what you're capable of. This won't change that."

She balled up a napkin and said, "*You* know what I can do. You and the rest of Pike's team are the only ones who do. Decoy's dead. The others look at me as a liability. I *know* how this will play in the team room."

Knuckles looked at me, and I shrugged, agreeing with her. *Fuck the Council.* He said, "This award isn't going to alter your actions on the Decoy tape. That's set in stone."

She flinched at the words, seeing the fight in her mind and not being sure what to say. I leaned forward into Knuckles's face, angry that he'd brought that up. It was an event she was still dealing with, alone at night, when the bad man comes.

"Don't go there. That's not right."

Knuckles said, "It *is* right. And if you were the team leader you claim to be, instead of protecting her as her *partner*, you'd see it. Her reputation has nothing to do with this ceremony. She already owns her reputation."

She said, "This has nothing to do with Decoy—"

He cut her off and said, "Yes, it does. At the end of the day, just like you told Pike, it's all about operating. All about permission. Stroke the Council a little bit. Make them feel good about what we're doing. Take off the edge of killer-commando crap and put on the pink ruffle of women's equality. Who cares if it's fake? The men in the team room won't, I promise. Pike's no longer there, but I am."

She leaned back, not liking the logic. I didn't either, but I saw it to be true. The Oversight Council was designed to execute Taskforce operations in the absence of politics, but in America, that was impossible. Politics always trumped the mission. Always. And that damn Decoy tape spoke for itself.

I said, "So Jennifer's going to be paraded in front of the Council tomorrow? What's she supposed to say? What's the message?"

Knuckles looked toward the door and said, "Ask the man yourself." I saw Kurt coming down the length of the bar. Knuckles grinned and said, "I'm just a team member."

He winked at me, and, for the first time, I wondered when he'd leave my team. After my fall from grace, then my return, he'd voluntarily turned over command of his team—my team—solely because of our relationship. We were closer than brothers, but hearing his words today, he proved again he was clearly smarter than 95 percent of the men inside the Taskforce—and they were some pretty smart individuals to begin with. Truth be told, he was smarter than me. And I was keeping him down by making him stay forever number two. How long would he be willing to remain there? The thought scared me.

Kurt approached the table, and Jennifer stood, giving him an embrace. He said, "How's my favorite female Operator?"

She said, "You mean your *only* female Operator? Apparently about to do a song and dance for you."

Kurt looked at Knuckles, and he said, "Hey, you didn't say it was classified."

I stood up, shook his hand, and said, "Apparently, this ceremony is so horrible you scared off the one guy who was supposed to get the award."

Kurt's expression became grim. "Something else scared Guy off. I just hope he's taking the time to deal with it."

★ 15 ★

Guy George laid out his new identity on the hotel bed, checking one more time to see if he could find anything indicating they were forged. Passport, credit cards, driver's license, and cellular phone, all in the name of Sean Parnell. And all looked perfect.

It was decision time. Kill or not kill?

It had been a week since he'd received the box with his brother's belongings, and he'd spent the days working in the Taskforce headquarters, studying intelligence and helping the analysts focus on various threats around the world. It was an easy, mindless task. No stress and no danger. In between, he focused on his target package, building linkages and fleshing out what he knew of the Qatari man Kurt had called Haider al-Attiya. The man his brother knew as Abu Kamal.

In the back of his mind, he'd toyed with the fantasy of hunting down the faces on the armband. A daydream that helped him to pass the time. Using his training and knowledge, he constructed exactly how he would do it, cornering the man in one climactic fight, having him beg for his life, then taking it violently. Eventually, he began working the problem back from the actual confrontation. Back to the beginning, occupying his mind with a fantasy to alleviate the pain.

How would he do it if he had no help from the Task-force? What assets would he need? How could he evade the very net he worked for? With an insider's perspective, he worried the problem like a piece of meat stuck in his teeth, day after day, over and over again.

The first hurdle was finding an ambush location. Qatar was the obvious choice, since the target lived there, and more than likely the other faces on the armband did too. The Russians had killed some Chechens there a few years ago, and he knew Doha pretty well. The primary problem would be accessing the target. He would be on Haider's home turf, and getting in, killing him, and getting out would be difficult. Not even the Russians had managed that. Not to mention, he'd need to interrogate the subject before termination. He would have to learn the real names and locations for the other pictures on the sleeve.

He decided he needed a different site, someplace neutral, where the target would hold no advantage. Which meant more research into the target's habits and movements. In his daydream, he set that aside for the moment.

Mindlessly working with the analysts, answering their questions and helping them focus on real-world targets, his daydreams began moving farther back upstream, focusing on the mechanics. What would he need for the mission? The actual nuts and bolts?

He'd done enough clandestine kill-capture missions to understand exactly what was required, and for this fantasy mission, it was easier than a Taskforce operation. He had no need to worry about exfiltrating with the target to some support facility for interrogation, or about infiltrating an entire team, or—worst of all—waiting on the Oversight Council for permission.

The more he thought about it, the more he realized that the entire mission profile would be much less complicated. In the Taskforce, the end state of an Omega operation was no evidence. No trace that a mission had even occurred. In his daydream, that didn't matter. He would leave the body where it lay. But he still needed some items.

Weapons he could get, even untraceable ones. It would require touching contacts he had made in the past while working for the Taskforce, and maybe a healthy dose of cash, but he could do it. With his savings he could buy cell phones, rent vehicles, and charge plane tickets. He could afford all of it, but he ran afoul of what that would require: Each purchase would be tied to him. To his identity.

This presented a significant problem. He had more than one target to kill, and if his name was attached to the first one, the Taskforce would be hunting him, using everything they had. For all of the information and knowledge he had gained working there, they had also learned about him. They had every bit of data on the life of Guy George that could be obtained, to include biometrics. They'd stop his ability to operate within seconds, yanking his credit cards, revoking his passport, and putting him on a no-fly list.

Greater than that, though, was the loyalty he owed to his country. He understood the implications of Taskforce exposure, and any investigation of him by a foreign intelligence organization would lead to his military history, then possibly to the Taskforce. He was aggravated by the cavalier attitude the Oversight Council and the Taskforce had taken about his brother, but he was still faithful.

Such an exposure would irreparably harm the defense of the nation he'd sworn to protect, and thus his mission would have the added stricture of protecting his men. His friends.

In his daydream, of course.

After work, he'd taken to doing research on the Internet, leading him to the stinking underbelly of the dark web, a place frequented by criminals and pedophiles. He'd learned that just about anything could be purchased, if the price was right. For instance, he could have a fake passport overnight, but it would fool only a bouncer at a bar. Getting one that would fool a customs official, with holograms and an RFID chip that duplicated a real US passport, required more time. And more information.

He needed a name and social security number that was valid, one that was already in the database of the giant behemoth of the US government, and wasn't in use by someone else.

He'd never considered the problem of traveling in alias before, with the myriad of databases that had to be cleared, simply because the documents he'd held had been provided by the US government. He hadn't needed to worry about someone checking if they were real, because they *were* real.

He toyed with the idea of stealing his Taskforce alias documents for his fantasy mission. After all, he was working in the headquarters and could draw them without question. He'd already memorized the fake life they represented, and it would shield the Taskforce from exposure, but it wouldn't solve the original problem: The Taskforce would immediately recognize they'd been taken, and then begin cutting off the ties that allowed him to operate, just as surely as if he were using his real identity.

He was forced to build from scratch, which meant a name and social security number. A person who was real, but no longer using them. And he hit on a stroke of genius.

Late one night, lying in bed, his mind toying with the problem, he had remembered a man he served with who had been killed in Iraq. His name was Sean Parnell, and he had gone to Ranger School with Guy in 1998. Before identity theft had become a problem.

Back then, the military used soldiers' social security numbers for everything. It was stamped all over, willynilly, on flight manifests, duffel bags, and on official Army orders.

Guy had gone to his closet and dug through his personal files, looking for his orders awarding him the coveted Ranger tab. He found it, holding it under the light of a bedside lamp. Name after name listed, with the social security numbers beside them. He found Parnell's name, then jotted down the number.

Just in case.

The next day, after work, he'd contacted a seller on the deep web, telling himself it was just for research. He wasn't really going to do anything with the passport. It was just an experiment to see how such things worked. The Taskforce, chasing terrorists, might want to know how easy it was.

Four days later, using a post office box rented with yet another alias name, he had his passport. A day after that, he had a driver's license. A real one, from Virginia, which allowed him to open a new bank account.

Two days after that, his alter identity complete, the

data from Pike's mission in the Caymans had floated across his desk.

Haider al-Attiya was supposed to be the one at the party, but according to Pike's initial report, he hadn't shown, so Guy had lost interest. Eventually, the finalized roll-up of the mission had arrived, including a photo of the man who *had* attended.

His name was Ahmed Mansoor, and nobody in the Taskforce had any data on him. He was a ghost. While the Taskforce focused on Brazilian mines, yacht trips to Key West, and Qatar conspiracies involving rare earth metals, Guy focused on the photograph.

It matched another face from the target package. One of the pictures without a name, and this man had gone to the Cayman Islands in lieu of Haider. It was proof positive that Haider was involved in his brother's death. The coincidence was too great to ignore. No way would both pictures be on his brother's arm in Afghanistan and now both be working with the same entity from Qatar.

He'd taken the information to Kurt, and his commander had given him a look of sympathy. With the additional information, Kurt had promised to bring it to the Oversight Council, but Guy had seen the futility behind Kurt's eyes.

That night, he'd lain in bed and made his decision. His first tentative step out of the daydream and into reality.

The next day, he'd put in for leave, claiming he now wanted to go to Montana for his brother's memorial. He'd avoided Kurt Hale all day long, and then had flown not to Montana but to Key West, Florida.

Ahmed Mansoor's current location.

★ 16 ★

Murphy's was starting to get rowdy, with happy hour in full swing. Kurt shook my hand and sat down, looking at the drinks on our table. He said, "Soda? What the hell, Pike?"

I glared at Jennifer and said, "She told me it was bad form."

Kurt flagged a waitress and ordered a round. When she'd left, he said, "Trust me, I could use a beer."

I said, "Because you're pimping out Jennifer like every other general with a female to hoist over his head?"

He rubbed his face and said, "No. Actually, I need a drink because I'm *not* a general."

I looked at Knuckles, but he was just as confused. I said, "What's up, sir?"

He said, "I've been fighting this traditional military architecture forever. Created our organization, then took it to the enemy, but the one thing I forgot is that we work *inside* that traditional architecture. Like it or not."

The round of beers came, and he took his, drawing a gulp. He said, "Blaine's getting RIFed."

RIF stood for Reduction in Force, and was something the military went through after every surge in recruitment due to war. Basically, the military expanded because of need, sometimes loosening recruiting requirements to fill the ranks. When the need was over, the military contracted, getting rid of those it deemed undesirable.

It had happened after World War II, Vietnam, and the "peace dividend" from the end of the Cold War. Now, after we proclaimed the wars in Afghanistan and Iraq "over," regardless of the fighting still going on, the military began its purges again, getting rid of those at the bottom rungs to meet the new congressionally mandated size requirements. But that made no sense for anyone in the Taskforce. No bragging, just facts, we were the absolute best of the best.

I said, "What's the RIF got to do with Blaine?"

"He got his SERB paperwork today. He's being involuntarily retired. Because I didn't protect him."

SERB stood for Selective Early Retirement Board. In today's military, anyone at the rank of lieutenant colonel or higher who'd shown no upward movement was placed in the crosshairs. The Army had no emotion about the matter. The men were shoved out the door like a guest who'd overstayed his welcome. But that wasn't us. Shit, we were the shiny edge of the knife blade, conducting complex operations all over the globe, and Blaine Alexander was the one who controlled all of them. The one who made national-level decisions in the span of a second. The guy who'd saved America's ass on more than one occasion.

Our unit was a little bit different from the ordinary military construct, to put it mildly. Not wanting the traditional military hierarchy, which led to traditional military inertia, Kurt had built a thinking, adapting organization. In the traditional military, when you reached a certain level, you had a certain rank and a certain predetermined job. In our organization, rank meant nothing. All that mattered was skill.

We were huge on the cover organization and support side, but really, really small on the tippy end of the spear. We had five teams total, comprising between five and ten men—all hand-selected—but we had literally thousands supporting us, be it in generating intelligence for targets, hacking for cyber penetration, or just cover organizations like Grolier Recovery Services.

Because we were so unique, Kurt had eschewed the traditional military mind-set of a pyramid, where the commander was in charge based on time-in-grade and not on the situation at hand. Sometimes, there was no reason to have *any* higher headquarters, and unlike the military, Kurt realized this. The greater military had spent the years in the War on Terror building one headquarters after another, until the warfighter was buried in bureaucracy, building PowerPoints for one useless layer after another.

Kurt had done the opposite. He'd let us run free, without an overarching command, trusting us to do what was right, but he'd picked one officer to be the man in charge when the time came, like plug and play. When we reached an endgame and were about to execute an action with national implications—what we called an Omega operation—the leadership meshed on top of us. And that guy was Blaine Alexander.

I said, "Why the hell is Blaine getting SERB paperwork? He's the cream of the crop. Well, at least as far as you officer types go."

Kurt smiled at the slur and said, "Because he's been shining a seat with his ass at the Joint Staff for the last four years. While his peers have been in combat."

"Yeah? That's his cover position. You don't have a way to protect him?"

Blaine, like all the members of the Taskforce—like I had done before I became a civilian—lived a dual life. They killed or captured terrorists in secret but were officially assigned to a real military unit. While they faced the guns and dying, they were given reports for some innocuous position inside the giant Department of Defense architecture. Actually, inside the greater government, as we had members of the CIA doing the same thing.

Kurt said, "I could have, but I fucked him. He was turned down for colonel on two promotion boards because, according to his file, he's done nothing. He didn't care, because he loves his job, but I missed the signals. I mean, he has a good file, but it's all fake-ass staff work at the Pentagon, while his peers have been commanding guys in combat. I never thought about how this would play out long-term. I figured he could stay forever. Turns out, the Army had a different idea. I screwed him."

Knuckles said, "Surely you can fix that. I mean, we *are* the Taskforce."

Staring into his beer, Kurt said, "Yeah, yeah. I can, and I will. He'll be okay, rankwise, but that doesn't alter the bigger problem. He makes colonel, and he's the same rank as me. We don't have a job for another colonel. There's no position for him. I can control the structure and positions of those below me, but I can't have him on my staff with the same rank. He'll have to go anyway."

I said, "Then you just go to general officer. Get your brigadier. Shit, we have the entire intelligence and defense establishment on the Oversight Council. How hard could that be?"

"I thought of that, and talked it over with Wolffe. The problem is that GO appointments are approved by

Congress. I also haven't been doing a damn thing for the last six years. As far as my records show, I'm nothing but a burned-out colonel on the staff of the J3 Special Operations division. Yeah, the powers in the Oversight Council could make it happen, but it would never pass without intervention, which will invite scrutiny."

He pushed a toothpick through the ring his beer had made on the table. He looked old. Older than I'd ever seen him look before.

He said, "Shit, have you seen the political knife fights that go on here? In this town? No way can I let that investigation get started. Some eager beaver opposed to the administration will tear into the nomination for political points, and possibly expose the Taskforce. Bring down the administration."

★ 17 ★

Kurt made the statement in such a manner that the promotion meant nothing at all. Which was what I would expect from him. All he wanted to do was solve the problem, as he'd been doing for decades.

Jennifer said, "What does the rank matter? I get I've never been in the military, but isn't that sort of the same BS you tried to get away from when you made the Taskforce? I mean, I don't have any rank, and yet you trusted me in the Caymans. *Pike's* no longer in the military, and he's leading a team."

I said, "Yeah. Why don't you just make Blaine a civilian? A GS-15 or something? Hell, your own deputy is a civilian."

Kurt said, "Wolffe is a standing member of the CIA. Hardly a civilian."

George Wolffe was a legend in the CIA, working inside the Special Activities Division, he'd been involved in just about every covert action the United States had conducted, both good and bad.

I said, "But Blaine is of the same mettle. Just because he'll become a civilian doesn't mean he's going to *become* a civilian. Any more than I did."

Kurt took another sip of his beer and said, "I'm not

worried about Blaine. Or you, for that matter. I'm worried about what I created. About the Taskforce. We're starting to get entrenched. Starting to be something other than a flash in the pan, and what we do now will solidify who we are."

"What's that mean?"

"It means I can't control the future. It means if I choose Blaine as a civilian because he's *Blaine*, someone in the future may choose another civilian who isn't Blaine. It means I've created something that needs to have left and right limits."

He took a sip of beer and continued. "Honestly, I'm worried about the precedent I've set with you. You *and* Jennifer. We had firm criteria to get into the Taskforce, and I broke that because of personalities. I did it for the right reasons, but someone behind me can abuse it. I have to prevent that."

I realized he was talking about things way, way above my pay grade. I said, "Are you saying you're leaving?"

"No, no. Not yet. But there's a presidential election coming up, and a change of administration one way or the other. President Warren *is* leaving, and we have to prepare for that. He created the Taskforce, and he's all we've known. This isn't like the Department of Defense, where the president changes over but the systems remain intact. When the new administration is read on, it'll be a new world. They'll focus on what's been established, and may— or may not—use it as it was intended. It worries me."

He looked at each of us in turn, then said, "I hand-selected each of you. I picked you, recruited you, then put you through selection." Jennifer leaned back, and he amended his statement, saying, "Okay, I didn't hand-select *you*, Jennifer, but I did let you go through selection because I'd seen what you held. Hear me out."

He toyed with his pint glass, thinking, then said, "I had that control, but I won't always have it. The next man may choose a different route, and all it will take is one man to go bad to bring this whole thing down."

He bored into me and said, "Like you almost did."

I felt like I'd been slapped. Yeah, I'd made an ass of myself, sinking into a morass of alcohol and self-hatred, but I'd never done anything to compromise the Taskforce. I said, "Hey, sir, all due respect, that's bullshit. I would—"

He cut me off with a hand and said, "There's a reason I asked both of you up here. Jennifer gets the award, but I need your skill. Your special skill."

The table grew quiet. Still fuming, I waited on his next words. He said, "You know Guy George?"

I said, "Yeah. You know I do. We were in the same troop when you were the squadron commander."

"I think he's going off the reservation. Understand, I have no proof. Just a vibe. The same one I had with you, way back when. I ignored it then, not knowing any better, but I don't intend to repeat that. I think he's got a vendetta because of his brother. I want you to talk him off the ledge."

I said, "How? Why me?"

He said, "The how is your damn information from the Caymans. I had him here in the headquarters, collating information, getting some downtime. He took your data from the castle operation, and sure as shit, the guy there was potentially one of the pictures on his brother's target package. Originally, he was convinced that a Qatari was behind his brother's death, some bigwig in the government, and we stood him down on that because of a lack of evidence. It was conspiracy theory stuff. Then, when your data appeared, showing another Qatari who was associated with the first, his face *also* on the target package, he went ballistic. He's convinced they killed his brother."

I leaned back and said, "Well, maybe they did."

Kurt took a deep breath, choosing his next words carefully. "Yeah, maybe they did. I want to bring the new evidence to the Council tomorrow. At Jennifer's award ceremony. I want to get sanction to chase them, and I will. The guys from Qatar won't kill anyone else, but they'll be removed from the chessboard by an official Taskforce mission. Not because of a vendetta. I need you to make that happen."

Confused, I said, "How? You want me to go hunt the guys from Qatar? I'm all ears, but I don't have a Taskforce target package."

"No. I want you to go to Montana. Go talk to Guy. He's about to walk off the cliff, and you've been there. You know what he's going through. Talk to him. You guys were in the same troop, and he respects you. Just don't let him do anything stupid."

The waitress came over and I asked for a rum and Coke. The beer wasn't cutting it. I knew that, in order to do what he said, I'd have to dip a toe into my own blackness. Hell, to succeed in bringing Guy back from the abyss, I'd probably have to roll in the blackness like a stripper in oil. It was something I'd worked hard to leave behind, and definitely didn't want to revisit.

Kurt saw my face and said, "Pike, I wouldn't ask. I really wouldn't, but I think this is important. Just go talk to him. Let him know where you were, and what happened. Let him know there's better ways of handling it."

I took a breath and looked at Knuckles. At my teammate. He nodded. Solemn.

I said, "Okay. I'll do it. If that's what you want, I'll do it."

I felt the tendrils of the beast, laughing at how easy it was to return.

When I'd lost my family, I became what some would call a sociopath. Before, I had been a trained killer at the apex of the predator chain, but with a moral compass. I did what was necessary to protect the United States. I was the White Knight keeping people from harm. After my loss, I was still an apex predator. That hadn't disappeared.

But my compass had.

If Guy was the same way, Kurt had a lot more worries than getting Blaine promoted.

★ 18 ★

Even in the wintertime, Key West was muggy. Cool and crisp in the morning, the early dawn had relinquished its grip, giving way to the heat of the southernmost point in the United States.

Guy sat on a park bench outside the Westin Resort, in front of a marina housing very expensive yachts, all in the shadow of a giant cruise ship. His eyes were on one boat in particular.

Finding a spot just south of the famed Mallory Square, now deserted by the street performers and sidewalk vendors who plied the tourists coming to watch the sunset, he'd been sitting in front of the docks, drinking coffee, since nine in the morning. It was going on noon, and so far, outside of seeing some crew members, there was no other movement on the boat. The only activity had been the cruise ship vomiting out its passengers for a day in Key West. His target had not shown, and Guy was wondering if he'd missed him, mistakenly relying on his earlier reconnaissance of the target's pattern of life.

The yacht itself was large by any standards except the cruise ship, with a line that stretched over a hundred feet, a sleek, modern vessel with sweeping decks that made it look somewhat like a large dart. It had been little trouble to locate. With the information Pike had turned up, all it had taken was asking a few questions of some locals, and a quick trip to major marinas in Key West that were big enough to house such a beast. He knew the vessel would have to register, having come from out of the country, and he found it after a little more than an hour of pedaling his rented bike up and down the island, talking to the dockmasters. The large marina in Key West Bight held many such yachts, but his target was not moored there. He'd eventually located it outside of the Westin Resort.

He'd watched it for one cycle of darkness, finding his target and shadowing him, still in the myth that he was just pretending. Just seeing if he could do what his brother demanded. Ironically, he knew the boardwalk in front of the Westin Resort intimately, as it was just south of Fleming Key and the US Army's Special Forces Combat Diver Qualification Course, a school he had attended not too many years ago—and one his brother was set to attend when he returned from Afghanistan. Nothing much had changed in Key West, but for what he needed to do, he had to remain completely anonymous, and the location wasn't advantageous.

Among all the quacks and hermits of Key West, he had a greater fear of bumping into a friend from Special Forces than he did of the target identifying he was being followed. Truthfully, that was always a perennial danger inside the Taskforce. They penetrated the most hostile nations on Earth, and there weren't that many people who could. The men and women who could do so would routinely know each other from a past life, and it wouldn't be the first time he'd run into some badass pretending to be a pipeline surveyor while he himself was pretending to be an investment banker. But now he would be the only one professing a false reason to be in Key West. Better not to ever meet, as the soldier would invariably invite him for a night of debauchery and take him away from his target. Not that he intended to do anything with the guy anyway.

At least that's what he kept telling himself.

By four in the afternoon, he'd had lunch, walked through the shopping area, and had gelato at an outdoor café in view of the dock. Even the cruise ship was gone, taking its passengers to another port of call, and Guy realized he was wearing out his welcome. While many, many people sat and watched the view at this location, none stayed as long as him. There were several hired security guards along the wharf whose job was to look for anomalies in the people walking about, searching for trouble, and Guy was beginning to feel his heat state. Beginning to back off his plan.

Since, well, he had no plan.

At fifteen minutes past five, eating his third gelato, he saw the target break the bridge of the yacht, talking to a crew member and wearing board shorts, a Hawaiian shirt, and flip-flops. The neatly groomed mustache completed the ensemble, making him look like every other tourist in Key West.

Guy exited the shop and sauntered around the dock, passing the wooden path leading from the boat to dry land. Guy took a seat in Mallory Square, knowing his target was headed to Duval Street. It was now closing in on sunset, and the tourist crowds were gathering around the street performers. Perfect for blending in.

He made as if he wanted to watch someone right at the tip of the square, a graying, long-haired man with a pride of cats. He had no idea what the draw was, but the crowd provided Guy the protection he needed. Pretending to watch catman, he kept one eye on the entrance to the square. He watched the target break out of the crowds near the dock and pass by him, oblivious to his presence.

Guy followed, now intent on tracking his prey. Or just following out of idle curiosity. He wasn't really sure which, and not looking too hard to find out. Deep down, in his soul, he knew this was ridiculous.

What was he doing? Really? Was he going to kill this guy in Key West? On US soil, all because of a grainy picture glued to an armband from Afghanistan? Seriously?

He was way outside of any official sanction. He was in the United States, where the Taskforce was forbidden from operating, tracking a guy who had no Taskforce mandate. Not even exploratory Alpha, and certainly not Omega, with a rider of DOA. It took many, many months and reams of evidence to give Omega for a capture mission, and an imminent threat to American lives to sanction the Omega authority with the caveat of Dead or Alive. He had nothing but derision from the Taskforce commander about his theory.

He pushed the questions to the rear and wove between the crowds, keeping his target in sight.

The man took a right at a juncture of the square and walked down a narrow alley lined with beer drinkers and incredibly bad acoustic musicians mangling Jimmy Buffett. Guy followed, wondering if there was some sort of gravitational pull for musicians that caused all caterwauling guitar players to end up in Key West.

The target reached an intersection with a park. Guy hung back, near enough to still be tormented by the music, watching and waiting. A waitress approached and he waved her away, seeing the Arab enter the park. Trouble.

No more than fifty meters across, it was a jungle of busts on concrete stalks, a history of the men and women of Key West, with a large sculpture in the center of the area. The target was reading the plaques below the busts, leaving Guy at a disadvantage.

The park had a separate exit, meaning the man could escape before Guy could react from the far side. Guy could either follow in, as the only other man to do so, or wait. If he followed, he'd be remembered. Not burned, but definitely remembered. He needed the burn to happen at execution. Not now.

But if he didn't follow, the target would exit on a different street. Away from where he was. He would lose him. Not a game changer, because odds were he could just repeat the stakeout the following day, but the risks increased with that, both because of the security guards remembering him and because he wasn't sure how long the target was staying in Key West. Guy might wake up tomorrow only to find the boat gone, his mission foiled.

And maybe that was for the best. But something in Guy didn't think so. Wouldn't think that way.

Guy penetrated the park, seeing the target reading yet another bust. He hung back, pretending to be interested, but he knew it looked odd. Two single men staring at busts of those long dead at sunset was not a recipe for success. One could explain his actions. The other could not.

It was the way of surveillance, and the reason nobody in the Taskforce did singleton follows. Nobody but idiots like him, out on a mission for reasons he couldn't articulate.

Guy was about to exit the way he'd come, calling the night a loss, when the target exited onto Front Street, walking with a purpose. Guy followed through the park, keeping his distance and wondering if the target had an ulterior motive for coming here. Board Shorts and Flip-Flops was moving with a stride he hadn't before, the target no longer walking as a tourist but now clearly with a destination in mind.

Maybe Guy wouldn't have to make a decision. Maybe the asshole was about to make it for him. Maybe he could get the evidence he needed.

Guy exited the park, feeling his pulse increase. The target walked across Front Street, down Greene Street, and strode right up to Captain Tony's Saloon, an indoor/outdoor bar known the world over. A tourist attraction. The place where Jimmy Buffett got his start and Ernest Hemingway drank his life away. The only good omen about it was the tree growing through the bar and out the roof. It was a hanging tree, a place where many evil shits like the Arab had met their fate in the distant past.

The Arab tapped the bartender's hand and took a seat. Disgusted, Guy slunk by him and found a stool across the bar, his back to the ubiquitous guitar player wailing away, with a pillar between him and the target.

★ 19 ★

So the asshole from Afghanistan is a boozing Arab. Guy should have known. Nothing nefarious was going on in Key West, and they were both pretending to be something they weren't. Guy that he was a tourist not out to kill, and the Arab that he was a tourist not out to embrace Allah.

It caused a spasm of anger.

Two rum drinks later, the target was on the move again, cutting across Greene to the famed Duval Street, Guy behind him, wondering why on earth he was still following. The anger was growing, a living thing, but he couldn't brace the Arab here, on one of the most heavily congested streets in Key West.

The freaks, tourists, and all-around weird were swirling about, something that would have been fun a decade ago but was muted on this night. Guy's wrath was palpable. Something real. Something dark, and looking for release. With this many drunks bumping about, Guy realized he'd be in a fight before the night was out, more than likely sending some poor schlub who didn't deserve it to the hospital. He needed to break contact. To reassess.

He could not.

The target passed Petronia Street, the crosswalks

painted multicolored hues, entering what Guy and his SF cohorts used to call Rainbow Row. The burlesque gay quarter. The next thing he knew, the target went inside a gay cabaret, taking a seat up front to watch the show. For Guy, the hypocrisy only heightened his anger.

The bar smelled of stale beer and sweat. He sat in the back and basically ignored anyone who so much as paid him a glance, growing more and more enraged at the actions of the target he was following. The man supported the Islamic State, an organization that threw homosexuals off of six-story buildings just to watch them shatter on the concrete below, their innards exploding like a dropped watermelon. They stoned to death women who were merely accused of adultery, and this sack of shit was here, in Key West, watching a drag show.

It made him want to cut the man's heart out right then, especially knowing he was here experiencing Key West, a place his brother was supposed to have enjoyed in six months, when he was to attend the Combat Diver's Course from the Seventh Special Forces Group. Following in Guy's footsteps.

The drag show went on, and Guy sat, stewing. Finally, it ended, with Guy not watching more than a few seconds, drinking rum punch and growing more and more angry, the blackness of the loss of his brother beginning to flow. He was losing the edge he maintained as one of the highest-trained killers in the world, and he didn't even see it slipping down the stream of rocks, bouncing farther and farther away. He was losing his judgment, and setting in motion events even he couldn't foresee.

Guy watched the target prepare to leave, seeing him talk to some of the clearly homosexual members in the bar, slipping one a note. Clouded by the liquor, he wanted to slice the Arab's throat right in the bar, just because he could.

But he let the target leave, taking note of his direction, then stood to follow. He heard a voice rising above the crowd, then laughter, but thought nothing of it, intent on following his prey. He began walking to the door and heard someone yell again. He realized they were talking to him. He turned back into the bar and saw a large man wearing a satirical version of the biker costume in the Village People. He smiled and waved his hand.

The man made a comment about him not enjoying the show. Guy had no patience for the sentiment, feeling the distance grow between him and his target.

Internally, Guy really didn't have a position on the LBGT community. It just wasn't something he thought about. You want to be gay, be gay. He couldn't care less, but the men in the bar took his attitude a different way.

Guy said, "The show wasn't as good as I expected."

With a smirk, the biker said, "Well, maybe I could show you something better."

Guy knew this was a no-win proposition. He'd spent enough time on Duval Street to get catcalled by the men outside the bars. It was almost a rite of passage of the Special Forces at Fleming Key, the men setting up the new guys for some heckling. Verbally fighting back was a nonstarter. Humor was needed here, but he was fresh out.

Guy said, "Save it for the Navy. They'll be here soon." And turned to go. The catcalls turned into a crescendo, the wannabe biker coming forward, crowding into his face, sneering and talking smack. Guy said, "Don't do this. Please."

The man continued his bullying, the others around him cheering him on. All thought they were just taunting a tourist, enjoying something they did nightly. Nobody expected the violence that sprang forth, least of all Guy.

The biker reached up to poke Guy in the chest, and he grabbed the man's finger, rotating it back fast enough to hear the snap of bone. The man fell to his knees and the bouncer swept forward. Guy simply pointed at him, holding the finger and shaking his head, while the biker whined like a small child. Guy let go, held his hands up, and walked backward out of the bar.

Someone from the back shouted about his "homophobia," misinterpreting what was driving his anger, but Guy was no longer listening. Nobody else made a move against him.

He reached the street, searching for his target, now fully enraged. He hadn't wanted to fight. Hadn't wanted to hurt anyone, but the fucking Arab had pushed him into it merely by making him follow into the bar.

He began walking back up Duval Street, toward the shore and the target's boat. The direction in which he'd seen the man go when he exited the bar.

The sidewalks were swollen, full of groups of inebriated partygoers. He pushed through them, threading when he could and shoving when he couldn't. Some reacted as if they wanted to retaliate, but one look into his eyes and they left him alone, instinctively knowing it wouldn't end well.

He thought his target might sail out of the harbor tomorrow, and a part of him wished it so. Hoped he had lost the trail.

He passed a covered market selling original artwork, located across from the ubiquitous American icon called the Hard Rock Café, then caught a glimpse of a Hawaiian shirt. It was the Arab, sitting at an outdoor bar next to the market, a smattering of tables surrounding him and an iron arch proclaiming CAROLINE'S CAFÉ.

Guy backpedaled into the market, a cloistered area with individual stalls selling everything from painted coconuts to handmade earrings. He pretended to shop, circling around and seeing that the café was basically sharing space with the market. He continued deeper in, getting a feel for the exits. There were none out the back, with both the café and market butting up to a fence with houses beyond. Closest to the rear was the men's restroom. Plopped on the ground at the end of a dimly lit gravel-lined alley, it was a stand-alone structure like an outhouse, connected to the kitchen by the roof.

His brain, a computer that was never turned off, automatically calculated the feasibility of a takedown, and the alley/restroom was perfect if one didn't care about exfiltrating with the target. If one knew the target was designated DOA.

He circled back around to the marketplace, threaded through the stalls, and took a seat at the farthest table in the back, his eyes on his prey. He ordered a beer from the waitress, then just sat, quietly smoldering, thinking about his actions in the other bar. Regretting them.

He toyed with the label on his beer bottle, finally turning his mind to the *problem*. Focusing on the enormity of what he was attempting to accomplish. He picked at the scab in his mind, forcing himself to admit that his actions were either borderline insane or they were justified in the name of his brother.

He wanted to believe his cause was just, but couldn't reconcile it with the soldier he was. He knew the man on the barstool was complicit in his brother's death, but the knowledge was tempered by twenty years of following a code that dictated his moral compass. Killing on the battle-field was war. Killing after the fact was murder. Wasn't it?

We preemptively kill people with drone strikes all the time.

But the "we" was a body of men, sanctioned at the highest level, after enormous oversight. Not a single man on a hunt for revenge. *But what's the difference between revenge and preemption? These fucks are going to continue killing. Motivation is irrelevant.*

Those twin forces were battling inside him when he saw the target stand. A waitress pointed toward the alley, and Guy's decision was forced upon him.

Guy stood, squeezing his hands open and closed. He took a half step, then turned back to the table, the demons inside fighting for control. He glanced toward the bar, but nobody was looking his way. He put in his earbuds and started the Pandora app. He heard the music, seeing his brother's smiling face, and the darkness floated up.

He entered the alley.

He walked fifty feet to the end, took a quick glance behind the building, seeing lumber stacked against a chain-link fence, but no humans. He faced the door and hesitated, his hand on the knife in his pocket. He withdrew it. A Zero Tolerance folder, it had a nearly four-inch blade, razor sharp, with a large belly designed for slicing. He flicked the knife open and stared at the dull gleam of the edge.

This is it. You cross the threshold, there is no turning back.

He paused a second longer, the demons battling it out. Finally, one rose triumphant.

He turned the knob.

★ 20 ★

George Wolffe drove, with Kurt in the passenger seat. Jennifer sat in the rear, as if she were being chauffeured, but she had no illusions about who was in charge. She felt small, like a child being paraded in front of other parents for bragging rights.

Pike had left her last night, taking a flight out to Billings, Montana, to talk to Guy. He was her expert on the Oversight Council, but they'd spent the afternoon talking about Guy and the threat he posed. Pike had been genuinely worried, something she rarely saw, so she'd heard him out. They hadn't talked at all about her ceremony today, the protocols involved and the land mines she should avoid, and now she was regretting it.

Wolffe pulled into the security checkpoint for the West Wing of the White House, flashing his credentials and reciting their names. The guard took the information, checked a computer, and waved them through, into one of the most secure spaces in the US umbrella. It was surreal to her. A guy could check a clipboard and let them in?

The only other time she'd been here had also been a Taskforce invitation, years ago, but she hadn't known it then. She thought she'd been arrested and was being dragged off to some top secret dungeon.

Kurt turned around and said, "Remember what we talked about. I'll say a few words, and then you graciously accept the accolades. No big deal. Don't go off script here. The whole point is to let me bring up Guy's new evidence. Chances are, you won't have to say a thing."

Jennifer nodded without conviction and Kurt said, "Hey, you okay?"

She looked at the West Wing to her right and said, "I'd rather be back home, in Charleston. Or in a gunfight."

Kurt laughed and said, "I know it looks imposing, but everyone here takes a shit just like you do."

She scrunched her face up at his words and he backpedaled. "I mean, they're just humans. I didn't mean they take a . . . they do . . ."

George Wolffe pulled into their designated parking spot and cut Kurt off, saying, "I think you've done enough."

He put the car in park and turned around, looking her in the eye. "Jennifer, trust me, you own this terrain. The men in this room all think they're important, but they don't ever risk their lives. That's what you do, and they want to touch the magic. They'll be fawning over you."

She nodded, and they exited the car, moving away from the West Wing and toward the Old Executive Office Building next door. Kurt and George showed their credentials again, and she was given a badge with a large *V* on it, meaning "visitor, escort required." They had passed through the metal detectors and begun walking upstairs when Jennifer's phone buzzed with a text. She checked the message, seeing it was from Pike.

Tell Kurt to check his phone. Guy never showed in Montana. Whereabouts unknown. Coming back now.

She thought, *That's not good,* and they reached a room on the second floor, a light above the door dormant, waiting to start blinking if the area was unsecure. Waiting on the meeting to begin. Mingling about outside were men of power. Jennifer said, "Kurt, hey—"

Before she could finish, he said, "Time to start playing the game." He walked up to the first man and said, "Hey, sir, how's it going? I mean your day, not your job."

The man laughed and shook his hand. She tried to place who he was, recognizing him but not knowing why. George leaned in and said, "Easton Beau Clute. Chair of the Senate Intelligence Committee. A friend. Someone we need, but not someone we want you talking to outside of the meeting. No telling what he'll ask."

A little nonplussed at the attitude, Jennifer simply nodded, allowing George to usher her into the conference room. She knew the members of the Oversight Council were the only people read on to Taskforce activities, and that those activities were volatile, but she didn't understand why she should be kept away from talking to the very men who authorized them.

She relinquished her cell phone before entering, putting it in a small locker designed for that purpose.

Locking up his own phone, George saw her look and said, "Nothing personal, but everything in this town is politics. You say one wrong thing, and that'll be the reason for doing something. Or not doing something."

"Then why did you bring me here?"

He showed her to a chair while other people milled around the room, looking at her, realizing she was the *one*, and he said, "Talking in front of the group is fine. Talking one-on-one is asking for disaster. Nobody here will ask you a question that isn't loaded. Trust me."

She nodded and he turned to go, fulfilling his own political duties. She grabbed his sleeve and said, "Hey, I just got a text from Pike. Guy didn't show in Montana. He wanted Kurt to know."

George nodded, showing no outward emotion, but she saw something behind his expression. A subtle fear. He walked away, shaking hands and making small talk.

Trying to sink into her chair, she surveyed the room. She knew that the Oversight Council was a select group, but the authority in this room was unprecedented. Comprised of only thirteen individuals, the members had been handpicked by the president himself, and each man in the room had a portfolio that far exceeded his duties here.

The secretary of defense, secretary of state, director of the CIA, national security advisor . . . the names just ran on, dripping with the power of the US government. She felt a little overwhelmed.

After a bit of time, as Jennifer sat patiently, the room coalesced around the conference table, the men taking their seats and Kurt walking to the front. He nodded at her. She noticed George take a seat in the rear, behind everyone else, and wondered if he'd passed the message.

A scrum of activity happened at the front of the room, and the president of the United States entered. Peyton Warren.

He shook Kurt's hand, then walked directly to Jennifer, scaring the hell out of her. He held out his hand and said, "Jennifer Cahill. It's been a while."

She stood, a plastic smile on her face. He turned

around to the room and said, "Some of you might remember Jennifer from that operation in Bosnia a few years ago. Some of you don't, but I'm sure Kurt will let you know why she's here. While we talk a good game in this room, she's putting it all on the line to execute. I want you people to remember that our words have consequences."

He took his seat at the head of the table and nodded to Kurt, saying, "Let's go. I've got another appointment to attend."

Jennifer was amazed at the nonchalance. She expected something more formal, but realized that, in the end, it *was* just a meeting. And he was just a man.

Kurt went into his rehearsed speech, talking about the activities of the Taskforce and how much they meant to the defense of the United States. He blathered on for a good five minutes, speaking about Guy and how he couldn't be there because of a death in the family, then got to Jennifer. He played up the mission in the Caymans, hinting that females were the new face of the Taskforce and making her seem like the second coming of James Bond. Eventually, he called her forward. She approached, standing next to him, and the room clapped. A nice, respectful sound, the men in the room looking at her in wonder. She felt like a piece of livestock on show.

She took in the applause, smiled at Kurt for the accolades, then returned to her seat, the entire purpose of her visit over in seconds. She realized why the men hated these ceremonies. The chasm between the Council members and what she did was as great as that of a fan watching the Super Bowl and the quarterback on the field.

Except the Council members in this room called the plays.

★ 21 ★

Kurt went into the meat of his talk, discussing ongoing operations. Occasionally, one of the Council members would steal a glance her way. Wanting to touch the magic.

Missions in the Maghreb, operations in Southeast Asia, problems with cover organizations, and issues with equipment. Kurt droned on and on, with a PowerPoint slide punctuating each segment. Jennifer faded out, wondering why she'd come at all. She heard the name Guy George, then her own name, and snapped back to the briefing.

". . . from what Pike and Jennifer gathered, I believe this man is a financier of Islamic State activities and a legitimate Taskforce target. He's funded terrorism in Afghanistan and is implicated in the death of at least four members of United States Special Forces."

President Warren said, "So what are you asking for?"

"Alpha. Let me explore. Let's find out what this guy is up to. I know he's killing people. I just don't know how."

Silent before, probably dozing off, Secretary of State Jonathan Billings exploded, "No way! Have you lost your mind? That's Haider al-Attiya! Son of Sharif al-

Attiya. They're both representatives of the Qatar Invest-ment Authority. Jesus Christ, you might as well accuse the Saudi Royal Family of being terrorists."

Kurt said, "Okay. I'm game for that discussion."

Billings stammered for a moment, then said, "You are an *idiot*. Like every other conspiracy theorist out there. You have no idea what is going on in the world. You're a hammer looking for a nail."

Kurt snapped back at his words, his face reflecting the contempt he felt. He said, "You want to hide behind their cloak of diplomacy, that's your mistake. I'm pre-senting facts. Pure and simple."

Billings raised his voice. "The Qatar Investment Au-thority is not funding terrorism. It has the backing of the emir. They have holdings all over the world. They're about to save the euro from crashing completely with their infusion of cash in Greece. You've lost your mind if you think they're spending their time killing soldiers in Afghanistan. Jesus, they're the ones who are bankrolling the building of our new embassy in London. They bought the old one."

Kurt took a breath and said, "Like I said, I'm present-ing facts. How do you explain not one but two pictures on a target package in Afghanistan? I didn't make that up. I didn't wish a soldier's death. I don't like it any more than you. But facts are facts."

"Allegations aren't facts. The pictures you have are nothing but wishful thinking. They're so damn bad they could be anybody." Billings turned to the president and said, "Sir, surely we aren't now talking about targeting a sovereign government based on some grainy pictures from Afghanistan? We know how often those are wrong." He looked at Kurt and said, "We know how often Spe-cial Forces soldiers kill civilians by mistake."

Jennifer saw the words hit home and thought Kurt was going to launch himself across the table, the tension in the room ratcheting up to the breaking point. She watched Kurt restrain himself, and wished Pike had been there. Billings deserved a thumping for his statement, even if Kurt couldn't dish it out.

Instead of using his fists, Kurt used words, and Jennifer finally understood why she was in the room. What Knuckles had meant about her doing some good. Kurt had been prepared for Billings, and she was weight in the fight. Kurt pointed at her and said, "That is a Taskforce member. One you just applauded. She is the face of what you're calling a murderer. Look at her and say that."

Truculent, Billings crossed his arms, saying nothing, his eyes remaining on Kurt. Everyone else in the room looked her way, and she could tell Kurt's words had had an effect. In the back, behind everyone else, George Wolffe winked at her. *Score one for the Taskforce.*

President Warren raised a hand and said, "Everyone take a breath. Kurt, how sure are you about this? You're asking for a delicate mission here. We aren't talking about some ISIS guy from Algeria."

Kurt turned away from Billings and said, "Sir, I'm not sure. That's why I'm asking for Alpha. I've got five faces and two names. Both names are in the QIA. The other three faces probably are as well. One of the names is in the United States right now, in Key West. We know that from Jennifer's mission."

Billings said, "We don't *know* anything. We're just guessing."

Kurt ignored him and continued. "I'm not saying I want to thump them in the head tomorrow. I'm saying I want to investigate." He nodded at Jennifer and said, "I'm saying let's use what our members have found."

President Warren looked at Billings and said, "And what's wrong with that?"

Billings said, "What's wrong with that? Sir, first, the Taskforce has no operational authority in the United States. I'm not looking to expand its mandate. I was against them even doing the mission in the Caymans. *That* was outside its charter. This is stretching things to the breaking point. As far as I'm concerned, the entire thing is fruit from the poisoned tree."

The secretary of defense spoke up. "Are you really telling us that we can't proceed against a terrorist threat based on some lawyer lingo? Seriously?"

The director of the CIA chuckled, turned to the president, and said, "Sir, not to paint too fine a gloss on this, but that's fucking stupid."

Jennifer inwardly smiled and saw Kurt relax, triumph assured. President Warren said, "Okay, okay, wait a minute. We're missing the point. Billings, why would it be bad to do this? Besides the precedent? What are you seeing from State?"

"Sir, the Qatar Investment Authority is about to dump money into Greece. They're willing to support the Greek government beyond the European Union. The EU has asked for draconian measures for debt relief. Measures the Greek government can't meet. If we do this, we're going to cause the investments to be withdrawn. And with that, the failure of the euro as a currency. If Greece leaves the European Union, the euro as a currency will most likely collapse. That will send the US economy into a recession. Possibly a depression. We can't let that happen."

President Warren said, "So if I don't help Greece avoid the very measures they need to emplace to stay solvent, I'm wrong? I have to watch one more Band-Aid be slapped on, or I'm the bad guy?"

Billings said, "Sir, that's not the way to look at this. As wrong as you think it may be, if the euro fails, it'll destroy any recovery we think we have. It's a national security issue. I've been working on this deal for damn near a year. And my point man is the target Kurt's got on the screen. You get rid of him, and you've lost the investment."

Billings glanced at Jennifer, then went to Kurt, saying, "Look, I'm sorry about what I said before. I have to put our nation's interests beyond a single attack. I'm not saying he was behind what you allege, because I really don't think he was, but even so, one death in Afghanistan isn't worth the destruction of the economy of the European Union—and the ripple effects into the United States. You remove him and you cut the legs out from under Greece. I'm sorry, but as you said, it's just a fact."

Billings turned to the president and said, "Sir, beyond all of the Greek problems, Haider is also the man I'm working with on that other issue. The delicate one."

Jennifer didn't know what that meant but saw that Billings's words held weight. Saw the twisted decision making of the US government right in front of her eyes. For the first time, understanding that lives of US citizens took a backseat to US policy. She saw the faces in the room and knew the answer before the president spoke.

Warren leaned back, surveying the council members and seeing concurrence for what he was about to say. "No Alpha authority here. We have enough targets to worry about. Focus on the ones that are a tangible threat."

Kurt said, "Sir? They killed a US citizen. They killed a Special Forces soldier. You want to just forget that?"

Jennifer was shocked at the insubordination.

Warren bristled and said, "We have no proof of that. Don't paint me in the blood of a dead American. You know better. You, most of all. You just briefed four other targets that we *know* have American blood on their hands and are a tangible threat. Did you not?"

Kurt retreated and said, "Yes, sir. We have four targets right now. Two ready for Omega."

"Well, then, it looks like you have your hands full anyway. You'd have to trade one known for an unknown. Deal with the current targets, then we'll revisit a Qatar connection."

Kurt nodded and President Warren softened his tone. "Kurt, I understand the personal connection here, but even if these guys were responsible for the attack in Afghanistan, they aren't a clear and present danger to the United States. They aren't a threat to the homeland. The Taskforce can only do so much."

Kurt said, "So forget Guy George's brother."

President Warren rubbed his eyes and said, "Yes. If that's what you want to call it."

Kurt muttered something that Jennifer didn't hear. She heard the asshat Billings drive home the wound, forcing the pain through his victory. "What was that, Kurt? What did you say?"

Kurt slowly turned to Billings. "I said it's easy to forget a man in here. When you have no skin in the game."

Billings started to respond, his pallid double chin quivering in anger, when the light above the door flashed. Someone was trying to enter. Kurt and Billings glared at each other while security clearances were checked, and the man was admitted. Jennifer expected him to go to the president, but he didn't. He walked straight to Jonathan Billings, the secretary of state, and leaned into his ear.

Billings jerked upright, then focused on Kurt. "You're already operating on the Qatari men, aren't you?"

He stood up and pointed at Jennifer. "Did you use her information? I can't believe I even considered cheering about her exploits. You sicken me."

President Warren said, "Calm down. What was that all about?"

Billings looked at the president and said, "Ahmed Mansoor? The guy from the Caymans? They just found him with his throat slit in Florida."

★ 22 ★

Haider tepidly picked at his Greek salad, the acid in his stomach stanching his appetite. In fact, the nagging fear that was producing the acid was overwhelming any joy from the rest of his senses.

Eating dinner at the storied Old Tavern in the Plaka of Athens, he was seated on the side of the Acropolis, in the shadow of the Parthenon, a cool evening breeze blowing across the open deck. He ignored it all, his mind having worried a tendril of dread until it had become a rope of fear.

Across from him sat Nassir and Khalid Mansoor, the "brothers" of Ahmed. In truth, they were all bastard children caught between fathers who refused to claim them and a society where the tribe's name meant all. They too showed little interest in the meal. They too held the fear, because Ahmed was as real a brother as blood.

Nassir hung up his cell phone and shook his head, the fourth time he had done so in as many hours. "Still no answer. I think it's time to call your father."

Ahmed had arrived in Key West two days ago. Haider had received one jubilant email praising the meeting on Grand Cayman, then nothing. Repeated attempts at contact had failed, and Haider had eventually been forced to release the crew to continue on to Miami, where the yacht was berthed.

Now he was concerned by the void in communication. All three at the table were feeling the angst, but unlike Nassir or Khalid, Haider's worry came from the potential backlash from his father. The elder al-Attiya had made it plain that sending Ahmed to the Caymans was a recipe for failure, and it looked as if he'd be proven right. At least in his father's eyes. Haider was convinced that Ahmed was more than likely doing nothing more than partying in the debauchery of Key West, but that alone would garner severe sanctions from his father. Especially since he'd used an official yacht from the emir to do so.

Haider said, "I'm not sure I should call. I mean, what can my father do? Ahmed will turn up. He's done this before. Remember Germany?"

Khalid said, "No, no, this is different. He's never been out of contact for this long. Yes, he's gone out on his own, but never without contact. Call him."

Haider said, "We have our mission here, in the next thirty minutes. We can't worry about Ahmed right now."

Haider saw the anger grow, and felt a new anxiety. Haider would never have feared Khalid before, but he'd seen his actions in Afghanistan. Seen his childhood friend develop a taste for violence. And a talent for it.

Hidden underneath Khalid's trimmed beard and manicured nails was an unbridled fury looking for release. Like Haider, all three of the "brothers" were Qatari citizens, but unlike Haider, they were outcasts. As such, they had been raised in the flowing wealth that the oil reserves of Qatar provided, but without the shield of a tribe or the honor of a name. Because of it, instead of taking the blessings provided by the coincidence of his birth, Khalid felt insulted. Cheated. Continually blaming others for his perceived misfortunes.

He'd found an outlet in a mixed martial arts dojo in Doha, one frequented by expatriates from the West, where he'd learned to fight hand-to-hand. And learned to hate. Whether it was directed at the Westerners or himself, Haider was unsure.

Khalid had gotten so good that Haider had begun to fear his outbursts of anger. And that was *before* they'd gone to Afghanistan. Before he'd seen what Khalid could do with a gun. And a knife.

Haider said, "Okay, okay, I'll call. Just don't make any noise. He thinks I'm meeting Nikos by myself. Don't let him know otherwise."

Khalid smirked and said, "Still afraid of your father."

Haider scowled and dialed his phone, thinking, *At least I have one.*

He looked away from Khalid as the international number went through its dings and whistles, then the call was answered without fanfare by his father, his caller identification giving Haider away.

"Tell me there isn't some problem. Tell me you are in Athens, conducting business and not calling me about the police in Key West."

Confused, Haider said, "Police? What about them?"

"Your idiot friend is dead. I just found out an hour ago. The consulate called the QIA, looking for answers."

Speechless, Haider said nothing. His father continued. "Luckily, he was not an official employee, but I still had to answer why he was there. What he was doing on a QIA yacht. I need the report he sent you about the Brazil initiative. And *you* need to prepare to explain yourself when you return."

Haider found his voice, surreptitiously glancing at Khalid. "How? What happened?"

"No idea. The American police are looking into it. Apparently, he was murdered. Killed in a botched robbery in that land of sin. Nothing good comes of walking with the infidel. You should have known that to begin with."

Haider was staggered by the news, but fought to keep his face neutral. The last thing he needed was Khalid to find out what had happened to his brother minutes before Nikos arrived for payment. Haider's father continued as if he'd just talked about missing dinner, saying, "You have the identification papers, yes? You have paid for the travel to Afghanistan?"

Caught off guard, still thinking about Ahmed, Haider said, "Yes . . . well, I'm meeting Nikos in a few minutes."

"But you have seen the passport? You have created the credit accounts?"

Haider snapped out of his trance and, with a little pique in his voice, said, "Yes, yes. The passport, credit cards, all of that is in the safe-deposit box with the others. I've created the bank accounts and wired the money through QIA accounts for activities here in Greece. It's done."

"Watch your tone. Are you sure nobody can trace it?"

Haider immediately became more subdued, but hated his father for not trusting him. "Yes. There are cutouts, and the monetary amounts are so small nobody will look. The only link is the database in the safe-deposit box with the other identification papers. Just like we did before, when I went to Afghanistan."

"Get rid of the link."

"Father, I can't. If I destroy the records, I can't recreate the system in the future. I can't possibly remember all of the cutouts and bank accounts on my own."

His father said, "We can talk about that later. For

now, you need to get the identification to Crete. This time, I *want* you to use one of our boats in the Athens harbor. I don't want you on any flight manifests."

"Crete? But I don't even know where or when the talks are going to occur."

"Our man is coming to Crete tomorrow night, hiding as a refugee on a boat from Libya. He'll break free once he's on Greek soil. You meet him there and give him the identification and travel documents. Get him to Afghanistan with papers."

"I can't go there tomorrow. I'm meeting the United States secretary of state. He called me, setting up a meeting tomorrow night. Something urgent. I think it's the peace talks."

Haider heard nothing for a moment, then, "What about your idiot friends? Are they in Greece with you?"

Haider thought about lying but decided against it. "Yes. I can send Nassir."

Nassir looked up, and Haider held a finger in the air, saying, "He can do it."

"Okay. I'll send you the instructions. Make sure he doesn't screw it up like your other friend. I don't mind if he kills himself, but only after the meeting."

Haider started to respond, then realized his father had hung up.

Khalid said, "Well, any news about Ahmed?"

Haider shook his head, hoping Khalid couldn't see through the lie, knowing he would break down and do something potentially insane. He was caught between the fear of failing his father and Khalid's actions, which would most certainly cause that failure. "No, but there's other news. Our contact from the Islamic State is arriving in Crete tomorrow night. We need to pass him his travel documents there."

Khalid said, "Who is this man? Why are we helping him? Keeping it secret is unlike you. This never happened in Afghanistan."

Haider said, "I'm sorry, but my father insisted. I'll tell you soon, but not now. Not until I've met Secretary Billings."

Khalid snorted, and Nassir said, "Have the man come here."

Haider drew himself up and said, "He's going to Crete on a refugee boat, acting as one of them. He can't redirect the boat. It's done." He pulled out a key from his pocket and said, "Nassir, I need you to get the documents, then go to the capital, Heraklion. I'll send you the specifics over email when I get them."

"How am I going to get to Crete?"

Haider smiled. "My father has a yacht lined up. It's an overnight trip to Heraklion. You should enjoy it."

Nassir smiled, until Khalid said, "Like Ahmed?"

Haider started to respond, then thought better of it. He said, "Go."

He watched Nassir disappear, passing by another man Haider recognized. It was Nikos Andreas, a black-market thug working with one of the Greek crime families in Athens, and was the man who'd provided the forged documents.

Haider waved, then stood up and stuck out his hand, saying, "Nikos, how are you?"

Nikos sat down, ignoring the gesture. "I'm not sure. You have the money?"

Haider withdrew his hand and followed suit. He held out another key and said, "Same box. Same bank. All of the money you asked for."

Nikos took the key, looking it over as if for something hidden, and said, "You told me the identification was for refugees. For people fleeing the chaos in Libya and Syria. Is this still true?"

Haider felt a bead of sweat on his neck, cool in the night air. "Yes, of course."

Nikos smiled and said, "Then why is there an American watching this meeting?"

★ 23 ★

Down the slope of the sprawling tavern, at a table tucked behind a tree, Guy George picked at his own meal, going from elation to confusion upon the arrival of the fourth man. Up the hill above him, among tourists eating their mussels and musing about the Acropolis, had sat the final three faces on his target package, all together. Absolute proof he was correct about the conspiracy of his brother's death, and justification for the killing he'd done in Key West.

He'd learned the location of just one face from the target package—Haider al-Attiya—and had to apply significant pressure to the man in the Key West restroom to get it. It hadn't been easy, and he hated himself for the action, both because of what he'd done and the fact that a small part of him enjoyed it.

He'd seen enough horrific debasement of humanity in the search for "truth" during combat to know what he'd done had the chance of being nothing but sadistic satisfaction, the man telling him whatever he thought would stop the pain.

The carnage he'd inflicted still ripped through his psyche, a permanent scar. He wasn't a pipe-swinger like the men in foreign countries he'd seen use the techniques.

Once, now long past, he'd been the soldier who broke up such things. Prevented his cause from being tainted with the very offal the enemy used.

Now he was that enemy.

When the man's essence had fled his carcass, a part of Guy's mind knew he'd crossed over, stepping past an invisible line that separated the righteous from the despicable. He'd shoved that part to the rear, listening to his brother's Pandora station and telling himself he was in the right. But deep down not believing it.

Seeing the men at the table above him brought vindication. A half step to redemption. He'd considered walking away right then, taking his digital photos and voice recordings with him. He could provide that to the Taskforce and turn them loose, but he knew he wouldn't. He'd have to admit to killing the man in Key West, and that, without sanction, was murder. Regardless, he was sure the Taskforce would not respond. Policy trumped blood. He'd already witnessed that, and he would never be forgiven. He was, to use a phrase, a dead man walking, and he was comfortable with the thought. His brother deserved what he could do, and his sacrifice would be worth it.

But not before he killed the three at the table.

He'd watched one of the men leave, then checked the level of his homemade audio-capture device, using an Android app and a directional microphone plugged into the micro USB port of his phone, and saw that the noise pickup wasn't nearly as strong as he'd wanted. When he'd returned his eyes to the table, he saw the fourth man arrive. A man he knew as Nikos.

Which was significant trouble.

In Key West, Guy had gleaned the one anchor point he needed—the Athenaeum InterContinental Hotel in Athens—and had immediately flown to Greece, successfully testing his new identity and credit cards. Before beginning surveillance on the hotel, he needed two things: technical equipment and weapons.

The tech stuff he'd managed to build off-the-shelf from a trip to a hobby store, a security boutique, and an electronics shop. It wasn't Taskforce sleek, but he'd managed to develop a crude beacon, surreptitious camera, a beam-focused digital recorder, and various cell phone exploit tools. None of the devices was as powerful or compact as the state of the art he could have drawn from the Taskforce, but they'd get the job done, as the commercial sector grew ever closer to the surveillance world that was once an elite domain of governments.

The weapons, on the other hand, were a whole different kettle of fish. No way could he buy guns on the open market. He'd had to turn to a different source, and risk exposure by doing so.

He'd called a CIA case officer he knew was working in Greece. She was an old girlfriend of his roommate, Decoy, and she'd kept in touch with him after Decoy's death, calling him for dinner whenever they were both in DC. She still didn't know whom he worked for, only that it was beyond her classification level, but in her world, she knew better than to ask. What really mattered was that she was now posted to the US Embassy in Athens. And she trusted him, something he intended to leverage.

As much as the congressional intelligence committees wanted the CIA to deal solely with upstanding individuals, the work of intelligence necessitated stepping into the cesspool of humanity from time to time, and while the portfolio of the Athens station would include terrorism, it was focused more intently on the internal struggles of Greece. The euro crisis, political strife, and yes, organized crime.

They'd had lunch, he hinting he was operational and she beating around the bush about her own work. Eventually, he'd asked the favor, and using contacts she had, believing Guy was doing good for the United States, she'd set up a meeting with Nikos later that first night.

After a myriad of security precautions, both on his part and Nikos's, he'd paid hard cash for a beat-up 6P9 pistol—a Russian weapon based on the Makarov, with an integral suppressor that could be broken down for travel—and a box of 9x18 ammunition. It would be enough to get him through the mission, but he wasn't sure about the function of either, the weapon old and worn, the bluing rubbed clean in several spots, and the cardboard box of ammunition looking as if it had been moved from location to location for years without use.

After the transfer, they'd conducted their security dance and had parted ways, and he'd never expected to see Nikos again. But now he was here, meeting Guy's targets. Which, from what he'd seen at last night's meeting, meant Nikos had put the entire restaurant under surveillance at least an hour before. There was no way he didn't know Guy was here. The only question was whether he thought Guy was a danger.

Guy knew the answer to that. Coincidence was a luxury neither believed in. If the roles were reversed, Guy would assume he was a threat, and would have actively prepared to neutralize that threat.

The biggest concern now was remaining anonymous from the other two men at the table. Guy had no idea why Nikos had arrived, and really didn't care. Nikos didn't know his name, but he did know what Guy looked like.

Before Nikos could point him out or do something else to expose him, he rose, shoving his equipment into a fanny pack, and throwing way more euros on the table than necessary. He slipped to the left, getting behind a tree and surveying quickly, regretting not bringing the pistol with him. He'd bought it purely for offensive action, and never thought he'd become the hunted.

Behind him was a cut-stone staircase leading sharply down the hill, the drop to the steps about fifteen feet. To his front was the regular exit of the restaurant, leading straight by the target's table.

Staircase it is.

He swiftly turned, strode to the stone wall that prevented drunkards from falling, and flipped over the side. He hung for a brief second, hearing a gasp from two pedestrians, then dropped.

He hammered the ground hard, one foot high, one low, rolling on his ankle. He glanced up and saw a couple, the woman with her mouth covered, and ignored them both. He skipped down the steps two at a time, seeing the flow of pedestrians on the street below.

Plaka, he knew, was an ancient neighborhood devoid of vehicles. An area made of twisting streets, tourist shops, and claustrophobic alleys, the only thing that penetrated the pedestrian throngs were minibikes and mopeds. He had to get to a taxi, and he needed to get out of Plaka to do so.

He glanced up the stairwell and saw two men appear, both with black leather jackets and beards. Not tourists. They began to follow.

Because of the way their own meeting had been arranged, Nikos had to assume he was official US government, but Guy had no idea how much weight that would carry.

He hit the road below and turned right, toward Syntagma Square and the coughing, congested streets of Athens.

★ 24 ★

Guy glanced back and saw the two rushing down the stairs, the shallow glow of the mercury lamps making them seem simian, their glide anything but innocent.

He darted into the crowd on the street, putting innocents between him and his predators. Walking quickly, he went through his options and decided that getting to Syntagma Square was his best alternative. They were pipe-swingers, no doubt, but they weren't *official* muscle. They had to worry about the authorities just as he did, so wouldn't attempt to harm him outright in the crowds. If he stuck to the main thoroughfares and stayed ahead of them, before they could present a threat, he could get out.

He wound down the hill, skipping past bars and restaurants, losing altitude and gaining confidence. He reached a T intersection, momentarily lost but knowing that downhill was safety. To his left he saw two policemen on BMW motorcycles, sitting on their saddles and smoking cigarettes, the deserted cobblestone road looking as if it had been built by Socrates. Just beyond them was an alley between apartments, which went sharply downhill.

Perfect. They wouldn't do anything in the presence of

the police, and might decide not even to follow him down the alley. He drew abreast, and one policeman sat upright. Guy felt a stab of adrenaline but kept his pace. The other turned toward him, talking into a radio. The first drew his weapon and shouted in Greek.

Jesus. They co-opted the police? How did they manage that?

He took off at a dead sprint, hearing the crack of a round just as he hit the narrow defilade leading downhill. He heard the motorcycles rev and knew he was in trouble. Not only from the motorcycles but from the radios the policemen held, and their knowledge of the terrain. And the fact that someone had called them to begin with.

He ran down the hill through the flickering moonlight and sparse vapor bulbs, realizing he'd channelized himself. He saw a splash of light on the cobblestones in front of him, his shadow in the middle, and knew the bikes were now behind him. He started looking for something to stop them. He saw nothing.

He reached another street and went right, running up the asphalt until another alley opened on the left, going straight downhill almost as steep as a staircase. He could see the lights of the main shopping area below and knew he was close to the endless traffic and taxicabs. Close to freedom.

He bounded down the narrow lane, moving so quickly that he could barely maintain his balance, seeing the flat ground of a street below, a market full of pedestrians beyond. He heard the motorcycles behind him, their headlights bouncing over him, and doubled his pace. He was within thirty meters of breaking into the crowds when three men appeared out of the moonlight, running up the alley straight at him.

Nothing remained but to fight.

They came at him as a pack, intent on preventing him from reaching the safety of the street, each dependent on the courage of the man to his left or right.

Guy had no such crutch.

The first reached him and swung a section of bicycle chain at his head. Guy caught the movement and ducked under, looping his arm over the man's elbow and torquing his right leg behind the man's knee. He swept his leg back and slammed him into the ground with his shoulder, hard enough to cause a dull thump from the skull. Not even registering the victory, he whipped backward with his left leg, catching the next assailant in the gut as he continued forward.

Guy heard the air leave the man's lungs as he turned to the final target, but he was moving too slow. The attacker swung a wicked fish priest, a short club with the head encased in metal, hammering him in the shoulder. The steel hit the brachial nerve near his collarbone, rendering his left side momentarily useless. Guy dropped to his knees, a panic for survival flooding him as the second attacker recovered from the kick.

The men leapt at him, Guy seeing both flash in a strobe effect of the bouncing headlights from the oncoming bikes, like something from a seventies disco. The man with the club swung, and Guy rolled to the right, putting his back to the rough-hewn stone of the alley and hearing the metal strike rock, seeing it cast sparks. He protected his left and lashed out with his right, throwing a cross with his full weight behind it. The man's head whipped sideways, slamming into the rock wall. He crumpled to the ground as the final man approached.

Guy saw the motorcycles gingerly bouncing down the

narrow lane, getting closer, the lights bobbing as if they were on stalks. He said, "I got no beef with you. Let me go. Tell Nikos this is a mistake."

The man drew up and Guy saw his size for the first time. Easily over six feet, with a wide girth and a bearded, acne-scarred face. In broken English, he pointed at the man with the fractured skull and said, "You missed the chance."

Hands to his front, the motorcycles still approaching, Guy's face curled into a death mask. "I don't have time for this shit. Bring it, you fuck."

The man did and, in the instant before he died, realized that size alone had nothing to do with the fight. He swung a bar-fight roundhouse, and Guy ducked under, pounding the man's right kidney with two deep strikes as he rotated behind him. The man screamed and Guy grabbed his hair, jerking him off balance. The target flailed his arms and tumbled backward like a felled tree. Guy dropped to a knee, controlling the head as the body fell, and the target's neck landed just above Guy's knee-cap. There was a crack, and the man was dead, his own weight having done the damage.

Guy let the man roll off his knee just as the first motorcycle reached him, the officer shouting from his bike but unable to engage with his weapon without losing control. Guy leapt down the alley, straight into the flea markets surrounding the Acropolis grounds.

Ignoring the stares from the myriad of tourists, he kept running until his lungs felt on fire, trying to remember the map he'd studied earlier. Trying to remember where Syntagma Square was, now that he was on level ground and free.

He stayed near Acropolis Park, cutting through musicians playing for euros and couples looking for romance, finally hitting the iron fence that surrounded the Acropolis itself. The sight brought him renewed courage, as he knew there were taxis at the entrance.

He saw the Acropolis Museum and realized he was close. Just a couple hundred meters to freedom. He cut into a path in the trees and picked up the pace, the fence to his right and the pedestrian street to his left. Ahead, he saw the circle for the entrance, people still milling about even at this hour. He saw the line of taxis and darted out of the trees just as two police motorcycles hit the circle from the city side, tires squealing as they hammered the brakes. They were followed by two more from his rear, the original hunters, who hit him with their lights.

He heard the shouts, the ones from the rear redirecting the new pair to his presence. With no other alternative, he turned into the park, running blindly, desperate to separate himself from the advantage of their motorcycles.

He heard the rev of engines behind him and felt the fear. The park was wide open, threaded with roads, and it was empty. He knew eventually he'd hit the same eight-foot iron fence and wouldn't be able to get over it before they hit him. Even if he did, he would be in the Acropolis. He would be nothing more than a corralled animal, lashing out until he felt the spear.

He ran on, the motorcycles' lights bouncing around him, his panic building. To his front, a hill of granite appeared. A giant, imposing knoll of stone with an iron staircase and some plaque that he wouldn't read even if he could in the dark. All he knew was that it was a break from the motorcycles.

He leapt to the stairs just as the motorcycles reached him, dropping their bikes and giving chase on foot. He sprinted up, finding the crest and running to the far side, the men no more than ten seconds behind him.

He reached a cliff, the grassy earth sloping fifty feet below.

He cursed and did a slow turn, searching for options. There were none. He looked across the cliff and saw a park below, full of archeological treasures, and recognized the Agora, Athens's ancient city center. On the far side was a cut for a metro train, a slice in the earth, and beyond was a street full of vendors.

Escape.

He heard the men scrambling up the rock face and decided. He'd either die from the drop or get away.

He lowered himself flat and slid off the side, seeking footing way too fast for safety. He used roots and outcroppings to make it fifteen feet down before his luck ran out. He felt the slide and tried to stop, but it did no good. He saw the police above him, shining lights in his eyes and shouting, and he screamed, falling into the void.

He hit the ground hard, bouncing once, then rolled down the slope, coming to a stop in a field of grass. He lay for a moment, unsure if he was broken, the lights of the police far above. He rose up, the adrenaline rocking his body, and found he was stable. Beat to hell, but no permanent damage. He took off through the field, the glow of flashlights growing fainter behind him, the police nowhere near insane enough to try to follow.

He came to the cut for the train tracks and leapt down, scrambling up the other side and reaching the pedestrian walkway, seeing tourists drinking beer in outdoor cafés. He climbed the fence, ignoring the shouts and iPhones pointed at him as he came over. He took the first street he could find, weaving deeper into the heart of the tourist-trap markets and restaurants, looking for a place to stop. To assess what had happened.

The man, Nikos, belonged to the Greek Mafia, and

they were known as the Godfathers of the Night because of their stranglehold on nightclubs in Athens, so any stop in such a place was basically suicide, but he needed to get off the street. To quit running once he had his break in contact. With the advantage of radios, moving now was the killer. He needed to hide until they grew tired of looking.

He hit a small alley, busting through the tattoo parlors and teenagers, and saw a sign ahead.

Salvation.

It read JAMES JOYCE IRISH PUB. A place where he could sit forever, and one definitely outside the neon and black lights of Mafia-controlled nightclubs.

He slid inside, pushing through the crowd of expats and taking a seat at the very back, his eye to the door. A waitress came over and, with a wonderfully safe Irish accent, said, "Poor thing, you look tuckered."

Guy gave her a crooked grin and said, "Yeah, sightseeing's a bitch. Can I get a Guinness?"

She left, and he rapidly assessed what he knew. Trained to thrive in chaos, the last few minutes of adrenaline faded like tide from a beach. No longer worthy of reflection.

He'd made some significant enemies inside Athens, but he still had a mission. He withdrew his recording device and put one earbud in, listening to the conversation before Nikos had arrived. He could make out little, the device nowhere near good enough to penetrate the wind and ambient noise of the other patrons. He strained to understand the mumbling about yachts, keys, and meetings, none of which did any good to focus his efforts.

But he did hear one thing.

Heraklion, Crete.

★ 25 ★

Secretary of State Jonathan Billings entered his hard car still inside the US Embassy compound in Athens, his six-man detail from the Bureau of Diplomatic Security doing a final check before the two-vehicle convoy rolled back to the hotel.

He'd had trouble staying focused on the endless briefings but gave the ambassador his praise and well wishes on the progress made on various fronts. Now, preparing to leave, he was running through his head the excuses he'd use to ditch his security detail. He didn't really think he needed them, but then again, someone *had* launched a rocket-propelled grenade at the front of the embassy here in 2007. Maybe ditching them wasn't the best choice, but he had to for his next meeting. Because no matter what those asshole hawks in the Oversight Council thought, he was going to warn Haider al-Attiya that a lunatic was after him.

Three days ago, he'd been roundly shut down with his accusations that the Taskforce was operating unilaterally inside the United States, assassinating Qatari citizens based on nothing but a bloodied target package from Afghanistan. One day later, Kurt had called an emergency meeting, something that rarely occurred, which caused all thirteen members to show. He'd stated that they had no proof of Taskforce involvement in Key West, but that he was missing a Taskforce member. A man had basically gone AWOL, and—conveniently, Billings thought—it was the brother of the soldier killed in Afghanistan.

Billings knew the whole damn thing was nothing but a show designed to cover up extralegal Taskforce operations—if there even was such a thing, given their extralegal existence to begin with—and had demanded that the family be informed.

Kurt had balked, saying he had no proof and was "taking steps to confirm or deny the situation."

Billings had said, "What does that mean? 'Taking steps'? Either the guy's on the loose or he's not."

"I've detailed Pike Logan to find him. To bring him in. My bet is he's on a bender somewhere in the United States. He lost Decoy, then his brother, and it took a toll. I saw it but didn't think he wouldn't go to the funeral. Pike will find him."

"Pike? Are you serious? You think he'll bring him in? Far from it. If anything, that psycho will give him pointers."

President Warren interceded at that point, saying, "Calm down, John. Kurt's doing what he can, and airing your personal grievances about individual Taskforce members isn't helping. Kurt informs us of the status, but the tactical decisions are his."

The secretary of defense cut in, "And he did save the damn pope last year. Give him a break."

Billings said, "Okay. Fine. But what about the Qatari guys? What about Haider al-Attiya?"

President Warren said, "What about them?"

"They need to be warned." He turned to Kerry Bostwick, the director of the CIA, and said, "Don't you have a protocol for sources or assets when you come across a death threat? Don't you have to warn them?"

Kerry shifted in his chair, clearly uncomfortable with the direction the conversation had taken. "This isn't the CIA. This is the Taskforce, and we have the means to control the outcome."

Billings looked at the president and said, "That's not what I asked. Sir . . ."

President Warren said, "Kerry, what's the protocol?"

Kerry placed his elbows on the table and rubbed his hands together, then said, "Okay, yes. If we come across a threat to a source, regardless of the source's orientation or cooperation, we warn them. But that's not this."

Billings said, "That's exactly this. The only difference is that it's not threat-stream reporting. It's one of our own guys."

Kurt interjected, "We don't know that. Give Pike a chance."

Billings cut him off. "Bullshit we don't know. We might not *wish* to know, but this is an unmitigated disaster. Haider is the one helping me with . . . that thing in Afghanistan. Haider's the member of the QIA that's willing to invest in Greece. We lose him—at our own hands—and it will be the worst foreign policy disaster in recent memory. And make no mistake, there have been some disasters."

President Warren said, "No warning. We handle this on our own. Let the Taskforce work it."

"Sir, I think we need to look at this holistically. The Taskforce has gone rogue. We are on the verge of bringing down this whole administration."

He paused and went from man to man, looking every member of the Oversight Council in the eye.

"Everyone in this room is looking at a jail cell. That's

a given, but we still have our duty to honor what we know to those threatened. It's unconscionable not to do so. At least let him prepare. Increase his own security."

And for the first time, the words were said aloud, thrown into the daylight from the dark. The true dilemma tossed into the room.

They had created a unique organization to resolve imminent threats, but in so doing, they had thrown out what made the United States what it was. Thrown out the oversight and the second-guessing. Thrown out transparency and democracy for the greater good. It had sounded responsible after 9/11, given the threat. Something that was needed, even if the US Constitution wouldn't allow it.

The Taskforce had worked like a well-oiled machine for years, proving its worth, eliminating one threat after another. A benign beast growing in strength, it had always done what was asked by the Council. But now it was off the rails, the beast looking for blood outside of the masters. A man recruited, trained, and equipped for missions at the national level, someone told repeatedly to ignore the laws of the land for the greater good, was now doing exactly what he'd been taught.

Every person in the room was under the knife.

President Warren said, "Kurt, thoughts?"

"Give Pike a chance. He'll bring him in. There's no reason to panic here."

Billings said, "I'm not panicking. I'm being prudent. Maybe we should also alert the FBI, get him in the system, use the CIA, or whatever else we can do to get his name out there."

Kurt glared and said, "We can't do that without the very compromise you fear. Anyway, I don't need someone else to put down a horse that belongs to me."

Billings rolled his eyes and said, "Sir, really? Now we're worried about egos?"

Warren said, "Kurt's right. No reason for extreme measures. No warning. Let it run its course."

Billings bit his lip but knew what he was going to do. He had a conscience, unlike the men around the table. Now, driving out of the embassy compound in Greece, he was about to step across the line. Put his own conscience in front of his obligations.

He drew strength from the example of Edward Snowden, another man who had bucked what the traditional establishment had said was right. He owed it to himself to do the same.

The small motorcade left the main road and rounded the snakelike streets, going through alleys and neighborhoods to the Athenaeum InterContinental. The hotel was not, to put it mildly, in the best part of town, and he would have stayed at his habitual haunt, the Hotel Grande Bretagne—where everyone who was anyone stayed—but Haider was booked at the InterContinental, and doing a meeting inside the hotel was the only way to avoid his security detail following him like a piece of gum picked up by his shoe.

They rounded the corner, and Billings saw the internal hotel security, aware of his presence and hoping to make a permanent impression. The two cars entered the small drive and he waited, one man exiting and opening his door, the rest fanning out. He shook the hand of the poor bellman, the guy terrified of screwing up.

They entered the expansive lobby, he in a bubble of security, his executive assistant one step behind, and everyone else staring at who had arrived. The hotel staff blocked off the elevator access, allowing him to ride alone, his detail talking among themselves in their radios.

Ridiculous.

He hated the security detail. It was exactly what wasn't needed as a diplomat. How could he encourage democracy and human rights when armed thugs surrounded him everywhere he went?

The elevator opened and his security entered first, pushing the button to his floor. Billings sank against the railing, running through what he would say to Haider. The elevator stopped and his assistant said, "Sir, did you want to go over the minutes for tomorrow's meeting now?"

"No, Leslie, we can do that later. Jet lag's hitting me. I'll call you for dinner." She smiled and went the opposite way from him down the hall, no security with her. Minutes later, he was at his suite, the room cleared by his detail. He went to his computer, pretending to work, giving them time to exit.

After the door had been closed for a minute or two, he dialed his phone and received a room number. He packed up his laptop and exited. The lone security man outside his door was startled, saying, "Sir, I thought you were in for the afternoon."

He raised his wrist to talk into the radio, and Billings said, "I am, I am. I'm just headed to the executive lounge to get a bottle of water."

"Sir, I can get that for you."

"I want to get it myself," Billings snapped. "Stay here. I'll be fine. I don't need a guard dog to go to the damn lounge."

The man shuffled his feet but did as he was told. Billings turned without another word and went to the elevators. He rode down two floors, then exited.

He found the room number and softly knocked. A man he didn't recognize opened the door, dressed smartly in a pinstriped suit with a well-groomed beard shaved close to his face. Billings thought he was nothing but a manservant for Haider—one of the many anyone important from Qatar would use—and came close to barging in as he was accustomed to do in his position, but the man looked him full in the eye. And Billings saw a little crazy leaking out. He waited outside.

The man said, "Sir, I am Khalid. Haider is waiting in the other room."

★ 26 ★

Billings traveled through the suite to the large bedroom, seeing Haider on the balcony outside, drinking tea. He stood, a large smile on his face, and embraced Billings with a traditional touching of cheeks. After greetings, Billings glanced at Khalid, and Haider said, "Khalid, could you check my computer for emails, please?"

Khalid nodded and left them alone. Haider poured Billings tea, and they made small talk for a few minutes. Eventually, they transitioned to Greece, discussing Qatari investment in a natural gas–fired power plant and other infusions of much-needed capital. Billings searched for an entrance, and finally received it when Haider said, "With the turmoil in the world, Qatar feels it irresponsible to not invest in Greece. It's sound policy." He smiled and said, "We don't need one more state falling into chaos."

Billings nodded. "That's wise. And another reason I believe Qatar can help with other conflicts. Remember the peace initiative I spoke of? Between the Taliban and the Afghanistan government?"

Acting disinterested, Haider said, "Yes, I do. I must say that it is out of my portfolio, but when I brought it up—" He raised a hand and said, "Discreetly, I assure you; my government was astounded that such a thing could be happening behind its back."

Billings said, "There is no great mystery. It's just the way of diplomacy. You remember the talks held in Norway between the High Peace Council and several Taliban officials from the office in Doha?"

"Yes, of course. They kept us informed of all of that, but it was unofficial. Just some women from Afghanistan demanding rights. Nothing came of it."

"Well, partially correct. What came of it was an overture from the HPC. They want to conduct serious talks, using the 'nothing' meetings as cover for the real ones. Too much pressure is put on the talks when they are officially announced. Too much is expected, forcing both sides to utter stupid things, preventing the very talks they want. This way, both can come secretly. Nobody is even looking at Norway."

Haider nodded, thinking. He said, "So a talk within a talk, without any official announcement. That might actually do some good."

Billings smiled and said, "I'm glad you feel that way, because the United States recognizes the power Qatar holds, and we'd like you to be the emissary. Unofficially. We can't have anyone known in the Qatari government show up in Oslo. It would defeat the entire purpose. Do you think you could do such a thing? Act as the go-between?"

Haider said, "I would be honored, and I thank you for the trust. When will this occur, so I may ensure my availability?"

"I don't know yet. The details are still being worked out, but the initial meeting will be soon. Days, not weeks. Understand, the Taliban office in Doha knows nothing, and it must remain that way. For security purposes."

Haider said, "Don't worry. If anyone understands security and secrecy, it's the Qatar Investment Authority. Whenever we try to invest overseas, if it becomes public knowledge, you Westerners—how do you say—'come out of the woods' to stop it."

Billings laughed and said, "I think you mean 'come out of the woodwork,' but I believe you."

He paused, on the threshold. The moment of truth.

Haider said, "What is it?"

"Speaking of security, there is something else I must tell you. I've learned through our intelligence agencies that there may be a threat against you."

His cup halfway to his lips, Haider paused, then said, "A threat? From your intelligence agency?"

Billings had decided that conveying the danger was good enough. In no way did he want to implicate himself or cause damage to all that he was doing by exposing the reality. He said, "No, no. Not from us. We just heard about it. We don't know who it is, but it came out of Afghanistan, and your name was mentioned. Something ridiculous about an operation you supposedly conducted. It could be nothing but coincidence. A mistaken name or something else, but you should take precautions. Please, I am breaking protocol for even telling you, but I felt it was necessary."

Haider said, "I appreciate the trust."

Haider watched the door close, Billings heading back to his room. Khalid said, "Well?"

"We're in, but there is a significant issue."

"What?"

Haider paused, not wanting another experience like he'd had last night. He'd finally gathered the courage to tell Khalid about the death of Ahmed, and as expected, Khalid was distraught, wanting to fly to the United States and kill someone just to relieve the pain. He'd eventually calmed down but now walked about with a permanent scowl, looking for a slight in anything the hotel staff did.

Haider made his decision. "Billings says there is a threat against me. He stated he didn't know from where, but it had to do with Afghanistan."

Khalid said, "The man last night."

"Yes. Secretary Billings is lying. He knows exactly who it is but is playing like a spy. He's too worried about our partnership to let it go but too stupid to realize I can see through him. It was the American from the restaurant, and apparently, he's hunting me."

Khalid said, "Does this have anything to do with Ahmed?"

Haider hadn't considered that. He thought about it, then said, "I don't see how. That was in Key West, Florida. The American is here, in Greece."

"Maybe it's not just a single American. How well do you trust Secretary Billings?"

"Enough. The logic makes no sense. If Billings had anything to do with it, why on earth tell me? No. He knows what it is, and he's afraid of anything happening to me because it will hurt him. It's no different than the tribal politics in Qatar."

Khalid nodded and said, "What do you want to do? You want me to interdict him?"

"Secretary Billings? No, no. That is the last thing I want. Call Nikos. He found the man once. He can do so again. We will fight fire with fire."

★ 27 ★

I sat back in disgust. "Are you telling me the greatest hackers in the United States inventory can't get me a lead on Guy George? That he's dropped off the face of the earth without a trace?"

My favorite computer geek, Bartholomew Creedwater—Creed, in Taskforce parlance—said, "Pike, I can't see into the guy's head. As much as you think I'm God, I can't penetrate the time-space continuum. I need a handle."

He glanced at Jennifer, making sure she knew that he was on his game and it wasn't his fault.

Creed was currently detailed to some computer operation involving North Korea, but when I'd been given this mission, I'd demanded his release, and Kurt had agreed. Creed was the best we had, and not averse to bending the rules, something I was sure I'd need on this shitty assignment. But he also had an unremitting crush on Jennifer, which annoyed the hell out of me.

She treated him like a little brother, and he responded to the attention. A couple of years ago, he'd seen her do some pretty incredible commando stuff on a mission in Colorado, and he'd fallen head over heels for her, thinking he was looking at the incarnation of the Black Widow from an *Avengers* movie. It was a little pathetic, but when I'd made a joke about it to Jennifer, she'd taken offense, calling me a bully. So now I had to endure his clumsy attempts at getting into her pants if I wanted his help.

Okay, that's not entirely true. I was willing to dangle Jennifer to get what I wanted. It's called leadership.

I said, "Come on, we own every bit of data on the guy. Surely you can find something. He's had to use a credit card, cell phone, bank account, or something."

"Pike, he's not using anything associated with his identity. Outside of that cash withdrawal over a week ago, he's done nothing. He's a ghost."

"How in the hell do you guys manage to find terrorists with nothing but a name but can't find this guy when we have his biometric data and every detail of his life?"

Creed looked at me and said, "He's well trained. He knows exactly what we're looking for."

Which scared the hell out of me, because it told me he wasn't just on a bender somewhere. If he had gone this far to hide his tracks, he was doing something bad. Stepping into the abyss. Once that path was crossed, it was very, very hard to come back. I knew, because I'd been there. And now I was supposed to put him down.

I kept thinking of that Clint Eastwood movie from the '90s. *In the Line of Fire.* Where the ex-CIA man and would-be assassin of the president says, *"What you didn't see, Frank, what you couldn't possibly know is, they sent my best friend—my comrade-in-arms—to my home to kill me."*

I'd always wondered who the real bad guy was in that movie. If maybe the assassin hadn't been justified. Now I was going to find out. The hard way.

I said, "Okay, okay, then we go to square one. Guy's

smart, I get that. Let's use it against him. He's got to operate, and we know he's not using Taskforce kit, so what *is* he using? He's going to have a drop phone, but it'll be a smartphone. He's going to use apps. He's going to leverage COTS stuff—and we can track that."

Creed sank back, not wanting to give his answer, but he did. "Pike, you're right. With the spyware embedded in most apps sending data to the host, we could find his location, but even with commercial stuff off the shelf, we have to know the name he's using to sign in. We can't hack an account without it. I can't just dig into Apple and find a ghost. I have to know what I'm looking for. Or, in reverse, we have to know his phone IMEI so we can crack the app, but if we had that, we wouldn't need the app."

I bunched my fists, and Jennifer stepped in, saying, "What about Taskforce apps? Has anyone downloaded those in the last few days?"

The Taskforce had its own cloud, with a bunch of apps that could be downloaded in a pinch if an Operator had lost some Taskforce kit and was forced to use an in extremis capability. They were definitely more robust than anything on the civilian market, but Guy hadn't used any of them. It was just one more backup to the backup in the Taskforce arsenal, and I'd already checked on their use.

"No. Nothing downloaded in the last few days, but he knows we can track that stuff. All of them have malware embedded, waiting to be initiated in case of loss on an operation. He wouldn't want the tether."

Jennifer nodded and kept at it. "Travel history? If he goes overseas, he's got to use a passport, and that will be tied biometrically."

Glad for the break away from tech stuff, Creed said,

"He hasn't left the United States. At least not with *his* passport. And we know he hasn't used any aliases from the Taskforce. They're all accounted for."

Jennifer looked at me and said, "That's something. At least we know he's in the United States."

Creed beamed at the supposed compliment from his statement. I glared at him and said, "Bullshit. We know nothing. I'm telling you, this target is the worst we've ever seen. He's smart, and he's skilled. An absence of data is proof of nothing. Creed, build me a list of off-the-shelf spy apps for both Android and Apple. Not the stupid baby-cam crap. The good stuff. That's what he's going to use."

Jennifer said, "Pike, let's not make this into something it's not. He's just an Operator. He's not Creed."

Creed looked at her like a high schooler gazing at a woman in a cosplay outfit who'd deigned to say hello, completely undone by the compliment.

I straightened up from staring at the computer and said, "Both of you listen to me, because it needs to be said. Guy George is every bit as good as me, and if he's truly on the hunt, he's going to figure out how to do it. Just like I would. Don't underestimate him. Especially his capacity for violence."

Jennifer looked unconvinced.

I said, "What did you think when we first met?"

Trying to deflate the atmosphere, she said, "I thought you were a drunk."

I locked eyes with her and said, "What did you think in Guatemala? When the blood began to flow?"

She got the point. I'd slaughtered many men to keep her alive, and I was sliding into the abyss even as I did it. Jennifer was the one who'd saved me from falling in completely. She kept her eyes on mine, then slowly said,

"I thought you were death. But you were killing for a reason."

I nodded and said, "Yes, but *he* thinks he's killing for a reason. That's what we're stopping, and I want to do it before Guy crosses a line he can't come back from."

Guy had come in brash and strong to my old Special Mission Unit, with a background from both the Ranger Battalions and Special Forces, walking up the military ladder of every unit worth a damn. He was one of those guys who just knew he was right, and was always fighting decisions because he had a better idea. You said left, he said right. If you had said right, he'd have said left. But he backed up the bravado with brains, strength, and skill. Not unlike me, before I knew better.

After that, I'd recruited him to the Taskforce, knowing Kurt would never put him on my team because we were too much alike. I knew he'd feel that that much unbridled arrogance on a team could cause a catastrophic event, so my team got Decoy, and Guy had gone to Johnny's team. In the end, it had been the right choice, as both teams flourished.

To me, the obvious decision was to have Johnny tracking down his own man, but Kurt hadn't seen it that way. The excuse was that Johnny's team was already deployed, and pulling them back would endanger ongoing operations, but I knew better. Johnny was too close to Guy, and Kurt feared his emotions would prevent him from doing what was necessary. Left unsaid was just what that might be. Kurt could give excuses, but I understood I was chosen because I had served with the target as well, yet I wasn't close enough to be clouded.

I told myself that, though I wondered if Kurt, having seen me at my worst, believed I was the only person capable of solving the problem because of my past. Like I had crossed a line once before and because of it, I was capable of returning there if he asked for it.

It was a thing I didn't want to even think about, but it hovered in the room like the stench of a dead animal. I wondered if Kurt thought I'd execute because I was the best at this and he trusted me, or because I had no soul.

It hurt.

Yes, I knew the target, but that only increased my fear. Guy George had been born fighting. A towheaded, rangy guy from a broken home in a small town in Montana, he was raised on bull riding and beer drinking. Not exactly what the Taskforce was searching for when they wanted someone to blend in in Amman, Jordan, but then again, neither was I. We recruited for diversity, trying to find men who could swim among various populations without leaving a ripple, but skill outweighed any other consideration. I had seen him operate in hostile lands all over the globe, finding ways to get the mission done regardless of his pure American looks. He had proven to be a cunning predator. Just like me.

And now I was hunting him. Possibly the only one in the room who knew the danger he truly represented.

★ 28 ★

I heard the door open behind me and saw Kurt enter, ripping down my little sign. He was followed by someone else.

He held out the computer printout, which read ALEC STATION, saying, "I don't see the humor. No jokes on this one."

Jennifer glared at me behind his back. When I'd hung the sign, she told me it was in poor taste, and, as usual, she was right. We'd been given our own top secret office to work our wonders searching for Guy, and I thought it had needed a name in case anyone came looking. Alec Station was the code name for the CIA's counterterrorist cell that tracked Osama bin Laden before 9/11. Given our mission, I'd thought it was funny.

Sheepishly, I took the paper and said, "Got it, sir."

He said, "Where do we stand?"

"Well, in the 'confirm or deny his location' department, we've done a lot of denying and very little confirming. He hasn't been to either his home of record in Montana or his condo in DC, and hasn't used anything associated with his identity. No checks, credit cards, E-ZPass toll use, car rentals, plane tickets, nothing."

"And we're sure he hasn't stolen one of his alias documentation packages?"

"Yep. Positive. He's moving, but we don't know how or where. He's just disappeared."

The man behind him stepped out. When Kurt had entered, I naturally thought it was George Wolffe, his deputy, and now did a double take when I saw who it was. Nicholas Seacrest, looking lost, and hesitant to even be in the room.

I said, "Well, well. If it isn't Veep." He grinned half-heartedly at his callsign, letting Jennifer hug him and awkwardly kiss him on the cheek. He freed himself from her embrace and shuffled from foot to foot. I looked at Kurt and said, "So he's a go? You're giving me permission to take him and show him the ropes?"

Kurt said, "That'll depend on whether you have any reason to use him or not."

I'd returned to DC about six hours after Jennifer's little award ceremony. Kurt had told me about the death in Key West and then dropped the bombshell that he wanted me to form a cell and find Guy. He still didn't believe that Guy would perform an extrajudicial killing, but he was covering his bases. I could tell a part of him was scared. Really scared.

He told me whatever assets I wanted were mine, and I'd given him my requirements. He'd relented at Creed but had balked at the mention of Veep.

Nicholas Seacrest was a Combat Controller—Air Force Special Operations—who had been taken hostage and held for ransom by a terrorist group. My team had been the one that had rescued him, and then he'd been instrumental in helping us rescue another hostage who meant a great deal to both me and Kurt. He'd performed very well under pressure, both in captivity and out, and when it was over, I'd subtly recruited him for the Taskforce, not saying anything to Kurt and never thinking he'd bite.

He had, and the Oversight Council had gone ballistic— because he had a little bit of a pedigree. He was the vice president's son. Which is why he was slapped with the callsign Veep.

After some wrangling, he was allowed into Assessment and Selection, which he passed with flying colors, something I'd never doubted he would do, because I'm a scary judge of talent. Just ask Jennifer. He was now in the training pipeline, learning all sorts of Jason Bourne tradecraft to survive as an Operator in the Taskforce. It had been sort of an unspoken agreement that he was coming to my team when he finished his training, but because of this mission, I'd asked to pull him early. Kurt had drawn the line at that, or so I'd thought.

A day ago, Kurt had said, "No way. He's not even on probation status. He has to finish training first, then go through all the alias documentation procedures, and still has to deploy for his check ride on an orientation mission before even walking across the hall to a team. Three or four months easily."

I said, "Sir, one of the reasons you gave me this was because Johnny was too close to Guy. That cuts both ways. He couldn't track Guy on the ground because Guy knows every one of his team members on sight. The same goes for me."

Kurt said, "Don't build this up into an Omega mission. All I want you to do is talk to him. Bring him back to the Taskforce."

"I get that, but I might have to track him to do it. Find him on the ground and determine his state of mind. We're not talking about a high school kid playing hooky. He failed to show up at his own brother's memorial. Something's not right, and you know it. I'm not going to run up to him at a bar and slap him on the back the first chance I get. I want to observe him first, and I need a clean team to do that."

"He doesn't know Jennifer. He hasn't met her, has he?"

"No. I've got both Brett and Jennifer, who are clean, as far as I know. Knuckles is no good, but he'll help when I approach him. I want to go two on one for that. But I need at least one more. Nick is squeaky clean, and he's worked with me before. I don't want someone from another team who I don't know."

"Pike, I'm having a hard enough time just keeping him in training. The Council only agreed to let him attend the course. They still haven't given permission for him to go operational. I'm taking it one step at a time, and broaching this now might mean he's *never* coming to your team."

"What's Hannister saying about it?"

Philip Hannister was the vice president, and an Oversight Council member. While in the Air Force, Nicholas had taken his mother's maiden name of Seacrest as a security precaution.

"He's good, from what I can see. He's not super comfortable with his son coming here, but it's no worse than he was when Nick was in white SOF to begin with. He's okay as a father. He's never fought what his son wanted. It's the professional connection that's got the Council concerned."

"Go talk to Hannister. Him and the president. You can get them alone and get concurrence. When you first gave me this mission, you talked about the changes coming to the Taskforce because of the presidential election. Start planning for it. Hannister is running and very well might win. What better way to set the tone for the Taskforce under a new administration than having the son of the president inside it?"

Kurt had raised an eyebrow and said, "I thought you hated the politics of the Oversight Council? Never want to get your hands dirty with the crap I have to deal with. That whole 'all I want to do is operate' thing is bullshit, huh?"

I'd smiled. "No, I do hate it. But that doesn't mean I don't understand it. All I want to do is operate."

★ 29 ★

Even after that conversation, I thought my idea had maybe a fifty-fifty chance of coming to fruition, but Kurt asking me if I had information worthy of employing the vice president's son could mean only one thing.

Nick looked slightly more relaxed after Jennifer pecked him on the cheek. I understood how he felt, given he was still in training. It didn't matter how big a badass you thought you were, when you came into the Taskforce for the first time, you couldn't help but feel somewhat inadequate. Especially if the commander of the entire organization pulled you from training. Nick probably thought he was getting fired.

I said, "Oh, I'll use him, all right. It looks like the conversation with Pop went okay."

"Yeah," Kurt said. "Let's just say the Council is a little concerned about Guy. You know pigs have started flying when they take *your* advice. Tell me you've got something beyond knowing he's not in Montana. Some magical Pike thread."

"Not yet, but I will. He's not using any special tools, which means he's relegated to commercial stuff. Still pretty significant, and I've got Creed trying to locate what apps he'd use, what technology he'd focus on to track a guy. There are a ton of useless 'catch my wife cheating' apps, but there are a few that are pretty damn devious, and that's where he'll gravitate. That is, if he's *really* on the hunt."

Kurt said, "Pike, Johnny called today. His team deployed on schedule, but he's missing one piece of kit. A Gremlin. He did a predeployment inventory, and it was there. Now it's not."

The Gremlin was a small device the size of an iPad mini, with a folding antenna and a plastic case on the back the size of a cigarette pack. Its sole purpose was to remotely slave a cell phone for the introduction of malware. If you knew the IMSI or IMEI of a targeted phone, you could trick the phone into talking with the device, and it would implant any program you wanted—with certain caveats based on the cell network and security settings of the phone. It being missing wasn't a good sign.

I said, "Hey, sir, let's not go on a witch hunt here. Maybe it's up in the team room. We can't assume that Guy took it."

Deep inside, I didn't want to believe what Kurt was saying. I didn't want to face the reality.

Kurt said, "Pike, you remember what you were like? Back in the bad days? After your family?"

Hearing an echo of what I'd said earlier, I caught Jennifer's eye and said, "Yes."

"Could you do this? Would you be capable?"

I said nothing for a moment. He said, "Pike?"

I looked at him and said, "Yeah. Yeah, I could do it. If it meant finding the murderer of my family, I'd have done it without looking back. But Guy isn't me. This is a different situation. My family was killed in the United States, not on a combat patrol. And . . . I was . . . a little screwed up. This has nothing to do with me."

Kurt took a breath, assimilating what I said, then dropped the hammer. "It has everything to do with you. Sorry, but you set the precedent. President Warren is talking about shutting down the Taskforce. Saying that our operational parameters are so far outside the law, we've inculcated a bunch of pirates. Men who don't know where the line is anymore, because we removed the line for them. And you're case study number one."

"What the hell? Seriously? I lost my way, but don't put this on me. My family was murdered in the United States. His was killed in combat. Guy is *not* my fault."

"Nobody's saying that. But they're looking at the comparison. At one time, you were the closest thing to bringing us down. And now, you're the closest thing to preventing that."

I sighed and said, "What do you want from me?"

"I want him home. I want him back in the fold."

I heard the words, but they didn't really express what he desired. What the end state could be. I said, "And if I can't do that? If I can't get him back in the fold? What do you want?"

He dodged the question. "What do you have to work with?"

I said, "Creed?"

The computer geek turned around, looking scared, and said, "We don't really have anything. I'm collating everything he could use, but we don't have usernames or accounts. We're fishing."

Nicholas Seacrest shuffled a bit, looking hesitant, then finally opened his mouth. "Maybe we're looking in the wrong place. Don't try to find specific surveillance apps. Look for apps everybody uses."

I said, "Like what?"

"Facebook, Instagram, that kind of thing. If he's using it mobile, we can get his location."

He saw us staring at him like a church group hearing rap music. He said, "What? You guys don't use Instagram? Snapchat?"

Nick was a full ten years younger than anyone else on my team. I said, "No. We don't. And neither will you in about a month. If you think Guy George is posting on Instagram, you've proven me wrong in my choice of teammates. Welcome to the real clandestine world, Air Force."

He sank back against a wall, looking like he wanted to crawl through it to the skull-crushing training he'd left, and Jennifer sidled up to me, pinching my arm, telling me without speaking that I was being too harsh. She'd lived in the Taskforce he-man world, getting beat up just like I was doing to Nick, and she didn't like it. I glanced at her and she whispered, "Calm down, commando. You might not be the smartest in the room."

I gave her a small grin, pulling back a couple of gears, because she *was* the smartest person in the room. But I wasn't done with Nick. I said, "Okay, okay, start over, Veep. He's not using social media, but he might be using something we can find. What else you got in your hipster tool kit?"

Nick looked at me like I was just baiting him for another insult. I said, "Cat got your tongue? You pining away for Kylie? Wishing you could just curl up in bed with her and get away from the mean people?"

Kylie was Kurt's niece, and the one I had been tracking to find when I rescued Nick. The one I'd really wanted to save. At the time, I couldn't have given a shit about him, but he'd ended up being pretty solid under fire, and it turned out he cared about Kylie as much as I did. In a little different way, of course.

Nick scowled, his face going crimson. Jennifer hissed, "Do you think that's helping?"

I said, "I want to know what Veep's got beyond just another face that Guy doesn't recognize. You have anything at all to contribute?"

Yeah, I was being an ass, but it was for a reason. I wanted to determine if what I'd seen before was real. If he could take the pressure he was under and produce. Even if that production would be nothing more than snapping back at me. I needed to see if he had heart.

I glanced at Jennifer, telling her to back off on supporting him. Letting her know she wasn't doing him any favors. She got it. She'd been there before, and understood.

Nick glanced at Kurt, then said to me, "Sorry, Granddad. I didn't know I had to spell it out. He's got a digital trail, just like you do. That didn't start with my generation. You ever bought anything on Amazon?"

I nodded, telling him to continue. He gained courage and said, "I promise he has a trail under his real name, and there will be a crossover with whatever name he's using now. Maybe he doesn't use social media—Twitter, Facebook, or Instagram—but he's using something. Uber, Spotify, something like that. He can stay away from what you're looking for, but he's using something you're not seeking. I promise."

When I didn't respond, he rolled his eyes and said, "Jesus, I'm not saying he's blabbing on Yik Yak, but he's using something."

I said, "What the hell is Yik Yak?"

Before he could answer, Kurt snapped his fingers and said, "Wait a minute. He might have a point."

He opened the door and snagged the first person he saw, saying, "Get me George Wolffe. Right now."

I said, "What do you have?"

"Nothing yet. But maybe something. George sat with Guy after our meeting, and he said something about a playlist."

George entered within seconds, saying, "What's up? I'm dealing with some serious blowback from the North Korea thing you handed me. Am I here to take Creed back? I could use him."

Kurt said, "No such luck. You remember when you were talking to Guy George after our meeting? He had earbuds in and ignored you?"

Wolffe looked confused, saying, "Yeah? He was listening to a Pandora station his brother had created."

Kurt said, "His brother? He was listening on his brother's account? You sure about that?"

"Yes, I think so. He talked about how his brother had created it, and it was the only thing he had left from him. Why?"

I smiled at Nick and said, "You'll do."

★ 30 ★

Turning to Creed, I said, "Does that help?"

He whirled to the keyboard and said, "As a matter of fact, it does. Pandora sends location information every damn time you use it. It's evil shit, but works for us. I'll have to find his brother's username, then crack his password, but with the information we have on him, it shouldn't be that hard."

Through a Department of Defense database, he pulled up everything we had on Guy's brother, including email accounts, AKO login, and anything else the DoD required of its soldiers, then used that to mine the web for associated usernames, hoping that he—like most people—duplicated passwords and login credentials. At the same time, he started a devious little program that began a brute force attack against the Pandora login, throwing everything he found at it. He started his work, digging deeper and deeper, and I turned to Kurt.

"Sir, what's the real mission here? I understand bring him home, but what if he's actually onto something? What if he's fighting the good fight?"

Kurt closed his eyes for a moment, then said, "Just get him home. Whatever he's doing, it's not right. We can't have individual justice. If he's correct on the death of this brother, we'll deal with it, but he can't do that unilaterally."

I took that in, considering just saying "Roger that" and driving on with the mission. But I couldn't.

I said, "Sir, he's got a lot of information on the guys from Qatar. My mission in the Caymans wasn't smoke and mirrors. I get he might be off the reservation, but they *did* kill his brother. They deserve to be put down. It's a Taskforce mission."

Kurt bristled and said, "Pike, don't go there. Don't. Just get him back. I can't throw away . . ."

I waited, but he didn't finish. I said, "Can't throw what away? This unit? Seriously? Is that what we've become? More worried about our own asses than what's in front of us? Sir . . ."

"Pike, leave it alone." He ran his hands through his hair and said, "Fuck, this is getting way out of control."

I said, "Nothing is out of control. You control your own destiny, and what's right is right."

He rubbed his eyes and I saw the absolute pain of what Guy was doing. What I had done in the past. He said, "You have no idea what you represent. We are an organization that is antithetical to everything the United States represents. You do what you can for the good of the nation, but you represent the worst. We have more power than any element in the United States arsenal, and every bit of that power is predicated on secrecy. We fight for the good, but Guy has become the bad. I'll burn down the organization before I'll take the bad."

The statement was so harsh I wasn't sure where to go with it. I said, "Sir, surely you don't think—"

Creed cut me off, saying, "I've got penetration. I've got the Pandora account. It was used mainly at Fort Meade for the last three months."

I heard the location and immediately thought of my own deployments, when I wasn't as top secret as I was now. Keeping my eyes on Kurt, I said, "That's the satellite dish from Afghanistan. The IP address reroutes to Fort Meade. Go later. What do you have?"

Creed said, "I got a trace here in DC. The latest trace, as of yesterday, is Athens, Greece. Before that . . ."

Creed didn't want to say it. I looked at him, knowing it would be bad. "Before that, what?"

"Before that, the login was from Key West, Florida."

The words sank into the room like a dismal fog. Kurt said, "Shit. He's gone over."

I now knew we had to make a choice. It wasn't just me talking a man off the ledge anymore.

I said, "Sir, what do you want me to do?"

"Bring him home."

"And if I can't? What are my rules of engagement? He's going after all of them, and he's going to find them."

Kurt paused, then said, "End it. One way or the other. There is more riding on this than just a single man."

I saw Jennifer fold inward, looking like she felt sick. I said, "Sir, I don't know if I can do that. I'm telling you up front. You're asking me to kill an American soldier."

He bristled, saying, "I *never* said that. Never. Jesus. I'd never ask you to do that. I'm asking you to solve the problem."

I faced him head-on. Looking him in the eye. "Sir. You know where this is going. I'll bring him back if I can, but you picked me for a reason. I know where his mind is. I know what he's capable of. And he's going to do it. He's going to kill every single damn one of those guys from Qatar. Unless I stop him, and I can't promise how that will occur."

Kurt said nothing. Just stared at the wall, feeling the disaster, and knowing he was the commander. The one to give the order.

Finally, he said, "Pike, I can't let it happen. Even if it's right in your mind. I need you to interdict him. Period. Can you do that?"

I glanced at Jennifer, seeing revulsion floating in her expression. Next to her, Nicholas Seacrest showed confusion, not sure what he was being asked to volunteer for.

I said, "Yeah. I can do it."

Kurt relaxed and said, "Thank you. Look, bring him home. I don't want any killing, of the Qatar guys or him. You're the only one who can do that."

Repeating a quote by the assassin from *In the Line of Fire*, I said, "Because we can't have monsters roaming the quiet countryside, now can we?"

★ 31 ★

Brushing his teeth inside his hotel room, washing away the grime from forty-eight hours of eating junk food, Guy heard his phone buzz. A three-phase jarring vibration, it was distinct, telling him the GPS fence had been broken. He was surprised, and pulled the toothbrush from his mouth. Not because it had triggered, but because of the time. It was going on six p.m., and the target had been back at the yacht for only a couple of hours. Guy still had preparations to make, but the alarm caught him short, making him wish yet again that he had a team. Someone to track the man twenty-four/seven. A group of Operators he could insert in and out, instead of just himself trying to maintain a blanket on the target.

After escaping from Nikos's thugs, he'd taken a commercial flight straight to Heraklion, Crete, getting out of the furnace of Athens. It was an overnight sail on a routine ferry, but only forty minutes by air. He knew two simple facts: One, his target was meeting a man on the island, and two, he was taking another yacht to get here. Not knowing where the meeting was to occur, or even when, Guy had conducted a stakeout of the Heraklion harbor. In truth, the boat could have docked anywhere, involving a three-hundred-and-sixty-degree search of every cove. It was an island, after all, but Guy had heard Heraklion mentioned, and figured a boat that size would not port at a simple harbor with nothing but a slip of concrete to moor against. No, it would anchor at a habitual place. Somewhere with electrical power and other amenities. Every coastal city in Crete had one, but Guy was betting it would be the Heraklion harbor, the one for the island's capital. He knew it was guesswork, but it was a fairly good one. Even given that guess, the surveillance hadn't been easy.

He had initially focused his reconnaissance effort on a location that would allow him to continually observe the slips. There was none. The harbor—like most harbors—jutted out from the city itself, surrounded by a seawall, without any place to camp out and watch. He'd hoped for a hotel overlooking the slips, but was out of luck, the closest he could find being a mid-price hotel called the GDM Megaron, which had a view of the sea but certainly wouldn't work for surveillance. It did get him close enough to react if the boat ever arrived, though, so he made it his temporary tactical operations center.

In Athens he'd purchased and downloaded a unique Android app that let him access thousands of open-source webcams around the world, from zoos to traffic cameras. It was a time-wasting way for the average user to gaze across the continents at a beach they would never visit, but it had a double use as a poor man's surveillance application. Guy had used it to search for cameras in the Heraklion harbor. He'd found one way out on the seawall, watching the entrance to the harbor and the large ferry lines that came and went, but none of the boat slips themselves.

The only thing this harbor had that others didn't was

an ancient castle, sitting in the water on the seawall about two hundred meters out, protecting the harbor from intruders who were no longer relevant. It was an archeological treasure, famed for its history, and not something he could use for the long term. But he could use it for pinpoint mechanics once the yacht entered.

He decided to split the difference, leveraging the webcam app to identify the Qatari vessel arriving, then the fortress for the start of a pattern of life. From there, he would—hopefully—inject the target's phone with another application, called OneSpy, which would allow him to covertly monitor the target, both for cell phone content and location, freeing him up from close-in surveillance.

The castle itself was something from the seventh century, and was connected to the land by a concrete walkway along the top of the seawall. He'd investigated and saw it was being renovated, with the backside blanketed in scaffolding and signs proclaiming construction hazards, but he saw nobody working. It looked as if they'd run out of steam and had just left the scaffolding in place. Easy to climb, and because of the renovations, it was closed to tourists for the foreseeable future. Especially with the horror show of the Greek economy.

He'd purchased a hide-site survival package of olives, salami, and water, then sat on his hotel bed, alternately watching the feed on his laptop and the BBC channel on the television. Living on room service, refusing to shower or to leave the monitor for more than a bathroom break, his enclosure beginning to take on the peculiar smell of hide sites in the past, he finally saw the boat he was waiting for. At dusk, a hundred-footer flying the jack of Qatar entered past the seawall.

He'd left his room, running to the harbor, the first

time he'd broken the plane of the door in a day and a half.

He'd watched the boat moor, taking note of the slip, and had sprinted back up, getting his surveillance package. Cloaked in the gathering gloom, the castle itself blocking the view from the harbor, he'd climbed the scaffolding lashed to the walls, reaching the rampart on the top. He laid out his kit, positioned his spotting scope, then settled in, doing the same thing he'd done in his hotel room.

Sitting and watching.

Eventually, dawn had broken, and the boat had begun to stir. He followed the crew members with his scope, then saw his target on the deck, eating breakfast. He waited until the man appeared to be close to finishing, then surveyed the base of the castle. On the land side, fishermen were repairing nets and prepping their boats for the day. On the ocean side, with the exception of a couple taking an early stroll on the seawall, there was nothing. He packed his belongings and waited until they'd turned around, heading back toward the city. He slung his pack and scrambled over the side.

He reached the rock walkway just as another couple rounded the corner. They looked at him curiously, but continued strolling. He ignored them, moving toward the land, his eyes on the towering yacht, the biggest in the harbor.

He saw a figure walking down the gangway but was too far to get a facial identification. He quickened his pace, intersecting the man at the juncture of the seawall, the gangway for the harbor funneling all straight to that point.

It was his target.

He fell in behind and began to follow, once again letting his quarry dictate his actions, thinking through his mission.

Killing a man was easy, especially if one didn't care about the future. But Guy needed to learn about the others. That's what he told himself, even if it didn't really explain his quest.

He wanted absolution. Needed to know what he was doing was just. Wanted to believe it, even without sanction, but the man in Key West had provided no information other than the location of Haider.

Guy had entered the bathroom in Key West with the naïve belief that the man would tell him what he needed to know. The man had not.

He had fought like a demon until the bathroom was bathed in blood, and Guy had learned only one thing: the location of Haider. He'd left the island wondering if he'd murdered an innocent man, not a small thing in his mind. Guy had killed many men in his life, but all in combat. In the line of fire. This one was eating at him, growing in power, draining his ability to continue.

Late at night, when the bad man came and he couldn't sleep, he told himself he wasn't a terrorist. Not a murderer. He focused on his brother's face to obtain blissful sleep, and then was tortured by his dreams. He desperately wanted to prove he was in the right. That required questions, along with staying alive to pursue the answers.

He followed the target most of the day, the man staying on foot for the duration. There were only three interesting stops, none involving a meeting. The first was at a car rental—one of the many dotting the city. The target spent twenty minutes inside, but left without a vehicle.

Guy had wanted to enter the facility and learn what had transpired, but he had yet to implant his virtual tether, so was forced to follow the target. Leaving there, the Arab wandered up 25 Avgoustou Street, the main pedestrian thoroughfare that went through the heart of the city. He went to the second stop of interest. The Alpha Bank of Greece.

Guy watched him go in, but didn't follow. He took a seat at a Starbucks on the corner, unable to escape the ubiquitous smiling green icon even here in Crete. The target exited twelve minutes later, carrying a zipped bank bag. A bank bag bulging with cash.

★ 32 ★

The target left the bank and wandered aimlessly up the pedestrian avenue, killing time and acting like a tourist. He passed city hall, Guy tracking behind, seeing youthful protestors and spray-painted bedsheets howling anti-austerity slogans. Eventually, they reached the outdoor bazaar, the smell of fish overpowering.

The target circled through the fish market, ignoring the vendors hawking their catches, and entered a section dedicated to trinkets and handmade crafts, bouncing in and out of the small tourist shops. Guy read his demeanor and surmised he wasn't meeting anyone here. If he had been, he wouldn't have bothered with the rental car office. Guy faded into the crowds and patiently waited for the target to stop longer than five minutes.

Eventually, the target started walking back toward the harbor, and Guy began planning how he could return to the top of the castle, feeling his mission slipping away. He needed help. But in his heart, he knew he wouldn't use such help even if he had it. Wouldn't ask anyone to bloody their hands on his quest. A part of him wanted the man to return to his boat and relieve him of the mission. Giving him an out for not completing it.

Another part, slithering deep in the abyss, wanted

vengeance, and the dichotomy was beginning to rip at his psyche. He decided to let fate do what it would. If the man gave him the chance, he'd take it. But if he didn't, he would fly home with his information, turn himself in, and let the Taskforce do what it would do.

And then fate stepped into the game.

Walking down a narrow alley, forcing Guy to give him a large lead, the target disappeared from view. Guy suppressed the urge to rush forward, knowing that the target wasn't the only threat. Once the man was dead, they'd look for connections, and he running down the street—caught either on a surveillance camera or in the memory of someone looking out a window—was a sure way to halt his mission profile.

He reached a narrow stairwell the target had escaped through and paused, staring into darkness in confusion, then saw a sign proclaiming the day's specials.

Restaurant.

The snake in the abyss twitched. *Time.* The target was giving him time. He went up the stairs slowly, his eyes adjusting to the gloom.

He entered a large room, open-air windows, and tables scattered throughout, all save one empty at the late lunch hour. The target was in the back of the room, next to an upright piano with nobody playing.

A hostess seated him and he pretended to peruse the menu. He ordered an appetizer just to keep the waitress away, then pulled out his stolen Gremlin. It looked enough like any tablet on the market, to include a Wi-Fi capability, that he had no fear using it. He asked the waitress the password for the restaurant Wi-Fi, then pretended to surf the web. In actuality, he initiated the Gremlin's true purpose, the parasitic device sniffing the air for cellular signals. Four phones registered. One was his. Two were a Greek country code. The last had to be his target.

He selected that number, and the device began attempting to exploit, working through Wi-Fi, Bluetooth, and the cellular network in an effort to penetrate the targeted phone. Guy kept one eye on the device and one on his target.

The man was flirting overtly with the waitress, looking like a cheesy disco boy from the seventies. Guy could only imagine the idiotic lines he was using. The waitress laughed and seemed to reciprocate, and an idea formed. Guy watched the target scribble something on a piece of paper and hand it to her, and he had his in. He would trap the man with his own sorry libido.

Guy started working through a plan, thinking of hotels he'd seen away from his own, when the Gremlin vibrated. It had penetration; the phone now slaved with the device.

Ordinarily, this would be the point when some nefarious Taskforce exploit would be injected, but Guy had no such thing. Luckily, the cheating spouses club the world over had engendered a lucrative business in cell phone spying, and the open market was replete with cell phone exploits. The application he'd subscribed to was called OneSpy, and it allowed him to literally take over the targeted phone like a ghost in the machine. Listening to calls, seeing texts and web pages real-time, and giving GPS locational data were all in its repertoire—even turning on the microphone remotely to hear conversations. And it worked in the background, unseen by the phone's owner.

No doubt, should the man do any sort of forensic scan, it would be found—unlike Taskforce applications— but he didn't need root access to deploy it, and he was fairly sure the Romeo across the room would never look.

Not knowing the type of phone the man would have, he'd purchased both iOS and Android applications. He scanned the readout of the slaved phone and saw it was an Apple iPhone 6. He linked the iOS into the Gremlin and the parasite went to work. Ten minutes later, it was done.

Still pretending to surf the web, Guy pulled up the OneSpy web page and logged in. Working through the menus, he pulled up the GPS feature and found a blinking blue dot sitting on top of the building the restaurant was in. The target.

He smiled. No longer would he have to keep the man in sight. He used the GPS fence feature, setting an alarm should the man leave his yacht, and relaxed, eating his appetizer as the target finished his meal.

When he left, Guy made no move to follow, instead waving over the waitress. Before she could speak, he said, "That man that just left works for the same company I do. In Qatar. He doesn't know me, but I'd like to surprise him tonight. I'll give you a hundred euros if you'll call him when I ask."

Looking hesitant, not wanting to upset a patron, she hesitated. In broken English, she said, "I don't do that. I'm not . . ."

Guy leaned back and laughed, then said, "No, no, no. You misunderstand. He was trying to get a date with you, yes?"

She nodded.

"I just want you to call him when I ask."

He peeled off a hundred-euro note and held it up. "You get this now. All I want to do is surprise him with some friends from work. A simple phone call. Nothing else. He's from Qatar. He'll never expect it, but my company wants to reward him, and I promise he'll be happy."

Naïve, but now returning his smile, she said, "He was cute."

"You call him, and if you want, I'll send him back to you tomorrow. After I've surprised him. You can apologize for the trick, and he'll be flattered."

She nodded, saying, "Is he rich?"

"Yeah. He's rich. He's on that big yacht in the harbor."

Her eyes widened, everyone near the harbor having commented on its appearance. She said, "Is he staying here long?"

Guy grinned and said, "Yes. He'll be here for the foreseeable future. I promise."

★ 33 ★

K nuckles and I exited the Megaro Moussikis metro stop and took a couple of seconds to get our bearings. He pointed north, toward what looked like a concert hall, and said, "She told me it was just on the other side of that."

We started walking, and I said, "You sure she's good to go?"

He said, "I'm sure she's trustworthy, but I don't know if she'll be any help. She was close to Decoy, and when he was killed, she became close to Guy. If he was getting any help inside Greece, she'd be the first one he'd call."

Carly Ramirez was a CIA case officer currently working out of the Athens station. A few years before, Knuckles had taken Decoy to Lima, Peru, for his orientation deployment—a final check before becoming a full-fledged Operator in the Taskforce, and the thing I'd talked Kurt into letting Nick Seacrest skip. While they were there, Decoy had hooked up with Carly—against Knuckles's expressed orders—and they'd dated on and off with a comfortable, long-distance relationship that had suited them both, right up until Decoy had been killed. I didn't push any further, because I knew Knuckles had been the one who'd delivered the news. He was close to her as well.

We'd flown out of DC the day before, using the last known trace of the Pandora application, an ISP in a hotel in Athens. The trace wasn't real time, only showing where the Pandora application had been used in the past, requiring us to wait until Guy decided to log into his brother's account again. In essence, it showed where he had been only after he was gone. Not good enough for a tracking operation.

We needed something more. A name he was using, or a real-time tracking capability, and the hacking cell was working on that. Apparently, through what little digital evidence Pandora kept, Creed had determined Guy was using an HTC phone, but nothing further. The SIM card was another roadblock. It had been purchased from a vending machine at JFK International, and if I knew Guy, he'd probably bought about a dozen of them.

There was one bright spot: Apparently, HTC phones used some type of evil diagnostic software called Carrier IQ. It was designed to monitor and report things like dropped calls and bad data connections for trouble-shooting purposes, but Creed called it a rootkit, and said it not only monitored the calls but allowed the carrier to remotely access the complete usage of the phone, to in-clude texts, web searches, key presses—basically anything done with the handset. Somewhere in that digital trail, we wanted to find a name. A tag. Something that would allow the hacking cell to dig out the alias he was using. From there, we could start a track.

First, though, Creed had to get into the phone. It was all black magic to me, but he said he could do it.

In the meantime, I'd sent Jennifer, Brett, and Nick to the hotel for static surveillance. It was tedious work, rotating in and out, and hoping the target showed, but it was all we had. Not wanting to go sightseeing around Athens, and feeling left out because we were no good for the surveillance effort, Knuckles had come up with the idea to hit up Carly and see if Guy had made contact.

Knuckles had set up a meeting at the embassy under the auspices of "just passing through," and she'd put us on the cleared visitor list. We could get on the grounds but couldn't get past Post One, the Marine Guard who was the gatekeeper for the interior of the embassy.

We reached the side entrance to the embassy on Petrou Kokkali Street and stated our purpose. The guard looked through a list of names, then pressed a button, letting us enter the guardhouse. Inside, it looked like a small airport, complete with X-ray machine and metal detector. We unloaded our pockets into a bin, followed by our smartphones. I pushed mine toward the X-ray and followed Knuckles through the metal detector. He started to shove everything back into his pockets when the back door opened, and I saw a woman enter. About five-three, with black hair that fell just past her shoulders, she had a healthy tan, a sprinkle of freckles on her face, and a little upturned nose that was cute for no damn reason whatsoever.

Knuckles's smile split his face open and he gave her a bear hug. *So that must be Carly.* I could see why Decoy had chased her. She was pretty attractive, in a tomboy, elfish sort of way.

I walked through the detector and began putting my belt back on, waiting to be introduced. Knuckles ignored me, saying, "What happened to the red hair?"

"Nobody has red hair in Greece." She turned to me and said, "This must be the infamous Nephilim Logan."

I showed some surprise at her using my given name instead of my callsign. She stuck out her hand and said,

"Decoy told me all about you. Don't worry, it was all good. Mostly."

I grinned and shook her hand, saying, "He didn't say a damn thing to me about you. Probably afraid he'd lose your attention once you met me."

She said, "No, no, I don't think that's it. Maybe because you're not my type. I don't really date Neanderthals."

Huh? I'd never even met this woman and she was going to insult me? Right in the embassy? I bit back my reply and Knuckles grinned, slapping me on the back and saying, "I told you she was a handful."

Carly looked past me and said, "This is it? Just you two? Where's the girl? Jennifer? I wanted to meet her."

Now I was really aggravated. There was no reason for Knuckles to tell a CIA case officer the makeup of the team we had here. All she needed to know was who was coming to the embassy.

Carly saw my look and said, "Don't blame Knuckles. Decoy told me all about Jennifer as well."

She glanced at Knuckles and I saw a little melancholy on her face. The sarcastic facade slipped a bit, and I saw the pain leak out. She said, "We had a unique relationship. He kept asking for tips on getting Jennifer into bed, because he said we were so much alike. Wanting to make me jealous, but he knew it would never work. I'm not built that way."

She turned back to me and said, "Besides, he also told me he didn't stand a chance because of the mighty Pike. He really respected you, you know. And he was very impressed with Jennifer. I just wanted to meet her. Not too often you get a chance to talk to someone in the arena, dealing with the enemy and you chauvinists at the same time."

She winked at me to let me know I was in on the joke, and in the span of about fifteen seconds, I went from being aggravated to warming up to her. I said, "Maybe you will. It's a small world we live in."

She said, "That it is. Come on."

We exited the guardhouse and walked down the sidewalk, moving past a newer building before turning into a courtyard with a few scattered picnic tables. Inside the glass doors, I could see Marine Post One.

Carly took a seat and said, "As far as we go." She held out her hands for Knuckles to take and said, "I've really missed you. Ever since I left DC, I never see any of you secret squirrels. Guy came through here the other day, and it reminded me of the good times we used to have when I was at HQ. The only saving grace in working there. When you called, I *knew* you guys were doing something here."

She saw us both tense up, and she chuckled, saying, "Come on, Knuckles. After that crap in Lima, you know I'm not telling my boss anything. I still owe you my career."

While on the orientation deployment, Knuckles and Decoy had become involved with a live hostage scenario and a terrorist group called Sendero Luminoso, and had solved the problem with Carly's help. Meaning they'd smoked the terrorists. They'd come out as the Taskforce heroes, fading into the darkness like Batman with nobody knowing who had done the deed. Carly had been hung out to dry for disobeying CIA orders and helping. Knuckles had pleaded to George Wolffe, the deputy director of the Taskforce and an old CIA hand. He'd made some calls, and put Carly back into hero land. She'd never forgotten it.

Knuckles smiled and said, "Yeah, sure. You wouldn't

tell your boss, but I'm pretty sure you spent some time after Lima trying to figure out who we were. Did you?"

She pursed her lips and said, "No. But I didn't look that hard. I don't need to know. Some things are compartmented for a reason, but it's still helping the United States. It's the same reason I helped Guy."

She saw the look again and narrowed her eyes, now catching on to why we weren't acting like this was a high school reunion. "You're not here just to bullshit, are you?"

Knuckles said, "No. We're here to find Guy."

"Why? What did he do?"

Knuckles shook his head slowly, saying, "Carly, I can't tell you, but it's not good. I need to know what he did here. What you did for him."

I saw her eyes widen, she now realizing that blind allegiance in the name of friendship may not have been the best course of action.

She said, "Jesus. It's Lima all over again. I'm going to get barbecued for helping you guys."

I said, "No. No, you're not, because *nobody* can know that you did *anything* to help Guy. This isn't like Lima. There is no good coming of it."

★ 34 ★

Carly went from Knuckles to me, looking for a joke that wasn't there. She said, "What's going on? What's Guy doing?"

I said, "What did you help him with?"

She jerked her hands away from Knuckles and said, "Don't go prosecutor on me. What's he *doing*?"

Knuckles looked at me, the team leader. Not wanting to voice it out loud himself, he deferred to my judgment on what to say. Carly followed suit, looking me in the eye and saying, "So you think Guy's over here exploiting the economic turmoil? He's in Greece using his government connections to make a windfall on the mess of the eurozone fight?"

It was the least possible of a bad situation. She didn't believe it even as she said it. I saw the hope in her eyes, wanting it to be something as simple as fraud. I hesitated for a moment, then said, "You know Guy. Would he do that?"

Her eyes on me, I saw the hardness come. The realization. She shook her head, saying, "No. He's not someone who would exploit anything for personal gain."

I nodded.

She said, "Then what?"

I glanced at Knuckles, wondering how far to go. I decided to take a step back. "All we need to know is what you did for him. We're trying to find him and don't have a handle."

She took that in and said, "Don't have a handle. . . . You can't even call him? He's your man. What's going on?" She locked eyes with Knuckles and said, "I deserve to know. I lost Decoy. Now I'm losing Guy. Tell me."

Knuckles glanced at me for help. I decided not to sugarcoat it.

"Guy is off the reservation. He's hunting men, and he's killing them."

She took that in, going from me to Knuckles, skepticism on her face. She'd seen enough of the intelligence world to wonder if maybe Guy had done something sanctioned and was now being cut free, with her helping to hang him. She paused at my words, considering, then said, "He's killing innocents?"

I leaned forward. "No. They aren't innocent. At least I don't think so, but they *are* innocent until proven guilty. He wasn't sent on this mission. He took it on his own, and he's killing people one by one."

She looked at Knuckles and said, "Guy wouldn't do that."

He said, "I know. It's complicated. He thinks he's in the right, but he's not. We want to stop it and need your help."

She repeated, "Guy wouldn't *do* that. He's not a murderer."

I said, "You don't know what he's capable of, but I do. I was chosen for this mission because I'm the one who knows what Guy is turning into. I'm the *only* one. And now I'm hunting him."

She studied me, looking for the lie. There was none. She said, "What do you want to know?"

Knuckles said, "Everything you do."

And she told us, going through their meeting and his subterfuge about a mission, detailing her complicity in setting up a meeting with a member of the Greek underground, a man who could get him explosives and weapons. Toward the end, I saw her hands shaking, sure she'd just facilitated the extrajudicial killing of men she didn't even know.

I stopped her and took her hands, saying, "Don't do this to yourself. You did what you thought was right. You trusted Guy, and that *was* right. You couldn't recognize the change."

I looked at Knuckles and said, "He didn't recognize it in me."

Knuckles rocked his head, looking at the sky and thinking. He said, "That's correct, to a point. But you left the unit before you became Guy."

I let a grim smile escape and said, "Yeah, yeah. I suppose that's true." I returned to Carly and said, "Look, you did nothing wrong. You used your judgment, and any other time it would have been correct. I need you to use it again. I need to find this man you turned him on to. Nikos."

She nodded and said, "I can do that, but if I do, Nikos is going to wonder what's going on. Why would I engineer two separate meetings? It makes no sense. He'll be waiting, and he'll be less than friendly. He's not a man to cross."

I considered her words and said, "Yeah, okay. That's probably a bad idea. No meeting. Yet. But give us everything you know about him. It might come in handy to find Guy. More important, Guy may contact you again. If he does, we need to know about it. Can you do that? Can you set him up for us if he calls?"

Knuckles's phone rang. He looked at the screen and said, "Creed." He stood up and walked away.

Carly let him leave and said, "What do you mean, 'set him up'?"

"All I want to do is bring him home. I've known Guy longer than you. I have no desire to harm him, but this has to stop. It's going to cause repercussions to the national interests. He's not hunting wannabe jihadists. He's killing government officials. No matter how much I might agree with the targets, he's in the wrong."

She slowly nodded, then said, "Maybe I can help, if he calls again."

I said, "That's all I'm asking."

Knuckles returned and said, "We've got to go. Creed cracked the Carrier IQ software. The good news is he managed to find the name registered with the phone, and we now own the handset. The bad news is Guy's left Athens."

"Where is he?"

"Crete."

★ 35 ★

Guy listened to the phone buzz its distinctive rhythm one more time, then threw his toothbrush into the sink and ran into the bedroom, pulling up the OneSpy application on his laptop. The target was on the move, the speed showing he was on foot, but Guy knew he wouldn't be walking for long.

He'd rented a car for a reason, and Guy was sure he was linking up with that vehicle.

This is it. The meeting.

Guy packed his bag, one eye on the digital display. The dot was stationary for a minute, then began to move, much faster than before.

On the road.

Guy jogged downstairs, ignoring the elevator, then speed-walked past the front desk to the sidewalk outside. He reached the narrow lane in front of the hotel, a mess of traffic cones and yellow tape marking road construction. Behind it was a line of scooters, something that was ubiquitous around the island, so much so that Heraklion Airport had a poster from the British consulate warning its citizens about getting drunk and wrecking them, apparently something that occurred frequently enough for an ad campaign.

After leaving the waitress at the restaurant, he'd debated getting a car and had settled on the scooter. Since there was no parking at the hotel, a rental wasn't responsive, as he'd have to have it delivered at a time he wanted to use it, then picked back up. Since he had no idea of a time, he'd opted for the ridiculous scooter, taking a risk that the target wasn't going to drive for hours. The only problem with it was they didn't take cash. He was forced to pay with his new credit card.

It would be a trace someone could use. He'd paid cash for the hotel, and cash for his plane tickets, but he knew he'd have to cross this line sooner or later. Couldn't be helped, and anyway, he'd had to present his passport for the plane tickets. If they had the card, it would be through the passport to begin with.

He looked at his phone, the OneSpy app showing the blue dot moving out of the city on the E75, the main east-west highway. A dangerous sign for Guy's little steed. He wheeled the scooter around and set out, feeling like Austin Powers.

Traveling at a blistering fifty-five kilometers an hour, being passed by all the cars on the road and getting his face pelted by flying insects, he drove for thirty minutes before pulling to the side of the road to check his phone. The target had stopped at a small coastal enclave called Sisi. Guy did a quick search and saw it was known more for its beaches and expats than anything else.

He pulled back onto the blacktop, continuing on. Twenty minutes later, he was off the highway, taking a left toward the coast on a bumpy, potholed piece of asphalt. He held his phone in one hand, zoomed to maximum, entering the town and then weaving left and right. Eventually, he ended at an empty field, the phone beacon just beyond, inside some sort of house near the water.

He parked and skulked through the tall grass of the field, kicking beer cans and bottles as he tried to remain quiet. He got closer and heard music, then laughter. He reached the front and saw a skull and crossbones pirate flag, two men on a balcony drinking.

It was an expat bar, called, appropriately enough, the Jolly Roger.

He entered a gate and swung around the back, seeing the ocean and the light of tiki lamps surrounding an open deck. In the corner, under a neon sign, he recognized the neatly trimmed mustache of his target. Next to him was a young man of about twenty-five. Medium height, swarthy skin, and sporting a scraggly jihadi beard as if he had the mange.

Between them was the banker's bag.

Guy took a seat in the corner, away from the strands of lights crisscrossing the deck. He ordered a beer from the waitress, a Brit who attempted small talk. He answered in short, clipped sentences, not mean but definitely not looking for conversation. He waited until the beer had arrived and the waitress had given up on him before drawing his camera. He took the best photographs that he could of the new man, knowing the lighting would cause havoc with the image, then settled in, watching from across the deck, the light strings above swaying in the breeze, alternately illuminating, then darkening the target table.

Eventually, the banker's bag was unlocked and opened. Guy watched a manila folder, three fat envelopes, and an old-school flip phone passed across. His target said a few more things, then stood to leave.

Guy felt the choice forced upon him. This was most definitely the meeting he'd heard about in Athens, and now his time for the mission was ticking down. The target had accomplished what he'd been sent to do, and might be driving straight back to the boat to leave. But the new man was intriguing.

He felt his target slipping from his grasp, but couldn't shake twenty years of operational deployments. Of eliminating the threat for those who couldn't. And this meeting had all the hallmarks of something bad. Something that should be reported.

He let the target leave, feeling the sliver of darkness coil, demanding he follow. He stuck with the new man. After twenty minutes, the man stood, pulling a bill out of one of the envelopes. Which gave Guy one answer on what had been passed.

Money. And lots of it.

Guy threw his own bills on the table and began to shadow the new man through the small town. Eventually, he entered a three-story cinder-block hotel, a mom-and-pop establishment for the lower stratum of vacationers. Guy stayed outside, and thought about his options. Thought about the conflicting pressure of the killing he wanted to accomplish juxtaposed against the problem in this hotel he wanted to solve.

He decided maybe he could do both. He waited until he was sure the man was settled in his room, then got his own. He checked it out, surveying the dilapidated bathroom and worn bed. He pulled a wooden chair from a corner and set it in the center of the room, thinking through his interrogation strategy. Satisfied, he picked up his phone and dialed another.

When the woman answered, he said, "Hey, you ready to earn that money?"

★ 36 ★

Haider smiled and said, "Yes, I got the email. Very good. So you had no troubles? You'll be coming home tonight?"

Nassir said, "No, no troubles at all. He was right where you said he'd be. He has the money, the identification, and the phone. He'll be taking a ferry tomorrow."

Haider repeated, "So you'll leave tonight?"

He heard a pause, then, "Uhhh, no. I'd like to stay the night and leave first thing tomorrow. If that's okay."

"Why?"

"I have a woman. Someone from Crete. She gave me her number, and she wants to meet at a hotel. I'm going there now."

"A hotel? And she's from Crete?"

Understanding the question, Nassir said, "Yes. She lives with her parents. All she asked was that I pay for the room."

Haider looked at Khalid, his friend leaning forward with a scowl, wondering where the conversation was going. He said, "No. Nassir, there have been things that have happened. I want you home."

"I'm already there. The hotel was in the same town I met the Syrian. It's a town full of foreigners. She wants to get away from Heraklion."

Haider put some steel in his voice. A fake confidence easy to do over the phone. "Nassir, you do this, you make your own way home. I'm telling the yacht to leave tonight."

Haider heard the whining begin, Nassir always being the obsequious one. "You get what you want no matter what you do. I never can. This is the one chance to act like I have a name. She thinks I'm royalty from Qatar. She thinks I'm like you."

Haider heard a car door slam and said, "Where are you right now?"

"I'm at the hotel. Going to the room. I'll let you talk to her, if that'll make you feel better."

Haider looked at Khalid and saw anger. He said, "Don't do this. You don't understand what's going on. There's someone looking for us. Looking for you. Because of Afghanistan. A killer."

Haider heard a shuffling, the phone going from one ear to the next, then, "What are you talking about?"

"I don't want to say on the phone. Not here. Just get back. Now."

Haider heard a noise and said, "What are you doing?"

"Knocking on the door. I'll pass the phone to her. She's something you'd like to bed. I promise."

Haider started to protest, then heard Nassir say, "Who are you?"

Khalid was stomping about the room, demanding answers. Haider held up a finger. Waiting on Nassir to say something. He didn't.

Through the connection, the voice as strong as if he'd been the one holding the handset, Haider heard, "Hang up the fucking phone."

Then nothing.

Haider dropped his arm, incredulous, the cell phone hanging uselessly by his side.

Khalid said, "What? What's going on?"

"It's him. It's the killer."

Guy heard the knock and looked through the peephole, seeing his target and feeling a flush of vengeance. He stared further and saw he was on his cell phone. Talking to someone.

He backed up, thinking. He couldn't open the door with the jerk talking on the phone. It was a trace. A last vestige of the target's life. He was expecting a woman to open the door, and when it was Guy, he'd inevitably say something into the phone. Something that couldn't be hidden when he came up missing.

He heard another knock, this one more insistent, and turned a small circle, cursing.

Let him go. Follow the man in the hotel. Do what's right.

He felt the pull. Felt the draw from his past, where the rule of law dictated his life. He leaned into the eyehole and saw the face from his brother's armband. The face of the man who had caused the death of an entire Special Forces team.

He leaned against the wall, his hands pressing his temples.

Do it. Don't do it. Do it. Don't do it.

The blackness twitched, uncoiling in his soul. He looked through the peephole again, and saw the target begin to move away.

He's going to leave. This is it.

Unbidden, his hand went to the knob. Like a thing from another body, he saw his arm open the door. Saw the look of shock on the man's face.

He said, "Hang up the fucking phone."

★ 37 ★

Khalid said, "What do you mean? The killer? He's there, right now?"

Haider nodded, mute.

"Are you saying he's killing Nassir as we speak?"

"Yes . . . No . . . I don't know. Nassir said he was meeting a female, then I heard another man tell him to hang up the phone. Then it disconnected."

Khalid said, "Look into your heart. Was it the killer?"

Haider nodded hesitantly, then with more power. "Yes. It was him. He's tracking us." He looked at Khalid and said, "How did he know? How did he find Nassir?"

Khalid said, "He works for the United States. This isn't a lone gunman. We need to capture him. Interrogate him. Find out what he knows."

On the verge of panic, thinking of his father, Haider said, "How? We don't know anything about him. He seems to know everything about us."

Haider put his hands to his head and continued. "He's going to find out about the Syrian. He's going to learn our plans."

Khalid turned cold. Clinical. "No, he won't. He will learn about the existence of the Syrian. In fact, he most likely already has, but you didn't tell Nassir what you told me after your meetings with the American secretary of state. Nassir doesn't know anything of value, other than the Syrian exists. And we can use that against the American."

"How?"

"When he learns of the Syrian, the man will want to hunt him. To kill him. It's impossible for him not to. We use his own desire against him."

Haider recoiled at the very notion, saying, "Khalid, I can't do that. If anything happens to the Syrian, my father will disown me. I should call him. Get his advice. Let him know what has transpired."

He brought the phone back up and Khalid placed a hand on his arm, stopping him.

"Don't call your father. He will tell you to send the Syrian as planned, and then disown you anyway." Khalid chuckled and said, "Don't worry. It's not too bad. I've been dead to my father from birth."

Haider ignored the comment. "I have to call him. This is too big of a problem. The man has killed two of us, and now might destroy my father's plans. If it festers, my father might do more than just disown me."

Khalid said, "Give it a day. Contact Nikos and have him send some men to Crete. I'll go with them. The American has Nassir's phone, and I'm sure Nassir has given him whatever passwords went along with it. Send Nassir an email detailing a new meeting for the Syrian. Someplace where he won't dare attack. Then call the Syrian and tell him to go there. The man will find him, and the Syrian will lead him straight to us, at a location we control."

Haider waivered and Khalid said, "Remember Ahmed. Remember Nassir. Your father doesn't care about them, but you do. We can avenge them."

Khalid placed his hands on Haider's shoulders, facing him square. Haider saw the crazy leaking out of his eyes. A small tear when they were in Qatar, it had grown larger since Afghanistan, like a split in a bucket. Khalid said, "You are my friend, but if you do not do this, you won't have to worry about your father. I'll kill you myself."

Guy returned from the small bathroom, carrying a rag damp with water. He walked to the man in the chair, taking his time. Letting the dread build.

Eyes rolling left and right, unable to turn his head, the man was sweating profusely. Using a roll of duct tape, Guy had strapped him to a chair like a mummy, both legs and arms cinched tight. He'd taken two broomsticks and run them up the back of the chair, strapping one behind each ear, then down the chair. His target was completely immobile, his shirt hitched high and his pants pulled down to his knees.

Directly to the front of the chair was a small end table. On top of it were all of the possessions the man had on him. Wallet, smartphone, change, and a laser-cut key. Next to the key was a pair of pliers.

Guy moved the table back a few feet, then squatted in front of the man and pulled out the rag he'd stuffed in the man's mouth. He said, "What is your name?" The man said nothing. Guy held up the rag and said, "Open your mouth back up." The man pursed his lips closed. Almost conversationally, Guy said, "You know the most sensitive parts of the human body? Your fingertips and your penis."

He picked up the pliers and said, "Oh, and your tongue, but I can't use that, because I need you to be able to speak. Now, I'm going to start with your fingers, the first just to get you to open your mouth. Then, once the rag is back in to muffle the screams, I'm going to apply some pressure so that you know what's going to happen. Then I'll start my questions. Some of them I already know the answer to. Some I don't. It'll be up to you to figure out which ones to lie to me about, but if you make a mistake, the penalty will be enormous."

The man began to cry. Inwardly, Guy felt the relief slip out, like a balloon losing air. This man was not nearly as hard as the one in Key West. After that episode, Guy had planned on each of his targets being die-hard fanatics. This man clearly was not.

Showing nothing but malice, Guy said, "So you know, I have more than ten questions, so eventually, if you don't answer correctly, we're going to reach little peter there. After that, I'll have to get creative."

The man closed his eyes and mumbled something. Guy thumped his forehead and said, "What was that?"

"Nassir. My name is Nassir."

Good.

"Now, that wasn't too hard, was it?"

Nassir mumbled, "No."

"Okay then, second question: When was the last time you were in Afghanistan?"

Nassir looked confused at the track of the question, and Guy raised the pliers, gently placing the tip of Nassir's index finger between the jaws. Guy said, "I'm not even going to pretend I don't know the answer to that question."

Nassir said, "Two months ago. It was the only time. I've never been there before that. I swear."

A strange mishmash of emotions flooded into Guy. Victory competing with sadness competing with anger. He felt the urge to take Nassir's murdering life right then, the snake coiling for vengeance, but the meeting that had occurred earlier pulled at the back of his brain. A need to learn if this cell intended to kill again. A responsibility to the duty he'd sworn to uphold.

And a yearning for absolution for what he was about to do.

He changed tack to throw off his subject, turning to the table and pointing at the key with his free hand. "Tell me what this goes to."

Whipped by the change in direction, Nassir stumbled for an answer, and Guy closed the pliers, shoving in the rag as soon as Nassir's mouth flew open.

A tortured grunt came through the rag, and Nassir released his bladder. Guy leapt up, yanking the rag from his mouth. Without any humor, he said, "That's not going to stop anything from happening."

Between sucking in great gouts of air, Nassir choked out, "It's for a safe-deposit box. A bank box."

The room reeking of urine, sweat, and the uniquely pungent smell of animal terror, Nassir stared at the pliers on his finger, waiting on the bite. Guy said, "Safe-deposit box? At the Alpha Bank here?"

Nassir tried to nod, the forehead moving a millimeter in its tape cocoon. "Yes, yes, the Alpha Bank."

Before Guy could ask another question, Nassir's eyes flew open and he shouted, "No, no. Not here. Not the one here. The Alpha bank in Athens. Please, please. I didn't mean to lie."

Guy realized the man had broken. Nassir was now correcting himself without any pressure being applied. He was done.

Guy set the key down and said, "Good, Nassir. Very good. I believe you."

Nassir sagged in relief, the tape alone holding him upright. Guy tapped his crushed finger, drawing a yelp of pain.

Guy said, "Don't take my kindness for granted. We aren't done."

Eyes wide, tears running down his face, Nassir waited. Guy said, "Tell me about this man you met today."

★ 38 ★

We hit the runway of Heraklion Airport and I immediately told Knuckles to call Creed, seeing if he'd gotten any more fidelity on the man we were hunting. Creed had managed to crack the Carrier IQ of the phone, giving us a wealth of data, including its location, but he was still trying to find out the man behind the phone. Or more precisely, the name of the man behind the phone. We needed that. Even in today's electronic world, an identity was paramount. It was something that could be hidden online but was necessary in the real world, and the real world still mattered in a manhunt. At least for a few more years.

Too many vendors required identification. Required some measure of proving who you were, from hotels to airlines to rental cars, and in foreign countries, that meant a passport. A US driver's license wouldn't cut it. In the end, you just can't fake it when you're talking to a human, and if we could find that name, we could track Guy.

We taxied to the FBO, away from the commercial terminal, and Brett stood up, saying, "What do you want downloaded?"

The aircraft we were in was a Gulfstream G650—a

Rock Star bird like the ones famous celebrities used to initiate unfortunate groupies into the mile-high club—and was leased to Grolier Services through about a thousand cutouts that eventually ended up at Blaisdell Consulting and the Taskforce. As much as I would have loved to test out Jennifer's propensity to be a groupie—okay, I didn't say that—its true purpose was to infiltrate our weapons and equipment through customs, with everything hidden in secret panels throughout the aircraft. Brett was wanting to know what to break out, since the concealment was a bit of a bitch to penetrate, with each category of equipment in its own little shell.

I said, "Surveillance stuff only. Cameras, cell phone penetration, and beacons. I want only one suitcase. I don't want to walk out of here like we're tracking an army."

"Weapons?"

I considered, not liking the thought, but knowing it was necessary. "Pistols. Suppressed."

Nick was sitting wide-eyed next to Jennifer, listening to the conversation. He'd taken that seat on purpose, I was sure, because he knew her and she was friendly. He was still scared of me, which suited me just fine. He said, "Are we going to do an assault here? On Crete?"

I said, "That'll all depend on him. Don't freak out on me here, kid. You just point him out. I'll do the rest."

Nick went from Knuckles, to Jennifer, to me. He said, "I'm not sure . . ."

I said, "Not sure of what? All I'm asking you to do is ID him for me. Jennifer will be with you. She'll work the kit. Don't make me regret bringing you here. I promise you won't get hurt."

I saw him take the words as an insult, and I realized I'd misjudged his reticence. He said, "When I was in Ireland, you showed a desire to do good. A ferocious will to rescue Kylie. It's why I came to the Taskforce. I'm just not . . . sure this is good."

I said, "Look, I'm sure you thought you'd be slaying terrorists left and right, but sometimes you follow orders, even if they're unpleasant. This doesn't make me happy any more than it does you. But you are doing good."

"How? We're chasing an American. We're hunting a guy in the Taskforce. Someone I'm supposed to emulate. Someone I should look up to. Instead, I'm wondering if I'm going to kill him."

I glanced at Jennifer, passing the ball. She took it seamlessly. She said, "You talked about Pike as someone you trust. Someone who got you to join this organization because you saw something in him that you wanted to follow. So did I."

I nodded, pleased with her using my leadership to get him to continue. Then she said, "But Pike wasn't always this way. When I met him, he was the sorriest human being I've ever seen, and I don't mean just because he was pathetic. He was worse than that. He was despicable."

I started to spit out something to get her to shut up, and she held up her hand, silencing me. Nick looked surprised at the action, which really aggravated me. Before I could explode, Jennifer said, "I saw him slaughter two men with his bare hands in a psychotic rage. I ran from him because I saw a sociopath. Then he saved my life at great risk to his own. He was not that man. And neither is Guy."

As serious as I've ever seen her, she said, "This is just like hunting terrorists, because you're going to save a life. Guy's life, and he deserves it. Pike picked you for the same reason you joined. He trusts. And I've been here before. Let's bring Guy home."

Nick looked uncertain, and I said, "Hey, this is a shitty mission all the way around, but I wouldn't have taken it if I didn't have a team to get it done. I chose you because of your judgment. Don't sell me short on the same thing."

Knuckles came forward, holding out the phone. He said, "We got him. He's currently at a tourist attraction south of Heraklion, inland. Been there for a couple of hours."

"Name? Did they get his ID?"

"Yeah. They think. They've found digital links to some guy named Sean Parnell, and they think it's him. He's used a credit card to buy a ferry ticket and a moped here on Crete, and the name came into Greece on the timeline we have for Guy. Nothing on hotels, though."

All I heard was the name, feeling a little sadness at what Guy had done. I said, "Sean Parnell?"

"Does that mean something?"

"Yeah. It's him. I knew a guy named Parnell in Ranger Battalion. Second Batt. No way is that a coincidence."

"So he's getting help from active-duty guys? They gave him a passport? You think this is a conspiracy?"

I shook my head. "No. Parnell's dead. Killed in Iraq."

★ 39 ★

Sitting just inside the entrance to the Palace of Knossos, an ancient archeological site detailing Minoan life on Crete, Guy kept his eyes on the ticket booth, waiting on his target to show. He glanced at his watch and saw it was nearly five p.m.—the time the tourist destination closed—and wondered if he'd put too much trust in the email. Maybe his actions last night had somehow altered the instructions the second man had received. Did they know his phone was compromised? Had they decided to change venues? Did they understand that the man who owned that handset was now dead?

It was a question he couldn't answer, and so he sat, waiting. Watching. Regretting letting the other man out of his sight. He consoled himself by thinking about the ferry ride. He would link up with the target there, whether he showed here or not. Worst case, he would miss a piece of the puzzle, but he hadn't lost the target.

He brushed off one more vendor looking to sell him bottled water or a postcard, glaring at the woman hard enough to make her scurry away. Or maybe it was just his appearance. A three-day growth of beard, no sleep, and the devil slithering through his soul.

He'd spent the better part of six hours interrogating Nassir, the subject answering all questions unhesitatingly.

Nassir told him he'd passed identification and money to the man he'd met, that the identification had come from a safe-deposit box owned by the Qatar Investment Authority, and that the man was up to no good. But he didn't learn what that might be.

Nassir didn't know, of that he was sure. During the interrogation, in between Guy's sessions of vomiting at what he was doing—the only break the subject received—Nassir would have made something up, if he was smart enough.

He was not.

Eventually, Guy turned to the table again, picking up the cell phone. Nassir gave up the passwords, scared of what Guy would find but more afraid of the repercussions if he remained mute. Guy had searched it, seeing justification for his actions. He waded through names, text messages, and PDF files, laboriously using Google Translate only to find all detailing normal activity. Then he'd come across a word document held on a service called Dropbox. When Google Translate finished, he saw it was a damn after-action review of his brother's killing in Afghanistan. A triumphant discussion of slaughtering the infidels in the quest for jihad.

And then a new email message appeared, about a meeting tomorrow. He'd grown angry at that point, losing his objectivity and his nausea.

He demanded answers for the email, but Nassir refused to tell him. Or didn't know. After the destruction was wrought, Guy was betting on the second reason.

When he felt he'd gathered all he could, Guy had dragged Nassir to the shower, still in his chair cocoon, placing his head near the drain, a gag in his mouth. Nassir had begged, thrashing in the tape. Guy had placed the barrel of his suppressed pistol up to the temple, saw the rolling eyes, tears streaming down, and couldn't do it.

Not with the man looking at him.

Key West had been different. There, the man had fought, pulling a knife and coming close to gaining the upper hand. The rage had been flowing, and it was almost self-defense. Man on man, with Guy earning the win. Nothing like this. Nassir had no fight in him, and was completely defenseless.

Guy had knocked him out at that point, hammering his temple with the barrel, getting the eyes off him.

And then had pulled the trigger.

Afterward, he'd distractedly turned on the shower, strangely feeling that it wouldn't be right for the maids to be forced to clean up the blood after it had solidified. He'd watched the red water swirl down the drain, feeling his soul going with it. He'd then curled up on the bed in the fetal position, trying to sleep.

Way past midnight, staring at the ceiling fan in a half sleep, he heard Nassir speak, asking for help. He'd snapped awake, sweat dripping down his back, straining his ears. He heard it again. He leapt out of bed, running to the bathroom and flipping on the lights. Nassir lay on the chipped tile, a gaping hole in his temple, his eyes unseeing.

Guy began to believe he was losing his grasp on reality.

He packed what little he'd brought, and went outside, leaving the PRIVACY PLEASE sign on the door. He'd rented the room for three nights, hoping nobody would check the room until he was gone, but if Nassir kept begging for help, the maids would hear.

The thought made him giddy and confused.

Losing it.

He slept on a makeshift bench built by workers at a construction site next door. When dawn broke, he'd awakened, retrieved his scooter, and began to watch.

At 0900, Guy saw a cab pull up to the hotel, a spike, given the small size of the town and the absolute absence of a taxi business. Someone had called him. At 0910, the target exited the hotel, his face now shorn clean, and got into the back of the cab. At 0912, the cab drove away, winding through the small roads of the town, heading back to the main highway.

Guy followed, glad to drive away from the voice inside the room. Glad to distance himself from his sin.

He strained to keep up with the cab, his mind not on his task but on the ghost in the hotel room. Wondering if it would remain or follow him.

They went back into Heraklion, the target stopping at the ferry terminal. Guy watched him from a distance, then let the cab leave, going to the terminal himself.

With two hundred euros, he learned the man was leaving tonight, and purchased a ticket himself. He'd then jumped back on his scooter and headed to the Palace of Knossos, the destination in the email. The meeting was set for four thirty in the afternoon, but so far, the man hadn't shown.

He watched a school group getting berated for not behaving properly, then the entrance of a family, two kids whining and the parents dragging them along, demanding that the trip to Crete become a learning experience instead of the vacation it should have been.

He took a swig from a bottle of water, and saw a cab pull up. He lowered the bottle, and saw his target exit. He patiently waited.

The target entered, and Guy let him get deep inside, where he stared at a map under a glass shield.

Planning for his contact.

Guy snapped a couple of shots with his little digital camera, and waited. The target moved up the path toward the ruins, and Guy followed.

For the average tourist, Guy figured it took about an hour to see everything in the ruins. More if you had a tour guide blathering on. Guy started the chronograph on his Timex, both to keep track of his potential heat state, and to determine a pattern of life for these types of meetings with the target. He needn't have bothered. Guy's target did a quick lap, moving among the trees and paths that surrounded the ruins, then stopped at a display of giant urns, just standing and waiting. Above him and to the right, behind an ancient mural, Guy held his breath and readied his camera.

Nothing happened.

Guy saw him check his own watch, then continue on, nonchalantly circling back to the parking lot.

Guy saw the signs and realized the meeting was busted. He had no idea why, but knew, with the man headed back to the entrance, there would be no linkup.

So intent was he on the target that he failed to see the female tourist shadowing them the entire way. Guy couldn't be faulted for this. He'd kept a wary eye out for a threat, and had found none. After all, there were plenty of tourists in the park, each taking pictures, so the woman didn't spike.

But he failed to notice that the woman included him in every frame.

★ 40 ★

Khalid heard Nikos's phone ding and looked up. Nikos manipulated an application, then smiled. Khalid said, "He's there? We have contact?"

Nikos held up his phone, saying, "Yes. He's on your man. You were right."

Khalid crowded forward, saying, "What's he look like?"

Nikos pointed him out, and Khalid said, "Good. Good. My man will be back in the city as his next stop. Are your men ready?"

"Yes. But there's still the matter of payment."

Khalid waved his arm, showcasing the opulence of the yacht stateroom and saying, "Does it look like we're lacking in money?"

Nikos said, "No, this boat is definitely a benefit. I appreciate not having to pay for a hotel room, but it's not a question of you being able to pay. There is the matter of how much. This man came to me from a contact in the United States government. I have to assume he has some connection with them, which raises the price considerably."

"You were going to capture him for free in Athens."

"Yes. Yes, I was, but that was to protect our interests. That transaction is complete, and apparently my interdiction prevented whatever he had planned."

Khalid focused on the Heraklion harbor for a moment, then said, "It did not."

"Why do you want him so bad?"

"He has information we need, and he's harmed two friends of mine. We will pay whatever you ask."

Nikos said, "The price will be high, I promise. I'll have to disappear for some time, and I don't like living in caves."

Irritably, Khalid said, "I just told you we would pay. I'm more worried that you can accomplish the task. You failed before."

Nikos smiled and said, "There is a major difference reacting to a surprise and laying a trap. We won't fail."

"He comes to us alive. He's no good dead."

"So you keep saying. Don't worry. If your man leads him to the café, my men will do the rest."

"How?"

"You pay, I deliver. My operational methods are none of your concern."

"Maybe in the past, but not here. My money brings me information. The café concerns me. Too many people. I won't tolerate another failure, and I won't pay unless I'm sure this has a chance of succeeding. Nonnegotiable."

Nikos considered, then said, "Okay. But the price just went higher. Maybe I'll retire permanently."

"Fine. How are you getting him from the heart of the tourist area to here? Do you own the police?"

"No, but I do own the manager of the café. When your target arrives, he will be served by one of my men. The drink—water, Coke, beer, whatever—will be spiked."

"I don't want him unconscious. We only have the sail back to the mainland to talk, and I intend to leave his body in the middle of the Mediterranean. Anyway, how are you going to carry him from there to here?"

"The drug only makes him lose motor control. He can walk, but he can't fight. We usually use it for . . . other reasons. The bathroom for the café is down a set of stairs right next to the delivery entrance. It's boxed in."

Nikos put a cigarette in his lips, lighting it. "When he goes to the bathroom for a piss—and he will, a side effect of the drug—we'll simply roll him up and bundle him out the service entrance. He'll be here in minutes."

Nikos blew out the smoke and said, "All you have to do is have your man stay long enough for the drug to take effect."

"How long?"

"Fifteen minutes. Twenty on the outside."

"What if he fights?"

Nikos laughed. "He can try. It won't help him. Trust me, I've seen women try to fight. At most, they mumble a little bit, then do what they're told."

Khalid said, "You sold him a weapon. He won't have to strike you with a fist."

"Won't matter. The weapon will be hidden. He's not going to go to the bathroom waving it about. When we get on him, it'll be too late."

Khalid nodded, saying, "All repercussions are yours if it goes bad. Until he's on this boat, we have no association or responsibility. That's part of the agreement."

Nikos smirked and said, "You have no faith."

Khalid glared at him and said, "I have an abundance of faith. So does this man. He is not a teenage girl. He's a killer, and you would do well to remember that."

★ 41 ★

Guy stayed behind the cab, wondering what the entire trip to Knossos had been about. Thinking through the implications, once again wondering if his interdiction had something to do with the missed meeting. Clearly, the target was supposed to do some coordination at the ruins with someone other than Nassir, but that meeting had not occurred. Why? Was it because Nassir hadn't responded? But the email had stated no response was necessary.

Greater still, why meet in a beach town, then plan another meeting later at a tourist location inland? Nassir had passed the bank bag, full of money and identification documents, and given instructions. He was the man on the ground. So why the second meeting?

It was poor operational security, and poor planning. It made no sense. Then again, not a whole lot made sense when dissecting terrorist actions. Guy knew he was seeing only a piece of the pie. It was like reading a text message with a bad autocorrect. You stared at it, wondering what the hell it meant, but only because you were missing a letter that would make it clear.

The cab stopped next to a short stone tunnel known as Arsenali Nuovi. It sat adjacent to the Heraklion harbor, a wonder from Venetian times falling into disrepair. The target exited the cab, walking into the arch, and Guy whipped his little scooter around, parking on the sidewalk next to two others.

He made a show of locking up the bike, even though he had no chain, fussing around and letting the target exit the tunnel, getting on to his destination. The man eventually did, walking up 25 Avgoustou Street just as Nassir had before, the pedestrian thoroughfare as clogged with visitors as it had been on that first day. Guy was convinced he was heading to the Alpha Bank.

Guy fell in behind, keeping a few tourists between them, thinking of how he could penetrate the bank with the target. He'd declined to risk it before, but then the mission had been simply to kill Nassir. Now he wanted to decipher whatever plot was occurring. Begging for it to be something evil. Something that would prove he was on the side of the righteous.

To his surprise, the target passed right by the bank, not even giving it a glance, continuing up the street. Eventually, he stopped at a café called Central Park, staring at the menu for a moment, then wandered inside. Guy followed.

The café was split half in and half out, with the outside area sprawling haphazardly next to a park, the patio covered by large individual umbrellas forming a makeshift roof and scattered propane heaters warding off the chill.

The target took a seat inside. Guy continued outside, taking a table with his back to the park and a view of the target's location through the window.

The day was rapidly fading, and Guy reflected on what could be happening. Another meeting, or just dinner? Either way, he knew the target had about an hour before boarding the ferry, so whatever it would be, it wouldn't take all night.

A waiter approached, wearing a green apron and a cheap earpiece attached to a radio on his hip. Guy ordered a Coke, then surreptitiously scanned the other waiters and waitresses, seeing they all had the same radio setup. He forced himself to relax. It was just a marketing ploy. They probably didn't even function.

The waiter brought his drink and he took a sip, surveying the crowd. Most were locals, but there were a few who stood out as tourists. French, English, maybe German, a tiny fraction still willing to test the waters of the Greek economy even with the troubles.

His eyes were tracking back to the window with his target when he saw an attractive dirty-blonde. The hair caught his eye—simply because he was a man—but the face registered in a different way. He had seen her before. Somewhere. Or she looked like someone he had seen before. He was unsure.

He stared intently, trying to place the woman, but failing. Something about her had ticked in his subconscious, and he'd learned to trust his instincts. He went to her partner, seeing a youngish male with close-cropped hair, sipping water. The man wasn't a fat tourist. He was fit, and he looked like he could handle trouble. Like he *had* handled trouble in the past.

It brought a spark of alarm. Had they come in after him? Or were they already here? Was he being tracked? Or being foolish?

The woman leaned over and kissed the man on the cheek. Guy saw him blush, and relaxed. *Paranoid*.

Jennifer came through my earpiece loud and clear. "Jackpot. I say again, Jackpot. I've got Runaway."

We usually gave every target we chased a nickname,

and we'd taken to calling Guy Runaway for obvious reasons. I glanced at Knuckles, making sure he'd heard, and saw he had. I clicked on. "Should we brace him right there?"

She said, "I'm not sure. He's wary, like a stray cat that's looking at everything as dangerous. He just gave me and Veep a hard stare. I mean hard. If I didn't know any better, I'd say he recognized us."

I looked at Knuckles and he gave me a quick shake of his head. *Impossible*.

He broke in, saying, "Koko, no way does he know you or Veep. Are you giving off a vibe? Something he can sense?"

Surveillance was an art as much as a science, and like ancient tribes who believed in witchcraft, we all believed you could project an aura that could burn you. Unspoken, unseen, but something there nonetheless. An aura a target could read.

Jennifer said, "No. No way. We're okay now. I kissed ol' Veep here on the cheek and got him to blush. Runaway lost interest after that. It just seemed like he could see through us somehow, but he didn't spike on Blood at all, so it's not our posture."

Blood was Brett Thorpe's callsign, and, as an African American, one he absolutely despised. He cut in, saying, "Maybe it's because I know what I'm doing."

He tended to believe his callsign should be Jason Bourne.

Okay, that's not true. He didn't have an arrogant bone in his body, but he did have a sense of humor about poking anyone else on the team. Truthfully, after hearing some of his stories, maybe his callsign *should* be Jason Bourne.

He continued, saying, "Pike, I think he's following someone. We ran a recce of the site, and nobody here remotely resembles the target deck, but he's definitely focused on a guy inside. An unknown."

Knuckles raised an eyebrow at the words. I said, "So don't brace him there?"

Brett said, "No. Let this play out. We know he's got a ferry ticket in an hour. My recommendation is not to do anything here. He's hyperalert, and he's looking for trouble. Let him get somewhere and relax."

Jennifer cut in, "Break, break. Runaway's up and moving."

★ 42 ★

Guy ignored the couple, focusing on the target in the window, disgusted at his paranoia. He ordered a beer, pushing the Coke away. When it arrived, he downed it in three large gulps, thinking about the future. He still had two men to kill, and he was fairly certain he could find them, given the electronic tether he had with Nassir's phone. He also had the key to the safe-deposit box in Athens, a box that was apparently a clearinghouse of false documents and bank accounts.

And a man in a café . . . decisions, decisions, decisions.

He ordered another beer, then felt his bladder, realizing he hadn't urinated the entire night, unwilling to use the bathroom the body was in. He stood up, moving toward the entrance, and found himself unconsciously leaning to the right, vertigo making him feel as if he were falling. He grabbed a table and steadied himself, shaking his head to clear it.

The sensation subsided, and he entered the café, following the signs to the restrooms. He reached the narrow stairwell, feeling his brain growing fuzzy. A peculiar half-drunk without the euphoria. He was close to the bottom of the stairwell when he slipped, sliding the rest of the way on his butt.

The room began to shift violently, and he realized he'd been drugged. *The woman outside. Should have listened to my instinct.*

He fought through the dizziness, swinging his hand about, trying to find purchase on the rail. He glanced up and saw his waiter standing at the top of the stairs, looking down in concern. He felt a cool breeze and realized a door had opened. Another waiter, pushing a keg of beer, came through. He could see the twilight outside, the setting sun bouncing off a delivery van, the engine running.

Incongruously, he wondered if the van would get a ticket for parking illegally, his brain refusing purchase on his situation.

The waiter with the keg bent over, and Guy held out his hand, mumbling for help. The man pulled out a pistol and pointed it at Guy's head, saying, "Drop your weapon. I know you have one."

Guy stared into the maw of the barrel, the darkness sucking him in, and a small piece of his mind clicked. A sliver of his true self broke free.

He reached behind his back and withdrew the worn 6P9, laying it on the ground. The man said, "Get up. No fighting, or you'll die right here."

Guy pulled himself with the rail, forcing his brain to engage. Forcing out the fog by sheer will alone. He wobbled and realized he would have one chance, and would most likely die right here.

The man waved the pistol to the door, and Guy took a step, then stuttered as if he were falling forward. He was not.

The man grabbed his shirt right at the collarbone, chuckling and saying, "Okay, okay. You're okay. You can walk."

Guy reached up and trapped the man's hands with both of his, then fell sideways for real, using his weight to torque the man's wrist in a direction it shouldn't go. The man screamed and Guy felt the bones snap.

He ended up on top of the man, uselessly scrambling to control his weapon. The man yelled again, bringing his gun hand forward, and fired, Guy knocking the gun high, the bullet slapping into the roof. With his left hand, he grabbed the long silencer of the 6P9 and swung the pistol like a tomahawk, smashing the man in the temple.

He heard another crack, and realized someone else was shooting. In slow motion, his body refusing to move with any speed, he turned and saw the waiter at the top of the stairs, holding another pistol.

Team. It's a team. I'm done.

The man fired again, and Guy flopped backward, reversing the 6P9 and aiming with a two-handed grip. The barrel wobbled all over the place like the hand of a conductor working a symphony. He couldn't get a sight picture. He squeezed off a round, the bullet traveling harmlessly into space. The man took aim again, and Guy knew he was dead. He waited on the strike, then saw the waiter's knees buckle, his head snapping backward as if it were attached to a string. Guy blinked and pulled himself upright.

It was the blond woman taking the man down from behind. She brought him to the ground and he watched her hammer the waiter in the throat. She looked down at him, her face hidden by her hair, illuminated in the harsh light of the overhead lamps, and the recognition came like a thunderbolt. It was something he'd seen before, duplicating this very scene. It was the woman from the Taskforce surveillance tape in Istanbul. The one who'd been with Decoy when he died. The one he'd watched over and over, not for her, but for him.

She was Taskforce. And she was deadly.

He stumbled backward, reaching the open door. He went through it, staggering into the street, looking for shadows to hide within.

★ 43 ★

I started the car immediately, jumping through traffic to get to the cross street at the base of the park. The area was blanketed with pedestrian-only thoroughfares, but the street below the park cut through them all. Where my team was currently running like hell to reach me.

Knuckles worked the radio, a hodgepodge of calls that only fleetingly told us what was going on. Two men down, then three men. Nick and Brett assaulting an armed waiter, then Jennifer eliminating another waiter shooting at Guy. Then all of them sprinting like looters into the park, panting on the radio for pickup.

I raced down the lane, seeing a fountain to my front. The park.

I hammered the brakes, causing the car behind me to honk. I ignored him, staring up the hill. I caught movement. Between gasps for air, I heard, "Almost out—you guys staged?"

I couldn't make out who the caller was, but Knuckles said, "We're in position."

I scanned up the hill and Knuckles said, "There. There they are."

Three figures broke from a tree line, skipping down

the slope in a loping run. Knuckles opened the sliding doors to our minivan, and I kept my eyes up higher. Looking for a follow-on force giving chase. I saw nothing.

They leapt inside, and I hit the gas, moving out of the kill zone and getting back into the flow of Crete traffic, away from the cloistered neighborhood streets. I let them get some adrenaline out before I began questioning, knowing they'd start talking among each other.

Nick said, "What. The. Fuck. Why did you smack that guy? What did you see?"

Brett said, "He was keyed on Guy. From the moment I entered. When Guy stood up, he started forward. Guy went inside, then I saw him put a hand on a gun."

"There was no gun. I mean . . . there was no way you could see a gun. How did you know?"

I looked in the rearview and saw Brett wink at Jennifer. He said, "Sometimes you just know. Thanks for helping out."

Nick said, "You didn't give me much choice."

Brett said, "Welcome to the Taskforce. You did fine. Although maybe you should have helped out Jenn instead of me. I had no trouble."

Jennifer said, "Don't do that. I was fine. If he'd have come to me, you wouldn't have been able to handle that third threat."

I finally cut in, "Okay, enough of the lovefest. What the hell happened?"

Brett said, "Someone is hunting Guy. Someone besides us, and it wasn't a bunch of Arabs. They were inside the café. They infiltrated the waitstaff. It was a planned ambush, and they were gunning for Guy."

"Who is it?"

"No idea, but it wasn't a target of opportunity. They

led him there with the man he was following. Led him into an ambush. If we hadn't been there, he'd be dead instead of on the run."

I turned onto the main east-west road and said, "Jenn, what about that? Where is he?"

"He fled out the back. No way could I have followed. He had a pistol and was looking to kill. But there was something else."

"What?"

"He was drugged. He was staggering around. Brett's right. They knew he was coming, and they infiltrated the waitstaff with a complex plan. It wasn't the Arabs. Or if it was, they have incredible reach."

I said, "Why, though? Why go to that trouble? Why not just kill him on the road? If they had that fidelity of where he was?"

Knuckles said what I was thinking. "Because he's onto something. They needed to take him alive for some reason. Find out what he knew and who he's working with. They think he's operating with sanction."

I shook my head. "Shit. That's not what I want to hear."

We rode in silence for a moment, all of us tumbling the information. Finally, Knuckles said, "What's the next step? What do you want to do?"

I pulled over, putting the van in park. I said, "I'm thinking we brace him on the ferry. We know he's getting on it because of the credit card purchase."

"How will we find him?"

I turned to Jennifer. "You burned?"

"I don't know. He stared at us hard, before the fight, but I think it was just because he's paranoid. He didn't get a look at my face during the fight. He was too busy escaping, but he's Taskforce. He might remember both me and Nick."

"Brett?"

"No. I'm completely clean."

"Okay. We go to the ferry."

I pulled up the ferry company website on a laptop, getting an amenities list. "There are only two places serving food. A restaurant inside, and a fast-food vendor on the deck. Sooner or later, he's got to get some food or drink. We stake out those two. Jennifer, you mix it up a little bit. Change your hair, put on glasses, something. You'll go with Brett as cover to mix up the profile. Nick, you go alone. You get the outside deck. It's cold out, so wear a hoodie to hide. Take a corner seat and just drink coffee. Look like a hippie backpacker."

Jennifer said, "What are you and Knuckles going to do?"

"Sit in a room until you call. He sees either of us first, and he's liable to go lethal."

★ 44 ★

Guy felt a hammering in his skull and finally awoke, disoriented in the darkness. He sensed movement, his body feeling as if it were shifting, and tensed for the vertigo.

Then he remembered.

He'd made it to the ferry. That's what he was feeling. He was on the ocean. He lay back in the small bunk, staring at the ceiling in the gloom, trying to collate all that had occurred. He leaned over the bed, seeing his small knapsack. He slid his hands down the rail and found the 6P9.

He was safe.

The movement back to his hotel, then to the ferry port, was a blur. Like a blackout drunk from his younger days in the Army. Only this one had deadly implications. He had vague recollections of packing, of checking out—the woman looking at him in concern—and staggering to the ferry. He'd arrived right after they allowed boarding and had managed to talk his way through the process. There were no customs or other law enforcement, the only gateway being a ticket agent and two stevedores. He'd moved inside the cavernous ship, walking by the trucks and other transport being loaded, and re-

ceived his room key. A single bunk in a claustrophobi-
cally small closet.

He remembered removing his shoes, then nothing.

Rubbing his face, he realized he could see the ceiling.
There was light coming through the small circular window. He looked at his watch and saw it was dawn. He'd
been asleep for twelve hours—almost the entire journey.

He felt his stomach rumble and sat up, the rapid
movement bringing on a remnant of vertigo from the
drug. He steadied himself, praying it wasn't something
that did permanent damage. The feeling passed, and he
put on his shoes. By his watch, they would be landing in
less than an hour, and he had a lot of thinking to do.
Decisions to make.

The attack at the café had been well planned, and it
hadn't been done by a bunch of Arabs. Whoever had
done it had connections in Crete. Enough so to co-opt
the staff and prepare an elaborate attack. It was amazing
it hadn't succeeded, and had all the hallmarks of a Taskforce operation.

But he'd been saved by the Taskforce. The woman
from Decoy's tape. Clearly, they were tracking him. Had
somehow found him, even with his precautions. They
were a threat, but it wasn't they who'd set the plan in
motion. Somehow, the false waiters had known he'd be
in that café. But why had he been in that café?

Because he'd been following a target. Someone under
the control of the killers from Qatar. They'd manipulated him to arrive, but even they wouldn't be able to
take over a café with that elaborate plot in twenty-four
hours. No. It had to be someone local. *Nikos.* And that
fucker would pay. One more for the target deck.

He stood, putting the 6P9 in the small of his back and
testing his legs, finding them strong. He left the room,

moving up the two decks to the cafeteria. He reached the open space of the deck, away from the narrow gangways, stepping over folks in sleeping bags, too cheap to fork over money for a cabin. He entered the cafeteria and took a quick survey, seeing families and loners all waiting to dock. He bought a pastry and a cup of coffee, wolfing down the first before touching the second.

He stood at the counter and methodically went over the room, searching for danger. He found it next to a black man in the corner.

A Caucasian woman sitting beside him, making small talk, dark glasses on her face and a scarf over her head. She made no outward show of even acknowledging Guy's presence, but he knew who she was. It radiated off her like heat from an open stove, a connection he'd found on a tape detailing a death that punctured his core.

It was the woman from Decoy's video. The one who'd saved his life. She looked nothing like she had last night, but he knew. He had no idea how, but he felt it.

She was here, on the ferry, which meant the man she was talking with was a killer as well. Taskforce, with a skill equal to his own.

He considered his options. He was on a boat that might be blanketed with Taskforce Operators. It wasn't like he could escape on the open ocean. The woman was already talking on a radio, alerting the team of his presence, of that he was sure. But she hadn't done anything against him. On the contrary, she'd saved his life. And she'd killed that fuck who murdered Decoy.

He was sick of hiding. Tired of running. He was doing what was just. It might not have started that way, but he was sure it would end in his favor. He wanted absolution, and he was looking at the only entity that could give it to him.

He made his choice.

He strode right up to their table, seeing the black man's eyes go wide. He raised a hand, saying, "No. Don't." The man relaxed, his hand at the small of his back, waiting. Guy turned to the woman and said, "Jennifer Cahill, right?"

She looked confused and said, "I'm sorry. I think you've mistaken me for someone else."

He said, "No. I'm not. I've seen your work. Decoy was my friend. I'm hoping you are as well."

★ 45 ★

Sharif al-Attiya held a finger up to the Skype call and said, "Don't say another word. Shut up." He turned away from the screen, feeling the beginnings of a throbbing headache. "Tarek, get in here!"

He waited for his assistant to arrive, giving his son nothing to indicate how incredibly angry he was. Out of habit, he awoke early every morning, but the time was usually his own, before he began his day with the investment authority. This morning had been different, with him waking up to three missed calls and an urgent text message for him to Skype his son. He had, and heard nothing but disaster.

Tarek entered the room, taking one look at Sharif's visage and becoming subdued. He'd seen the volcano Sharif could become, and knew whatever was happening, it was not good news.

Sharif turned back to the screen and said, "Okay, idiot. Continue."

Haider stumbled for words, then said, "Do you want me to repeat what I told you?"

"No, you donkey. Just keep going."

"Yes, sir. . . . Nassir is missing, and we're sure he's dead. We missed capturing the American, but we're searching Crete. Nikos has men at the airport and is combing the hotels. He has a lot of penetration. A lot of help. We'll find him soon."

Tarek's face showed confusion, and Sharif said, "My idiot son found out that he was being tracked for his actions in Afghanistan. Instead of calling me, or leveraging whatever help we could provide, he decided to use our *shahid* as bait. The mission failed, and now our Syrian is compromised."

His face slack, Tarek said, "What?"

Spittle flying from his lips, Sharif barked, "He put our mission in jeopardy! He tried to capture the American, and all he did was expose the Syrian. Now the American is running loose."

Trying to catch up without asking any more questions, Tarek said, "Is the Syrian on the ferry?"

From the computer, Haider said, "Yes, yes. He wasn't harmed. Father, it was the US secretary of state who told me about the plot. I decided to intervene. It should have been easy, but he had help. Someone helped him escape."

"So it's a team? An American team hunting the Syrian?"

"No, no. Father, he—they—are hunting me. Me and my friends. And they've killed two."

Sharif waved that away with a hand, saying, "What does the Greek, Nikos, know?"

"Nothing. He only knows the documents we paid for. He's used to working outside the law. He tried to capture the American in Athens, when he spotted the man conducting surveillance on our meeting."

Sharif exploded again. "The American was there two days ago? And I'm just now finding out?"

Haider ducked his head on the screen, saying nothing. Tarek said, "Sir, let's focus on the problem. What's done is done."

Sharif said, "How do you know the man is still on Crete?"

"He was drugged. He wouldn't have had the capacity to purchase a plane ticket. We believe he's either in a hotel or passed out in an alley. We're looking."

"What about a ferry?"

"It left too soon. Nikos says he wouldn't be coherent enough to buy a ticket that quickly."

"What if he already had one?"

"He was following our man because we sent a message to trap him. He didn't know where the man was staying. He captured Nassir, but Nassir knew nothing of the plan. The only lead he had was the meeting we set up. There's no way he knew the Syrian was leaving. He was following the man for a reason, and the *shahid* could have stayed for days."

"What was that reason? Because he wants to prevent a plot, or because he wants to kill you?"

Haider glanced back into the room and Sharif snapped at him, "Who's there with you?"

"Khalid."

"Bring him forward. I don't like talking to people I can't see."

Khalid sat next to Haider, looking nowhere near as timid. He said, "Sir, it was my idea to capture the American. And it was a good idea. You would have done the same."

"Shut up. I'm not addressing you. Sit still."

Khalid showed no indication the words had any effect, but he remained silent.

Sharif said, "Son, answer the question. Is the man hunting you, or is he trying to penetrate our plans?"

Truculent, Haider said, "Which one is worse to you?"

"Don't trifle with me."

"He's after me. Khalid and me. Secretary Billings said it was because of Afghanistan. A vendetta."

Sharif nodded and said, "Okay. So we just have to keep you alive a little longer. Make sure he's chasing you and not the Syrian. Maybe I should serve you up like you did our *shahid*."

"Father . . ."

Khalid said, "You won't be serving me up." He paused a beat before adding, "Sir."

Sharif waved his hand at the screen and said, "Don't tell me what I will or will not do. You sons of dogs have no business here anyway. Haider, what did you learn of the peace deal? Do you have a location in Afghanistan?"

"It's not in Afghanistan. It's in Oslo, Norway, but I don't know when. I have a meeting with Secretary Billings in two days. I should learn the timeline then."

"Oslo? Did you send the Syrian to Afghanistan as I ordered?"

"No. He's coming here. I thought it prudent."

Sharif nodded. "Good. Good. At least you did one thing right."

Haider let slip a tiny smile and Sharif said, "Can you continue? With this man on the loose?"

"Yes, of course. He's on Crete and I'm in Athens."

"Okay. Do so. Get control of the Syrian, meet the secretary of state, then *report back*. Is that understood?"

Haider said, "Yes, sir." Sharif ended the call with Khalid looking on in disdain.

Tarek said, "That man Khalid has no respect. Especially given his station."

Sharif said, "Yes, but he has more courage than my own son. I almost wish he were the one in charge." He tapped a finger to his lip for a moment, then said, "Do you think we should continue? Do you think our Syrian remains viable?"

Tarek thought for a moment, then said, "Yes. We can continue. If the American is chasing our man, the plan might fail, but so what? All they have is a refugee who fled Libya and ended up in Crete. There is no connection between us. Let the Syrian move forward. Let the meeting go as Haider plans. There is no downside."

"There is one, and we need to deal with it."

"What do you mean?"

Sharif looked at his trusted confidant and said, "Start scrubbing my association. Start building everything on the back of my son."

The implications sank in, and Tarek said, "Are you sure?"

"Yes. Don't look at me that way. At one time, I was willing to give my life for the cause. Why would I not be willing to give my son's?"

★ 46 ★

I heard the phone buzz through a half-conscious mind, my brain making it part of the weird dream I was having involving weapons, Knuckles, and a sociopath on the loose. Knuckles slapped me and said, "We're on."

We'd boarded the ferry right before it left, buying two three-man rooms, earning me a little jab from Knuckles about how Jennifer and I always managed to get the leftovers, allowing us to sleep in the same space.

He made fun of our relationship just because he could, but he was coming to grips with the new normal, meaning I was capable of making decisions despite my feelings for Jennifer. Or more precisely, because of my connection to her.

Anyway, it wasn't like we'd had the chance to use the damn room. The team had staked out the two food vendors soon after boarding, and nothing had happened for the duration of the trip. I had become convinced we left Guy on Crete.

I came fully awake and said, "Who's texting? Veep or Koko?"

"Koko. Runaway is in the room."

We'd been on the damn boat for close to twelve hours, with Veep outside freezing his ass off, and Jennifer and Brett acting like the other folks who were too cheap to buy a room, hanging out in the cafeteria instead of the cattle call of the seats crammed together in the coach section.

We'd relied on text messages because we knew that Runaway would recognize the Taskforce Bluetooth earpieces we all used. It made the contact slow, but it was better than the guy seeing the clues and fleeing.

I picked up my phone. The text read, *Runaway here. Buying coffee.*

I texted back. *Atmospherics?*

Good. Not a lot of people around. Let him take a seat.

I looked at Knuckles, feeling the adrenaline. Knowing that the next few steps would be crucial. I texted back. *Give me a lock-on when he sits down.*

Roger.

We waited, staring at the phone. Wanting a good end. Wanting this decision to be one of the good ones. Like every mission, I was thrown a curveball. The phone vibrated with: *He's walking to us. Straight at us.*

I waited a moment, then, when nothing else came in, I texted, *What the hell does that mean?*

My phone rang with a verbal call.

I looked at Knuckles and he shrugged. I answered, and heard "Pike, I'm here with Guy. He'd like to talk."

I took that in, and like a high school cheerleader whispering about a date, I said, "Can he hear me?"

"No."

"What the fuck is going on?"

"Get up here. I'm with him now."

We moved out, Knuckles in the lead. Going up the gangway, he said, "What's the call with this? What do you want to do?"

"Same as before. We wanted to isolate him and talk. He beat us to the punch, but it's still the same game."

We entered the deck and I found Jennifer at a table toward the rear, looking concerned. Brett was next to her, a little smile on his face and his hand at the small of his back, telling me he was ready to draw, if necessary. I'm not sure anything would cause his blood pressure to rise.

I saw the back of Guy's head. When Jennifer focused on us, he turned around, and I was shocked at his appearance. He looked like a cancer patient, drawn and papery. Like something was eating him from the inside out.

I walked up with a confident swagger and said, "Hey, Guy, guess you found us out."

He stood, and I saw a dislocation. A feral projection that told me he wasn't whole. A projection I'd seen before. Looking in the mirror during the bad days.

He was being torn apart.

He said, "Hey, Pike. I'm glad it was you. I wanted to talk to you. I wanted to talk to anyone in the Taskforce, but you're the best choice. You know what I'm doing. You understand."

Not a good way to start.

He continued, "I have information on a potential attack. I'm following a lead. I'm doing what's right."

He was staring at me with a weird glow, and I knew he was sliding over the edge. I had no idea what he'd done, but I knew it wasn't good. All that remained was pulling him back up.

I shook his hand and said, "Guy, good to see you. Kurt asked me to find you."

I saw his eyes narrow, reevaluating. We sat down.

He said, "Yeah, yeah. I knew you'd be coming, but, fuck, I never thought you'd get to me this fast."

I gave him an easy smile, trying to reconcile in my mind what I was seeing in the flesh. Nobody around us could recognize it, but I was looking at disaster. The man was a caricature of his former self.

I saw Knuckles's face, and realized I was wrong. Some others could recognize it as well.

★ 47 ★

He went between Knuckles and me, ignoring Brett and Jennifer for the men he knew. He said, "I understand you want to bring me home. I get that. But did you hear what I said about a potential attack? I think we're missing something."

By his saying "we're," I got a handle. He believed I was with him. He believed I was in his family, which could prove all the difference.

I said, "Okay, Guy. I'll hear you out. What do you have?"

He pulled out a cheap digital camera and turned it on, flipping to a picture of a thin, swarthy youth of about twenty, with a scrub beard. Not one from the target package. He said, "This man. He's doing something against American interests, and it's tied to those fucks from Qatar. The ones who killed my brother."

He told me the story of tracking one of the faces on the target package, watching the linkup, then switching to the unknown. He ended with email intercept and the trail from the ferry to the café. The story had definite spikes of suspicious behavior, with the bank money and identification, but he'd glossed over something pretty significant.

I said, "What happened to the first guy. Nassir, was it? Where is he?"

I saw the weird glow again, and he said, "He's where he should be. He admitted to killing my brother."

Everyone mentally flinched at the words. We'd hoped we could interdict him before he did something awful, but we'd clearly failed. Softly, barely above a whisper, I said, "What about the man in Key West?"

He just looked at me. No questions in his eyes. He knew exactly what I was talking about.

I said, "Guy, you can't do this. Come with us. Let me take you home."

He said, "Did you even hear what I said? There's an attack being planned. This isn't about my brother anymore."

"Yes, it is. Come home with us and let me bring it up to the Oversight Council. This isn't the way."

I saw the blossom of anger, and knew I was losing. I needed to bring him in of his own volition, not forcibly. I had enough people with me to prevent any damage, but I couldn't hog-tie him here, in the middle of the deck.

He said, "Really? Is that what you said in Istanbul? When Decoy was killed?"

"Don't make this about me."

He scoffed and said, "Yeah. Right. You went on a rampage, killing anyone who'd been involved in that operation. You did it against orders. *You* did it. And now *I'm* the murderer?"

What he said was true, and it was unsettling to hear Kurt's fears borne out by a man I'd been ordered to bring home. I said, "We stopped a nuclear device from killing thousands."

He leaned forward. "And that's what I'm doing as

well. You went after the Russians because they killed Decoy—I would have too—and in your path of destruction, you found a threat. I'm doing the same thing. I *have* done the same thing. Help me here."

I glanced at Knuckles, and Guy caught the look. He followed the gaze, talking to my second-in-command. "Don't *you* go all high-and-mighty on me too. I know what happened. I know what you asked Pike to do. You begged him to kill every one of those sorry sons of bitches involved in Decoy's death."

He returned to me, the heat radiating out of his eyes. "And you did."

I said, "Guy, don't twist this into situational ethics. That mission has nothing in common with what you're doing. The two are not the same, and you can't justify the one by talking about the other. Don't even go there."

He leaned back into the cushions of his chair. He studied me for a moment, then said, "So that's how it is. You kill whenever it suits *you*, but you're still on a leash for fucks who have no idea what we do. They say jump, and you do."

"What the hell are you talking about? You can't go around killing just because *you* think it's right."

"But it's okay when you do it."

"That's not what I mean. I listen to the Council. They exist for a reason. It's not about a vendetta. It's about national security."

The words sounded hollow even before they left my mouth. He was right about everything he'd said, and my actions in Istanbul were proving Kurt correct on the dangers of the Taskforce.

He said, "Think about it. We get Omega authority from the Council, and it's game on, our consciences salved by some fat fuck with a pen. How many times have you been denied Omega because of some overarching political bullshit? Not because the target wasn't worthy? So by a stroke of a pen, we can take a guy out, but without that blessing, we're murderers? Based on some political crap that has nothing to do with the target? How is that right?"

I felt the gap growing between us, his earlier hope at seeing me slipping away. I tried to stop the slide. "I hear you. I really do, but we live in a land of laws. We can't just decide when or what law we're going to follow, and sometimes that 'political crap' proves more important. It's imperfect, but it's the best system in the world."

The statement fell flat on him. I tried again, "Tell me about the target you've found. What do you have for an anchor? Maybe I can get the Oversight Council to let me loose on it."

He said nothing for a moment, and I saw I'd lost. When he did speak, it was exactly what I didn't want to hear. "Pike, I respect you. But we both know what you say isn't true. They won't let you chase it. Not with me running loose, and I'm not coming in until the mission is done. If I give you the information, all I'm doing is giving you the ability to interdict me."

The people around us began to rise, and I realized we had docked. I was running out of time. Guy stood up. He looked at Jennifer and said, "Thank you for what you did for Decoy."

He came back to me. "And thank you for hunting down the rest of the vermin that killed him. I'm going to do the same, for my brother. For his men."

I grabbed his arm, and he let me. He said, "Are you going to take me down right here? How is that going to be explained, when I start screaming about top secret commandos out to kill me? You think the police will just let us go without any answers?"

I said, "You wouldn't. You aren't that far gone."

He pulled his arm away and said, "I *will*, because I haven't lost view of what's right."

I remained seated, wondering how I'd let this get out of control. I said, "You can't continue. I know the name you're using. We'll find you. Do you think Sean Parnell would approve of you making him a murderer?"

He paused for a moment, then shouldered his pack and said, "I'm going to walk right off this ferry. It goes without saying that if I see you or this team again, I'll know why you're there. I'll start shooting and consider it self-defense."

Knuckles spoke for the first time, saying, "Decoy wouldn't want this. You're spitting on his legacy. What he believed in."

He said, "Not true. Decoy would have done the same if the roles had been reversed and you'd been murdered. And I know my brother doesn't mind what I'm doing now."

He entered the flow of people leaving the ferry, and we simply sat, watching him disappear into the crowd of people.

★ 48 ★

Perched on a couch inside the Oval Office, Kurt Hale waited patiently for President Warren to finish toying with his iPad. To his left, George Wolffe provided some much-needed moral support. Across from him sat Alexander Palmer, the national security advisor and an unknown vote in the room. Nobody else was present. No other Oversight Council personnel had been invited, and Kurt intended to use that to his advantage.

He was here ostensibly to discuss manning issues, and thus the full Council wasn't necessary, but he also had some explosive information that he wanted to present one-on-one to the president, getting a read on his mindset before throwing the stinking carcass onto the briefing table for the full Oversight Council.

It was not how the Council was designed to be used, and in fact was counter to the charter under which the Taskforce operated, but Kurt had done it in the past for sensitive operations, and this one was most definitely sensitive.

The president finally looked up and said, "Where were we? You said you had a solution for the Blaine dilemma? You have someone else in mind?"

Kurt glanced at George, then said, "No, sir. I want to

keep Blaine. I want him to go ahead and SERB out, as if he was forced to retire, then hire him on as a contractor."

Palmer said, "I thought you'd already discarded that idea. We're going backward here. When we last spoke, we agreed you'd cull the records and find someone else for Omega command. A fresh body. Someone new."

In presenting the arguments to keep Blaine on active duty and inside the Taskforce, Kurt had basically sabotaged his current plan. When it had become clear that there was no good way to retain Blaine without an inquiry into what he'd been doing and exposure of Taskforce operations—in effect, giving up the organization to prove that he wasn't just a homesteading staff officer at the Pentagon, coasting through his career—Kurt had agreed to let him go. Then he'd thought about Pike's words in the restaurant. After multiple consultations with George Wolffe, he'd decided it was—while not perfect—the best solution available.

Kurt said, "I know, sir, but I've thought about it, and I don't think we should attempt to train up another person for the Omega operations. It's the crux of the Taskforce mission, and the greatest single point of failure. We need someone on the X who understands both the tactical and strategic dimensions of a hit. Someone who knows when to proceed and when to quit, and that's Blaine. He's learned too much to simply let him go. We talked about hiring him as a contractor just to keep his expertise, but that very expertise is wasted sitting at headquarters."

President Warren said, "I thought you were concerned about precedent. About opening the portals of the Taskforce too wide. You have a cut line of who is eligible to even try out for the Taskforce. By doing this, you're potentially abusing your own rules. What's to say, years from now, when you and I are both gone, the commander decides to hire someone based on friendship? Someone not from the DoD's Special Mission Units or CIA paramilitary world?"

"Sir, that's a risk, I know, but I think it's a greater risk to replace him. We aren't a plug-and-play unit like an Infantry command. His skills weren't learned at Ranger School or Command and General Staff College. I'm actually looking at the long-term health of the Taskforce."

Palmer said, "Or you're just kicking the can down the road."

President Warren said, "How would it work? How can you have a civilian leading active-duty members?"

"It works because of his reputation. It's not like he wears a uniform on the job with his rank. The men listen to him because of who he is, not because of his title."

"I don't know if I want to start outsourcing to contractors."

"Sir, you already do, with Pike Logan. He's a civilian too, but he's in charge of a team of active-duty guys."

President Warren imperceptibly nodded, thinking through the ramifications, and Kurt pressed. "Sir, technically, *you're* a civilian. But you're also the commander in chief. Vice President Hannister is running for your job. He knows the terrain, but you have to admit that he's going to need all the experience he can get if he wins."

President Warren had been elected on a national security platform and had brought Phillip Hannister to the ticket because of his economic expertise and domestic experience as an effort to round out the campaign.

Palmer laughed and said, "Let's not get ahead of ourselves here. The election is months away."

Wolffe spoke for the first time. "It's not that far off, and we need to plan for the future. Whatever that future may be."

President Warren said, "Okay, you guys, we'll take a look at it. We've got time to sort this out." He stood, indicating the meeting was over.

Kurt rose as well and said, "Sir, I've got one other thing to talk about."

"What is it?"

"Pike's located Guy George, and it's bad."

President Warren said, "How bad?"

"You might want to sit back down."

He did so, and Kurt laid out everything he knew, detailing Guy's killing spree in Key West and Crete and the attempt to capture or kill him in the restaurant, ending with the confrontation on the ferry.

Palmer was stunned, his mouth slightly open. He found his voice and said, "So Pike had a chance to bring him in and didn't? After he learned about the killings?"

"It's not that simple. Pike couldn't have taken him down on the ferry, in front of the crew and passengers from a foreign country. Guy threatened Taskforce exposure. Pike did the correct thing here."

"Maybe he picked a wrong time to approach. Hell, earlier you were using him as an example of a civilian with needed experience. I would have thought Pike would know better."

Kurt started to answer and President Warren interrupted with a question. "Would Guy do that? Expose the Taskforce?"

Kurt said, "I don't know, honestly. He told Pike he would, but the strange thing is, Pike didn't go to *him* initially. Guy sought out the Taskforce on his own. He recognized Jennifer from that Decoy tape that's floating around, and walked right up to her. He introduced himself and stated he hoped she was a friend. Pike thinks he was looking for help. Looking for a way out. At first, he was friendly and it looked like it would be a good ending, then he changed. It's like he's bouncing between the good and the bad. I just don't know what he's capable of."

Palmer said, "Jesus Christ. So we have a lunatic on the loose? Billings was right?"

Kurt said, "I'm not sure I'd call him a lunatic just yet. There's more to this than meets the eye. He told Pike he was onto a plot. He was following a guy on the ferry. Someone who'd met the second man he killed and received identification and money. He told Pike he'd quit once he'd solved the problem."

President Warren said, "And I'm supposed to take what he says at face value? An unstable, trained killer who's murdering members of the Qatar government?"

"Sir, Pike believes he's really stumbled on to something. Believes that in his quest for revenge, he actually found something bad, and there's enough smoke out there to warrant further exploration. No matter what Secretary Billings says, we know for a fact that the one he killed in Key West and the one that Billings is in love with in Greece both bear a striking resemblance to the men on his brother's target package. We don't know which one he killed in Crete, but Guy said he admitted to being in Afghanistan. Admitted to killing his brother.

"On top of that, someone besides us tried to capture Guy. Someone with a motive and real skill. I know we have other equities in play here, but the problems in Greece shouldn't supersede the evidence of wrongdoing. We can't just walk away. They've killed Americans, and might be planning to kill more."

President Warren pursed his lips and glanced at Palmer. Palmer shrugged, then said, "Tell him. Can't hurt anything."

★ 49 ★

Kurt said, "Tell me what?"

"The Taliban and the government of Afghanistan are holding covert peace talks. Not the ones you read about in the press in Pakistan or with China overseeing. Real talks, held in secret in Oslo, Norway, without the pressure of public results or posturing on Twitter. Since the announcement of Mullah Omar's death, things have sputtered, with the Islamic State working the fractures inside the Taliban. We can't allow them a foothold. Haider al-Attiya is our go-between with the government of Qatar. Billings thinks he's crucial to the outcome because of the weight Qatar carries."

Kurt said, "Seriously? Who gives a shit what Billings thinks? We're talking about a potential attack, and he's kissing the ass of a terrorist? I'd exclude him from the discussion because he's no longer impartial."

President Warren bristled and said, "I'll remind you he's the secretary of state. *I* care what he thinks."

Kurt backpedaled. "Sir, sorry. There's just something else that's been nagging, and Billings is at the heart of it. The assault on Guy in the café was extremely complex, and involved local players. It has to be tied into what

Guy was doing, but there's no way a group from Qatar would have known they were being hunted in enough time to establish such an elaborate plan. The first man, in Key West, is held as an unsolved murder, and the second was still warm by the time of the assault."

"What are you implying?"

"Someone had to tell the Qataris they were being hunted. I think it's Billings."

Palmer exhaled and said, "Preposterous. He was given a direct order not to."

"Like I said to Billings at the last Council meeting, I'm not making up the facts. There is no way that attack on Guy could have been planned and executed without forewarning."

President Warren rubbed his face, saying, "I don't know if it's preposterous. After his outburst, I could see him doing that. Thinking he was in the right. He has a strong moral streak and a disdain for the use of force. It's why I like his voice on the Council."

Palmer said, "What do you want to do about it?"

"I'll handle Billings. These talks could be the beginning of the end of combat in Afghanistan. It is crucial for them to continue."

Kurt said, "At the very least, don't let him meet with Haider by himself anymore. Make him take a CIA case officer. Someone who can judge what's going on from both sides. Billings doesn't have the experience for that."

Palmer said, "That's not a bad idea."

President Warren said, "Okay, Palmer, talk to Kerry at CIA." He looked at Kurt and said, "You mourn the loss of Guy's brother, but I have to look to the future. Intercepting Haider right now may mean the death of more people down the road because these talks fail. They may not be American lives, but they deserve a chance at peace. I don't like it any more than you do, but I have a greater responsibility."

"Sir, I'm not asking for Omega. Just Alpha authority. Let me explore with Pike's team. It may be a way to bring in Guy. He came looking for help, and when Pike ignored him, he went on his own. If he thinks we're onboard, maybe he'll come in."

Palmer said, "Just tell him that. Tell Pike he's got Alpha, then, when he pulls in Guy, call him off."

"You want me to lie to Pike?"

"What's a lie matter when we've got this calamity on our hands? You lie on a daily basis about everything you do."

"Sir, you order me to do that, and you'll destroy the Taskforce. We've been talking around this issue since I came in here today. We need good men like Blaine. Men we trust to do the right thing on the ground, but that's a two-way street. Guy feels like he's been betrayed, but he's mistaken. If I lie to Pike, it *will* be a betrayal. No matter the greater good you envision, it will be corrosive to the unit. Nobody will trust anything I say, thinking they're being played, and in our world—in a world where we *do* lie for the greater good—it will destroy the essence of who we are."

President Warren held up his hand, stopping the argument. "I get it. I understand completely. I'm not asking you to lie to Pike, but if you want Alpha authority, it'll have to go to the Council. Which means Billings."

"Can't you cut him out? Hell, he misses half the meetings anyway."

"Not with your target deck. We have trust at our level as well, and with him dealing personally with Haider, he needs to be informed."

"You sure that trust at your level is working?"

Kurt saw the president's face grow dark and held up his hands in surrender. "Okay, okay, sir. Just tell him we'll only explore. We won't do any Omega operation until after the peace talks, but it's our best chance to bring in Guy. If the Council says no, I still have that problem."

Palmer said, "And? You have all the authority you need for that right now. The Council has already voted, and he needs to be stopped. Permanently."

Kurt leaned forward and said, "We here in DC use words like 'stop him' and 'permanently' without spelling out what that means. Stopping him may include DOA approval. It may mean pulling the trigger from a distance, and I don't have the authority to order that. Shit, I'm not even sure I have the *courage* to order that, and I don't know if any team I own will execute."

Alexander Palmer seemed shocked at having it spelled out. Kurt continued. "Guy told Pike that if he saw him again, he'd start shooting first, in self-defense, and Pike believes him. I want the Council to make that call. I want them to think about it. I want them to understand what happens based on their words."

President Warren said, "You expect them to say no?"

Kurt turned away from Palmer and looked squarely at the president of the United States. "I want them to understand that if they say no to an Alpha mission, they are ordering the execution of a United States soldier, and it's not just the man who pulls the trigger who has blood on his hands."

He stood and said, "We all do."

★ 50 ★

I lay in bed staring at the wall, blessed sleep hiding just beyond my reach. I'd made the call not to attempt to follow Guy, and we'd left the ferry, moving straight to a hotel. Since we'd all been awake for close to two days, I'd ordered the team to rack out, then had reported in to Kurt.

It had not been a good conversation.

After finishing, I'd closed the computer, then simply stared at Jennifer's slumbering form, reflecting where I'd gone wrong. Wondering what I was going to have to do to accomplish the mission. I wanted to wake her and talk, but we needed the rest. I thought about going to Knuckles's room, and discarded that as well. The biggest impact on crisis decision-making was lack of sleep, and I'd seen the effects when lives mattered.

I'd crawled into bed beside her and closed my eyes, waiting on the sleep to come. It would not.

Guy's words on the ferry were eating at me. Forcing me to choose between my duty to the Taskforce and my own past. After some uncomfortable back-and-forth, with Kurt alluding to what I might be asked to do, he'd said he would bring my information higher, asking for permission to go after Guy's target—and in so doing, hopefully rein in Guy's thirst for blood—but I understood the implications if they failed to act. I was going to be ordered to take out Guy.

Take out. Right.

Euphemisms abounded in our world. "Eliminate the threat." "Reduce the risk." "Execute kinetic options." "Clear the target." "Limit collateral damage." *Take out Guy.*

Like I was removing the trash.

All of the words were tidy, clinical descriptions of what in reality was anything but. They involved killing, pure and simple. And I wasn't sure I could do that.

I stared at the wall, then felt Jennifer roll over, her leg rubbing against mine. It reminded me of where I was in my life, and that following through on an order to remove Guy might destroy everything I'd worked so hard to build.

Guy's words rang true to me, touching a core that I didn't want to reflect on. Did I use the power of the Oversight Council approval as absolution for the deaths I'd caused? When I'd ignored them in Istanbul, was I right? Or a murderer like Guy?

I'd done some seriously bad things in the name of protecting others, but it had always been for what was right.

Hadn't it?

I wasn't a particularly religious man, but I believed in a higher being. I believed that if I did what was just, I'd be measured on it in the end, the scales of my actions deciding my fate. Had I died a few years ago, when I was in the abyss like Guy, I'd have been found wanting, but now, I was back in the land of the living. Doing what was right and protecting those who couldn't protect themselves. And this mission could alter the balance. Could alter me. I'd been where Guy was, and I'd learned in Istanbul, once you touched the abyss, it was always a part of you. Waiting to take over.

Out of nowhere, Jennifer's voice split the quiet, startling me. "Pike, you awake?"

I rolled over, saying, "Yeah. I am."

She pulled her hair out of her eyes and I saw they were red. She hadn't slept either.

I said, "Jenn, you need to get some rest. We have a pretty bad mission coming up, and for some reason, Guy has a connection to you. I need you one hundred percent."

She said, "That's what I want to talk about."

She started to speak again, then thought better of it. I said, "What?"

"I can't do it. I can't use his emotions to kill him. I won't."

She bored into me for a moment, then said, "And I don't want you to, either. This is bad. Evil. There is no goodness in any of this. It's bad what he's doing, and it's bad what we're planning. It's evil all the way around. I feel like I'm swimming in raw sewage."

That caused a grin to slip out. "Swimming in raw sewage. Eloquent."

She took my hand and said, "I'm serious. I saw you with Guy. I saw what his statements were doing to you, and that was just a talk. You go through with this, and it'll be permanent. To all of us."

I flopped on my back, and said, "He's not like me. He's not . . ."

She said, "He's *just* like you. Nobody but me saw you at your rock bottom. He *is* you. And, like you, he doesn't deserve to die. This is bigger than him. I don't want to lose what we have."

I propped up on an elbow and said, "What's that mean?"

She looked at me for a moment, then said, "In Rome you worked magic. There might be a total of three men on Earth who could have done what you did with this team. Maybe even fewer. The Taskforce is pure. It's real. It's concrete. But it's only as good as the men in it. I came into the Taskforce because you asked, but I stayed because of the good we do. It's about saving lives. We execute this mission, and it's going to be about death. I can't do that."

I was taken aback at the words. I had pushed her reluctantly into the Taskforce because I saw an innate skill, and she'd fought it the whole way, only staying because I asked. Or so I thought. It was the first time she'd ever talked about the mission in the absence of our relationship.

She said, "You *are* the Taskforce."

I lay back down, thinking about the mission and my place in it. Thinking about the growing decision I'd have to make.

I heard a knock on the door. *Jesus. Don't the maids read the "Do Not Disturb" sign?*

I glanced at Jennifer. She shrugged. I padded to the front barefoot, looked out the peephole, and saw Nick. *Shit.* I thought about ordering Jennifer back to her connecting room, but just didn't have the energy. I opened the door.

He said, "Hey, can we talk for a minute?"

"You need to get some sleep. I want you on your toes. We can talk in four hours."

"No, we can't. I can't sleep."

I swung the door wide and he entered. He did a double take on Jennifer in the bed, wearing nothing but an oversize T-shirt. I said, "Yeah, yeah, it's Jennifer. Fucking get over it. What's on your mind?"

He went from her to me, saying nothing. I said, "Spit it out. You're cutting into my sleep. Is the Internet not working in your room?"

Hesitantly, he said, "I want to talk about the mission. About Guy. I'm not sure I can do this."

I started to respond, when someone else knocked on the door. I held up a finger and went back to the peephole, seeing Brett.

What the hell.

I opened the door and said, "What is it about you guys not wanting to sleep?"

His face was as serious as I'd ever seen it. Usually jovial, with an easy vibe, he was all business. He said, "I need to talk to you about what happened on the ferry."

I rolled my eyes and said, "Come on in."

★51★

Brett entered, saw Nick, then Jennifer in the bed, and his laid-back attitude finally surfaced. He said, "Well, well. Not what I expected. A threesome with the vice president's son?"

Nick blushed furiously, saying nothing. Jennifer threw a pillow at Brett's head, but he blocked it. I said, "Come on, people. I need some damn sleep. What do you want?"

Brett turned serious again and said, "I've seen some shitty things happen in my time. I've been *involved* in some shitty things. Bad guys we manipulated. Good guys we abandoned when the political winds shifted. People whose motivations we didn't even understand, just using them when we could. But we never did anything like this."

Brett had been a Recon Marine before joining the Special Activities Division of the CIA as a paramilitary case officer. He'd been involved in more dirty operations than even me.

He continued. "This mission is the worst of the worst. We need to take a look at what we're being ordered to do. Reflect on it."

My phone vibrated. I tapped the screen, seeing a text from Knuckles. *You awake?*

I held my finger up to Brett and texted back, *Yeah. Can I come down? We need to talk.*

I rolled my eyes and texted back, *Come on down.*

Brett said, "Who's that?"

Then we heard a knock on the door. He'd texted from the hallway. I opened it, and Knuckles said, "Jennifer here?"

"Yeah."

"We need to talk about this mission, and I want to do it one-on-one."

I stepped aside and held my arm out, saying, "We're beyond that now. Come on in."

He entered, looking confused for a minute at the entire team assembled in my room, wondering what was going on and whether he was being left out. But he knew better than that. He opened his mouth, and I said, "They all arrived in the last two minutes. All wanting to talk about the mission. About Guy."

Knuckles nodded, and said, "Good. Good. That's exactly why I'm here."

I said, "And?"

"And based on the fact that everyone came here on their own, I don't think I need to say a word. But I will. This mission is shit."

He was right, but I was still the team leader, with a team leader's responsibility.

I said, "It may be. Cancel that. It *is* shit. But I can't pick what we do. We don't always get the James Bond mission in the Cayman Islands, Knuckles. You know that."

Then Knuckles used my own sounding board against me.

He looked at Jennifer, sitting in the bed with her back against the headboard and the covers pulled up high. "You good with this?"

If he'd have asked Nick, he'd have gotten a wishy-washy response, the new man caught between his loyalty to the chain of command and the mission. Even Brett wouldn't outright confront me in front of the team. But Knuckles knew Jennifer. Knew exactly why I connected with her. She had a moral compass that didn't care about the chain of command.

She said, "No. I'm not. Nobody in the room is good with this. I'm not good with Guy killing, and I'm not good with us killing him to stop him killing. It's disgusting."

She paused, catching my eye, and we were the only two people in the room. She said, "Pike's not good with this either."

Everyone focused on me, and I felt the pressure of disobeying an order I hadn't even received yet. But I'd disobeyed orders before. In Istanbul. Only this time, I wouldn't be doing it to kill. I'd be doing it to save a life, as Jennifer had done with me.

I said, "Everyone listen to me. You don't follow the orders we're given, and you're done in the Taskforce. They will replace you with someone who will. They've done it to me before."

I looked at Nick, the newest member. He nodded, not backing down. Comfortable with the choice. I continued, "But nobody argues with success. I've seen that firsthand. You can ignore an order if it makes everyone else look good in the end."

I went eye to eye with the team, ending with Jennifer. I said, "I'm not killing Guy just because the Taskforce says so. He's coming home."

I looked at Knuckles. "You want to solve this problem the right way?"

He nodded, a slow smile spreading on his face. He said, "Yeah. No matter what the Council says."

I said, "Okay, then, since all you geniuses want to keep me from sleep, how do we do that? We're all burned for surveillance, and he'll start shooting the moment he sees us."

"Where do we stand with Taskforce assets?"

"He's ditched his phone. Not surprising, since it's the first thing any one of us would do. The Taskforce has cut off his credit cards and frozen his bank accounts under the name Sean Parnell, but we don't know how much cash he has. With the bank problems in Greece, he probably came over here with a sizable amount. Which, I guess, is saying we don't have a hell of a lot to track with. It was a mistake to confront him on the ferry."

Brett said, "Aw, that's bullshit. Don't second-guess that. We were always only getting one shot at a meeting, and it was the perfect spot for the endgame you envisioned. Didn't work out. What else we got?"

"Kurt's taking my report to the Oversight Council. If we are sanctioned for Alpha against the guy on the ferry, we'll get complete Taskforce assets for tracking, and that also might be the leverage we need to bring him in."

Nick said, "But he's the only one who knows who the man is. A catch-22. We can't even identify the target without Guy pointing the way."

"That's exactly what I mean. That's what I'll tell Guy. We have Alpha to explore, but we need his intelligence. We need him *on* the team, not fighting the team."

Knuckles said, "You think he'll buy that?"

"Best I can do."

Nick said, "Doesn't fix the primary problem. We don't know where Guy is or how to get in touch with him."

Brett said, "Yeah, yeah, we don't have a handle, but it wouldn't be the first time. Something will break. You work with Pike long enough, and something always does."

Nick looked skeptical, but was afraid to say anything as the junior member of the team.

Brett laughed at his expression and said, "Trust me. It'll happen. Him sleeping with Jennifer is some kind of magic."

Jennifer scowled, still under the covers, and Brett said, "Hey, babe, you got to contribute somehow."

I grinned at the ribbing and said, "Okay, enough. What we need right now is rest. We can't do anything until the Oversight Council meets anyway. Everyone, head on back to your rooms."

No sooner were the words out of my mouth than I felt my phone vibrate with a text. It was from Carly, and it was succinct.

Guy just called me. We need to meet.

Knuckles saw my face and said, "What is it?"

I passed him the phone. "We aren't getting any sleep."

Brett looked at the text, then at Jennifer, eyes open in mock amazement. He said, "You've been busy."

This time the pillow found its mark.

★ 52 ★

Guy felt the cold seep into the car, the cooling engine ticking its drum of surrender to the outside air. Shoehorned between two cars on the frontage road next to Andrea Siggrou Street, he watched the front entrance to a four-story building, the bold sign outside proclaiming THE COTTON CLUB SEX THEATER.

He was farther away than he wanted, with eight lanes of traffic complete with median separating him from his target, but the alternative was to park on the eastern frontage road right next to the target and risk being seen. He was forced to use optics, but he felt more secure.

He'd been in position for two hours and had seen little in the way of movement in or out of the building, but that was to be expected. The disco didn't even open for five more hours, remaining still until the darkness came like a brood of vampires waiting to wake, but sooner or later, Nikos would show.

Carly's information had been vague, but he was sure it was accurate. They were too close personally for her to play any silly spy games. She would have just told him no outright. She'd given him the bare minimum of what he wanted, clearly trying to help, but there was something about the call that was off, and he wondered if she was growing suspicious. She'd seemed distant during the conversation. Hesitant. He'd asked what was wrong and she'd proclaimed work, then said she couldn't talk about it. At one point, he thought she was about to ask a question, then she'd backed off.

It troubled him, but he knew she would never turn him in, both because of their friendship and because she didn't even know who to report him to. The CIA was absolutely out of the question, and she didn't know how to contact the Taskforce.

But Pike did. And that man was devious. In addition, he had Knuckles as his 2IC. Knuckles had been as close to Decoy as Guy. He was the man who'd recruited Decoy to the Taskforce in the first place, and had been the man who provided the notification of Decoy's death to Carly. She knew him as well as she did Decoy, which was to say as well as she knew Guy. There was a chance they'd find her here and question her.

He doubted she would proactively turn him in, but Pike was a different matter. Guy had heard the stories, and seen the results. If there were a weak link—for which Carly qualified—Pike would find it. He was somewhat supernatural in that respect, but even if he did, it no longer mattered. The endgame was approaching rapidly— much quicker than Pike could decipher, even with his skills. Guy would kill the final two men soon, and it did no good to try to determine who was on whose side. Pike, Carly, the Taskforce, Billings, Nikos—none of that mattered anymore. For him, there was only one side now.

His.

After leaving the ferry, Guy had disappeared into the crowds around the dock, moving swiftly to escape whatever net the Taskforce might have attempted. He'd considered throwing his phone into the back of the first passing Bongo truck, leaving it on and transmitting, but then thought better of it, settling for breaking it into pieces.

After moving steadily north for thirty minutes, losing himself in the concrete and cinder blocks, he'd caught a cab and asked for a cheap hotel. The man had dropped him off at a seedy establishment crammed on a side street, between a butcher shop and an auto repair garage. With only eight rooms and a sign that proclaimed nothing more than hotel, he thought it would work.

He'd checked in using cash, leaving him about a thousand dollars in euros. He tipped the wizened man behind the counter fifty euros to forgo the passport requirement. The clerk had balked, thinking he was an illegal alien or smuggler, until Guy allowed him to inspect his US passport. Guy proclaimed he was afraid of identity theft, and the man believed him. Or, more precisely, with the troubles in the Greek economy, he believed the fifty euros.

After checking in, he'd set about replacing his phone, attempting to find an ATM that would dispense money from his credit card. His was declined. Initially, he thought it was just a function of the Greek economy, as all ATMs had a limit on the amount a local could withdraw, and thought maybe this bank was saving that limit for Greek citizens, refusing to deliver because his credit card was based in the United States.

He'd tried two more ATMs with the same results. He'd found a cell phone provider and attempted to purchase a phone directly, using the card under the name Sean Parnell—not something he wanted to do because of the linkages—and the card was declined.

So they'd frozen his bank accounts and credit cards. The Taskforce was on the move, just as Pike had said they would be. No matter. He knew their rhythms. Knew how they operated, and it was way, way too slow to interdict him. He reverted to his limited cash supply, buying two five-hundred-dollar pay-as-you-go credit cards.

By midday, he'd burned through most of one with a new cell phone and a rental car, and figured the second would last long enough. All he needed was a max of two days to complete the mission.

He saw a knot of men approaching the front door to the Cotton Club and raised his small binoculars. A scrum of guys in black leather and denim, all sporting thick beards. One of the men resembled a face on the target package, but he was too far away for Guy to be sure.

He saw a preening man in the center, wearing a goatee and a flaming-red suede jacket.

Nikos.

First target in Athens.

★ 53 ★

Guy still had his mission to take out the final two from the target deck, but couldn't accomplish it with Nikos on the loose. The man had too many connections. Too many ways to counter him. He needed the targets from Qatar separated from any help. It was the primary reason he'd chosen Greece instead of Qatar to begin with. He'd debated and finally decided Nikos had to go. It was a complication, but a necessary one.

Guy told himself it was based purely on the mission, but the blackness sliding through him, like ropes greased in a charnel house, told him differently. That asshole had picked the fight. Chosen his fate.

Guy counted the men. Five total, including Nikos. Probably two or three hired security, with the remaining being friends or ass kissers begging for Nikos's attention. One held the door, and they all entered. Guy gave them five minutes. From a distant memory, he saw his brother over a board game, tired and cranky, saying, "Give me the dice. I'm going on a suicide run."

Guy started the car and headed to the small underground tunnel that would allow him to cross the broad thoroughfare, thinking of the past with his brother. Actually smelling the cans of Schlitz beer they'd pilfered from their father's fridge on those days long ago.

Two years apart, they'd had a space of time in high school where they'd become infatuated with the game called Risk. A contest of strategy, it involved using armies and dice to attempt to take over the world. The games themselves could last days, but only if his brother retained interest.

Guy would play his heart out to the bitter end, no matter if he was losing or not, going on until his plastic armies breathed their final breath. His brother, on the other hand, would get dispirited and quit if he felt he was on the losing end with no recovery. When he became tired of the fight, he'd simply look up and say, "Suicide run," then put all of his plastic tokens on a single country, rolling the dice and attacking each enemy country with the full force of his men, risking all of them until he either won or was demolished.

It used to aggravate the hell out of Guy, because one out of ten times, the tactic worked, all based on the chance of the roll of the dice, like doubling a bet on every spin of a roulette wheel. No skill, no thought, no strategy. Just brute force and luck.

And now he was going to do the same.

He parked on the back side of the building, driving the car up over the curb on its two right wheels and blocking the ability for the other cars to leave. He didn't care. Odds were, he wasn't walking out alive anyway.

He circled the block, playing his brother's Pandora list. Feeling the pain. Drawing energy from the anger. He walked up to the door of the Cotton Club, passing by windows that were blacked out, hiding what was inside. He tried the aluminum door handle, pulling it an inch and finding it open.

He paused for a brief moment, removing his earbuds and adjusting the long barrel of the 6P9 under his left shoulder, getting it ready in the makeshift holster he'd built. He took two deep breaths, controlling the anger and channeling the adrenaline.

This is it. Five men. Only five.

He knew that was most likely wrong, but also that he held the edge. The men inside this building understood violence, but only on their terms. They had no idea of the pain he could bring. The skill he held.

He opened the door and went inside, letting his eyes adjust to the gloom. The interior was dank and smelled of spilled beer and mildew, the tables looking chipped and dilapidated in the harsh light of the sun before the night settled in and the vampires began to roam.

To his front was a stage, the center portion spearing out between the tables, the length interspersed with floor-to-ceiling poles. On each side was a bar, the one on the left dark and empty, the one on the right lit by small overhead bulbs. He saw a man talking to two women, the man dressed like the usual pipe-swinger—leather jacket, cropped beard, and scarred, meaty hands. The women were dressed as if they were going to a costume party, one as a flapper from the 1920s, the other like an Egyptian pharaoh's concubine. Neither was particularly attractive.

All three were staring at him from the light he'd caused to explode by opening the door. He walked to them, feeling the weight of his pistol. The women looked hesitant. The man looked aggravated.

Guy said, "Hey, I'm here to see Nikos. Is he around?"

The man glowered and, in broken English, said, "No. Nobody here by that name."

Guy turned to the girls and repeated the question. They became surly, with one, in much better English, saying, "Never heard of him. Maybe he'll show when we open."

Guy nodded, almost robotically, thinking of the size of the building. Thinking of how long it would take to clear without information.

The man said, "You go."

Guy said, "Unfortunately, no. I saw him enter. Either call him or send me up. I'm not leaving."

The girls laughed, the one closest to him leaning over, showing her cleavage and saying, "You going to leave. Trust me."

The man reached beneath the bar and pulled out a fishing priest with a head encased in a sheath of metal. Just like the one used on Guy days before. He said, "Get out now, or pay."

In one fluid motion, Guy withdrew his pistol. He placed the long suppressor against the man's forehead and pulled the trigger, spraying the back of the bar, the bullet a muted spit. The man dropped straight down, folding like a slinky with the wires bent.

He turned to the girls, the barrel held in the air. He said, "Do I need to repeat the question?"

In hurried speech, talking over each other and clinging together as if that would protect them, they told him where to find Nikos's office.

He said, "Lay your phones on the bar."

They did so and he said, "Get the fuck out of here, now."

The '20s flapper said, "You going to die. You can't come in here and do this. You going to *die*."

He smiled, a twisted, crazy thing, saying nothing. They fled, spilling the light in again. He let the door close before he moved, cloaking himself in the blessed darkness again.

Suicide run.

★ 54 ★

Nikos said, "By herself? Or with an escort?" He listened, then disconnected from the call. He saw the Arab tense at his words and mentally sized him up. He recognized that Khalid wasn't the same milquetoast as Haider. This man had steel in him, and might actually have the skill to back up the attitude. He glanced at the two men on either side of the door, giving them an unseen signal. They both withdrew pistols, keeping them between their folded hands in the front, only the barrel poking out.

Khalid said, "Is it like we thought? She's going to a meeting?"

Nikos said, "Haider was my employer. I don't answer to you."

Khalid said, "I speak for Haider, and I heard the call. You answer to our money, and we have offered a significant amount for the death of the American. You still owe us for that."

Nikos leaned back in his chair, an ostentatious bit of leather designed to showcase the man. Present him as a king on a throne responsible for the fate of anyone brought in his presence. The desk in front of him was much larger than necessary, a burnished, solid oak behemoth, and littered with small signals of intimidation. Little indicators of his ability to kill. A replica guillotine, a paperweight shaped like a skull, and a letter opener in the form of a miniature Japanese Katana. The centerpiece was two M67 fragmentation grenades, both with a rubber band on the spoon, indicating the pin had been pulled. Showing that he lived without fear.

Nikos picked up the letter opener and played with the edge of the blade, saying, "You've paid me nothing. I attempted in Crete, and yes, I failed, but it cost you nothing. It cost me a great deal. A lot of cleanup. I'm not sure I want to continue with the same agreement here in Athens, especially when it involves a spy from the CIA. It's not good for business. Besides, he's probably still on Crete. I have men looking."

"He's not on Crete. You don't believe it, and neither do I. Yes, you attempted to catch him, and how long do you think it'll take for him to decipher who was responsible for that failure? You are now on his list, just like we are. He's coming here, and you should be afraid."

Nikos scoffed, saying, "He's but one man. He can do nothing to me."

"Then why did you place surveillance on the US Embassy? Why did you just receive a call telling you that the American's contact was leaving by herself?"

"I keep tabs on her because of my business. Nothing more. I need to ensure she's not causing an inadvertent problem. We both have equities. I provide her information, and she provides me leeway to operate. I aggravate her, and she could provide the same information to my government. It's a significant risk to my business. You must understand. I scratch her back, and she scratches mine."

Nikos saw the anger flash, Khalid leaning over the

desk. "She set up my men. She set *you* up. She is the catalyst for the American interdicting our meetings. He's here, and she's going to meet him. *Right*. *Now*." The last two words were punctuated with a stab of a finger into the desk.

The men at the back of the room released their hands, freeing the pistols. Nikos waved, telling them to back down. Khalid saw the action and turned, eyeing the men. He said, "You think your security can help you? Haider lives in a world of giving, where money gets what he wants."

He turned back to Nikos and said, "I live in the world of taking. You *will* find this American. You do, and you get the money. More than enough to live out the rest of your days with whores and wine. You don't and you get me. If the American doesn't find you first."

Nikos was a bit unnerved at Khalid's complete lack of fear of the two men at the door. But he still owned the room. He chuckled, playing down the threat. He said, "Okay, okay, Khalid. I see you are afraid of him, but I am not. Here's the deal. You want me to commit to the woman, and it'll double the price. The American was tied to the United States somehow, but the woman *is* CIA. I know this for a fact."

"She is our only link to the killer. I need to interrogate her."

"And is this from Haider?"

"Don't worry about him. As I said, I speak for him."

"Maybe I should call him first."

"Maybe you should get some men moving toward the woman."

Nikos showed anger for the first time, saying, "I can't snatch her off the street! This isn't Qatar, where you can run over whoever you want if you're a citizen. We have laws here."

"She's not working on CIA business. This man we're after is rogue. She's trying to contain it. Anything that happens to her can be blamed on him."

"How do you know this? Where is your information coming from?"

"From the highest levels of the United States government. It's valid. And so is our money."

The phone rang again, and Nikos answered. He listened for a moment, then said, "No, don't follow her inside. Get the men ready." He hung up, saying nothing. Thinking.

Khalid said, "Well?"

Nikos toyed with the letter opener for a moment, then said, "I want half up front. If I move on her, I want the money right now. And I won't do anything else. The woman is my final operation. If it goes bad, I leave, taking your money with me. Nonnegotiable."

"What's she doing?"

"She's acting strange. You may be right."

Khalid smiled, and the sight was unsettling, reminding Nikos of a cat toying with a mouse long after the creature was dead. Khalid dialed his phone and spoke in Arabic for a moment. He hung up and said, "The money is transferred to the account you gave."

Nikos nodded, realizing he was crossing a void from which there was no return. He picked up his own phone and spoke a few words. He placed the handset slowly on the desk and said, "Okay. It's done. She will be brought to a warehouse. I'll turn her over to you, and we are through. You find the American on your own after that."

Khalid said, "I go with your men. And *that's* nonnegotiable."

★ 55 ★

After giving everyone thirty minutes, we met in the lobby of the Hilton Hotel. I handed out bumper locations for the countersurveillance effort and gave them a chance to look and ask questions. There were none.

Initially, I was just going to take myself and Jennifer, but Brett and Knuckles were having none of that. And then Nick decided that he had enough balls to tell me he wanted to go as well.

I thought about ordering them to stand down, but I knew they wouldn't get any sleep until we returned anyway, and I wasn't worried about Carly compromising anything. If she were going to do that, it would have already happened regardless of whom I brought to the meeting, and she wouldn't have scheduled the meet in the middle of the National Gardens. She would have brought us inside the embassy, where she could control any outcome. Clearly, she wanted to hide this as much as we did.

We exited the hotel in two-minute increments, moving in singletons and pairs, with Jennifer and I going last. The countersurveillance effort would take the metro, but we would walk, giving them time to set up.

The National Gardens was really a park, similar in style to our own famed Central Park but without the scope. It was crisscrossed with footpaths and various attractions like an aviary and a central lake, and Carly had picked a gazebo near the very center. Nick would come in from the west, Brett from the south, and Knuckles would position on the east edge, watching us enter. They'd pick up bumper locations that would allow a three-hundred-and-sixty-degree view of the meet location, keeping eyes on anyone who passed to see if they were interested in what we were doing.

Jennifer and I would be the stationary element. Carly would come in last.

The texts with her were unencrypted, so I had to be circumspect when coordinating the activities. I'd asked her if she was bringing her friend for Knuckles to meet—meaning was she coming with a security package—and she'd said no. I trusted her—to a point—and told her that was good, because Knuckles had his own date, and I didn't want to see a catfight. Meaning *I'll have security, but I don't want to end up spiking on some hidden CIA clowns crashing the meeting.*

She'd sent back a smiley-face emoticon. I'd chuckled at the absurdity of planning top secret meetings in the age of Apple. Honestly, I didn't feel there was any threat from the meeting, but it was good to be prepared and it gave me a chance to train Nick in our way of operating.

Jennifer started walking south, and I followed. We went past the war museum, then cut west, down a road next to the presidential palace. We hit the park right next to a Greek soldier standing guard in what looked like a wooden phone booth. Wearing traditional Greek attire from what appeared to be World War I, his fez made him look a little bit like a Shriner waiting on a miniature motorcycle for a parade.

We entered the park and consulted a large map behind glass, like we were just a couple more tourists. We found the gazebo on the map, confirming what our overhead imagery had already told us, then wound our way through the trees and rocks, passing the bird sanctuary and the lake, waiting on a call. Knuckles finally said, "Good track. Nobody on you. Moving to my bumper."

I nodded at Jennifer and said, "Roger all. Blood, Veep, give me an up."

"East side is clear. Nobody of interest. Meet site is clean."

"Roger."

Brett came on, saying, "Pike, this is Blood. South is good."

The area opened up a bit into a clearing, and I saw our gazebo. I tried to spot my team but could not, which is exactly what I wanted. The shelter had four separate tables with bench seats surrounding each. None was occupied. We took a seat, and I put a Texas Longhorns ball cap on my head. I said, "In position," and heard "Standby."

Carly was coming from the south, so I knew she'd bump into Brett first. It happened five minutes later. "Pike, this is Blood. Spook is inbound."

Guy heard the door open upstairs, then the pounding of feet coming lower. He vaulted over the bar, landing on the body of the man he'd killed earlier. He crouched in the shadows, weapon ready. He heard a shout in Greek, someone looking for the bartender or the girls. He heard a man approach and flattened against the edge of the bar, sliding as much as he could into the shelving while keeping his weapon available for instant use. He held his breath, catching shadows against the walls.

The man above picked up one of the cell phones of the girls, and Guy cursed himself for not bringing them over the bar when he leapt. The man said something else in Greek, then Guy heard another voice speaking English. With an Arabic accent.

"I need to leave *now*. What are we waiting on?"

The other man said, "Your car. Unless you want to run."

The Arab voice said, "What do you mean? Are you not coming?"

A third voice said, "No. Our driver will take you to the park. We aren't foot soldiers. We stay here with the boss, in case you decide you want to return."

Guy saw a flash of light against the wall, the outside door opening, then heard more Greek. Finally, one of the men said, "Go. He will take you to the other men."

The light splashed again, then he heard muttering in Greek, followed by a laugh. He waited, and heard two sets of feet going back up the stairs.

He remained still for a full two minutes, then slid quietly out, climbing over the chipped wooden top. He dropped lightly to the other side, noticing that the two cell phones were gone.

He had no idea what had just transpired, but knew he was running out of time. Sooner rather than later, someone else was going to enter the slut shop and he didn't want to kill anyone who didn't deserve it.

He found the stairs, thinking of the noise the men had made coming down them. He went to the rail, spreading his legs until each foot was as close to a support beam as possible, and began waddling up the staircase.

He reached the top and paused, looking down the narrow hallway. Illuminated by a single bulb midway down, most of the hallway was in shadows. According to the women from below, Nikos's office was the last one on the left side of the hall, adjacent to the only fire escape attached to the building. Which made sense, as he'd want a way to flee if raided.

The problem was that in order to reach it, he had to pass other rooms, and he didn't want to leave an uncleared area behind him. It was asking to be attacked from the rear.

But he had no team with him, and couldn't possibly assault each room without alerting his primary target. He needed speed and surprise, which he would lose the minute he engaged anyone, whether it was a noncombatant or not.

He counted down the hallway, seeing three doors on the left and three on the right. Only two had light spilling out from the threshold. The target's door at the end of the hall and the one closest to him.

Decision time.

★ 56 ★

I acknowledged the call from Brett, glancing to the south. I saw a family of four about a hundred meters away, then saw Carly wandering through the trees, looking for the safe signal. My ball cap. She saw it, then sauntered over to us. She sat down and raised her eyebrow. I held up a finger, then heard, "She's clean. Nobody's on her."

I said, "Roger. All elements stand by."

Carly said, "So you didn't find my secret agents?"

I said, "No. They must be very, very good."

She stuck her hand across the table and said, "You must be the infamous Koko. Decoy told me all about you."

Jennifer took her hand and said, "Well, clearly not *all* about me, or you'd know I hate that callsign."

Carly's face froze for a moment, like she'd made a faux pas, and Jennifer let her off the hook, saying, "Decoy was a good man. Even when he was trying to get my clothes off. I miss him."

Carly said, "I do too. Believe me. And I don't want to lose Guy the same way."

I said, "So what's up with the contact? Did you tell him we'd talked?"

"No, no. Not at all. I thought about it, but I believe it would have only spooked him. He asked for information."

"What information?"

"He asked about Nikos. I'd set up a meeting between them initially, but this time he didn't want that. He asked for specifics. Where Nikos worked, how deep his connections ran, what were the limits of his turf, and where he spent most of his time. Basic bio-data stuff we keep on all the members of organized crime here in Athens. The same dossier you wanted."

That's not good.

"Did you give it to him?"

She slid a piece of paper across the table to Jennifer and said, "I did. And before you say it, I know he's not using it for a sanctioned operation, but I had to give him something or he would have become suspicious. I offered a few crumbs. Not nearly as much as you got, so he's going to have to work a bit to develop a pattern of life to use Nikos as a link to whatever else he's doing. I texted you right after."

She saw my face and said, "Pike, I had to make a decision. You asked me to help you bring him in, and this was the best way. I get him busy chasing his tail, and you develop actionable intelligence to bring him in."

She finished the statement by pointing to the paper in Jennifer's hand.

Jennifer held it up, and I saw a complete breakdown of the handset he was currently using. IMSI, IMEI, make, model, where he'd purchased it, how much it cost, and the cellular plan it was tethered to. She'd obviously been using government resources at great risk to herself. Getting such data would be a significant breach, involving more than just the CIA.

But it might not be enough. I said, "Carly, someone attempted to capture Guy in Crete. Someone with significant host-nation assets and capability, and no restraint about violence. It wasn't the guys from Qatar."

She took that in, drawing the lines between the dots and beginning to look nauseous. She said, "Nikos?"

"Yes. I think so. Well, I can guarantee that *Guy* thinks so."

She put her head in her hands, saying, "Jesus Christ. Every time I help you guys, I end up doing more harm than good."

Jennifer put her hand on Carly's shoulder and said, "You didn't know, and we needed this information. You just cut our search time by an order of magnitude. If you hadn't played out your hand, he would have ditched this phone as well."

I said, "Did you give him enough to find Nikos? If he wasn't trying to use Nikos as a lead for follow-on operations, if he was using it as an end itself, could he do so?"

She deflated, like a pet that had been scolded, looking for support from the very person who had punished her.

"Yes. He could."

I said, "Okay. No biggie. We've still got time. Don't worry about that right now. You made a call, and it was correct. I need everything you gave him."

She said, "Pike, if he kills Nikos, it'll rupture some very tightly wound alliances. It'll be a disaster."

"I got it. I'm more worried about the guys from Qatar because of international repercussions. A dead mafia guy is the least of my concerns."

She didn't look convinced, and I said, "Was Nikos a valuable source for you guys?"

She shook her head. "No. He's a shitbag. We can't prove it, but he's into child prostitution, gunrunning, and false identification to a host of bad folks. We used him more as a hedge to prevent stuff from going down. You know, have a meet, ask some pointed questions in such a manner that he'd back off from certain things. I always got the impression he'd kill me if it suited him. The only reason he didn't was because he knew I was with the US government."

"Then quit worrying about him. Worry about Guy. I'm going to need your help to bring him in. He trusts you. Can you take a few days off? For 'personal reasons'?"

She shook her head, saying, "Bad timing. I have to go to a high-level conference tomorrow with the secretary of state. He's meeting some schmucks here in Greece one-on-one and the National Command Authority doesn't think he's capable. I'm hand-holding."

That made no sense. I said, "They need CIA talent for a state meeting? You don't even speak Greek."

She said, "Yeah, I know. That's not why they want me. It's a back-door thing involving a contact from another country. I can't really tell you more than that. I'm just not available."

I started to reply when Nick came on the radio, saying, "Pike, this is Veep. I have some activity. Two men coming your way, and they're acting strange."

Veep was in the west position. Neither Carly nor I had come from that direction, so they couldn't have pinged on us. It was nothing, but I didn't want to stifle his willingness to report. I said, "Keep eyes on. Almost done."

Brett cut in. "Pike, Pike, this is Blood. I got one coming your way as well. Not a tourist, and I got a printing on his clothes."

Meaning he could see the outline of a gun.

I looked at Jennifer, seeing her begin to slide her own

hand down to the hidden Glock in her purse. Carly saw the movement and said, "What's going on?"

"You armed?"

"No. We don't carry in Greece. What's happening?"

Knuckles came on. "Pike, I got two from my side. One of them is an Arab from the target package. He's not here out of coincidence. Someone must have seen Carly enter, but didn't follow. Now they're hunting. Beating the bushes."

My eyes narrowed at the words. I looked at Jennifer and said, "Get her out. You're her PSD. Take her to the north, toward the parliament building."

There were no northern exits from the park, but there was a slew of security around the parliament building. Carly said, "What the hell is going on?"

"You're being hunted. They're trying to find Guy, and they're using you to do it."

Jennifer stood, putting her hand on Carly's bicep and pulling her to her feet. Carly said, "Wait, what are you going to do?"

I unholstered my own weapon and said, "Fight."

★ 57 ★

Guy slid to the closest door with light spilling out and gently put his ear to it. He heard a woman and a man talking. *At least two.*

There was a sign in Greek on the door, complete with a silhouette of a nude dancer. *A dressing room. Hopefully . . .*

Each of the offices had a large window looking into the hall, which the club had painted flat black. In places, the paint had chipped away, letting light through and, hopefully, giving Guy a way to confirm his thoughts.

He crouched down and duckwalked beneath the sill, putting an eye to the nearest crack in the paint. He saw a rack of costumes and the edge of a mirror over a desk, then a woman, completely nude, her hair in curlers. She plucked two tissues from a box and wiped her mouth. Guy heard the man in the room laugh, then watched the woman pull something off the rack.

Guy hugged the wall, letting her move back deeper into the dressing room. Clearly, they were focused on each other, but ignoring them left his escape route compromised.

He decided to leave them alone, even with the man in

the room. If he moved swiftly enough, he could kill everyone in Nikos's office, then exit down the fire escape.

If it was there.

He moved in a crouch below the window, then stood, his weapon raised. He shuffled forward, sliding his feet to maintain a solid firing stance, his eyes on the final door. He reached the middle of the hallway, directly underneath the anemic incandescent bulb, and heard the door behind him open, the girl chatting with the man inside.

He whirled around, the sights of the 6P9 settling instinctively on the woman's nose. She was wearing nothing but a teddy, one curler hanging low, out of place with the rest. He saw her mouth drop into a perfect little O, and time stood still.

His brain screamed at him to pull the trigger. To silence her before she could compromise the mission.

He could not.

She shrieked louder than an actress in a horror movie, then stumbled backward, finding the stairs and racing down them.

The man burst out at the noise, a pistol in his hands, sliding right into Guy's sight picture. Guy squeezed twice, the suppressor making a muted spit. The man's head snapped back, and he fell without uttering a sound.

Behind him, a door burst open, and the light from Nikos's office invaded the hallway. Guy heard a man shout. He whirled around, dropping to a knee and firing at the silhouette framed by the illumination. The man did the same, firing where Guy had just been. He felt the crack of rounds splitting the air above him, then saw the man topple over, wounded. The man began crawling backward, pulling himself into the office.

Guy fired into the body, stilling the movement.

Guy had a choice to make in the span of a millisecond: Use the escape route behind him, or press the fight.

Suicide run.

He stood, raced toward the open door, and the black window shattered, an object coming through. Something bounced against the wall and hit the floor. Guy recognized the object instantly, and slid to a stop, incredulous. *Grenade.* He turned and kicked the nearest door beneath its knob, the jamb splintering open.

He dove inside just as the grenade went off, feeling shrapnel slam into his legs, the explosion whipping him sideways into the doorjamb. He rolled over, the ringing in his ears blocking out everything else. He shook his head, trying to clear the fog. He checked his legs, relieved to see each still attached. His right calf was peppered in blood, looking like someone had repeatedly stabbed a fork into it. He tested it and found it would support his weight.

He pulled up to the corner of the door and peeked out, wondering how many grenades Nikos might have, feeling the press of time. He knew speed was of the essence, as the concussion most assuredly would attract the attention of others, either police or more foot soldiers.

He saw movement, a man ducking below the shattered window, and slithered out of the room on his belly, high-crawling down the hallway, using his elbows and knees. He reached the office doorway and backed into the wall, glancing inside.

He saw a massive desk, two chairs to the front, but no men.

Underneath the window.

He coiled his legs, then leapt through the door sideways. He landed on his left side, his barrel aimed at a man stunned by his appearance. He pulled the trigger twice, watching the bullets slam into the man's head and explode out the back.

It wasn't Nikos.

Guy rolled over, swinging the weapon in an arc. He found no other threats, but saw the ladder outside the window. *Escape.* He pulled into a crouch, then leapt on top of the desk, aiming the gun on the other side. Nikos was cowering behind an ostentatious leather chair, his hands out front, trying to ward off the death.

He said, "Don't, don't, don't . . ."

Guy said, "Where can I find the Arabs?"

"I don't know . . . I just call them and we meet up."

Guy crouched down, picking up the remaining grenade. He tested the rubber band, then put it into his jacket pocket. He said, "Give me your phone."

"It's on the desk." Guy picked it up, and Nikos gained courage from the fact that he was still alive, mistaking the delay as fear on Guy's part. "You harm me and you'll be hunted until the day you die. There is no place you can hide. When my father finds you, he will kill you very, very slowly."

Guy said, "I guess you're a bad man, huh?"

Nikos sat up, straightening his shirt and running his hand through his hair. "That's right. I'm not someone to trifle with. Let's talk business. I owe no allegiance to the Arabs."

Guy heard noises down the hall, then footsteps on the stairs. He said, "Are the Arabs still at the Athenaeum Hotel?"

Nikos heard the men coming and stalled, saying, "I'll take you to them. I'll help you kill them."

Guy raised the barrel and Nikos said, "All right, all right. Yes. They're at the Athenaeum InterContinental just up the street, okay? Now what?"

Guy cocked his head toward the man on the floor, the blood and brain matter congealing on the wall, reminding him of Nassir in the shower. Reminding him of Nassir calling to him in the night. The deaths he'd caused flashed through his mind, the tendrils of the abyss wrapping him tighter.

He said, "I guess I'm a bad man too."

Puzzled, Nikos said nothing.

Guy raised the barrel and said, "It's not a good day to be a bad man."

★ 58 ★

I called all elements, telling them to maintain eyes on their respective targets, wondering if we weren't missing other hunters searching elsewhere in the park, something that could prove catastrophic. In military operations, one of the worst things you could do was to plan solely against the enemy you'd confirmed, only to see your carefully detailed operation eviscerated by some element you didn't know existed, and so hadn't anticipated.

I needed to get Carly out clean, without bumping into either the ones we knew *or* the ones we didn't. Thread the needle, as it were, escaping and letting them search an empty park. I could handle the problem right now, but if there were more stalkers than the ones we saw, all of them would race to the first sign of trouble, swarming on us like flies to roadkill.

Thank God for Veep. If he hadn't been new, I would have winged this meeting. And missed the trap.

Carly was the linchpin. The key. They knew her, but they didn't know my team, and it made me sick that I'd put her in danger. She'd come because she was trying to help Guy, and now she was being hunted because of it. There was no way I'd let any harm come to her.

The thought broke open a nascent truth, like the final letters in a crossword puzzle spilling out a hidden connection. The *Arab* was here. And he was hunting *Carly* in order to find *Guy*. But the only way the Arab would know Carly existed was because of her connection to Nikos. Which meant he would have to know that she'd set up a meeting between *Guy* and Nikos.

Guy was right. There was a conspiracy threaded through all of this, and it wasn't just because of some Mafioso-done-wrong scenario. The Arabs were doing something. Something bad enough to hunt a CIA agent to prevent Guy from interfering.

Jennifer and Carly were almost out of sight, winding through the paths at a rapid clip. Carly glanced at me once, questioning what she'd become involved in, but Jennifer never looked back. Scanning every bush, she walked with her hand on her purse as if to keep it protected from pickpockets, but I knew what she was "protecting." Her ability to withdraw her suppressed Glock 27 and blast the shit out of anyone in her way.

I remained on my bench, waiting on the hunters to cross my path in their search for Carly. Waiting on whatever endgame they had planned. Then I realized I was playing *their* game. Why did I give a crap what *they* had planned? The damn Arab from Guy's target package was in the park, and *he* should be worried about what *I* had planned.

The Oversight Council hadn't given us Alpha authority yet, but this situation wasn't of my creation. One of the men Guy was stalking was in the park, had coordinated with a known organized crime figure, and was targeting a CIA agent. *And it isn't my fault*. I couldn't be blamed for capturing a guy out to kill Carly.

I clicked on the radio, saying, "Koko, Koko, hold up."

She came back, saying, "What? Threat to my front?"

"No. Just stand by. All elements, all elements, give me a status."

Knuckles said, "Still got the Arab in sight. He seems to be controlling things. He's not searching, and the guy with him is deferring to his commands."

Brett said, "I'm on my man. He's searching the south end of the park. He's in cell contact with someone. Most likely the Arab."

I said, "Roger all. Veep?"

"I got my two. They're closing in on the gazebo. You should have them in sight shortly."

I stood, seeing a bench hidden underneath some low-hanging shrubs. I moved that way, saying, "Any other indications? Any unknowns not previously tagged?"

I heard nothing. I said, "Okay, everyone listen up. I want Koko to bring Spook back down to my location. Go past Veep's targets. Let them see her. Then continue south where the footpaths get narrow and turn into spaghetti. The thick area of the park."

Nobody responded for a moment, and I could imagine what they were thinking. I waited. Knuckles came on. "Pike, what's going through the granite in your skull?"

I said, "Remember that op in Sri Lanka?"

"The Rambo operation?"

"Yeah. That's what I've got in mind."

"I know this doesn't need to be said, but we've got no sanction for that."

I said, "I can't help it if these assholes chose to interdict our *sanctioned* mission. You think we can do it? Here?"

Knuckles said nothing for a moment. I was about to ask again, wanting his opinion—truthfully, wanting his approval—when he came back on. "Yeah, I think so. With a little luck, we can do it. The guys I'm with are the key. They're controlling this thing. They need to go last."

I said, "Understood. That's exactly what I was thinking. The Arab is the end state. We're taking him with us."

Jennifer broke her radio silence. "Pike, we don't have even Alpha yet. You're talking about an Omega mission on foreign soil. Using an uncleared person as bait."

Meaning, Carly would see what we were doing.

I started to answer, when the two pipe-swingers from Veep came into the clearing. I said, "Break, break. Veep, your target set has one with a beard, one with glasses? Wearing a cheesy tracksuit?"

Nick said, "That's my target set. Uhhh . . . What are we doing?"

"Stand by. Break, break, Koko, hold what you got. I don't want them to see Carly too early. Brett, are you clear of the gazebo? No chance they can intervene?"

"No. We're way south, but I'm echoing Veep. What are we doing?"

Shit. I realized that only two people on the net remembered Sri Lanka. Knuckles and me. It would be much easier to give orders based on a historical mission we had all participated in, but nobody else had been in the Taskforce at that time.

I said, "Okay, everyone listen close. This is like ten little Indians. We're going to take each team one at a time. Koko is the rabbit, and she'll lead them one by one into a kill zone in the south of the park, where it's overgrown. Veep, you're up first. Pick an ambush spot and mark it on your phone, then coordinate with Koko.

She'll drag them in, and you take them out. Be sure you can stash the bodies."

I heard nothing. I said, "Veep, you copy?"

He came on, a sharp tone in his transmission. "Yes. I copy. But you want me to kill someone? Here in Greece?"

I was shocked at the comment, then realized he wasn't yet an official team member. He'd had no probation missions. No easy tasks to get him seasoned, and no operations with a mentor to make sure he understood our ethos. He was being thrown into operations without the trust of our organization built through experience, and was now questioning what we stood for. At this point, he was probably wondering if we hadn't killed JFK.

I said, "No, damn it. No lethal actions. Haven't you seen *First Blood*?"

I heard nothing for a second, then, "Seriously? That old movie?"

"Yes. Jesus. *That* old movie. Remember when he hunted all the guys in the forest? Taking them out one by one? That's what we're doing. Can you execute?"

Brett had picked up the game plan immediately and, because he's a smart-ass, came on in an imitation of Sly Stallone's voice. "I could have killed them. I could have killed them all. Let it go or you'll get a war you won't believe."

I said, "Yep. That's exactly right. Ten little Indians, taking them out one by one, but no killing. Veep, can you execute?"

Brett cut me off. "Break, break, Pike, Pike, this is Blood. My target just entered a perfect kill zone. He's stumbling around in the woods searching. I can execute without the rabbit. You want me to do so? Do I have authority?"

Perfect.

"Oh yeah. Get rid of him. Veep, Veep, you ready?"

I was putting a lot of pressure on our new member, but it couldn't be helped. I needed to remain out of contact because I was going to take down the Arab with Knuckles. Which was critical. The whole purpose of the operation. I knew if I bagged him, I could all but guarantee bringing in Guy, solving the problem. I couldn't afford to expose myself beforehand.

Nick came back, a little fear leaking through the radio. "Yeah. I think so. I have a site. I think I can do it, but . . . Pike, there were two of them."

I said, "I understand. You've got Koko leading them in. She'll take one. You take the other. Can you do it?"

"Yes. I can do it."

He didn't sound that confident. "Mark your position on your phone. Koko, you copy?"

She sounded much better than Nick. Instead of fear, I got a little aggravation. I knew she was doing it precisely to give Nick a boost of confidence, something he was sorely needing.

"Yeah, I copy. You are definitely buying the beer tonight. Break, break, Veep, I've got your mark. I'm inbound. I'll pass, you hit. I'll key off of you. Don't worry. This is easier than the House of Pain."

He took the words in, and came back a little stronger. "Roger all. I hit, you assist. Easy day."

I smiled, then heard Knuckles say, "Pike, the Arab gets the call of a lock-on, and they're going to move. What do you want me to do? Follow? Or interdict? There's no good place here. Nothing hidden like in the south."

The plan in motion, I stood, saying, "I'm coming to you. Just keep eyes on until I'm there. They start moving, you track."

"And if they break out? Start running?"

He was asking all the right questions, covering the contingencies. Unfortunately, I didn't have an answer for him. Well, I did, but it wasn't something the Oversight Council would approve of.

I said, "Take them down. For Guy. That fucking Arab is going into a bag."

★ 59 ★

Nick Seacrest felt the sweat build on his neck, the cold weather belying why it was forming. He was scared. No two ways about it.

He'd moved to the south of the park, and just as Pike had said, the footpaths went from wide, twenty-feet-across affairs, to small, single tracks threading throughout the trees and shrubs. If he weren't careful, he'd become lost in the maze.

He'd found a park bench tucked underneath a row of bushes and flanked by two ancient trees. The foliage was spilling out more than it should, unkempt and threading through the slats of the bench, looking like a man who used to be able to afford a salon haircut but now just lived with cutting it himself. Another casualty of the Greek economy, but something that worked in his favor.

He'd glanced behind the bench, but couldn't penetrate more than four feet into the undergrowth. Perfect for . . . whatever he was supposed to do.

He sat on the bench, waiting, analyzing the coming fight, trying to rehearse in his mind how he would attack. He scrambled to remember the hundreds of incapacitation moves he'd learned on the mat in the gym, all of them running through his mind in an endless loop as he considered, then discarded, then considered again.

He'd had plenty of training in hand-to-hand combat, and could defend himself in just about any situation—in fact, *had* defended himself—but this was different. In the past, it had been in the heat of combat, with his life on the line and the fight forced on him, screaming and clawing while a battle raged around him. Here, he was supposed to clinically render a man unconscious without raising an alarm to anyone else wandering through the park. By himself.

This is insane.

His earpiece clicked, startling him. "Pike, Pike, this is Blood. My target's down and hidden."

"Roger that. Good work. I need you to return to the hotel and get our car. Stage on the southernmost exit on the east side. The one away from the presidential palace and the guard force."

"Could take some time. Can you maintain control until I get back?"

"Yeah, I think so. There's another gazebo down there where we can hold up. Between Knuckles and me, we should be good. We'll keep the Arab company. Just don't take too long."

"Roger all."

Nick then heard his own callsign. "Veep, Veep, you still good?"

He mustered his "radio voice," the one he used when talking to aircraft. The one that always sounded calm and collected, no matter the bullets flying around or the begging of teammates for steel on target. "This is Veep. Roger."

"I got Koko in sight. Your targets are going to get visual in about ten seconds. You have control."

Nick took a deep breath and said a final "Roger."

The pressure was incredible. It was unlike anything he'd experienced in the past. Nick was a Combat Controller and he was damn good at his job. He'd been on the tip of the spear for close to ten years, and had seen combat in both Iraq and Afghanistan—where he'd had the misfortune of being blown up by an IED.

He'd fought to stay in Special Operations after that, but his national pedigree of being the vice president's son had intervened. Everyone was too worried about what the headlines would be if he was killed. Too worried about the press. He'd been forced to reclass into another, safer military occupational specialty. He'd hated it. Then, out of the blue, he had met Pike Logan and had back-ended an invitation to the Taskforce. A unit that didn't even exist. And he'd been allowed to train. Now he was wondering what he had been thinking.

One minute they were seriously discussing killing an American Taskforce member, the next he was in a park preparing to take down a man he wasn't even sure was bad. And the speed of operations was something else again. He'd started the morning doing nothing but countersurveillance but now was going to end it as either a hero or a goat. It was a different world, and it brought fear, but not about the fact that he was preparing to go hand-to-hand with two armed men. No, it wasn't the danger. It was a massive fear of screwing up. Of letting down Pike and the rest of the team. Of proving once and for all that he wasn't worthy of membership in the most exclusive club on Earth.

Jennifer came on, saying, "Veep, I've got your marker. We're one minute out. We're dragging the two anchors behind us. You take Tracksuit. I'll get the other one."

Controlling his breathing, clenching and unclenching his fist, Nick said, "Roger. I got Tracksuit."

He decided he'd attack with a come-along joint lock to bring the man to his knees, then subdue him with a rear naked choke. Simple, basic moves that he knew well. His adrenaline was so great he was afraid of losing the fine motor skills required for anything more complex. Those two moves were muscle memory. Easy to execute.

He mentally went through the motions in his head, visualizing exactly how it would go down. He wondered if Jennifer was doing the same thing. Then the fact that there were *two* men coalesced.

She's got the second guy. What if she can't take him down?

For the first time, he had doubts about something besides himself.

Can she do it? He remembered her words about the House of Pain, something he'd barely managed to survive. It was a culmination event at Taskforce Assessment and Selection, whereby the candidate had to initially fight one, then two, finishing with taking on three Taskforce Operators, all acting as role players in a hand-to-hand slugfest, fighting through each level until he either succeeded or was knocked out.

How did she know about that? *Surely she hasn't done the House of Pain.*

Has she?

★ 60 ★

Nick's earpiece came alive. "Pike, Pike, this is Knuckles. My target set is moving south. Deeper into the park. They aren't following behind Carly."

"What's your read?"

"I think they're going to try to cut her off. Get a team in front and a team behind."

"Inside the thick area?"

"Yep."

"Perfect. I'm moving your way."

Nick heard the calls and was amazed at the smoothness. Almost as if they were deciding on a movie to see instead of conducting three separate hostile takedowns in a foreign country. It was a skill he yearned for. A unit he desperately wanted to prove capable of joining. And he'd know in the next few minutes.

Jennifer came on. "Thirty seconds. Get ready. Anchor is about twenty feet behind me. I'll pass you, then pause to look at something. They should stop right in front of you, waiting on me to move."

"Roger all. I'm set."

"Tracksuit is on your side. Take him down quickly. Once I commit, I'll be occupied. I can't deal with both."

You'll be occupied? It dawned on him that she was worried about *his* capabilities.

"Got it."

He caught a flash of movement on the trail, and saw Jennifer and Carly walking abreast, brushing the bushes on either side, walking as if they had more concern of the weather than what was about to occur. They passed him, and Jennifer glanced his way.

She winked.

He couldn't believe it.

His eyes tracked behind her and saw the two men. For the first time, he sized them up for a fight. Tracksuit was a slender man of about five-six, while his friend was closer to six feet, with a large beer gut. Neither one was that imposing.

On the plus side, they were the same ones he'd spotted before, giving him some comfort. There was no way they would be following if they bore no ill will. They drew abreast of his bench and stopped suddenly. He looked down the trail and saw Carly pointing into the shrubs. He wondered what she was looking at, then realized it was the execute order.

Go time.

Tracksuit was directly in front of him, right foot back, left foot forward, half facing him. *Joint lock, right wrist, right elbow.*

He sprang up and leaned forward, slapping one hand on Tracksuit's wrist and the other on the man's elbow. He slid his thumb over the joint of the man's middle finger, then drew out, holding the elbow. Nick quickly rotated, expecting the man to drop to his knees from the pain.

He did not. Instead, he shouted and turned with the

move, spinning in the same direction as Nick and ripping his hand from Nick's grasp, then clamping his other hand on the one Nick had at his elbow, clawing to pry it free.

Nick was stunned, his plan of attack in disarray. Like reliving a bad car wreck and trying to ascertain what had gone wrong, Nick couldn't comprehend how the man had escaped. Then his brain exploded with the answer: *You rotated the wrong way. You had no lock. You had no control.* He'd screwed up in the most amateur way possible. Instead of bringing Tracksuit to his knees, all he'd done was telegraph his intentions.

Desperately trying to regain the momentum, fighting for control of the arm he still held, he threw a weak jab to Tracksuit's face, seeing something fly through the air in his peripheral vision.

Jennifer landed on the second man's back like a demented baboon. In the span of a millisecond, she rotated her legs over the man's shoulders, riding his upper back like a teenager in a failed swimming pool chicken-fight. He flailed his arms ineffectually, trying to dislodge her, and she locked her legs under his chin, using her shinbones to cut into his carotid arteries. She reached over his shoulder and grabbed her foot, pulling it up and burying his neck into the blade of her shin.

Before Nick even registered that Jennifer was in the fight, Tracksuit swung a roundhouse that connected with his nose, causing an explosion of stars. He stumbled back, raising his fists to protect himself. The man came in strong, throwing jabs and kicks, most connecting in one way or another. On the defensive, Nick blocked what he could, knowing he was losing the initiative and trying to formulate a new plan of attack.

He was failing.

Behind Tracksuit, Nick saw Carly kick Jennifer's target behind the knees, and he collapsed like a felled tree, Jennifer still locking out the blood to his brain in an iron grip. Tracksuit reached behind his back, and Nick knew the threat that was coming. He forgot all about his plan, resorting to pure size and fury. And an adrenaline borne of fear.

He charged forward, ducking low, wrapping up Tracksuit's arms and driving him back like a blocking dummy on a football field. The man shouted, and they hit Nick's bench at full speed, Nick driving Tracksuit over it backward. They landed hard in the shrubs, Nick's weight knocking the air out of the man below him. Not giving any respite, Nick slapped the weapon out of the man's hand, then jackhammered Tracksuit's face over and over, like an MMA fighter waiting on the referee to end the match, the other fighter clearly done.

Jennifer did so, jerking Nick's arm before he could land another blow. He looked up, nose bloody, breathing heavily. She said, "You won. Help me with my guy."

He looked down, and Tracksuit's face was a gory mess. He was out cold.

Nick wiped the red snot from his own nose, and Jennifer offered her hand. He rose, a little unsteadily, then helped her drag her target into the brush.

Embarrassment seeping through, he waited on her to make the call, knowing it would be trouble for him. She keyed her radio and said, "Pike, Koko. Both targets down." She winked at him, then said, "No issues."

Nick felt the relief flow. It was over, and he hadn't screwed up.

Jennifer said, "Let's clear out of here."

Face flushed with adrenaline, Carly nodded. "Good call."

Jennifer said, "Thanks for the help on that take-down."

Carly smiled and said, "I thought I was a badass, but, man, that was some Jason Bourne shit."

Nick shrugged and said, "Thanks."

Carly raised an eyebrow at his words. "Seriously? You thought I was talking about you? I've seen better fighting from a third-grade schoolyard."

Nick felt the flush climb up his cheeks and Jennifer laughed. "Don't worry, Veep. I've been there. You've got some pressure as a newbie, and you did fine."

He smiled back, surprised at her deference. She had shown considerable skill, and could have hammered him like Carly, but she did not.

He genuinely liked her.

He grinned and said, "You didn't do too bad yourself."

★ 61 ★

I was slipping through the trees, closing in on Knuck-les, when I got the call from Jennifer. *Two down. One to go.*

I saw Knuckles ahead and heard Jennifer say, "Targets are hidden, but they're armed. You want us to take the weapons?"

"No. Leave them on the bodies. Give the police something to hang on them when they're found. They're no threat to us now."

"Roger all. You guys need help?"

"Nope. Get Carly out of here. Blood's bringing an exfil vehicle. All I need is Knuckles. I want you to prep for reception. We can store him in the van, but I need some life support equipment and a guard roster."

Jennifer said, "Roger all. I can do that."

"One other thing: Get Kurt on the line. Let him know what happened, and that we have a detainee."

She said, "Through no fault of our own?"

"Well, of course. I can't help it if the man Guy's hunt-ing is now hunting us. Works out."

She said, "I can do that. See you at the flamefest."

Meaning the after-action review when we were done.

She was not-so-subtly telling me she was going to have an issue with this operation.

I smiled and said, "See you there."

I caught up with Knuckles on a park bench, tossing bread to the pigeons and looking like he was just killing time. I slid in next to him, saying, "Where are they?"

"Straight through the trees to the left. By that fake pond. They're talking on the phone."

I laughed. "Or more likely *not* talking on the phone. All targets down, and they're trying to figure out what to do. They can't get anyone on their team."

"As far as we know. They might have a hundred people in here."

"No way. If they did, they'd have reacted differently. There might be one more team to the north, but they're no threat."

I couldn't see who he was talking about because of the trees. I said, "I need eyes on."

He said, "Switch with me. You can see them. They aren't moving."

I did and focused on the Arab. He was about five foot seven, but looked solid. Like he lifted weights. Not something I was used to seeing in a terrorist target. The other man was a nondescript pipe-swinger with the ubiquitous leather jacket and thick beard.

I watched the Arab's actions for a minute, then said, "That guy works out."

Knuckles knew exactly what I meant by the statement. Anyone who worked out consistently had a discipline, a control over his destiny that most did not. It may be just to pick up chicks, but an Arab doing so was an indicator. Not necessarily in a bad way, but an indicator nonetheless.

Okay, given that he was in a park, with a known Greek

organized-crime man, hunting a CIA agent, it was in a bad way.

I watched a little bit longer, then said, "And he's hyperalert. He's looking for the bad man." I focused on his face, but couldn't make a connection to the pictures we had. He was simply too far away.

I said, "You sure he's one of the guys from the target package?"

Knuckles laughed and said, "Hell, no. Those pictures weren't the best, but there was something about his eyes. Remember the intel pictures on the armband? Three guys looking like the usual inbred terrorist fuck, and that one guy looking like a mug shot, where he wanted to kill the photographer?"

I nodded. "Yep."

"That's this guy. I don't know when that picture was taken, but this guy has the same look. Same eyes. Like he's pissed off at the world."

I considered his information, then gave him my ultimatum. "Okay. They're the same-looking guy. I think it's him, but I'm not betting my career on it. What do you think? Is this good enough for Omega for you?"

Knuckles looked at me. "You want permission? From me?"

I said, "Yeah, I guess I do. Carly's out clean. Mission accomplished. But Guy is still out there, and that Arab is involved. Do *you* think taking him down is worth it?"

He sat for a spell, then said, "Yeah. Guy's worth it. And that fuck is the key."

I heard the words and felt a swell of vindication. Knuckles deflated it fairly rapidly. He stood and said, "Besides, this won't be the first time I've done something stupid. But it's always with you, for some reason."

I rose up and said, "Okay, okay, no reason to rub it in.

I'll take the Arab, you take beard guy. Rip his ass quickly, because I'll be jamming a barrel into the Arab's ribs. I need him to see he has no alternative. I don't want him to even think about a fight."

He said, "No issues. You want to do it here? Or let them move?"

"Hang on a sec." I got on the radio and said, "Blood, Blood, what's your status?"

"Got the vehicle and I'm inbound. I can circle the block a few times, but there's no parking. President's palace takes priority. I do a couple of loops, and I'm going to draw some stares."

Knuckles said, "Guess that answers the question."

"Yeah, it does. They're parallel to the southern exit right now, and nobody's around. I say we take them."

"Someone shows up, and we're done."

I started walking to them, saying, "Yeah, yeah. Story of my life. Just take that guy down quickly. Then we're moving straight west, both of us controlling the Arab."

I keyed the radio and said, "Blood, we're moving to interdict. Status?"

"One block over. Standing by on your call. Be advised, there's an armed security guard on the building adjacent to the exit."

"Doing what?"

"Doing nothing but standing. No idea why, but he's got an MP5. Looks old and worn, like it's passed from man to man, but the building is something worth the investment."

Knuckles heard the words and glanced at me. I raised my brow, and he just shrugged. Telling me to go ahead.

I picked up the pace, closing on our targets. The Arab was standing stiffly, looking annoyed. The Greek was dialing his phone. I knew he would get nothing. They were both on the edge of a man-made turtle pond, the concrete cracked and worn. To their left was a stand of shrubs, about ten feet away. Where we'd stash the body of the guy on the phone.

We hit the apex of the lake, the path leading us right at them, and I looked at Knuckles, an unspoken command.

Showtime.

I unholstered my pistol, a compact Glock 27, chambered in .40 caliber. Knuckles quickened his pace, getting one step ahead of me.

We got within five feet of our targets before they noticed we were there. They ignored us, intent on their phone conversation. Or lack thereof. Knuckles came abreast of the Greek and whirled, roping his arm over his head and kicking his knee at the same time, the man's neck taking his full weight in the bend of Knuckles's arm. Knuckles tucked his shoulder into the man's head, forcing it down, then used his other hand to lever the arm, scissoring it into the carotid arteries and cinching tight.

The Arab saw the action and gasped, starting to react. I threw my arm over his head and pulled him close to me, jamming my Glock into his kidney. I spoke into his ear, saying, "Easy, easy. Don't move."

He froze for an instant, then surprised the hell out of me.

In one fluid move, he stepped to the right, hooking his leg behind mine and bending down. With his right hand, he swept my weapon out, pushing the barrel away from his body, at the same time jerking upward with his leg, breaking my balance. He coiled, then threw himself backward.

He landed on top of me and swiftly rotated, attacking

my weapon arm with both hands, clamping the hand and trapping my elbow. His head burrowed into my chest to protect himself, he began working the hold, now inches away from an arm bar that would shatter my shoulder.

He locked the hold together in a classic paintbrush and began to sweep the ground with my wrist, the entire action happening so fast I was stunned.

I lost the weapon.

He was strong, and Jesus, *he could fight*.

I felt my shoulder begin to give, and instinct kicked in. I rolled my body toward the sweep, breaking the tension on my shoulder and punching him in the back of the head with two jabs. He continued to work the hold, and I knew I needed to get him to focus somewhere else. Punching wasn't working.

I reached across his head with my left hand and clamped it onto his forehead, searching for his eyes with my fingers. I pulled his head backward, gouging the eyes as hard as I could from my weak position. He screamed and jerked upright, giving me immediate relief.

I pulled my arm free and clamped my legs around his waist, then reached across his body, grabbing his shirt collar with both hands, my arms forming an X. I yanked out and saw his eyes bulge. He tried to pry my arms open, wrenching and grunting to no avail. I pulled harder. He hit me in the face, but I didn't quit. Huffing like a bull, he rose with brute strength, holding me in the air, my legs around his waist and my arms still cinching his shirt into his neck.

He slammed back into the ground, my body taking the full force of both our weights. One of my hands broke free, and it was enough of a respite for him to continue. He collapsed on top of me and we began swimming our limbs, both fighting for position, arms and legs moving in and out in a game of action and counteraction, neither one of us gaining dominance, the only noise the slapping of skin and the hissing of our breath.

In desperation, he went back to attempting to pound my face, forcing me to tuck my chin and block with my arms. I rotated one leg high, slamming it against his neck, trying for a triangle choke with my thighs. He swam an arm under, preventing it, and I immediately reversed and torqued with my body, flinging him over with my leg against his head. He landed on his back and mule-kicked with the strength of both thighs, throwing me off.

He leapt up, doing a Bruce Lee kung fu flip-up like he was being filmed. He saw Knuckles sprinting toward him and took off, running flat out into the park.

I rose, breathing heavily, the whole fight lasting no more than a minute. Very few things were as exhausting as grappling with someone who knows what they're doing, and the entire event was something of a shock.

I said, "What the fuck took you so long?"

He said, "Me? My guy is down. What the hell were *you* doing?"

I wiped the sweat from my face, dusted off my clothes, and picked up my useless Glock.

"That guy can fight. If there's a terrorist camp out there teaching his skills, America's in trouble."

★ 62 ★

Guy popped another Red Bull and slugged half of the can, absently scratching the bandage over the puncture wounds in his calf. He needed the caffeine, given that he was definitely running on a lack of sleep. But today was the endgame. The trap was set. All he had to do was get back inside Haider's car to arm the device. A perfect final piece of justice, mimicking the way his brother had died. Only, Guy's attack would be surgical. No massive explosion. No dead civilians. No collateral damage whatsoever.

He'd been very, very busy the last thirty hours.

He'd left Nikos and the rest of the dead where they lay, fleeing down the fire escape to the street below, pausing just long enough to use his socks as an improvised bandage on his leg, then blending into the crowds on the main avenue fronting the sex club. He'd left his car where he'd parked it, preferring to walk the six or so blocks to the Athenaeum InterContinental Hotel.

Wanting to start the mission immediately.

He'd entered, completely calm, ignoring the pain in his leg and the surreptitious glances at the blood on his jeans. He knew if he acted relaxed and normal, they'd logically connect the color to paint or some other stain. Nobody who was wounded would be acting as he was.

The attack of Nikos was already behind him, giving him no other thought than he'd purchased breathing room to accomplish his mission. It had been bought with blood, but he was fairly sure he'd cauterized any threat from local forces. His only concern was that it would alter his target's planned actions. They might even flee back to Qatar.

He didn't think so, because he was convinced they had a mission to accomplish. Some greater obligation that would force them to remain. But that wasn't a given, which required rapid action.

The hotel lobby was huge, stretching out in all directions, marble walls and pillars dominating the space. He'd looked for a spot to set up, out of sight of the exit, and found two escalators to the right of the reception desk. They went down an additional two floors, below street level, to a section of meeting rooms and scattered tables for breaks from conference panels. The top was open to the lobby, like an indoor mall, but he doubted his target would look down. And he didn't need to look up.

He'd used Nassir's phone history to program the Gremlin with the number Nassir had been talking to when he was captured—clearly another target—and had set an alarm to notify him when it was in proximity.

He'd sat for a little under an hour, reading a stray English newspaper and impatiently staring at the tablet screen of the Gremlin. He was running through other options for tracking the target, considering an attempt to locate his room, when the Gremlin had triggered, surprising him.

The phone was in the lobby, and the Gremlin had automatically attacked it, attempting to insert the same malware Guy had used to trap Nassir.

The signal strength from the Gremlin told him it was too weak for a rapid insert. At this pace, it would take fifteen minutes, and he was sure he didn't have that time. He needed to close the gap. It was a risk, but he wanted eyes on to determine a profile of his target anyway.

He ignored the escalators, as they spilled out right into the heart of the lobby, and instead moved to the elevators in the rear. He exited behind the reception desk, looking at his screen. The handset was still captured, and the signal strength was growing.

He moved adjacent to the concierge desk and saw three men outside the glass doors of the entrance, talking to a bellman. Two were from his brother's target package. One was the man he'd followed in Crete. All of them together, waiting on a vehicle. Exactly what Guy wanted to see.

A valet brought a car around, and Guy trained on the model, needing crucial information. It was a late-model Audi A7. A very expensive automobile, with very unique security components. But no automobile was completely safe, if one knew the weaknesses. In the old days, it would be a physical, metal key or a slim-jim and a hot-wire. In modern times, it was all about the digits. He watched the men enter, noting the positions, as his primary target's location would be critical.

They settled in and drove away.

He'd learned three things he needed to know: One, the make and model of the car. Two, that they used the valet, so the key would be stored with every other valet key. And three, his primary target took the passenger's seat, with the man from Crete driving and the other man from the target package taking a seat in the back.

He'd retrieved his car, retreated to his hotel, and got online. In the not-so-distant past—say, less than a week ago—he would have had Taskforce assets to accomplish what he wanted, but that time was gone. Luckily, the Taskforce didn't do research and development in a vacuum. They relied on Operators to determine the direction and focus, relied on the men who would use the equipment on the ground to test and refine.

All Taskforce Operators were trained in "obtaining" vehicles in the absence of a key for in extremis use, but they'd realized that they were learning rudimentary skills suitable for a B movie made in the '80s, with the car industry moving leaps and bounds every year, just like everything else in the Internet age. In between deployments, Guy had been detailed to an automobile cell, created to teach the means for stealing a car with the latest electronics and security. They'd developed workarounds for just about every make and model, a tiring slog, given the number, but in the process Guy had learned one thing: The crooks were already ahead of them.

And that's where he turned now. People in the past who had provided unwitting assistance to a unit they didn't even know existed.

He sent an email to an account in Beirut, Lebanon, that manufactured the two devices he needed, asking for a "dealer" in Athens, Greece. The man's website sold the products to "help" locksmiths "recover" vehicles, but given the features touted, the legality was thinly veiled. Things like "clone a key within forty seconds," "immediately render safe the alarm system," and "container can be shaped in a multitude of forms"—a bunch of features that would have no bearing if the owner were standing nearby.

He closed the computer, letting the message do its work, then reserved a room at the Athenaeum with his final pay-as-you-go card. That done, he went to an electronics store for the components he'd need for his trap. Nothing special, and all commercial, off the shelf.

By the time he'd returned, he had his answer for a contact in Athens, the man in Beirut not even bothering to ascertain why he wanted to know or whether he was law enforcement. Two hours later, he had the equipment he needed to access the car. In truth, during the transaction, he'd had more fear he was dealing with someone who knew about his connection to Nikos than the man did about his being out to set him up. Clearly, nobody in Greece cared about car theft.

He was running on fumes, but he was set. He needed only two more pieces of information: where they stored the keys for valet, and where they parked the car.

He'd returned to his hotel, eating a soggy gyro for a meal and waiting until nightfall, catching the only three hours of sleep he'd get for the foreseeable future. After midnight, he'd returned to the Athenaeum. He sat across the street and waited, watching the movements of the valet drivers taking the vehicles from the rich after a night on the town. He located a closet just inside the front door, where they placed the keys, the same one that was used to temporarily store luggage from guests.

Perfect.

★ 63 ★

After identifying the location of the key storage, Guy entered the garage, searching for the valet spaces. There were just two floors, and the valet spaces were fairly easy to find. In minutes, he located the Audi in a corner, away from the lights, one of only seven cars parked in the valet spaces.

Even better.

He checked for cameras and found two, one near the entrance to the garage, and one near the elevators. None focused on the valet parking.

He returned to his car and retrieved his equipment, then went to the front desk, dragging a carry-on roller and holding a briefcase. He checked in, got his keys, then said he was late to meet a friend at a bar—delayed plane and all that—and had no time to go to his room. Would they hold his luggage until he returned?

Of course they would. He watched to ensure that the bag went into the same closet he'd seen before, then exited the hotel, taking the briefcase.

He walked around the block, then penetrated the garage, now moving swiftly. He went straight to the Audi, going around to the front, against the wall, and opened the briefcase, pulling out a black box with an antenna and a digital readout. He turned it on, and saw a read of three different codes from three different cars.

Modern-day vehicles have an enormous amount of encryption technology embedded into the key fobs they use. Rolling codes, time-outs, shifting encryption, all were designed to defeat the latest cat-and-mouse game of stealing the transmitted unlock signal and, for the most part, did prevent him from doing that very thing. But his target also used an RFID transmitter, whereby if the physical fob itself was close to the car, a person could unlock or lock the vehicle simply by touch, without sending a code. It was considered the perfect security, because the signal was so low that the fob had to be present for the door to unlock—within a meter or two—and if the fob was present, it must either be stolen or be from the owner.

If it were stolen, then no amount of encryption would matter. After all, if someone stole the keys to a 1970 Volkswagen, the same thing would occur. So it wasn't something to worry about. Except ingenious thieves had found a work-around.

His contact in Beirut had developed an amplifier that would take the weak signal of the key fob and transmit it over four hundred meters to a mated receiver, which would, in turn, transmit the same signal to the car. In effect, tricking the car into thinking the fob was present, the computer inside not realizing the fob had turned into the size of a briefcase.

It wasn't exactly easy, as the amplifier had to be within two meters of the key fob, and had to be there for the length of time it took to enter the vehicle. Not a technique that would work with someone moving around with the key fob in his or her pocket. But something that was easy for a key fob locked in a valet closet.

He clicked the first signal, then touched the handle of the driver's door. The car remained locked. He clicked the second, and touched. The headlights flashed, and the doors unlocked. He smiled.

Money well spent.

He pulled the handle and slid into the footwell. He withdrew a blank Audi key fob and a small device with a circle of plastic on one end and a data connection on the other. He rotated on his back and pulled open the ODB II port that was used for diagnostics of the vehicle's engine via the car's central computer. The one that controlled everything about the vehicle. Including its security codes.

The key fob's security was designed to prevent the codes from being stolen out of the air, while in use, not from inside the vehicle itself. Access to the car laid bare the entire system. After all, even owners needed a way to program a new fob, and that had to happen in conjunction with the vehicle itself. The ODB port was the gateway for doing so, and was mandated to work with a standardized software program to prevent the manufacturers from building in a proprietary system that would force the owner to only use their service centers for diagnostics. It was a bit of legalized egalitarianism that worked in the car thief's favor.

He plugged in the data connection, waited for the LED light to flash, then placed the key fob blank into the plastic circle. He sat just over a minute, then saw the LED strobe for five seconds before shutting off.

He unplugged from the port, then held up the fob.

Moment of truth.

He pressed the button, and the door locks snapped shut. Now under the command of his new fob.

He had no idea if the car would start, and no intention of trying. The man in Beirut claimed it would, but also stated that there were "variables" in models he couldn't control when it came to actually driving the car. Just getting in was assured, but running the vehicle was out of his hands. A disclaimer, you know, because he truly cared about helping out the owner with a new key fob.

Guy didn't care. All he needed was a way to access the car on the move, without the laborious briefcase trick.

He put the fob down and withdrew his final items from the briefcase: the hand grenade he'd taken from Nikos's office, a digital, battery-powered capacitor, and a section of wire colored black and white.

He'd already rigged the grenade for an electrical charge instead of the friction primer that was normally used, drilling out the spring that rotated the firing pin, rendering the grenade safe before continuing.

From the driver's seat, he taped the digital capacitor to the body and connected the wires running out of the fuse set. He pushed a button, checking the battery on the capacitor and the connection with the fuse, making sure he had a clean circuit. A light flashed green, telling him the capacitor could store the electrical charge he'd need, and the circuit was good.

He went to the passenger's side and opened the door, flicking off the overhead light. He spent thirty more minutes underneath the seat, securing the grenade under the cushion and splicing the leads into the air bag release system, his chosen form of initiation.

In all modern cars, there was a small pressure switch in the passenger seat that let the computer know if someone was occupying that space, which, in turn, told the computer to arm the air bag. This was what he leveraged.

When he was done, he had a perfect pressure-plate booby trap. Should someone sit down, they'd close an electrical circuit, and in so doing, initiate the grenade. He tested the components for electrical flow, saw it was good, then disconnected one of the leads, defusing the system. He wouldn't arm it until he was sure his target was in the vehicle, which was the point of the new key fob.

It wasn't foolproof, as the grenade fuse would still require four to five seconds to explode—enough time to escape if someone were switched on to a threat. In addition, the seat itself would mitigate the blast, but he was sure it would kill whoever was inside the car and he thought the mitigation was a good thing. He didn't want any collateral damage from innocents walking by the vehicle. Or because someone different used the car. Which was why he was sitting on Perikleous Street, just down from the Embassy of Qatar, slugging Red Bulls and waiting on his targets to exit.

He'd watched the Audi appear early in the morning at the Athenaeum Hotel, and was pleased to see the same package as yesterday: The driver from Crete, the primary face from the target package in the passenger seat, and the secondary one in the backseat. He'd begun to follow, just waiting for the chance to arm his trap. Sooner or later, they'd stop for lunch or something else, and he'd get the chance to turn the expensive ride into a death trap.

Today was the day.

★ 64 ★

Haider not only heard the displeasure through his father's chosen words, but he also recognized the disgust in his father's voice even through the VPN connection, the enunciation leaving no doubt that the man on the other end thought he was talking to an idiot.

"So you actually had your friend attempt to interdict a meeting with the CIA? And you thought this was prudent?"

"Well, honestly, he did it on his own."

His father's answer surprised him. "At least he tried something, for as little good it did. Does he understand what the CIA is?"

"Father, I have a man attempting to kill me and my friends. He's already succeeded twice. Our intersection is Nikos, and he said the killer was tied to a CIA contact. It was how Nikos had met the man. Nikos was following her, and agreed to help us help eliminate him. *After* the meeting with the CIA."

"And yet you failed. For the second time."

"Father, we didn't know they would have an entire *team* there. We just thought it was a meeting between two people. It was a way to stem the bleeding, without exposure. We weren't doing anything to the CIA agent."

Haider saw his father lean back, the screen making his actions jerky with the weak connection. Sharif rubbed his face, then said, "You broke up a CIA meeting. A meeting you *knew* was CIA. Why do you now think the team was out to get you? *Of course* they had a team. That attack on your friend wasn't because they were hunting you. It was because you *interrupted a meeting with the CIA*."

"We didn't interrupt anything. We were going to track the man that's doing the killing *after* the meeting. They struck first, without us doing anything. Khalid said that they tried to capture him. Does that sound like a team providing protection?"

"Shut up and use your head for a change. I swear, how you survived in Afghanistan is beyond me. Khalid entered the park. *Khalid* attempted to interdict the meeting. How can you possibly say they were out to capture him? Do you mean they actually set up an enormously complicated trap, feeding Nikos information, knowing that he would feed it to you, and that you would be stupid enough to react?"

In the cold light of day, his father's logic crushed the conspiracy theories from the discussions the night before. Maybe they *were* reading too much into the attack. But that didn't alter the fact that two of his friends were dead. One for sure, and another who had simply disappeared.

He said, "Father, you might be right, but I want to leave here. Yesterday may have been my fault, but there is still a team chasing us. Still someone who wants to see me dead."

Sharif shut that line of discussion down. "No son of mine is a coward. At least your friend Khalid has the courage to attempt to capture the American, even if he failed. You will not flee from the operations simply because it has become dangerous. Do you understand?"

The words were as abrupt as a physical slap. *Coward? Who said anything about fear?* He said, "No, I don't understand. Staying here, waiting to get attacked, is stupid. It's not helping anything. Courage and stupidity are two different things. In fact, it might be hurting the very mission you want. I should go to Oslo to prepare."

Tarek, his father's confidant, showed the hint of a smile. Haider took it as a good sign. Sharif waved his hand as if he'd had enough of the discussion. He said, "You can't go to Oslo until you know when the meeting is to occur."

"I think I'll learn that today. I have a meeting with Secretary Billings today, and I think the peace talks are soon."

"Do you have the *shahid*? Is he ready?"

"Yes. He's acting as my driver, the same thing he will do in Oslo. The problem is, he has no way to get into the country. He has a passport from Afghanistan, and no visa for Norway. We paid for the documents before we knew where the peace meetings were going to occur."

"Go back to Nikos. Money is no object. Pay what he wants."

"Nikos has disappeared. He won't answer the phone or the email he gave us. Khalid thinks the park mission scared him and he's gone underground. Either way, he's no help."

Sharif thought for a moment, then said, "Talk to Secretary Billings. Tell him your predicament. Tell him you have a confidant well versed in Afghanistan affairs, both from the Taliban and from the government. He's your inside man, and he's necessary if they truly want an unbiased look from Qatar. Tell him he has an Afghanistan passport and that he's going to act as your driver to deflect attention, but he needs a visa. The government of Qatar can't help, given how secret this meeting is."

"Father, he's not going to provide a visa from Norway for an unknown man from Afghanistan."

"Yes, he will. He likes the intrigue. He wants to be secretive, thinking he's manipulating events outside of the primary participants. He wants to do something like this, or he'd have never asked for your help. Trust me, I have dealt with men like him many times."

Haider heard the words, and for the first time in his entire adult life, he felt pride in being his father's son, and admiration at the Machiavellian manipulation proposed. His father understood the levers to pull without ever having met Secretary Billings, and Haider, having worked with the secretary, knew what his father said rang true.

Haider said, "I can ask, and see what he says."

"He'll say yes. He's infatuated with his own importance. He wants to report back to his president that he's in control and manipulating events for the United States. Make no mistake, he believes he needs you more than you need him, and I think it is absolute poetry that we will use him to facilitate the means of his own destruction."

Haider said, "Okay. I'll do my best. What about the car? Is it ready?"

"Yes. I've arranged for you to pick it up. Just tell me when."

Haider nodded and said, "We'd better go. I have a bit of a drive. I hope you're right about the American secretary of state."

"I am, but the results will depend on you. If you fail and cannot get your *shahid* to travel with you, you can be the one who drives the vehicle."

Haider laughed, but the look on his father's face left doubt as to whether he was making a joke.

★ 65 ★

Guy found himself nodding off, his head actually hitting the driver's-side window. He snapped awake, looking toward the small guard shack. He saw a blip of activity from the bored Greek national inside. The man was staring at the ramp leading under the building. Something was happening, the guard shack alone belying that this was a simple office building.

It would seem strange to an American who was used to seeing the power projection of the United States overseas, with embassies full of flag waving and imposing blocks of granite, but the Embassy of Qatar was located on the third floor of an office complex built over a bike shop and auto parts store, out on a lonely stretch of road in the northern part of Athens. One wouldn't even know the building had anything to do with Qatar except for a lone flag flying on the roof and a restricted entryway guarded by the Greeks.

Like a lot of countries in the world, Qatar had no need to advertise their presence. In fact, doing so would only open them up to security risks they had every reason to avoid. And so they had an embassy inside an office building, with minimal indication it even existed. It worked fine for them. Unlike the United States, there wasn't exactly a line of people fighting for a visa from Qatar.

Guy focused on the guard's actions. When he saw him press a button, and the drop bar to the concrete ramp rose, he leaned forward, hand on the ignition. As he saw an Audi crest the steep drive from the underground garage, he turned the keys. When he saw the man in the passenger seat, he pulled out, tagging two cars behind.

He dragged anchor as they moved through traffic, going steadily north. He thought the car would head back into the city, but it didn't, and he regretted sitting and waiting, wasting his chance. Infiltrating the underground garage beneath the building would have been a significant challenge, but he might have missed his opportunity. While they didn't advertise their presence, Qatar had invested heavily in security. He could probably penetrate, but he was positive he'd be on camera after the killings. Something for the police to tear apart. So he'd opted to wait.

The Audi drove steadily, now heading west. Thirty minutes later, Guy wondered where it was going. He thought it was to one of the suburbs surrounding the city, perhaps to continue their criminal activity—something he would really love to interdict—but the car entered 75, a major highway that threaded out of the city to the hinterlands of the rest of Greece. Clearly, they had a purpose, and it wasn't in Athens.

Guy stayed behind them, the trip passing an hour and the car continuing on the highway. His mind drifted, thinking of the endgame. Thinking of the destruction, and the follow on, or the lack thereof.

He was going to complete his mission—kill his man—and get nothing from it. Nothing but revenge. He had the safe-deposit key, but couldn't access it by himself.

They drove on, steadily going northwest, the road stretching out, passing tourist buses and making him wonder where they were headed.

His mind toyed with the mission over and over, trying to feel the vindication he had before. He thought about Pike Logan. About the meeting on the ferry. He had so wanted them to join him. So wanted absolution. Pike, of all people, understood what he was doing. Pike had lost family, and had exacted his revenge. Nobody talked about it out loud, but everyone knew he'd killed a man in interrogation isolation. A devil who was a terrorist and deserved it. But also a man who'd murdered Pike's family.

Pike was a stone-cold killer. An Operator whom some people in the Taskforce feared but everyone respected, and Guy believed he was the same. He *knew* it. He just wanted someone else to tell him it was so.

Pike's face sprang into his memory from when he'd walked away on the ferry. A mixture of fear and pity. He did not want to be remembered that way. He didn't *deserve* to be remembered that way.

Two hours into the trip, blindly following the Audi in front, winding into the mountains of northern Greece, he made his decision. He'd kill the fucks who'd murdered his brother, then turn himself in. He still had the key to the safe-deposit box, and he was sure it would vindicate him. Once the Taskforce found the information it held, they'd back off.

He was in the right. Just like Pike.

He came out of his thoughts when the Audi pulled to the side of the road, into one of many parking slots that had appeared while he was lost in thought. He passed by it, ignoring the passengers and staring straight ahead, finding the next available spot on the small, two-lane road.

He pulled in, then assessed where he was.

A tourist spot, of that he was sure because of the number of cars. He glanced around, and found a sign just outside of the parking area, proclaiming the hours of a museum.

Delphi.

The target had parked downhill from the archeological site of the famous Delphi ruins, but why?

The answer came as soon as he thought of the question: The target was conducting a personal meet, and using the expansive grounds as cover.

Which meant they'd all leave the car.

He picked up his cloned key fob, rubbing it with his thumb like a talisman.

Perfect.

★ 66 ★

The encrypted tunnel for our computer hookup made Colonel Kurt Hale's voice sound a bit mechanical, but it was doing little to hide his anger. He was pissed, and not in the usual "Pike will be Pike" way.

"Before I cut your nuts off and serve them to the Oversight Council on a platter, I want to be sure: You saw some people you *thought* were bad, and then interdicted them? In the hopes of interrogating an Arab that you had no Omega authority to capture? And the asshole escaped? Did I just summarize that correctly?"

Wow. When he put it that way, it did sound sort of bad.

We'd come back from the operation a day ago, and I'd opted to wait for the scheduled contact to report, mainly because we hadn't captured anyone and none of our team had any injuries. We'd escaped clean, and I was fairly sure that the Arab wasn't filing a police report. For her part, Carly would say nothing, as she was operating outside of the CIA, and so I'd decided that no flash message was necessary. A report right after wouldn't have altered anything on my end, but it could have altered a vote on Alpha authority from the Oversight Council. Because of that, I'd decided that reporting early wasn't in the team's best interest, or Guy's. All I'd catch was the wrath of Kurt Hale, and I could wait for that. Hell, it wasn't like he was going to tell me anything new. I'd already had a hammering from the teammates at the after-action review.

Back in the hotel, we, as a team, held a clinical, antiseptic inspection of every detail of the mission to learn what went right, and what could have gone better, the point being to spread any lessons across the force. As team leader, I made sure that nobody was immune from criticism—me included—but also that nobody was attacked out of anger or animosity.

Five minutes in, I was thinking maybe this one wasn't that necessary, since the only consternation seemed to be my deciding to hit the guys in the park in the first place. Knuckles was on my side, with Jennifer saying it was absolutely counterproductive. Jennifer's points—that we could have evacuated Carly without any drama, and we had no Omega authority for a takedown—were valid, but had it gone the other way, it would be a whole different conversation, which meant that it wasn't worth dwelling on. But for some reason, Jennifer did.

Brett backed up Jennifer, and poor Nick sat in the middle, afraid to commit either way. Jennifer really didn't want to talk about the actions themselves, which piqued my interest. I certainly didn't want to detail what had happened to me, but I did, because the team needed to know what they were up against with that Arab. It was embarrassing, but necessary, and I was curious why Jennifer was staying away from her fight, preferring to harp on the overarching decision.

She was hiding something.

I asked her to walk me through her part of the mission, and she did, which sounded pretty solid. She brought up some points about communication and flow, and it sounded fairly normal. Like the takedown hadn't been any issue at all.

I asked, "So how did Veep here get his face clocked?"

Nick's nose had been bloodied and he had a cut below his eye, meaning something hadn't gone smoothly. Before he could speak, Jennifer defended him, saying, "He did just fine."

I looked at Nick, waiting. Embarrassed, he glanced at Jennifer, then said, "Okay, okay, I wasn't ready. I lost control of my target and I almost cost both of us."

His hangdog face was almost comical. He looked like he was waiting on me to hand him a plane ticket home, not realizing it was the perfect answer, and that I was pleased. I could tell he'd already internalized the lessons and that the admission was very, very painful.

There was nothing like thinking you're the hero only to have to admit you're a zero.

Jennifer was glaring at me, daring me to tear into him, like I did it for sport. I realized she was still learning. Still thought these AARs were nothing more than an Alpha-male dick-measuring contest. It could be a teaching point for both of them.

I smiled and said, "Well, at least your guy went down. I'm still chasing mine."

I saw the relief flood through him, and Knuckles gave me a wink. Jennifer looked a little shocked that I didn't rip him apart, which I'd correct once we were in private. When I could rib her a little bit about her lost-puppy protective instincts. It wasn't doing Nick any favors.

After the AAR, we'd spent the rest of the time tracking Guy's phone and spitballing various courses of action for bringing him in, waiting on the Oversight Council to give us our big ticket for the attempt: Alpha authority against the Arab contingent.

We'd identified his hotel, then followed his phone signature around the city, just keeping tabs, but I never got the call from Kurt. Finally, I'd reached my window of contact with the Taskforce.

When I reported in, the commo guy on the other end had said, "Hang on, Pike. Colonel Hale told me to get him when you called." Which wasn't what I wanted to hear. And now I was *really* not hearing any love.

I said, "Sir, okay, maybe it wasn't the best decision, but you want Guy back, the Arab is on his target deck, he was hunting Carly because of her connection to Guy, and it was within my in extremis authority. It was a good call, but it didn't work out."

"Didn't work out. Really."

The sarcasm was so thick I could have put it on a bagel. I waited, mute.

Kurt sighed, then looked at the ceiling. He returned to the screen and said, "So you didn't bother to call in this little escapade because, why?"

"Because it was no harm, no foul. It didn't require a flash message."

"You mean because it would have affected the Council vote on giving you Alpha for the very Arab you attacked."

He wasn't asking a question. I said, "Well, yeah, sir. I knew you'd have to report it."

He chuckled at my honesty, shaking his head. "Okay . . . you'd have been right. No way would they have given Alpha with those shenanigans. Especially with Billings on the vote."

I perked up. "Are you saying what I think you are? They did?"

"Yeah. They did. President Warren weighed in, based on my judgment, which in hindsight looks a little suspect."

Brett knocked on the door, saying, "Coming in."

Kurt heard and said, "Who is it?"

I said, "Brett," then turned from the screen. "What's up?"

"Guy's on the move again, and it's way north. It's a spike. He's not running around the city anymore. Knuckles thinks he's operational."

From the computer, Kurt said, "North where?"

I scooted over, letting Brett slide into the screen. "Way north of Athens. Like two hours away."

"Near Delphi?"

Brett looked startled and said, "Actually, yeah. Not 'near' Delphi. He's stopped at the Delphi ruins."

Kurt became brusque, all business. "Pike, Secretary Billings is meeting the first target on Guy's list. A man named Haider al-Attiya. It's a clandestine linkup to discuss a potential peace deal with the Taliban in Afghanistan, and it's happening at the Delphi ruins. He *cannot* interrupt that."

Holy cow. That's bad.

Guy had no idea, I was sure. In his quest for revenge, he was about to aid the very terrorists he hated.

I turned to Brett. "Get the team up and moving." He went running out of the room and I returned to the screen, saying, "Sir, they're two hours away. I don't know if I can interdict Guy in time."

He said, "Do what you can. I'm on it. I'll warn Billings."

"That's not going to be enough. Billings is like a damn petulant child. He'll probably ignore you, if he even answers his phone."

"Best I can do. I never trusted these back-channel diplomacy things, so I convinced the president to at least send a case officer with him. He should be able to do something even if Billings won't."

Carly's words about a meeting came back. *Jesus. She's the case officer.*

"Sir, that case officer I was telling you about in the park—Guy's friend from Decoy's past—she's the one on it. She told me, but I didn't put it together before. I was going to use her to pull in Guy, but she told me she was committed with the SECSTATE. It has to be this meeting."

"You got her number? That would cut through some red tape."

"Yeah, yeah, I got it. I'll call her on the move. We need to get Billings to stay in the park until we can get there."

"I'll do what I can, but like you said, he doesn't really listen to me. Call me secure from the road."

I glanced back, making sure the room was empty, then returned to the screen. About to disconnect, Kurt saw the change in my demeanor and said, "What?"

"Sir . . . I saw what Guy has become. He's got the skill and he's got the desire. He's going to kill his target, and there's nothing on earth we can do about it."

"I don't need to hear that shit. *You* were like him, and you came back."

I squeezed my eyes shut and said, "I know. I know. That's *exactly* what I mean."

I looked at the screen, my boss uncertain where I was coming from. Kurt not wanting to believe, but the tendrils of the beast inside me knew it like an absolute truth.

I said, "Someone's going to die today, and nothing you or I do will alter that."

★ 67 ★

Guy watched the three men from the vehicle walk up the stairs to the museum, losing them from sight as they passed behind a thatch of landscaping at an outdoor café. He waited an additional ten minutes, then slipped out of his car. He hugged the stone wall, walking in front of the vehicles parked nose-in to the museum lot, using the granite as cover to stay out of sight of anyone coming down the stairs.

He glanced around as he moved, casually surveying his surroundings. He saw packs of families taking the walkway from the museum to the ruins proper, but no one in the lot. He reached the front of the Audi and slipped his hand into his pocket. He pressed the key, seeing the locks pop up.

His casual demeanor shifted as he rounded the car. He ducked low, moving swiftly, scuttling like a crab. He opened the door, sliding into the seat, his head below the dash, staring at the indicator above the console. He saw the "passenger air bag off" light flick out.

Sensor working.

He slid into the footwell, wanting to spend no more than three seconds arming his system. He rotated his head to the left and slid his hand under the seat, feeling for the loose lead. He found it and threaded it into the plastic slip-lock, snapping it closed and completing the circuit. He pressed the button on the capacitor and saw a light flash green.

The trap was set.

He rolled upright and caught movement in the side mirror. A two-car convoy pulled up behind his vehicle and stopped. He slid back into the footwell, cramped with the door barely open, carefully avoiding the seat and its pressure sensor. The cars remained still. He crawled across the center console as if he was playing a game of Twister, pulling the passenger door closed behind him. He slid into the driver's seat, focusing on the mirror.

A small entourage arrived from the steps of the museum, walking to the vehicle. Four men spilled out, wearing black suits and sunglasses.

Protection. What the hell?

A man with a sizable gut and a thick double chin exited, and Guy recognized him. *Secretary Billings? Here? Right now?*

He couldn't believe his luck. What on earth had the gods put in his coffee to cause him to attempt a trap at the exact moment the US secretary of state paid an official visit to the Delphi ruins? He slid lower in the seat, positive that he wouldn't be recognized by Billings, but also knowing the personal security detail would be watching every single twig blown by a breeze. No way could he exit now.

Then his world shrank even further.

While Billings was glad-handing the museum people, another person exited. A woman. Guy focused on her, and felt an electric jolt.

Carly?

From his hunched-over position, he couldn't be sure.

He slid his hand up to the controls for the mirror and began manipulating, trying to confirm.

It was her. And she would most definitely recognize him.

What the fuck is she doing here?

He crouched down, waiting on the PSD to move, feeling the seconds tick by, wondering if his targets would return to the car and find him in it. It was the most excruciating two minutes of his life. Eventually, the entourage walked away, the Greeks looking like a school of fish circling a sinking piece of bread, all of the members fawning over the secretary of state, he in the middle and Carly off to the right flank. They went up the steps to the museum, and the two-car convoy looped around, parking about fifty meters away in a roped-off section Guy had missed before.

He slid out of the target vehicle and locked it, walking toward his own car as if he belonged, opening the door and taking his seat. He watched the entourage disappear and wondered what was going on.

★ 68 ★

Carly walked up the slabs of stone in the path that wound across the mountain, climbing steadily higher, looping back and forth, the switchbacks seemingly endless, the stadium on top their ultimate goal. She was invigorated by the ruins, having had little time to sightsee since she'd come onboard with the Greek station, spending most of her days in the seedy underbelly of Athens.

The view to the south was incredible, the mountains falling away and looking remarkably like the Blue Ridge chain on the Appalachian Trail, with even some low fog to complete the image. The problems with Guy and her ongoing work had initially caused aggravation at being tasked to set up a professional meeting for Billings, but now she was glad for the mission, enjoying her short day trip.

She couldn't say the same about her charge.

Billings was huffing like a bull in a matador contest, putting his hands on his knees at every step and pressing down as if his arms could help his legs continue, the security detail and his personal assistant walking robotically around him.

She said, "You want to take a break, sir?"

Sweat rolling down his jowls, Billings just glared at her, saving his breath for the climb. They paused at four separate points, letting the chosen tour guide spout a monologue on the various relics and structures scattered about and giving the secretary a brief respite. Eventually, they rounded the bend leading to the stadium at the top, the crumbling structure running over a hundred meters, amazing Carly at the ability of ancient man to construct it on top of a mountain, all for panhellenic foot races lost to history.

The tour guide started her spiel, and Carly faded to the back, outside the ring of security, watching. She saw her contact standing next to a placard describing the grounds, at the head of the stadium fifty meters away. A man named Haider al-Attiya, dressed exactly like the men in Billings's security detail.

When she'd initially been tasked the responsibility for setting up the meeting, she'd analyzed it using standard operational procedures for a personal source meet, and found one glaring problem—the overt movements of the secretary of state.

She'd debriefed Billings, keeping her thoughts to herself on his amateur attempts to slip his security earlier, endangering not only himself, but the source as well. She'd gone over his itinerary and designed a plan to incorporate the source meet under the noses of the ubiquitous Greek government officials greeting him at every turn. A way for them to ensure the final meet location was hidden, yet still blend in with Secretary Billings's schedule.

She broke from the pack, moving toward Haider, and felt her phone vibrate. She glanced at the screen, recognizing the number for Pike Logan, and shunted it to voice mail. Now was not the time to discuss anything about Guy.

* * *

Having waited more than an hour, Guy was growing impatient. Whatever the Arabs were doing, it was taking forever, and the secretary of state's arrival was complicating his plan. After successfully returning to his car, he'd kept a wary eye on the two drivers of the convoy, but both simply leaned against their car doors behind the ropes fifty meters away, clearly bored. They were far enough out that his improvised explosive device would cause no harm, but he was worried nonetheless. With his luck, they'd pull the convoy up behind the Audi, and the secretary of state would walk by the passenger door the moment Haider sat down.

He was feeling the lack of sleep, knowing his judgment was slipping and urgently wanting to get to the endgame. Kill the targets and let him rest for a week.

He thought about the key in his hotel room. The one for the safe-deposit box. The one that would allow further exploitation of the operational cell from Qatar. And it was a cell, of that he was sure. He knew his actions would short-circuit their immediate plans, but there was probably a trove of threads inside that box, waiting to be pulled.

He couldn't do it alone, though. After this, he'd give himself up. Hand over the key and take the punishment, hoping that the exploitation by the Taskforce would vindicate him. Even if it didn't, he had no energy to continue. No fire left after the mission today. He wanted back into the land of the good, even if it meant living behind bars.

He began to run through his head how he'd get in touch with Pike, and the actions he'd take to turn himself in. Maybe he could go through Carly. Surely, she could work a contact through the station. Maybe get her to send a back-channel message to the director himself. He was on the Oversight Council, and from what Pike said, they were all in a panic about his actions.

His phone vibrated in his pocket, startling him. He pulled it out, and saw it was Carly.

What the hell?

★ 69 ★

Carly walked over to Haider, pretending to look at the placard. Even though she recognized him, she continued with her bona fides to give him confidence.

"They have this placard in every language but Arabic."

He replied, "No matter. I speak English."

She stuck out her hand and said, "I'm Carly. I'll be handling the meeting."

He shook it and said, "I don't know why we're doing all of this . . . as you would say . . . cloak-and-dagger."

"Just a protection. Listen, I don't have a lot of time. The guide will lead the group down here soon for the tour. After, when we start back down the mountain, you blend in with the security. Don't try to act like you know what you're doing, just walk on the perimeter down to our vehicles. When the crowd breaks up, stay with us. You'll load into the secretary's car and we'll drive to that quaint tourist town on the way back to Athens. You have a car and driver as instructed, yes?"

"Yes."

"Have them follow. We'll stop in the town for lunch, you can talk to the secretary, and when we leave, you stay behind. Is that clear?"

"Yes. It's clear."

Carly smiled and said, "Sounds complicated, but it's just a precaution. Here they come."

The group approached, Haider and Carly relinquishing their position next to the placard and fading to the back. The tour guide began talking again, with Secretary Billings theatrically raising his eyebrows her way. She nodded slightly, exasperated in him, wanting to say, *You do realize everyone's looking at you, right?*

Eventually, the guide wound down, the tour was over, and they began the march back to the bottom, moving more swiftly now that it was downhill and there were no more programmed stops.

Guy stared at the screen of his phone. *She must have seen me.* He considered not answering, but knew, if she were calling, it was to keep him in the shadows. She could have just walked right up to him if she wanted. And still might.

He answered, confused again when a man's voice came on.

"Guy? Is that you?"

"Who's this?"

"It's Pike. Pike Logan."

The words sent him spinning, trying to find an anchor as to what was happening. How did he have Carly's phone?

Before he could speak, Pike said, "Sorry for the subterfuge. I had to make sure you'd answer. I had the office spoof the number."—"Office" meaning "Taskforce," Pike speaking around the issue on an open line.—"Look, I know you're on the hunt, and I know where you are. I'm about ten minutes out, and I need you to back off."

Guy looked at his watch, factoring the time. He said,

"I told you on the ferry, I can't do that. I'm almost complete here."

"Guy, the office has agreed to let us explore. The man you're trying to buy is not a final yet. Do you hear me? Get back on the team. If it pans out, it pans out, but we don't decide that. We bring the evidence, and the office decides."

So they gave Pike Alpha authority. The words held a weight, Pike telling him in code that he wanted Guy to join him in the exploration of evidence, but that it wasn't up to them to decide on taking out a target. It was up to the Oversight Council. The ones who had refused before. *What if this was nothing but a ploy?*

He wanted to believe. Desperately wanted to cross back over, but his brother was still in the balance. He said, "Pike, I hear you. I'm willing to talk. There's a key in my hotel room to a safe-deposit box in Athens. I did the research and located it, but I can't get in by myself. It's the future of this thread. The past is the past."

He heard relief in Pike's voice. "So you're standing down?"

"No. I'm sorry. That man is part of the past."

Guy saw the entourage of the US secretary of state, the personal security detail, and the gaggle of Greek authorities, all coming down the stairs. He saw Carly in the back, walking next to a security man.

Only it wasn't.

What the hell?

Pike's voice became dark. "The man you're looking at is *working* with the office. You need to stand down, now."

So that's what's going on. Duplicitous bastards.

"Pike, I don't work for them anymore, and I can't believe you'd use a lie to get me to stop. That fucker is gone, just like my brother."

★ 70 ★

Carly hung in the back next to Haider, watching Secretary Billings thank his hosts and receive a small token of appreciation. He shook a few more hands, then signaled for his vehicles. As they pulled around, he motioned for Carly to come to him.

He said, "Look, I want to talk to Mr. al-Attiya alone for a minute. You and my security will ride in the second car."

Mildly aggravated, she said, "Sir, that's not the plan. I'm here for a reason."

He showed displeasure, saying, "You're *here* to support me. Period. I'm just talking about the ride to the restaurant. Twenty minutes."

She said, "Sir, we can't all fit into the second car. There's not enough room."

Billings waved Haider over, saying, "Go with his people. Someone needs to make sure they know where we're stopping anyway."

Now alarmed at the breakdown of the plan, she said, "Sir, that's not a good idea."

With Haider approaching, he hissed, "Don't question me on what's good or not. I'm doing it." He pointed at his personal assistant chatting with a Greek. "Would you prefer I sent Leslie with them to give you room? She doesn't know what we're doing."

Haider arrived and she remained silent. Billings said, "Where's your car? Carly here is going to make sure it knows where to meet us."

Haider pointed, and Carly saw a late-model Audi, two men standing by the trunk.

Pike said, "Don't do it, Guy. I'm not lying to you. I would *never* lie to you. Carly is working it with your man, but we *do* have permission. You're going to hurt her. Come back over and let's attack this together. Do it right."

Guy stared at the group by the convoy, the Greeks moving back up the stairs and waving, the car doors opening. He said, "I know Carly's here. I see her."

The security men went to the second car, cramming in all five. The lead car had only Secretary Billings, Haider, and Carly. He felt his breath increase, knowing he was within seconds of initiation.

Go. End the meeting. Get this over with.

Secretary Billings held out his hand, and Haider entered the car. Guy snapped upright, not believing what he was seeing.

Shit.

Carly began walking toward the Audi, looking back at the secretary's car. The convoy began moving, leaving the parking lot.

No, no, no, no.

Pike was still shouting in the phone, but Guy was no longer listening. He watched Carly move at a slow pace, stopping at the back of the Audi and talking to the two men there. His two targets.

She shook their hands, then moved to the passenger door, snapping Guy out of his trance. He was almost a hundred meters away, with no time to reach her.

He cut into the diatribe on the phone, saying, "Pike, forgive me. Find the key."

And started his car.

Carly portrayed calm on the outside, but felt the anxiety she always did on a source meet, where she never really knew the motivations of the men she was courting. The driver appeared normal enough, but the other passenger—introduced as Khalid—was a bundle of energy with piercing eyes, like a bird of prey constantly scanning, constantly on the hunt.

She said, "We'll be following about a minute behind. You remember that town about fifteen kilometers back on Highway 48? We'll be stopping at a restaurant there."

Khalid said, "Okay. You ride up front. Show him the way."

She moved to the passenger's door, keeping one eye on him. She opened it, then saw him turn. She focused on his line of sight and saw a small Fiat screaming across the parking lot. She was about to sit down when she recognized the man behind the wheel.

Guy George.

There could be only one reason he was coming: *Targets.*

She screamed, "Get in the car, get in the car!"

His door half-open, Khalid whirled around, facing the vehicle. The other Arab jumped up on the curb, moving toward the stairs. Carly slid into the seat, slamming the door. Guy exploded from the car, disregarding the Arabs and running right at her, shouting at her to get out.

His eyes were bloodshot and wild, and she realized

Pike was right. He'd crossed over. She locked the door. Khalid jumped on Guy's back as he came by, but he ignored the attack, staggering forward. Guy bashed the window with his elbow, spraying Carly with glass.

She raised her arms and Guy ripped at the door locks, screaming, "Get the fuck out of the car! It's going to blow!"

Khalid wrapped his arms around Guy's neck, and Guy whirled backward, slamming Khalid into the body of the Audi and causing him to drop.

His words sank in. Carly frantically fought the door handle, managing to get it to pop open. Guy kicked the edge, swinging it wide, grabbing her by the hair and shirt and jerking her forcefully out, flinging her body to the ground.

Khalid stood up, arms raised, snarling, but Guy ignored him, instead jumping onto the passenger seat until his body covered it. Khalid charged, and the seat exploded in a blinding flash, throwing Khalid backward.

Carly covered her head, pieces of glass and bits of metal raining around her. She heard nothing but ringing in her ears. She rolled over and saw Guy slide out of the car, his body black and red. He hit the pavement and she saw his arm rise up.

He was alive.

She crawled to him, surveying the carnage, not knowing where to even begin because of his massive wounds. Blood was everywhere. His jaw was askew, white bone lancing out of red flesh. His abdomen was ripped open, internal organs spilling out onto the pavement.

He grabbed her hand, his eyes fluttering.

Seconds later, she saw his soul flee his body.

★ 71 ★

The mood inside the Oval Office was somber and hushed, without the usual back-and-forth talking among the principals committee of the Oversight Council. All waited on Colonel Kurt Hale to continue.

He clicked a slide, showing the Audi twisted open like a tuna can. "Sergeant Major Guy George died of his wounds. Pike arrived shortly after the explosion and provided immediate damage control. Due to the sensitive and urgent nature of the discussions between Haider al-Attiya and Secretary Billings, I had briefed Pike on the current meeting with Secretary Billings and deployed him immediately to do what he could. He knew about CIA case officer involvement, and he evacuated Carly Ramirez for cover purposes."

Kerry Bostwick, the director of the CIA, said, "I appreciate that. Her being there would have only complicated things with the authorities."

Alexander Palmer said, "Other injuries? Was Sergeant Major George the only one hit?"

"Haider's friend, a man introduced as Khalid, apparently received a slight cut to his forehead, but he and the other man fled the scene, refusing treatment."

President Warren said, "And our exposure?"

Kurt knew that question was coming and had spent the majority of the last twenty-four hours mitigating disaster. "So far, we are okay, but it's tenuous. The press is calling it an attack against the United States secretary of state, since he'd left there seconds before. The problem is that the IED was embedded in an Audi rented by Haider al-Attiya."

"So he's going to be linked? Charged with this?"

"Not with some luck. I had the Taskforce computer network operations cell manipulate the rental data for that car—basically erase it. And we did it messily, so they'd know it was hacked, trying to make it look like it was preplanned. The strike wasn't a suicide attack, so we hope it'll look like someone covering his tracks. The rental agency is a high-end one, not like a Hertz. You arrange your car, and it's delivered to you. This vehicle was delivered to the Athenaeum Hotel as a two-package deal for two different customers, with both given to the valet. There is a risk that someone in the chain will remember who that car was for, but Haider al-Attiya was never physically seen or contacted, and there are now no physical or virtual records. The only man the valet saw was the driver that Carly met, after the car was delivered. It's not perfect, but there's enough smoke to diffuse things."

President Warren said, "That *does* sound a bit tenuous."

"Best we can do, but we expect the Greeks will have a preconceived notion of where to look for villains, and it'll probably be along local lines. It won't be with the Qatar Investment Authority if they want to keep the money flowing. There are a couple of loose points, though."

"What?"

Kurt said, "Carly, for one. She's not a risk, but I took the liberty to have Pike read her onto the program. She's made a bunch of leaps in her head, I'm sure, and most probably aren't correct. She's damn near become a member of the Taskforce anyway with her help, and honestly she's pretty good at what she does."

In a small bit of humor, Kerry said, "Always cherry-picking my talent. I can see where this is going."

Kurt said, "Just trying to plug the holes."

Kerry looked at President Warren. "Sir?"

"Yeah, that's fine. Read her on, but also have her sign the usual nondisclosures."

"The read-on's complete. The nondisclosures will have to wait. Pike doesn't travel with them."

The president waved his hand, indicating that was minutia. "What else?"

"Haider al-Attiya and his cohorts. They need to be told to shut the hell up and get out of the country. I'm assuming Billings has control of them, correct?"

Palmer said, "Yeah, he didn't even realize the attack had occurred until way later. His meeting went according to plan. Haider's agreed to go to Oslo and has the timeline. There were some issues with visas, but Billings says he can handle it."

Kurt said, "Okay, then, let him press about how he's going out on a limb to protect them, then put a gag on them. Cover their tracks and get them out of Greece. I don't care what they think they know, Billings needs to shut them down."

He paused for effect, then said, "Unless you want to throw Haider and his guys to the wolves. That would save me some Alpha mission work with Pike. We could let the Greek authorities tear those assholes apart. They'll find the terrorist connections and use Guy George's attack to hang 'em as an assault against the secretary of state. But I doubt Billings will go along with that."

Palmer said, "You still think they've got something to do with Guy's brother's death? After how crazy Guy acted?"

"I can't prove anything at this stage, but yes. I actually think it's more than that. What I know is that a man who was one of the most highly trained terrorist hunters on the planet believed it, even if he went rogue to prove it, and—besides that new driver—all of those assholes are on a target package from Afghanistan."

Palmer said, "Well, we'll go with your first option. We can't have them talking about rogue American super ninjas trying to kill them under a Greek interrogation."

Kurt said, "Why would they talk about that? They have no idea. I mean, Billings never said anything about Guy to his friends, right?"

President Warren raised his hand and said, "We're not going to revisit that. I talked to Billings and he denied telling Haider anything. That's enough for me. And that means it's enough for you. Understood?"

Kurt bit back a retort, only saying, "Yes, sir."

Alexander Palmer said, "And we need to discuss the Alpha authority Pike was given. With Guy George dead, there's no reason to continue pursuing it."

Kurt said, "What are you talking about? Nothing's changed with Haider al-Attiya. Yeah, Billings can run his little ego boost in Oslo, but our exploration is based on evidence of future planning. Not on bringing in Guy George."

He went from face to face, and felt a sickening realization. He said, "Right?" He looked at the president and said, "Right, sir? You didn't give me Alpha as a ploy, did you? Tell me you didn't make me lie to Pike."

President Warren said, "No, of course not, but all operations are predicated on the environment. We're going to need to evaluate the current atmosphere within Greece and perhaps revisit Alpha at a later date. Those Arabs are not an imminent threat worth forcing potential compromise. We've done enough in Greece."

"Sir, that's not true. Pike has nothing at all to do with any of this. He's not involved in the attack or any of Billings's meetings. He's not tied into anything, and not a risk of compromise."

"Kurt, enough. We'll make a decision at the Oversight Council meeting in two days. I'm not going to use this forum for something that should be an Oversight Council discussion."

Kurt remained quiet, understanding the intent, but not wanting it voiced out loud. Saving himself an out.

President Warren continued, "But speaking of Guy, where do we stand with him?"

"Innocent bystander caught in the blast. Nothing more. We're getting him home using the alias he had in Greece. Turned out to be a Ranger Battalion buddy that died in Iraq. When he gets here, we'll switch him back. His parents will learn of the death as a training accident."

President Warren said, "How many other siblings did he have?"

"None. Both sons are dead."

President Warren looked at the secretary of defense and said, "I want something done for the family from you. Something personal. They've lost two sons in the span of a month. We can't tell them about Guy's contributions, but I want his death to mean something."

Kurt Hale appreciated the sentiment, but not in the way President Warren intended.

Guy's death will most definitely mean something.

★ 72 ★

I closed the laptop lid and said, "So now you know who we are. What we do."

Carly said nothing, glancing at Jennifer, then at me. I said, "You'll have to sign some nondisclosure statements for the bean counters, but I don't have them here."

She finally spoke. "I've done some classified activities in my time, but this is beyond belief. I'm . . . sorry I agreed to be read on. I don't want to know about this."

I laughed and said, "Too late for that."

She said, "Pike . . . this is illegal. Signing a nondisclosure or building a snazzy briefing makes it look official, like any other covert action, but it's not." She looked at Jennifer and said, "Is this what you knew before you agreed to join?"

Jennifer said, "No. Not really. Pike sort of tricked me into joining based on our cover organization. I'd get to do scientific research, and occasionally my company would be used to enhance United States security. I joined for him, but I stayed for the mission."

I said, "Oh, bullshit. She pretends to be above it all, but you saw her in the park. She loves this shit. Yes, it's illegal, but we control the outcome. It's kept small, and we hire only the best."

Carly's face clouded over and she said, "You mean like Guy."

I said, "Yes. Like Guy."

A cycle of darkness was now between us and the death of Guy George. The aftermath had been brutal, because we had failed. It was something that would hang over my head until I laid it down for the final time.

Driving in our rental van, all of us kitted out for a hostile takedown like we were going against an imminent threat, we had planned on the move. Nobody wanted to escalate into lethal force, and we'd loaded down with nonlethal options. Guy had stated he'd start shooting the minute he saw us, but I didn't think that would be the case. At least I hoped it wouldn't be.

After failing to get Carly to answer her phone, I'd decided to mitigate the risk by reaching out to Guy directly. I'd had the Taskforce spoof Carly's number, and was talking to him on the phone when we rounded the final mountain bend to Delphi. I could see the parking spots about a mile ahead, the thin road threading the side of a ridgeline and bulging out in front of the archeological site.

During the conversation, I was growing confident that Guy would stand down. I could hear it in his voice. Then, the discussion went south, his final words chilling. We were close enough to see the explosion, and arrived within a minute of its going off, the staff of the museum and random tourists just starting to react.

We pulled up in a rush, the man I'd fought in the park passing by, running the other way and looking back, a cut over his left eye bleeding freely. We leapt out, but there was nothing to be done. Carly was cradling Guy's body, and he was destroyed. Carly was covered in blood, and I wasn't sure if it was hers or Guy's. The place turned into chaos, like an anthill kicked over, with people screaming and running back and forth.

Without words, the team deployed into a security perimeter and Brett, our designated medic, ran to the side of the car. He took one look at Guy and turned to Carly, breaking her away. He found her to be physically okay, and we loaded her into the van. Knuckles had the presence of mind to scoop up a pistol lying on the ground next to Guy's body, but that was all we could recover. We drove off, masked by the confusion.

Leaving Guy's body behind.

I'd called the Taskforce immediately, giving them a SITREP and passing the pictures of the vehicle Guy had destroyed. I'd then debriefed Carly on the drive back, and learned that Guy had sacrificed himself to save her.

In the end, I'd been right. Someone was going to die at Guy's hands, and there hadn't been a damn thing I could do to stop it.

Kurt had called back within five minutes, and I walked him through everything I knew. The conversation was short and clinical, like describing a failed science experiment instead of the death of someone we both considered family. It ended with him telling me to sterilize Guy's hotel room and to read on Carly, getting her under control.

Using Guy's historical trace, I'd ordered Knuckles and Nick to track down his hotel room, sterilize it, then maintain eyes on for a night to see who else showed up. I decided reading on Carly to our operations could wait. She had been through a significant event, and her mental state took priority.

I'd let her call in to work, going secure on her phone and telling her boss what had occurred. Needless to say, it was a long conversation, the station having already heard of the incident, and losing their mind over the implications. When she'd hung up, she told me Secretary Billings was fine and that the two men from the museum had somehow linked up with him. Her voice sounded like it was business as usual, but her eyes were hollow. I refused to let her leave.

We'd spent the night talking, just letting her get her feelings out. Brett surreptitiously monitored her, with Jennifer and I providing a sounding board. At one point, she'd demanded to know what we were about. I'd told her to wait, that it wasn't worth the effort now. All we needed to discuss was Guy. And Decoy.

Eventually, Brett had given her a sedative, and I'd given her my bed. I sent Jennifer to Nick's room, and I slept on the couch.

In the morning, she had seemed much more herself, stating she had to get back to work—reports to write, people to talk to—and I knew I couldn't stop her with just my incredible persona, but I had a briefing that might.

And, boy, did it ever.

She stared at my laptop screen and said, "Who else knows about the Taskforce?"

"That's a little tricky. We have plenty of shell companies and cover organizations—doctors, boat drivers, pilots, that sort of thing—but very few are read on to the whole program. They know they're doing something classified for the government, but they're either working under a cover within a cover or are just doing it blindly because it's helping out national security."

I saw her face and said, "Don't look like you're shocked. You do the same damn thing. The Oversight Council, of course, knows all, as do the Operators. And now you."

She said, "Why are you telling me this? I really don't

want to know. This thing is a gross violation of everything I've ever learned. It's exactly what we laugh about when we hear the conspiracies about the CIA. Do you know how many congressional committees I've had to testify in front of on things that were benign? This would cause a complete meltdown. The destruction of the presidential administration."

"Yeah, I know. Believe me, I know. That's why Guy going rogue was so important."

"But why me? If nobody else knows about it?"

"Because of your position and your support on past operations. You had to know we were something different when you saw Decoy and Knuckles in action in Peru. We've read on a few others who have been involved in operations unwittingly."

I paused, then smiled. "But only if Kurt wants to recruit them."

Carly shook her head, saying, "Don't tell me a read-on means recruitment. No way. Decoy's dead. And now Guy." She looked me in the eye and said, "You talk about this organization as if it's ironclad do-gooders, but Guy almost killed me. Because he was on a vendetta."

Jennifer spoke up. "Hey, wait a minute. I wouldn't be here if I thought this organization was evil. Like you, I had my doubts, but you have no right to judge. Guy was wrong, no doubt, and I wanted to bring him in, but he was onto something."

"What do you mean?"

I said, "We've been given authority to explore the relationships of those three assholes doing business with Secretary Billings. Guy was convinced they were involved in his brother's death in Afghanistan, and when he was hunting them, he found what he said was evidence of further terrorist activity."

"Then why is Secretary Billings dealing with them? You just told me he was a member of the Oversight Council. Don't tell me *you're* rogue as well."

"No, Billings knows what we're doing. Why that jerk-off is continuing is beyond me. He's always had his head up his ass, convinced he knows more than anyone else."

She squinted her eyes, not liking me disparaging a cabinet official. She clearly hadn't had to deal with him in an official capacity. I backed off, saying, "Okay, okay. He's using them to help stabilize the Greek economy and apparently thinks they'll help with some peace overtures in Afghanistan. He thinks he's Henry Kissinger dealing with Black September in Lebanon at the same time they're blowing up Israelis. Nobody believes they're an imminent threat, but the bottom line is we still have Alpha authority."

She had another question, but before she could broach it, the door to our room opened.

★ 73 ★

Knuckles barged in, about to blurt something out, then saw Carly. Nick said nothing, shifting from foot to foot, still the new guy. Exasperated, I said, "And?"

Knuckles said, "And we're clean. We policed up some electrical components and other odds and ends, including a box of Russian ammo, so I guess that nails down who owns the 6P9. We left his clothes and other travel stuff, only taking anything compromising."

"Anyone show?"

"Yeah. Took a while, but they've obviously identified the body. Some beat cops came in, then a guy that looked like he was from the US Embassy. Nothing spiked. Looked like a standard investigation, so we let 'em go."

"That's fine. Did you find anything of value?"

Knuckles glanced at Carly again and I said, "She was just read on. You're not hiding anything anymore."

He grinned and said, "Good, because I was about to blow a gasket without being able to say anything. We got the safe-deposit key, and Guy's research to track it down. We know the bank, and we've got all of his digital photos he's taken. He was right. Those fucksticks are into some bad shit. I don't know what, but he wasn't kidding about that new man." He nodded at Carly, saying, "The one you said was driving? Guy's got photos of him getting a ton of cash and new identification. On the island of Crete. How much do you know about him?"

She started to answer, and my phone rang with the peculiar ringtone telling me it was a secure call. The rest of the team heard it and knew what it was as well. They looked at me like a pack of hounds tracking a guy waving bacon.

I answered, then mouthed, *Kurt*.

"Hey, sir, I was just about to send you a report. Knuckles just got back."

"Let's have it."

"First, looks like Guy's alias is holding up. Knuckles watched the room overnight, and it's not spiked with anyone other than local forces."

"Well, that's good news. From our end, keeping him as a tragic victim is shaky."

"Nothing bad seen from this end. You do your magic, and we should be good. Carly's read on to the program and good to go. She's headed back to work to answer any further questions, but from her end, Secretary Billings's meeting with Haider al-Attiya was kept out of the attack. His two friends managed to escape without getting rolled up."

Kurt said, "Yeah, I know. I just got out of a briefing with the principals. Billings is headed to Oslo, Norway, and he's taking all three of those guys with him."

"You're shitting me."

"Nope. He's even managed to convince the president to let him put pressure on Norway's ambassador to give Haider's driver a visa for Oslo. Apparently, that guy's Haider's go-to man for Afghanistan."

"Sir, that's the second thing I wanted to talk to you about. We've sterilized Guy's hotel room, and we have digital proof that that 'driver' got his documentation in Crete days ago. He's not some genius on Afghanistan politics."

"Pike, anything that Guy came up with is not going to sway Billings. The man was running crazy."

"Well, tell him to buckle the fuck up, then, because I've got a key to a safe-deposit box, and what's inside isn't going to be good news for his friends."

"Pike. I need you to start looking at exfil options. Prepare to come home."

I said nothing for a second, not sure I'd heard correctly. "What? We're on an operational mission here. Yeah, Guy's dead, but we got Alpha before that. And it's *because* Guy's dead that I'm continuing. He saved Carly's life. Did you know that? In the end, he had a pretty fucking good trap, and Secretary Billings screwed it up. Guy gave his life to fix what he'd done wrong. He's going to go down in history as evil, but he's onto evidence about those guys, and I'm rooting that shit out."

"I hear you . . . Pike, they're going to pull Alpha authority. Shit, they've actually already done so. I just chose to not hear it."

"What's that mean?"

"President Warren said they wanted to revisit the Alpha authority at the next Oversight Council meeting. He meant he wanted me to stop all activities, then put it back up to a vote to reauthorize it, if they agreed. Which they won't."

I saw where he was going, giving me an out. "But he didn't say that, did he? He didn't *say* that he was rescinding Alpha *until* the vote, did he?"

I heard nothing but breathing, and I knew my friend

Colonel Kurt Hale was about to step into Pike land. I said, "Sir?"

"No. He didn't say that, explicitly."

"So we have until the Oversight Council meeting before they can rescind it, right?"

Nothing.

"Right, sir?"

"Yeah. I guess that's right."

I broke into a smile. "When's the meeting?"

"Two days. You don't have anything in two days, and you're done."

"Oh, I'll have something. Don't think I can't read between the lines here. Those fucks gave you Alpha just to bring in Guy. They played with Taskforce loyalty to get what they wanted."

"Pike, that's not true. They're just making decisions based on the information they have. There's a lot at stake here with Greece and Afghanistan."

"Oh, bullshit, sir. They're looking at the benefit of these guys like a neighborhood looking at the good the Mafia does, conveniently forgetting the murders. Guy was right. And we still do what's right, don't we?"

I saw Carly staring at me intently. I turned away. She might be read on, but she didn't need to hear the inside baseball of what life in the Taskforce was really like.

Kurt said, "Pike, you get me something in two days, or we're done. Guy's sacrifice will mean nothing."

I said, "Easy day, sir. They can forget about his brother, but I'm not forgetting about Guy."

I hung up and everyone looked at me, waiting. I said, "We have two days."

Knuckles said, "Two days to do what?"

"Rob a bank."

★ 74 ★

Khalid flipped through the Afghan passport, seeing nothing but the new visa for Norway. He said, "Sabour Jarden. A Pashtun name. What city?"

Sipping tea and eating a fig, Sabour said, "I'm from Palmyra, Syria."

"But we were given this name for the passport. Specifically given *this* name. Why?"

Sabour smiled and said, "I don't know. I guess because we were going to Afghanistan. My first name is Sabour, but Jarden is made up. A tribal name."

Khalid laughed and said, "How on earth were you supposed to infiltrate anything in Afghanistan?"

Sabour set his tea down, a movement made delicate by his long fingers. Khalid thought everything he did was delicate, like a bird. He was slight, with a sad smile perpetually on his face, and so far had not questioned a single thing, as if he had completely given his fate over to others. A fact that intrigued Khalid.

Sabour said, "I was the only one in our camp that had ever been to Afghanistan. I spent a year in Gardez."

"And now you're with us in Oslo instead. Do you have any doubts?"

The sad smile slipped out again. "No. Allah has chosen me for a great mission. I go where he tells me to go."

Khalid laughed again and said, "You believe Allah is speaking through Haider and his father?"

"Yes. Do you not?"

When Khalid didn't answer, Sabour said, "Why are you here, if not for the caliphate?"

The question was confusing, precisely because Khalid had never really given it any thought. In the end, simple anger drove him forward. He was not seeking anything more than to prove his own self-worth. He wanted to be like Sharif, a self-made man, and so he continued leveraging Haider for a lost cause of tribal affiliation. He was Muslim, of course, but other than its providing an outlet for his hatred of the West, he'd never really given Islam or the caliphate much reflection.

Khalid said, "I do what I do for my own reasons. I'm curious about you, though. You know what you're here for, right?"

He didn't say it out loud, as if the fact that Sabour's success involved giving his life was somehow not to be verbalized.

"Yes. Of course."

"And you have no qualms? No fear?"

The smile appeared and left, like a shadow. "Of course not. All I am doing is moving on to something greater. I'm leaving this mortal land for paradise. Most must endure a lifetime before entry, but I will be granted access by virtue of my sacrifice."

Khalid nodded as if he understood, but he didn't. Haider's phone rang, and Khalid picked it up, seeing the country code for Qatar. He knew who it was, and expected the usual excoriation from Sharif. He was pleasantly surprised.

"Where is my son?"

"Sir, he's with the secretary of state. They're talking about the peace meetings."

"Good, good. You are the one I wanted to talk with anyway. You had no trouble getting into Oslo with the *shahid*?"

The statement confused Khalid, but he didn't let it show in his voice. "No. Secretary Billings took care of his entry, just as you said would happen."

"And Haider knows the meeting location?"

"Not yet. He's finding out now . . . sir, what did you mean, you wanted to talk to me?"

"Write this down." Khalid grabbed a pen, and Sharif relayed an address in the Gronland section of Oslo. He had Khalid repeat it, then said, "That is an automobile shop in the city near the Islamic Cultural Center. The men there will give you the keys to a Range Rover. You will bring it back to the *shahid*."

"Yes, sir. Do I pay them?"

"No. They have been well compensated. But you will go alone."

Khalid's instincts kicked in at the words. Sharif had shown him only scorn in the past, so if he wanted Khalid to go alone, there was a reason, and it probably involved protecting his son. He said, "I'll need the *shahid* to learn. I'll take him with me."

"You can teach him when you get back. You go alone. There will be a man named Abdul-Haq, and he'll also provide you weapons for emergencies. I want you to use them on him."

Khalid said nothing. Sharif said, "Khalid, can you do this?"

"Why?"

"He is a link. A weakness. I want him removed to protect the mission."

Khalid didn't respond. Sharif continued, "Khalid, you have shown a willingness to do what's necessary, and an intelligence to get it done. You killed in Afghanistan, correct? That's what Haider tells me."

"Yes. I did."

"The Americans? You killed the one they captured?"

"Yes."

"And you survived the attack in Greece without panicking. Haider said the *shahid* was a bundle of nerves afterward, but you were in control. Is this true?"

"I guess . . ."

"Khalid, Haider does not have it in him. If I send him, he will fail. You do this, and you will become my second son."

Khalid could not believe the words. The promise it held. He said, "Are you toying with me?"

"No. I mean what I say."

"Okay, sir. It will be done."

Sharif disconnected and Khalid set the phone on the table, lost in thought. The door to the room opened, and Haider entered.

The first words out of his mouth were, "Sabour, never, ever speak to the secretary again. He's starting to question."

Sabour nodded and Khalid said, "From the plane?"

"Yes. From the plane flight."

After takeoff, the first thing Secretary Billings had done was question the attack at Delphi, playacting as if he had no idea why it had occurred and ensuring they knew that the United States had protected them by eliminating their connection to the Audi. No mention was made of the man who'd died, Secretary Billings acting as if he were the innocent bystander proclaimed by the press.

Khalid had thought it was ludicrous, as both of them knew it was the work of the United States, but for whatever reason, Secretary Billings preferred to pretend. As long as he kept facilitating their mission, Khalid would let it go. Especially since the man who'd been hunting them was now dead.

Eventually, the talk turned to the meetings, and Secretary Billings had given Sabour a greeting in Pashto. When Sabour had simply looked at him, Billings had asked where he was from, in English. Haider had translated into Arabic, and, puzzled, Billings had asked why he was using that language instead of Pashto. Thinking fast, Haider had said he didn't speak Pashto, and Sabour didn't speak English, so they would use Arabic to talk. Billings had taken that in, and then asked questions about the Taliban sects and the fractures after the death of Mullah Omar.

Haider had pretended to hold a conversation with Sabour, then gave out general platitudes. Not satisfied with the answers, Billings had probed deeper. Eventually, when the answers remained shallow, Billings had quit asking, looking as if he were doubting Sabour's expertise. Khalid had redirected the conversation to the attack at Delphi, and Secretary Billings became recalcitrant, no longer eager to talk. They flew the rest of the way in silence.

Khalid said, "Is it going to be an issue?"

Haider waved his hand and took a seat, looking out at the Oslo cityscape. "No. He just thinks I'm stupid for bringing Sabour. He doesn't suspect us of anything."

"Where are the talks? Here, in the city?"

"No. They're in the old town of Fredrikstad, about an hour and a half away. He's got some work here in Oslo tomorrow, then we'll travel down the day after tomorrow. He asked if we wanted to go with him in his vehicles."

"And what did you say?"

"What do you think? I said we had our own vehicle arranged by the QIA. Any word on that from my father?"

"Yes. I pick up the car tomorrow. By myself."

★ 75 ★

Jennifer ate the last of her Clif Bar and wadded up the wrapper, tucking it into a pouch attached to her hip. She checked the time, seeing it had crawled past eleven p.m. She clicked her radio and said, "Pike, Pike, this is Koko. I'm ready to move. Does Creed have control yet?"

"He's getting there. Hang on. It's taking some additional work."

She shifted on her metal I-beam, biting back a retort. She knew everyone else was on the net, and it wouldn't do to snap at Pike. Even though he deserved it.

Four hours, my ass. Which is what Pike had said. She'd been stuck up in the ceiling above the ladies' toilet for close to ten hours, smelling grease and hearing toilets flush, holding her breath every time the door opened. Things had slowed down after five, and then had begun to crawl by seven, but Pike refused to let her leave until Creed—their magic little hacker—could penetrate the internal security cameras for the bank, in effect giving her fair warning as she moved about. Irritated, she whispered, "I thought Creed said that damn slave device was going to alleviate all of this hacking work?"

Earlier, as soon as she'd entered through the ceiling tiles, she'd found a bundle of fiber-optic lines running through the space between the floors, and, guided by Creed, she'd spliced into one with a digital slave device that was supposed to make penetration easy.

Pike said, "It is, it is. According to Creed, without it, we wouldn't stand a chance of breaking encryption. He's working it. Just a little longer."

Little longer. I should have taken Knuckles's job. Let him do this.

She and Knuckles had entered the huge Alpha Bank complex between Panepistimiou and Stadiou Streets, near the university and the national library, ostensibly to rent a safe-deposit box. This, of course, they did, but their true purpose was twofold: one, determine the layout of the bank, to include the safe-deposit room, and two, for Jennifer to remain behind, setting up the escape.

After filling out the necessary forms in the old granite wing of the bank, they'd traveled four floors underground, to the vault area. Accompanied by a bank manager the entire time, they'd passed through a giant vault door like one seen on a movie set, and another steel cage door, then entered the safe-deposit-box room. The manager had given them a quick tour, then showed them their box. He'd turned one key and Knuckles the other, withdrawing the box. The manager had given them privacy at that point, whereupon they'd placed exactly nothing in the steel container.

They'd repeated the trip back to the first floor, thanking the manager and heading on their way. As soon as he was out of sight, Jennifer had split off. Knuckles had exited, and Jennifer had walked to the elevator. She took it to the fourth floor, entering a small lobby and seeing a closed double door with a keycard reader mounted on the wall. To the right was a pair of restrooms, one for men and one for women, just as Creed had said.

From her purse, she pulled out a device the size of a US quarter and peeled off a strip of paper, exposing adhesive tape. She'd pretended to try opening the door while sticking the device on the side of the key reader. Feigning disgust at not being able to enter, she'd then "gone to the bathroom."

She'd been hiding ever since.

Pike came back on, "Koko, Koko, you ready?"

"Is that a joke? Yes."

"Okay. You're a go. We have God's eye of the place. It looks empty on your floor. Some security below, but nothing with you."

She came close to saying, *Yeah, I heard them all leave,* but didn't.

Pike continued, "You've got a camera on the northeast corner near the elevator. When you leave the restroom, hug the wall. It's got the door in view, but not the reader. You'll be on camera for a second, but that can't be helped. Once you're through the first door, there's another camera midway down. It's focused on the offices, but I can see the edge of the server room door. I don't want to see you on that one."

She started slinking toward the tiles she'd used to get into the ceiling, saying, "You won't."

"Let me rephrase. Creed only got access to the feed. He hasn't penetrated the system yet. If you're on them, you're getting recorded."

She removed the tiles, hung for a minute in the dark, then dropped to the floor of the bathroom. She said, "Tell him he's no longer on my favorites list. That'll get some work out of him."

Replacing the tiles, she heard nothing from her ear-piece, then Brett came on. "Jeez, Jennifer, you're getting cold and crusty for so little time here. Pike wouldn't be so harsh."

She smiled and crept to the door. "Okay, okay, don't beat him up. He's still my favorite. But I'd really like to know if there are any motion detectors. Can he help with that?"

Pike said, "Yeah, he's got them, and they're all on the ground floor, where the bank is. Nothing on your floor."

She peeked out the door and said, "He's back on my list. You can tell him that."

She heard the aggravation in Pike's voice even through the radio signal. "Would you screw all that 'list' shit and get on with the mission?"

She slipped out the door with a real grin breaking out, realizing Pike was right. She *did* love this stuff.

Brett said, "Pike, I think when you say 'screw all this list shit,' that's what she meant. It gives Creed hope."

She slid down the wall, her back to it, eyes on the northeast corner. She said, "Moving."

Pike came on. "Everyone clear the net. Clear the net. No more jokes."

She reached the keycard access and peeled away the device. She heard Brett say, "Man, talk about no hu-mor . . . ," then Pike, "Clear. The. Net."

She said, "About to attempt entry. Brett, you ready?"

"Yep. Engine's running. You call, I'll be waiting, but you still have to get out."

"Roger all."

She held the small device to her phone, waiting on it to register with the cards that had used the key reader while she was hiding in the ceiling.

The majority of keycard readers used throughout the

world were fairly secure, with massive encryption designed to prevent anyone from hacking the system, but most used a protocol that had a glaring flaw when the card actually talked to the reader. Since the distance was literally inches, it hadn't been seen as a problem when the protocol was designed in the late '90s. But like everything in the modern world, build a vulnerability and the hackers will come.

Her little device, based off something called a BLEkey, intercepted the communications between the card and the reader in the nanosecond they talked, then translated the key. You couldn't get the information from the reader without a two-thousand-year brute-force attack, and you couldn't get it from the card, but when the two talked, it was as if they were speaking unsecure. All she had to do was download the results to her phone and she'd now have access.

Theoretically.

The downside was that if this was one of the few that had mitigated such attacks, the card reader would know it and would send an alarm when she tried to penetrate. Which is where Brett came in.

She saw the algorithm register in her phone, then manipulated an app. It asked if she wanted to duplicate, and she tapped yes, then held the phone to the card reader.

The light went from red to green. She was in.

She pushed open the door and slid down the wall, stopping short of the first door on the left. In the dim light of the hallway, she saw the dome camera Pike had mentioned. She leaned forward and touched her phone to the keycard reader outside the door. It flashed green. Before turning the handle, she manipulated the screen of her app, bringing up a separate protocol. She turned the handle, opened the door, then touched the card reader with her phone again.

The light switched off.

She entered a room full of blinking servers, fiber-optic cables, and other mishmash, a short hallway leading off in the darkness. She keyed her radio and said, "I'm in. Keycard reader to this room is down."

She heard the relief in Pike's voice. "Good job. Saw you enter the hallway, but no reaction from security. They missed it. Let me know if Creed's floor plan is correct. Everything hinges on that."

She said, "Roger," and put on a small Petzl headlamp, the tiny LEDs barely illuminating the hallway. She went down it slowly, finally ending at a dead end, a large access panel held in place by wing nuts to her front, looking as if it was used for the HVAC system. It wasn't.

She unscrewed the wing nuts, removed the panel, and was staring down a giant shaft, multiple cables running up through the center of the space.

She said, "It's good. I'm looking into the south elevator shaft. I can execute."

Brett said, "Roger all, Koko. I'll let Creed know he gets a favor from you. Can I roll?"

She smiled and said, "Let Creed know he did well. Nothing more. And yeah, you can roll."

Pike came on. "Koko, get some sleep. You got the hard job. We'll be coming in between noon and one, whenever the crowd's the largest."

She said, "Roger that. More Clif Bars for breakfast."

"I'll buy you a steak dinner. If we actually make it out of there."

The words reminded her that this wasn't all fun and games.

★ 76 ★

Khalid folded his napkin and saw that Haider was conflicted by Sharif's demand that he travel alone to retrieve the vehicle, but also knew that Haider's father understood the same thing that Khalid had in Afghanistan: Haider wasn't a killer. He wanted to impress his father, but he didn't understand the sacrifice expected.

Haider was not cut from the same cloth as his father. He was anointed as a son by simple fate, but Khalid understood that having a name didn't mean one was worthy to wear it. He had none, and yet Haider's own father saw the difference. A name indicated nothing about the true essence of a man, but in his world, it held a power like none other. And he was going to earn one.

Khalid said, "Haider, I told you. Your father wants to protect you. I'm expendable. I get the car and bring it back. You wait here. It's what he wanted."

"Why didn't he tell me this? Why did he give you the order directly?"

"You told me to wait for his call. You were in a meeting. He called. That's all it is."

Khalid saw the suspicion blossom and said, "Haider, I'm with you. I'm with your father. I am dedicated to the mission."

"That's what concerns me. You never liked my father before. You called him one more bloated citizen. You talked me into going to Afghanistan *because* my father said it was a bad idea."

Khalid said, "We all learn. We grow. Let me get the car, and quit worrying about things that don't matter. You have to see the secretary today. Let that be your focus. Let me do what your father asked."

Haider squeezed the napkin in his fist, then threw it into the middle of his breakfast. Khalid sat still, waiting. Knowing that Sharif was right. Haider did not have it in him to fight.

Haider fumed, glancing around to see if anyone had seen his actions, then said, "You'll bring the car here, right?"

Khalid said, "Yes. Of course I'll bring it here. Why would you ask that? We are brothers."

Haider said nothing, waving him to the door. Khalid left the hotel out the side exit, on foot, not caring anymore about Haider's feelings. He was on a new path, and if that meant pushing Haider out of the way, so be it.

The cold slapped him as soon as the door closed, a light dusting of snow coating the streets. He shivered and tightened his overcoat, cursing under his breath. He looked at his map, then began walking. In minutes he'd left behind the pure Norwegian world of Oslo and entered the new reality of Gronland. An area densely packed with immigrants from a variety of Muslim countries, it had become a hotbed of tension between the newly arrived and the native Norwegian population. While the same snow fell here, it was a small microcosm that resembled Beirut more than Oslo, with the same fault lines.

Layered underneath the conflict with the government

was a battle between radical and moderate Islam, with most immigrants wanting nothing more than to live their lives, but a small minority espoused fanatical views that were vocal enough to seem to represent them all.

In 2014, one such group threatened a new 9/11 if Gronland weren't made into a Sharia state ruled by the Quran. Their manifesto proclaimed, "Bar this city quarter and let us control it the way we wish to do it. This is the best for both parts. We do not wish to live with dirty beasts like you."

It was a mere ten blocks from his hotel, but a universe away culturally, with women wearing niqabs and children in head scarves because of belief rather than the weather.

Truthfully, he felt more comfortable the deeper he penetrated. He passed by the Islamic Cultural Center and saw his garage at the end of the road.

Located in a small spit of parking lot with a roll-up door, it was sandwiched between two more respectable establishments, one selling secondhand clothes and the other plying halal grocery products.

He went to the door on the right and rang the bell. A teen answered, his effort at toughness belied by his pathetic attempt to grow a beard. Khalid said, "I'm looking for Abdul-Haq."

He heard a voice deeper in asking in Arabic who was at the door. The teen answered, and an older man of about sixty came down the hall. Khalid said, "Abdul-Haq?"

"Yes."

"I'm from Sharif al-Attiya. I believe you have a vehicle and some other items for me."

Abdul sent the teen away and opened the door. Khalid entered, and Abdul said, "How is Sharif?"

"He's fine."

"I haven't seen him since our time in Afghanistan. He

has done well for himself. I was surprised to get the request. I would not think he would want to soil his hands with such direct engagements."

Khalid was taken aback at the connection, and realized why Sharif wanted him to eliminate the man. He was making sure nothing led back to him, and he was willing to kill a friend to do so. The fact spoke volumes about Sharif's commitment, and far from causing Khalid to wonder about Sharif's loyalty to follow through on his pledge to Khalid, it made him more resolute. He would need to be as strong as Sharif if he were to earn the right to work by his side.

They entered a small bay with a late-model Range Rover filling it. Abdul said, "Here it is, and it's a work of art. The explosives are double sealed in the fuel tank. Not even a trained canine will detect them."

He opened the driver's-side door and leaned in, reaching beneath the seat. He pulled out a metal container the size of a cigarette box. In the center was a spring-loaded hinge. He flicked it open, revealing a metal on-off toggle switch and a button.

Abdul said, "It's simplicity itself. One, flick the switch to on. Two, press the button. That's it."

Khalid said, "Nothing else?"

Abdul closed the protective cover. "No. Sharif said he wanted it simple and direct. There are no timers or anything else. Obviously, someone will have to be in the vehicle to detonate, and the ignition must be turned on."

"How big will the explosion be?"

"It will obliterate the car, that's for sure. Anyone near it will be killed. Speaking of which, the only way someone will suspect anything is by the fuel gauge. The tank now holds only five gallons, but will show full. If you run out of gas, it will look strange."

Khalid said, "And the weapons?"

Abdul went around to the rear, opening the hatchback. He rolled a section of the carpet away, revealing a hidden container set into the body of the vehicle. He opened it, and Khalid saw two folding-stock AK-47s and a Czech CZ 75 pistol.

Khalid withdrew one of the AKs and cycled the action, making sure it functioned. He did the same with the pistol and Abdul said, "You have experience with this, I see."

He replaced the weapons and said, "A little. I understand payment has already been made?"

"Yes. I won't ask what you intend to do with these weapons, but give Sharif my support. If he is involved in this directly, I'm sure it is something important."

Khalid closed the hatchback, then rotated until Abdul was between him and the vehicle. He said, "I will, I promise," then wrapped his arms around Abdul's neck, jerking backward sharply.

Abdul's eyes bulged and Khalid felt his neck snap, then smelled a foul odor as Abdul's bowels released. Khalid gently laid him on the floor.

He knelt next to the body and yelled for the teen, saying Abdul needed him. The youth sauntered in, all bluster and bad attitude, then saw Abdul.

His face registered shock and he ran to the body, shouting, "What happened?"

Khalid waited for him to kneel down, then said, "I killed him."

It was the last thing the boy ever heard.

★ 77 ★

Sitting on a park bench across from the main entrance to the commercial section of the Alpha Bank, Knuckles said, "Doesn't look like the noon rush is what we thought it would be."

I said, "Yeah. I hear you. I wanted more folks than this, but I guess nobody goes to the bank anymore after the shutdowns last summer."

I wanted a crowd of people inside to generate a lot of press, with folks running to the nearest TV camera to breathlessly detail the insane American inside. But it didn't look like I was going to get it.

Knuckles said, "Want to initiate now, or wait a bit?"

"Let's give it a couple more minutes. Maybe the lunch crowd shows up later than in America."

"We wait too long and Jennifer's going to need some more Clif Bars."

"Yeah, I know." Truthfully, I was feeling the pressure of our plan, and wasn't so sure I wanted to initiate. It was borderline insane.

Knuckles had rented the safe-deposit box yesterday, wearing some Hollywood makeup, with his nose longer, his cheeks stuffed with cotton, and a cheesy handlebar mustache. He had it on again today for his little play, and it made him look ugly. He was no longer the hot hippie SEAL.

For my part, I had on a wig of rat-tailed hair, a soiled ball cap on top of the matted mess, and dark sunglasses. In my case, I *wanted* to look like an Occupy Wall Street hipster.

Knuckles said, "I sit out here much longer, and my glue is going to start peeling off."

I laughed and said, "Just make sure your squibs are ready to fire."

He said, "The squibs will fire just fine, but damn, this sounded a hell of a lot easier in the hotel room. Looking at the size of this place now gives me a little pause."

"It's still the same plan. Doesn't matter how big the bank is; all we need to do is get to the elevator and get underground."

He was right about the size. This branch of the Alpha Bank was huge. It took up a whole block between Panepistimiou and Stadiou Streets, five stories tall, with a myriad of offices handling everything from venture capital to insurance concerns. The commercial branch on Stadiou Street was built of modern glass and stone, grafted onto the rest of the bank's old architecture stretching north to Panepistimiou.

The problem we had was that we needed to get into the safe-deposit box owned by the Qatar Investment Authority, but we couldn't do that without a manager's key. Two were required to open the box, and there was no way to get that key in the limited amount of time we had. Hell, I wasn't sure there was a way to do it given a year. So I'd opted for a frontal assault.

After kicking around the problem for about two hours, going back and forth, I'd decided we were looking for the wrong solution. We needed the information inside the safe-deposit box, and we were beating our heads against the wall trying to do it clandestinely. I decided a covert approach was just as good.

A clandestine operation, by definition, meant that the opposing force never knew it had occurred. A reconnaissance before an assault, a death engendered by "natural causes," or a plane crash caused by a "mechanical failure" were all clandestine. At the conclusion of the mission, nobody was any wiser that an operation had occurred, and that was exactly what we wanted here, but it was impossible.

So I'd opted to embed the clandestine part of our mission into a covert one.

The term *covert* was used ad nauseam in descriptions by the press, but it had a specific definition. It was the close cousin of *clandestine*, meaning that someone knew the action had occurred but had no idea who had done it. A coup in Guatemala where US involvement was unknown, a bridge explosively destroyed without a fingerprint from the perpetrator, or an assassination without anyone claiming credit were all covert. And that was where I decided we needed to go.

Attack the bank, knowing that the action would be all over the news, but cloak the reason for the attack within the attack itself. It was risky as hell, mainly because we couldn't hurt anyone on the mission, but it was the only solution I could find.

At the end of today, they'd definitely know we'd been inside the bank, but I didn't really care. The *why* we were inside was all I wanted to camouflage. In no way could I let word get out that we'd targeted a specific safe-deposit box, with the QIA realizing they'd been breached. That would cause all sorts of repercussions for the follow-on chase.

The biggest problem we had now was that they'd have Knuckles's and Jennifer's information on the rental of our safe-deposit box. It was all fake, of course, but a thread nonetheless. Nothing I could do about that, and it was a risk I was willing to take.

Talking about it today was a smidge of too little too late. After all, we already had Jennifer inside prepping for our escape.

I keyed the radio and said, "Koko, Koko, you a go to execute?"

She came on immediately. "This is Koko. Roger. The sooner the better. I'm ready to get out of here."

I called Nick, currently monitoring all of the video feeds and shouldering the responsibility of shutting down select ones when asked. "Veep, we still have control?"

"This is Veep. Roger. Creed's got complete control now. No record."

That was good news. The last thing I needed was to be seen on the nightly news in a grainy surveillance video.

I said, "Roger," then switched to Brett, currently hiding in a sliver of alleyway two buildings over. "Blood, Blood, you secure and ready?"

"This is Blood. Roger all. I'm tucked in tight behind a Dumpster. I can stay for a little while, but don't push it. I keep seeing folks leave the building to smoke. Sooner or later, one's going to come over to the van and ask me what I'm doing."

"Good to go. We'll be in and out in less than an hour."

Knuckles followed up with, "We hope."

I smiled. Off the net I said, "You ready?"

"Ready as I'll ever be."

"Okay. Let's rob a bank."

He stood and said, "For Guy."

I bumped his fist and said, "For Guy. See you on the inside."

He walked away without looking back. I saw him disappear from the street, going into the side entrance of the old section of Alpha Bank. I gave him a minute, then stood up, shouldering a black duffel bag. I walked toward the modern granite-and-glass structure of the commercial entrance, keying my radio.

"All elements, all elements, it's showtime."

★ 78 ★

I pulled open the glass door, noting the guards, but nobody bothered to say anything about my bag, which was good since it held a bunch of strange climbing gear. Not to mention a sawed-off shotgun.

I heard Nick say, "I got you and Knuckles. Feed's good."

"No recording?"

"No. You're clean."

There were two lines of people waiting on a teller, and I ignored them both, moving to the left where my mental map told me was a short staircase leading to the old section of the building. I went up the first small flight, then turned the corner and waited. The next flight was only about seven steps, and I could see the doorway Knuckles would pass through, as well as the elevator bank he would access to go the four floors below.

I withdrew an envelope that had POLICE written in bold block letters. It was my "manifesto," explaining why a lunatic American was causing havoc in a Greek bank. A bunch of drivel about how the rich man was getting richer and the poor man was getting poorer and how the EU was forcing austerity just like a Wall Street banker screwed over the downtrodden in the United

States. The end state was a demand for Alpha Bank to redistribute its wealth to the people. Yeah, it had enough radical craziness to make someone believe I was here for the long term.

I saw Knuckles break the plane of the door separating the old building from the new. I took a deep breath. It was time.

He was walking with the secondary bank manager—the man required to open the safe-deposit box—chatting amicably as if he didn't have a care in the world. The manager pressed the elevator call button, and I withdrew the shotgun, waiting, my breath increasing. I saw the elevator arrive, and went running up the stairs.

I reached them, wishing that the bank was much more crowded. I needed a response to what I was going to do next.

The manager finally caught my approach and turned, puzzled. I raised the shotgun barrel in the air and squeezed the trigger, the noise deafening against the marble walls. He shrieked and sank back. I heard the small crowd in the old section stir, but not nearly as much as I had wanted.

I jabbed the barrel into Knuckles's stomach, forcing him into the elevator, then grabbed the manager by the collar and jerked him in. I pressed sub-basement four and tossed out the manifesto as the doors closed.

We started down and I yelled at the manager, cuffing him in the head and calling him names straight out of the '60s. I said, "When we get to the bottom, you're going to open the vault. I know it's down there."

That was true, but I also knew he was unable to open it.

He knelt down, cowering, and said he couldn't do that. I jammed the barrel into his head and said he'd better find someone who could, because I wasn't leaving until that happened.

For his part, Knuckles just sat with his arms over his head, whimpering.

We reached the bottom and I said, "Act like nothing's wrong and get the security guard to the elevator. Screw this up, and you're dead."

I heard Nick in my earpiece. "Pike, a lot of activity, but nobody's stopped at the manifesto. They just ran through the hallway like they weren't sure where the noise came from."

Just perfect. Shit. Nobody saw me.

The manager shouted outside the elevator in Greek, and I pressed into the corner, out of sight. When the guard appeared, I stepped out, shoving the barrel in his face and shouting. I had him throw his pistol away, then turned to Knuckles. "Reach in my bag. You'll find a package of zip ties. Get them. Now!"

He did and I pressed the stop button on the elevator, leaving my bag inside. I said, "All three of you, move to the vault room."

The main vault of the bank was to the right, and the safe-deposit-box room was to the left, both behind a secondary cage. I wanted to show no interest in the safe-deposit boxes. Yet.

I had Knuckles zip-tie the two men, then himself, both the ankles and the wrists. In my earpiece, I heard Nick say, "Koko, Koko, climbing kit is in place."

At the fourth-floor elevator access, Jennifer put on a pair of thick gloves, the palms and fingers reinforced with extra leather. She swung her arms back and forth twice, then lightly leapt into space, snagging the three cables that worked the elevator. She wrapped her boots together, the cable cluster in the center, and began a hand-over-hand slide down the cable.

She reached the top of the elevator and said, "On the ground. Getting gear now."

She opened the access hatch at the top and dropped into the car. She grabbed Pike's duffel bag and slung it over her shoulder, climbing back up through the access panel. Using her headlight, she withdrew three sets of peculiar-looking clamps with two long stirrups attached. She attached the first one as high as she could reach, then the other two beneath it. She tested the hold of each, then put the duffel over her shoulder.

She stood, putting a hand in each of the clamps of the first set. She pulled herself up, then slid her feet into the stirrups, standing up and letting them take her weight. She began walking up the cable, sliding one hand and bending her knee, then straightening up and repeating the process with the other hand, moving up the cable in a high-tech prusik climb.

By the time she reached the topmost ceiling of the building, she was completely winded. She paused for a moment to get her breathing under control, then grabbed the ironwork under the ceiling. She monkey-crawled to the roof access door and opened it, throwing out the duffel bag. She crossed back over, retrieved her climbing gear, then exited the door, putting her gloves in the eave to make sure it didn't lock her out.

She slung the bag and got her bearings, scanning for the path they'd researched in the satellite photos. She scrambled across the roof, running in a crouch and searching for her little alley cut. She found it after climbing and dropping over several different ventilation systems, the bank itself two buildings behind. She looked down and saw her van, Brett inside, relief flowing through her.

She tossed the duffel to the ground and pulled out three coils of thin kernmantle climbing rope, threading each around an anchor point. She laid out three harnesses by the ropes and keyed her radio.

"Exfil in place."

★ 79 ★

The bank manager had calmed down a little bit, getting his wits about him since I hadn't shot anyone yet. He said, "What do you want?"

I made sure to spray spittle with my answer, striving to look crazy. "Want? I want you to quit raping the people. I want that vault opened and the money distributed to the people, and make no mistake, I'm prepared to die for that."

He recoiled, suitably scared, then repeated, "I cannot open the safe. I'm not authorized. It's on a time-lock system, and I don't even know the times. They shift."

I turned to the security guard and withdrew the radio from his belt. I said, "You speak English?"

He shook his head no. I handed the radio to the bank manager and said, "Tell them my demands are in an envelope outside the elevators. Tell them I've booby-trapped both the stairwell and the elevator bank. Do it in English. Anyone comes down here, and you die. You say anything in Greek to indicate anything other than that, and you die."

He relayed and I made a pretense of disappearing into the vault room, turning the handle on the giant door. I returned and said, "Did you find someone to open the vault?"

"No, no. You didn't tell me to do that."

I cuffed his head and said, "Do it," then turned to Knuckles. "What are you doing here?"

He said, "Please, please. I'm just here to get into my safe-deposit box. It has some official papers."

I looked surprised and said, "You're American?"

He nodded. I said, "Rich American?"

He shook his head no. I slapped him and said, "Bullshit. Let's go see what's in your safe-deposit box."

He said, "It requires two keys."

"So?"

The manager looked stricken and I said, "Give me the other key."

He did. I cut Knuckles's ankles free and jerked him to his feet, saying, "Move."

We entered the safe-deposit room, and I pulled out the key we'd found in Guy's hotel room. I ran to box 1307 and inserted both keys. The box opened. I ripped it out, seeing three thumb drives, a wad of banknotes, a bank ledger, and four or five passport shells. I began taking photos of the passports and the ledger while Knuckles used his phone to download the files on the drives.

We were done in less than five minutes. Nick came over the earpiece saying, "Finally got some local SWAT guys. Building is getting sealed. Might want to move."

I looked at Knuckles and said, "You ready to die?"

"The sooner the better."

He pulled a thin wire with a small pad from under his shirt. I raised the shotgun, aiming into a corner. I pulled the trigger, and he pressed the pad. The Hollywood squibs went off and his chest exploded with red, as if he'd taken the brunt end of some double-ought buckshot. He winked at me and said, "See you on the other side."

He staggered out of the room, wailing and screaming, then collapsed in front of the stunned guard and manager. I came jogging out, eyes wide and crazy. I shouted, "I didn't want to do that! He lied to me. There was nothing in his box but paper."

I pointed the gun at the manager and said, "You'd better get someone to open that safe. I'm running out of patience."

He said, "I'm doing it. There's a man up top who wants to talk to you. An American."

American? Shit. Embassy. Time to go.

I took the radio and cut the manager's ankles free. I said, "I'm going to show them what happens if they try anything. Help me with the body."

We dragged Knuckles to the elevator, me grabbing his hands and the guard struggling with the feet. We dumped him in the elevator and I aimed the shotgun, saying, "Get back to the vault room."

I followed him, then cinched his ankles again, taking his radio and saying, "I'm sending that elevator up to the ground floor. When I get back, I want you to tell them to come get their prize."

I ran back to the elevator, finding it empty, but the access panel open. I slung the shotgun over my shoulder and chinned myself up through the hatch. Above me I could see Knuckles whipping his legs back and forth as he climbed the cable. I found the last harness and raised the clamps to eye level, then began the climb myself, talking to Nick for the first time.

"Veep, Veep, we're in the shaft. Is the exfil vehicle outside the perimeter?"

"Roger. Looks like they're debating an assault. It's all over the news now. Man, that manifesto I wrote is awesome. They're reading it every five seconds."

I said, "You're making me wonder."

I passed the fourth floor and looked up, seeing Knuckles disappear out the roof access. Then I heard something mechanical. The cable began moving. I was rising.

Shit.

It would have been great four floors below, as I wouldn't have had to work to go higher, but now it was about to jam me into the cable access on the roof for the elevator motor. Aside from definitely killing me, it would cause an investigation into our escape route.

I started pumping my legs and arms, left, right, left, right, attempting to climb down, but only slowing my rise. I said, "Veep, Veep, how is the elevator moving?"

"Stand by. . . . Pike, looks like they've got a team outside the elevator and are using the fireman's override."

In between strokes I said, "That . . . would . . . have . . . been . . . nice . . . to . . . know."

"I was scoping the perimeter. Pike, when they don't find a body, they're going to start wondering."

Cutting our getaway time in half. I'd intended to get at least a ten-minute wait from the bank manager before he generated the courage to try to escape, which is why I'd taken the radio. Someone in charge must have made the call, disregarding my booby-trap bluff. But that was the fifty-meter target. The ten-meter target was literally ten meters above my head, and getting closer by the second.

I huffed and struggled, wondering if the car was going to stop on the first floor or come all the way up. I couldn't match the speed of the cable, and began planning my escape. I looked to my left, seeing the open access door. I came level with it and leapt, slamming chest-high on the sill and slapping my hands outside the doorjamb, holding myself up, my legs dangling into space. I waited to hear the elevator motor chew through my metal prusik device, but nothing came.

I looked behind me and saw the cables had stopped with about six inches to spare.

Story of my life.

Knuckles came on the net. "Pike, Pike, we're set out here. What's your status?"

"At the door. Need to retrieve my climbing gear."

"What's taking so long? You that out of shape?"

I felt the metal of the jamb biting into my flesh and knew I'd bruised a couple of ribs in my leap.

I climbed out, biting back my reply.

★ 80 ★

Khalid carefully watched Sabour handle the detonation switch, making sure he didn't accidentally do anything stupid or clumsy. He had the ignition off, but he wasn't betting his life solely on what Abdul-Haq had said.

Khalid said, "Any questions?"

His eyes shining, finally meeting his means of destruction, Sabour said, "No. It seems simple enough."

Haider said, "That's it? That's all there is to it?"

Khalid said, "Yes, that's it. The only issue will be getting to Fredrikstad. Google Maps shows it to be about a hundred kilometers away. We'll have to stop for gas more than once to get there."

Khalid locked up the Range Rover and they made their way back to their hotel rooms, stopping on the fifth floor to let off Sabour. The doors opened and Khalid said, "I'll call you later."

The remaining two continued up in silence, not speaking until they were safe behind the closed door of Haider's room. Khalid tossed the Range Rover keys onto a table and said, "So, Haider, what's the plan? I got the vehicle. Now what?"

Khalid seemed to be acting more and more as if he was in charge, and Haider didn't like it. He said, "Secretary Billings left today. He's renting a cottage in Fredrik-stad, and he's given me the address. I told him I'd meet him there tomorrow."

"Then what? Do you know where the meetings are occurring? What's the schedule?"

"No, but I don't need to. Secretary Billings will take us to the meeting. Remember, the peace talks are being cloaked by a discussion on Afghan women's issues. He's keeping everything close to his chest on this to protect the secrecy. They started yesterday, but Billings said it was mainly just formal introduction speeches by the participants. At some point, the secret peace talks will begin in a separate room, away from the public meetings."

"So how is this going to work?"

Haider felt as if he was being interrogated by his father. He finally became piqued at Khalid's tone. "It'll work how I say it works."

Khalid said, "You don't know, do you? How is Sabour supposed to attack? We don't even have the basics for the mission."

"Did you want me to ask Billings where we could park a car bomb? Yes, we have some details to learn, but we can do that tomorrow." Haider sat on the couch and said, "All Sabour has to do is make sure he doesn't kill us along with the Afghans."

Khalid said, "Did you tell your father this? That you don't know anything?"

"No. He doesn't need to know. Why do you care? Two days ago, you were telling me *not* to call my father. Now you want to talk to him every step of the way?"

"Your father entrusted us with this mission. We cannot fail."

Haider took that in, then said, "He entrusted *me*. Not us. He entrusted his son."

Khalid bared his teeth, and Haider felt a glimmer of fear at the rage he'd seen before. Khalid said, "Yes, he gave you the mission, but he told *me* to help execute, and I will not fail him. He didn't *entrust* his son. He's afraid of you disappointing him. And I'm here to make sure that doesn't happen."

"What are you talking about?"

"You know. He's *your* father. And if we don't fail, he'll be mine as well."

Haider waited, and when Khalid didn't continue, he said, "What does that mean?"

Khalid went to the minibar and withdrew a Sprite, opening it and taking a sip.

Haider said, "Khalid, what did my father tell you?"

"If we succeed, I get the power of your name. We'll become brothers."

Instead of joy, Haider felt fear. His father was pushing him out, the weak bird forced from the nest. "He said that?"

"Yes. It's why he had me get the vehicle. I had to kill two men there. He knew you wouldn't do it."

"Wait . . . you killed two men? Here in Oslo?"

"Well, a man and a boy. To protect the name al-Attiya."

Khalid said it so nonchalantly that Haider had a hard time believing it. But he knew his father, and he'd seen Khalid in Afghanistan.

Haider tried to regain his role as leader. "Whatever he's told you, I am the one in charge. This is *my* mission. Not yours."

Khalid took another sip and said, "I understand. But remember this: We *will* succeed. You've had a name your entire life. I'll now have mine, and if that means taking it from your dead body, I will."

★81★

Sitting on the couch in my sweats, I flipped through the channels on the television, looking for another news story of the dramatic bank hostage crisis. I found one, but it was the same sorry footage from another broadcast, and it was in Greek. I switched to the BBC and caught a teaser of the bank heist. My little show was coming up next.

Wearing a loose sweatshirt, yoga pants, and socks, Jennifer sat down next to me and handed me a beer. She said, "Can't get enough of yourself, huh?"

I said, "Hey, come on now, it's not too often you get to rob a bank on behalf of the United States. This is a Taskforce record. We're going down in history."

She grinned and said, "Yeah, until we get caught."

"That ain't going to happen. They had their chance."

We'd made it out of the bank just fine, rappelling down the narrow alley shaft on the ropes Jennifer had emplaced. She'd done a simple loop, with the center of the rope on the anchor point, so when we hit the ground, all we'd had to do was pull one end, then stow everything in Brett's van.

We were exactly fifty meters outside of the police blockade, which was perfect, and after getting a call from

Veep that the coast looked clear, we'd simply entered the traffic and driven back to the hotel, looking at the circus in our rearview mirror.

We'd uploaded everything we gleaned to the Task-force, then had conducted an after-action review, which, honestly, involved mostly boasting about our incredible prowess. After that, we'd had a few beers swapping lies about the mission, with Nick Seacrest hanging on every word and looking at us like we were superheroes. Which, of course, we were. He'd missed most of the fun because I'd made him stay in the hotel running the tactical operations center, giving him experience on the overarching big picture. Developing him for the future.

We had Creed on a VPN live stream just to throw him a bone for helping out, with Jennifer doing the thanking because Creed worshipped her. Honestly, it was a little cruel since he stood no chance, but I guess a man can hope—and he had done some good work. While she was talking, a shadow appeared in the background, then Kurt Hale's head broke into the screen.

Jennifer had recoiled and we'd all shaped up pretty damn quickly. Kurt had said, "Jennifer? Is that you?"

Offscreen, she said, "Yes, sir. How are you doing?"

He'd said, "Where the fuck is Pike?"

Which didn't sound too positive.

I took the seat in front of the screen, saying, "Right here. What's up? You crack the data we sent?"

He rolled his eyes, saying, "I'm more concerned how you got it," and then he punctuated every word, saying, "You. Robbed. A. Fucking. *Bank*?"

I glanced at Knuckles off camera. He grinned and shrugged. I said, "Well, yeah, sir. I told you we had a safe-deposit key, and you said we had Alpha."

"I thought you were going to just walk in and use it!

Jesus Christ. You're all over every damn TV channel in the universe, with the exception of maybe China."

"Sir, we couldn't 'just use it.' We needed the manager's key. It worked out fine. We were in and out. No harm, and no foul."

He looked incredulous. He shook his head and said, "We talked about the Alpha authority. It's tenuous. It's not really even there, except for my ignoring the president's intent. And your solution for that was to rob a bank?"

"Sir, if I had a week or two, I could have figured out a way to do this without drama. I didn't have that. If the Oversight Council wants to bitch, it's their own fault."

He looked at me, his eyes squinting, but I could see a little admiration. At least I hoped it was that and not just a bad connection. "I have no idea how you've lived as long as you have. It's uncanny."

I couldn't resist. I said, "You should have been there. It was a piece of art. An operation that will never be topped. Sir, they have no idea what happened. We cloaked it and we disappeared. It'll be the talk of the town, but we'll be gone tomorrow, mission accomplished."

He said, "You know I've got the Oversight Council meeting in a few hours. I'm going to have to sit there with a straight face and say you *robbed a bank*. I mean, I'm not sure I even want to enter the room."

I said, "Get the data translated. Do the analysis. It'll be the best defense. Those fucks are bad people, and it'll prove Guy was in the right. That's all that matters."

He nodded, a rueful smile on his face. He said, "You'd better hope so, or we're both going to be fired."

I said, "Sir, trust me. Guy deserves this. This is his redemption. You recruited him and you trained him.

Trust those instincts. You were right then and he's right now."

Kurt said, "Okay, Pike. I believe you, but you'd better get me a SIT-REP in the next hour of everything that happened. I need some facts. The good, the bad, and the ugly. And you need to get out of Greece."

I said, "Sir, already planned. The Rock Star bird is inbound, and we'll be out of here tomorrow morning. I'll send the report, but for what it's worth, I've got your back. There was only good. No bad and no ugly, unless you count Creed talking to Jennifer. The best thing is to get someone on the data we sent."

He signed off, and everyone looked at me like we'd done something wrong. Except Knuckles. He said, "What the hell. You guys look like you just got caught shoplifting. Veep, break out the beer. We did good today."

I said, "You got that right."

We'd spent an hour or so shooting the bull, me taking grief for my leap out of the elevator, and Nick taking a little heat for not warning me it was coming. It was some much-needed downtime after Guy's death. We should have been packing and preparing to leave, but the venting was necessary, so I let it continue. Eventually, it wound down, and I kicked everyone out, getting one snide comment from Knuckles about Jennifer staying and Creed not even being in the country.

Par for the course with him.

We should have gone to bed, but I really wanted to see what the press was saying about the bank heist. And so I kept flipping through the channels. I waited on the BBC report and said, "That data is going to be good. I just wish we could be the ones doing the Omega operation on those assholes from Qatar."

She smiled and said, "Well, maybe it'll take a cycle or

two to figure out what they're up to. Maybe we'll be back in the hopper by then."

I nodded and said, "Maybe." Then, "So you're finally going to admit you like this shit?"

She smiled and said, "Yeah. Yeah, I am. This team is pretty good, and that mission was something out of a movie. And I was a necessary part of it."

"Yeah, you were. I just wish Guy hadn't had to die to do it."

We sat in silence for a moment, then she said, "You did well with Carly. She needed that support."

I rubbed my face and said, "That was hard. I mean . . . I've done that before, but it was one of the hardest. She talked all night about Decoy and Guy. It was crushing."

"She wants to come to the memorial. She's got leave coming up. She wants to be there, especially now since she's read on."

I sat up. "How do you know that?"

"We talked. Girl talk."

I leaned back and closed my eyes. "That will be one more slap to her face. I don't think Guy's going to get a memorial. The Taskforce wants to bury his memory, and they will."

Jennifer said, "That's not right."

I said, "It is what it is."

She stood up and said, "Enough for tonight. I'm sick of the bad things. You ready for bed?"

I said, "You mean sleep, or some celebration for our super-secret mission?"

She gave me her incredibly sexy squint and said, "What do you think?"

I felt a grin split my face and said, "I think I'm ready for bed."

And then my phone rang with its unique ringtone, meaning an encrypted call.

Meaning trouble.

I answered, expecting to hear a Taskforce analyst. I recognized Kurt Hale's voice immediately.

"Pike, you awake?"

"Yeah, yeah, what's up, sir?"

"You were right. We translated the data from the thumb drives, and those fucks are bad, but it's not a slow burn like everyone thought. The guy from Crete has a false passport from Afghanistan, and the name matches the guy who Billings got a visa for entering Norway."

"Yeah, so?"

"He's listed as a *shahid* on the spreadsheet from the bank. They brought in a suicide bomber, and he's traveling with the United States secretary of state."

I had no response. The thought was incredible.

Kurt continued, "Talk to the analysts at the Taskforce. They've got a complete data dump for you."

I looked at Jennifer and said, "I take it the Oversight Council meeting went okay."

He said, "Oh yeah. They're having heart attacks. It's fluid—no Omega yet—but they let me get Blaine Alexander in the air. When your bird gets there tomorrow morning, I need you to get your ass to Norway."

I said, "You just said I have no Omega authority. What's the mission?"

"I honestly don't know yet, but I want you on the ground for whatever it is. The Council is skittish right now, so plan on some problem solving without guidance. Blaine will provide command and control, and you'll provide . . . what you always provide."

I said, "Sounds about as solid as Jell-O."

"It is. We've got Billings in the middle of it."

I smiled at the thought of that idiot trying to vote on an Omega mission that involved him being tied to the terrorists. Couldn't make up something that stupid. I said, "I love this job. Talk to you in the morning," and hung up.

Jennifer said, "What was that about?"

"Billings fucking up my celebration, that's what."

★ 82 ★

Khalid watched Haider and Sabour enter the hotel breakfast nook together and wondered if Haider was cooking up a scheme separate from him. It would do no good. Khalid had had a long talk with Sabour after the meeting in Haider's room, and Sabour, like Khalid, understood commitment.

The two sat down, and Khalid exchanged strained pleasantries with Haider, then ate in silence. They finished breakfast, then started the hour-plus drive to Fredrikstad. They stopped for gas twice on the trip, the last on Highway 110 just before it intersected with 111, the open fields blanketed with snow and giving the air a quiet feel.

Haider went to the men's room and when he returned, Khalid was leaning against the SUV, rubbing his hands in the cold. He said, "We're close to the old town. Where from here?"

"It's about five miles away." He glanced at Sabour in the driver's seat, making sure the window was up, then said, "Look, Khalid, we are friends. We cannot continue fighting each other and expect to succeed. I don't want to do that."

Khalid said, "Neither do I, brother. Neither do I."

Haider smiled and held out his hand, saying, "My father is right about you. You *are* my brother."

The words reinforced the steel in Khalid's soul, forging yet again the desire to please Sharif and earn his place at the table. He became emotional, his eyes misting. He said, "Let's make our destiny."

Haider opened the passenger door and said, "Let's do it."

Sabour put the Range Rover into drive, and Haider opened a sheet of paper, reading directions. He said, "You'll go for another mile on this highway. Look for a side road on the left that disappears into the woods. Billings said it would be easy to find because it's the only road that goes into a stand of forest. All the others go into bald fields."

They pulled out and continued, passing an occasional car on the left and some Norwegians walking on a footpath on the right. They entered a lightly wooded area, the barren trees looking like skeletons, and Haider said, "Slow down. Keep your eyes out. It'll be a gated road."

Ahead, a tall wooden fence began tracking the highway. They traveled down it for about half a mile, and then saw a thin ribbon of asphalt slipping into the woods.

"That's it," said Haider.

They turned onto the road and drove for about a quarter of a mile through the woods before the asphalt ended, hitting another gate with a gravel drive beyond it and a two-story stone house about a hundred meters away. At the second gate were several men dressed in suits and overcoats.

Sabour pulled to a stop.

One man came to the window and said, "Haider al-Attiya?"

Sabour said nothing. Haider said, "I am al-Attiya.

From the Qatar Investment Authority, here to meet with Secretary Billings."

The man said, "We've been expecting you. Please, I need all in the car to exit for a search."

That had never happened before. Haider said, "Of course, of course," and opened the door. Khalid did the same, but watched closely.

Before he'd even exited the vehicle, a two-man team was sweeping the underside of the Range Rover with a mirror attached to a pole and another man was working some sort of electronic tablet, aiming it at the vehicle and watching the screen. The interest in their vehicle brought something new to the game, and Khalid wondered if they should be worried.

On the one hand, it might simply be new security procedures because of what the American had done in Delphi. A knee-jerk reaction to protect the security force's own reputation, since they'd failed to do anything about the assassin in Greece.

Or it might be something more sinister.

He saw a man slide into the driver's seat and begin manipulating all of the controls, making sure they worked as intended. Two other men moved all three of them away from the vehicle, then searched them, apologizing as they did it.

When that was complete, one man used a clipboard and began questioning them, having them produce passports and other identification. They seemed to spend an inordinate amount of time on Sabour's passport, asking specific questions about where he'd received it and how long he'd used it, focusing on the fact that the only visa was for Norway.

Khalid interrupted, saying, "Look, sir, I understand the protection, but Secretary Billings is the man who worked to give him that visa. We are here on his invitation. If you have questions about that, you should direct them to him."

Khalid couldn't see the eyes behind the dark sunglasses. The security man said, "You and Haider can go to the house. Your driver will wait here."

Showing concern, Haider said, "Why? What has he done?"

Khalid waved his hand and said, "That's fine. Do we just walk right up?"

"Yes. Ring the bell at the front door. Another member of our detail will meet you."

To Sabour, Khalid said, "Wait here. We won't be long."

He flicked his eyes at Haider, willing him to calm down. They began walking down the gravel track that led to the house and Haider said, "That has never, ever happened before. They know."

"Calm down. If they *knew*, we'd be lying on the ground in handcuffs. It's just because of that attack at Delphi. The dog American that Billings told you about is the root of this. It was Billings's problem to deal with, and he didn't, leading to the attack. Their intelligence agencies are probably all blaming each other over the mess, and searching for scapegoats. They are no different than our own royal family, looking for people to blame."

He gave Haider a hard stare and said, "Don't let it interfere."

They reached the front door of the stone manor and Haider rang the bell. Another man answered and asked for their passports, incongruously wearing sunglasses indoors.

They both presented their documents and were allowed into the foyer. Khalid glanced around, seeing Billings's ubiquitous assistant—Leslie something or other—but saw no other security. The man led them into a great room and said, "Take a seat."

They did, Khalid feeling a little angst with the formality. Wondering if it was a reflection of the location, or something else.

They sat for twenty minutes, the dark wood and heavy drapes of the house feeding Khalid's anxiety. The cottage was not an inviting place. More like something out of a Grimms' fairy tale. He looked at Haider and saw the same worry reflected in his expression. He thought about standing up and leaving, but knew that was impossible. Not if he wanted to earn the respect of Sharif's father. He was committed, and he would see it through. But he could prepare, just in case.

He said, "Is there a bathroom I could use?"

The security man said, "Yes, down this hallway, first door on the left."

Khalid glanced at Haider, then followed the directions, looking for other security. Trying to determine what he was up against. He reached the bathroom and saw two men reading magazines in a bedroom, both glancing up when he approached. On the table between them was an HK MP7 sitting next to a vase of flowers as if it was just one more decoration.

They were definitely security. So three at least.

From the attack at Delphi, he remembered that the secretary had a detail of about five shooters, not counting the drivers and other hangers-on. The gate they'd passed through had six people, but most were probably specialists on antiterrorism and installation protection, not personal security. Meaning they were paid to prevent bad things but wouldn't react if the bad thing happened. But at least two were shooters. So it was a good bet that he faced only three inside the house.

He left the bathroom and found Haider engaging the lone security man in conversation, talking about trips abroad, the assistant ignoring them both. The security man laughed, relaxed and enjoying the discussion. Khalid felt the fear slip away. He was being paranoid.

He sat down and Secretary Billings appeared. He nodded at Khalid, then said, "Haider, could I talk to you for a moment in private?"

Khalid watched them disappear, wondering. He saw Billings glance back at the security man, then at him. And it became clear.

He knows.

★ 83 ★

The Gulfstream hit the tarmac of Moss Rygge airport, only about thirty minutes away from Fredrikstad, and I immediately began issuing orders. Basically repeating what I'd already said, but hell, that's what leaders do.

Repeat shit over and over.

"Okay, we have no idea what we're doing here, so I need a split evacuation of the aircraft. I want both long guns and surveillance kit. We might be going offensive, or we might just be tagging and tracking. When the customs guys get here, Brett handles them. We're members of Grolier Recovery Service, and we're here to look at the fortifications of Old Town Fredrikstad. That's all you need to say."

Knuckles had already moved to the rear of the aircraft and had begun making a list of what to remove after customs was through with their inspection.

Nick said, "I'm . . . not really read in to the whole cover story of Grolier. I can't fake it."

I said, "Just fake the fact that we hired you for aircraft purposes. You can do that with your Air Force background. Anyone asks you in-depth questions about GRS, you point at Jennifer and tell them she's the spokesperson. You're just the hired help."

He said, "How is that going to solve anything?"

I looked at Jennifer with a "help me here" glance. I knew she'd studied up as soon as she learned where we were going. She said, "Fredrikstad was originally founded in the sixteenth century by King Fredrik II. The old town is the finest European example of a fortified city. It was originally built—"

I waved a hand, cutting her off. I said, "Trust me, she can talk the talk."

Knuckles issued orders, organizing the load-out, knowing the pressure we were under. He got the team moving, doing what they could before immigration showed up, then sat down across from me, looking for answers. Answers I didn't have.

He said, "What's the play here? What are we doing?"

I said, "Knuckles, you're asking for a miracle with that question. I don't know. You heard my conversation with Blaine. *He* doesn't even know."

I'd spent the night getting one data dump after another from the Taskforce, all indicating something evil but, outside of the term *shahid*, nothing specifically pointed to a smoking gun. The thumb drives had showed unequivocally that the al-Attiya clan was involved in some seriously bad activities, but none of it involved what we'd call "actionable intelligence."

There were lots of potential connections to both past and future operations, but no black-and-white order to kill the secretary of state or blow up the peace talks. No outright proof of malevolent actions, which is really what always occurred. No terrorist in his right mind talked about his actions in the open. At least no terrorist who wanted to live beyond a day and a half.

It was all innuendo, requiring massive cross-checks and linkage exploration. After the initial analysis of the data, we had a ton of smoke, which would have been good enough to continue watching the QIA team, but not solid proof for anything more than that. With the exception of one thing: the word *shahid*.

It was an Arabic term meaning "witness" but had, in the modern jihadi world, evolved into meaning someone who died fulfilling a religious obligation. Someone who had become a martyr in the course of jihad, and it had been used as the notation beside the fake Afghanistan passport. It could mean only one thing: He was going to kill himself for Islam. Meaning he was going to kill more than just himself.

Once airborne, I'd called Blaine, himself flying out of Washington, DC. He was the officer in charge of Omega operations, but we hadn't yet been given that authority, so it was a little strange, though I'd be lying if I didn't say I was happy Kurt had sent him. He was a backstop I might potentially need.

He'd answered the call mid-flight, saying, "So I guess I'm heading into operations with my favorite team. Thank heavens for that."

I'd laughed, because he said that to every team he was going to control, then I countered with, "I'm not so sure about that. From what I hear, the Army is giving you your walking papers. Not sure I want to be under the command of someone who can't even get promoted."

He said, "It's already done. I'm on terminal leave right now. It could cause a conflict of interest, since I'm working a government job paid for by the Oversight Council while still on active duty. Hard to say if anyone will pay attention to a lowly lieutenant colonel, though."

418 / BRAD TAYLOR

I took that in, trying to make sense of it, then said, "Sir? The Army really pulled the trigger? Fired you?"

He said, "Well . . . yes and no. I took Kurt's option. I'm now a civilian like you. But if you think I'll take your shit because of it, you're sorely mistaken."

That brought a grin, because he'd been covering my butt for years for things I'd done, taking more than his fair share of Pike trouble. I said, "That's the best possible solution. Welcome to the real world. You ready to slay some monsters?"

He said, "Oh yeah, but I'm not sure that's what we're looking at."

I said, "We're looking at a clown who received a fake passport to kill people. It's pretty clear."

Blaine said, "Yeah, I'm with you, but the attack may be months from now. I mean, why give him an Afghanistan passport? Maybe they're prepping him for that theater."

"Why bring him to Norway, then? Where the peace talks are happening?"

I heard my voice rising as I talked and regretted it. I needed to remain unemotional.

Blaine said, "Pike, I hear you, but you're forgetting that we control Billings. He has an entire diplomatic security team there. We've been in contact with Billings, and he's read on to the threat."

"What's that mean in real terms?"

"It means there *is* no immediate threat. The only immediate threat is the peace talks, and they won't be allowed to go to them. Best case, we've solved the problem with a phone call. Worst case, Billings has a threat against him, personally, but we have the men there to neutralize any attempt. They have the ball. Honestly, I don't see this as a Taskforce mission. I'm glad to play, but I don't think we're worth putting on the field."

I said, "Maybe. Maybe you're right, but you're forgetting what Billings is like. Forgetting what he's done in the past. That assclown will neutralize his own security."

"Pike, come on. He might be a jerk, but he's not going to let them get near the meetings. He's got marching orders from the president of the United States."

"So they're going to arrest the guys from Qatar when they show up?"

"No. Hell no. Of course not. What proof do we have to do that? Nothing. A thumb drive from a bank we never entered. Secretary Billings doesn't even believe the evidence we have, and he's certainly not going to explode the peace talks with allegations of infiltration of a Qatari suicide team."

I'd taken that in, which was about what I'd expected. I said, "So we're back at square one."

"Well, yeah, except I'm in the air, and you're about to be on the ground. I'll be an hour behind you. You can call that square one, but I call it endgame."

I'd disconnected the call and rode the aircraft onto the tarmac, ignoring the stares from the team.

Now on the ground, Knuckles was asking a valid question: What the hell were we doing?

Our conversation was interrupted by the arrival of the immigration officials, forcing all of us into cover mode, answering their questions politely. Led around by Brett, my crew went through the usual pathetic customs inventory that anyone gets as a chartered aircraft in a European city, and the men left, satisfied that we were who we said we were.

Knuckles got the team moving, breaking open panels on the interior of the aircraft that exposed a host of James Bond surveillance kit, along with our lethal tools in case surveillance turned into assault.

Satisfied the team was executing his orders, he sat back down, facing me.

"Pike, I understand the pressure, but you've got to give us some focus here. Talking long guns and surveillance isn't cutting it."

I thought about my response, and Guy's face appeared out of nowhere, demanding the same answer. I realized I didn't care about protecting Billings or the peace talks. I wanted vengeance, pure and simple. Knuckles saw the change. Recognized where I was.

He said, "Pike, are we sure about this? Don't let Guy's death cause you to make a decision you'll regret. Maybe Billings is right for once."

I sat for a moment, quelling the beast. A strange thing that was now a part of my essence, but something that I'd learned to control, almost at will. Almost.

Knuckles said, "Pike?"

I said, "Okay, for starters, we'll just deploy to the secretary's location. We'll get eyes on the targets and continue with our Alpha mission. Surveil them for follow-on operations. It'll probably be nothing. Billings agreed not to take them to the meetings. Problem solved."

But I didn't believe it. And neither did the beast. From the data we'd found, I knew the Arab I'd fought in Greece was here, and he was looking for trouble.

We finished the load-out, all equipment stowed in innocuous suitcases, and moved to the rental car counters. I told Knuckles to get two cars, not that we needed the space but because we might need the flexibility.

I saw a counter for motorcycle tours, advertising

BMW bikes for running around the fjords. I said, "Veep, you've done mobility stuff in your units, right?"

He quit fidgeting with his bag and said, "Yeah. Why?"

"You do any biking there in the special tactics squadron?"

"All the time."

Knuckles came back with the keys to two vehicles, one a van, the other a sedan. Brett was standing next to me, and I knew he could do what I was asking of Nick.

I said to Nick, "How about renting two of those Beemers for a few days? You and Brett."

Knuckles said, "Why?"

I said, "Because I want the flexibility. I don't believe a word I said to you earlier. I don't care what Billings thinks. Those assholes are here for a reason, and the fight is coming to us."

★ 84 ★

From his facial expression, Khalid was bored, but his heel unconsciously rapping on the hardwood floor gave away his anxiety. Every few seconds, he glanced reflexively at the closed doors Secretary Billings and Haider had disappeared behind, waiting on the outcome. The security man with the indoor sunglasses sat stoically one chair over, glancing at the door as often as Khalid. For her part, the assistant Leslie ignored them both, tapping away on a laptop.

Khalid stood, startling the security man. He rose as well. Khalid said, "I don't know what's taking so long. What's this about?"

The man said, "Just routine. They'll be out soon."

Khalid smiled and said, "Because we're Arabs, right?"

The man shook his head and said, "No, not at all. Can I get you something to drink? We have soda, coffee, or water."

Khalid said, "Yes, actually, if it's not too much of a bother. I'll have a glass of water."

The man left the room, and Khalid considered asking Leslie about the meeting, but decided he'd get the same answer. So far, nobody had shown any outward animosity, but that meant little. He heard the security man's footsteps in the kitchen, then saw the office door open. Haider came out first, his eyes fearful, darting left and right.

Not good.

Secretary Billings followed him through the door, looking almost comically stern and authoritarian. Khalid said, "So? We go now?"

Haider clasped his hands together and said, "No. Apparently, we've come to Norway for nothing. Secretary Billings has changed his mind on allowing us to help. He now feels it will be counterproductive for us to attend the meetings."

Khalid said, "Why?"

Secretary Billings said, "It's just the way of things. The representatives of the Afghan High Peace Council don't feel it will be helpful to have members of Qatar observe the talks. I made a mistake. I still believe you can contribute, but I can't go against their wishes."

Khalid saw the fear leaking out of Haider's expression and knew something else had been said in that room. Haider said, "Secretary Billings has agreed to reimburse our travel expenses, but this trip was in vain."

Khalid saw his new life floating away like a lost balloon released by a child. They were going to fail. He said, "This is ridiculous. We can still simply observe. We flew all the way here."

Khalid knew his protest sounded weak and desperate, which was exactly what he didn't want to highlight. But he *was* desperate.

Billings said, "No. I'm sorry. It's not going to happen."

The security man returned with his water, sensing something was amiss. He raised the glass, and Khalid made his decision.

They would *not* fail.

He reached for the water with both hands, an innocuous gesture. He clamped them on the man's wrist, spilling the water and trapping the hand. He ducked under the arm, rotating it in a direction nature hadn't intended, snapping the joint.

The guard screamed in pain and Khalid slammed his foot into the groin, dropping the man to his knees. He let go of the arm and hammered the guard in the temple. The guard fell forward, unconscious, landing straight on his face.

Khalid flipped up the man's suit jacket, revealing a holstered Sig Saur P250 pistol. He snatched it and then stood, the entire action taking no more than a few seconds. The two men from the back of the house burst into the room, looking for a threat. They found it.

Khalid fired twice, hitting each one in the chest and causing them to fall.

Leslie shrieked and dropped to the floor. Haider screamed, "Stop it, stop it! What are you doing?"

Billings looked as if he was going to pass out, his jowls quivering in fear.

Khalid said, "We are going to that meeting."

With his weapon still raised, Khalid pulled a radio from the unconscious guard's belt and tossed it to Billings. "Call the gate. Tell them that the Range Rover can come forward."

Billings said, "I will not."

Khalid raised the weapon and said, "This isn't diplomacy. I'm not asking for a debate. It's war. You press that radio button, or I'll kill you right here."

Haider jumped between them and said, "Khalid, have you lost your mind? Stop it. Stop right now. My father would never want this."

Khalid said, "Move away, brother. We aren't really family yet."

Haider raised his arms and said, "No. We aren't doing this. Let's get back to the airport and go home."

Khalid gritted his teeth, realizing the dilemma he'd put them in. It was too late for that. They were committed. Stopping now would do nothing but guarantee the loss of his future patronage from Sharif, and yet Sharif's son sought that end in front of him.

He said, "Brother, move away."

Haider pressed his hands out in a gesture of surrender and slid forward, saying, "Don't do this. You and I can still fight another day. This isn't the end that you want it to be."

Khalid realized that Sharif was correct. His son had no steel. No courage. Haider was worth more dead than alive as a lever of intimidation for Billings.

Khalid pulled the trigger, hitting Haider just below his left eye. The bullet tracked through his brain, exploding out of the back and whipping by Billings's head, missing the secretary by inches and embedding in the wall. Haider's brain matter sprayed out, a snap of moisture as if someone had popped a wet towel, the offal coating Billings in a thick mist.

Leslie screamed again, curling up on the floor and covering her head. Billings stood with his mouth open like a fish, shocked, afraid to close it and ingest the gore.

Khalid said, "Press the button on the radio, or you will be next."

★ 85 ★

After only thirty minutes of tarmac time, our little caravan of vehicles left the airport, heading south toward Fredrikstad. Knuckles and I were up front in the sedan, Brett and Nick on two BMW G 650 touring bikes in the middle, and Jennifer in a van bringing up the rear, the back loaded with all of our kit. Knuckles said, "We've got about a forty-minute ride, which means we might beat Blaine to the cottage. You want to go laager outside the town, burn off some time?"

My phone vibrated and I said, "Speak of the devil. Blaine must be on the ground." I answered, saying, "About time, Showboat. We're inbound. What's your status?"

"Waiting on customs. I can see your aircraft, and given what little time it took you to get on the road, I take it they're not that thorough."

"No. Thirty minutes max. Did you get any further guidance, or are we still flapping on this thing?"

"Still flapping, but I'm sure you've come up with a plan. Oversight Council's working it through Billings. They still haven't given Omega, but they want these guys under close watch. It's a little political, to say the least."

"Yeah. I figured. Listen, I'm going to need some information from Billings."

"Okay. Like what?"

"I need to know where these guys are staying. I want to put a full blanket on them. Bug their rooms, tag their vehicles, and penetrate their communication systems. The usual. Build up a case for Omega, and Billings can help with that. He's still talking to the targets, right?"

"Yeah, but he's a diplomat, Pike. I don't know if I can convince him to use his position as a lever to facilitate Taskforce operations. He'll make decisions as part of the Council, but he won't turn into a commando just because you asked. I think it's going to be an issue of principle with him."

"I only need him to do two things. One, give me the hotel. Two, set up a meeting with his boys, then keep them there for an hour. Half the team will crack into the room while they're meeting, the other half will identify the target vehicles and get a handle on their cellular communications. After that, he's done. It's not like I'm asking him to start slinging lead, and we wouldn't even be in this position if he'd have listened to Guy in the first place."

He said, "Let me give it a go. Don't show up at the cottage until I'm done. Seeing you might set him off."

"Because he's jealous of my innate skills?"

He said, "Because he hates your guts," and hung up. I radioed the team, telling them we were pulling over for a spell. We corralled at a gas station and I told them what I knew, along with where I envisioned the mission going. We'd been waiting no more than ten minutes when Blaine called again. I looked at Knuckles and said, "That's either great news or Billings has told us to pack sand."

I answered, saying, "Tell me Billings has decided he'd like to attend Assessment and Selection."

I heard no humor coming back. "Pike, something catastrophic has occurred. I can't get Billings on the phone. I got his assistant, a woman named Leslie, and she's almost catatonic. Get to the cottage, ASAP."

I circled my hand in the air, telling everyone to load up, then said, "What's happened? What am I walking into?"

"I don't know. I need you to figure that out. All she kept shouting was that Secretary Billings was gone, and people are dead."

I hung up the phone, seeing Brett and Nick getting on their bikes. I reversed my command. "Hold up." I looked at Knuckles and said, "Surveillance just went out the window. Kit everyone up for assault."

"What's going on?"

"All I know is that Showboat says there are dead people. We're headed straight to the cottage to sort it out, and we're going armed."

His eyes widened slightly, but he said, "Beats the hell out of following those turds for days."

He turned away from the hood and waved over Jennifer. "Bring the kit around. We're going in loaded for bear."

Five minutes later, the motorcyclists were each outfitted with a suppressed Glock 23. Knuckles, Jennifer, and I had a Primary Weapons Systems MK109 chambered in .300 Blackout, a folding-stock AR rifle with a Gemtech suppressor that made the cycling of the bolt louder than the bullet.

I pulled up an overhead image on a tablet that showed the thread of the road leading to the cottage. I said, "Okay, the house is about four miles away. Brett and Nick will lead."

I used a pen to point on the tablet. "Head down this asphalt road and get a feel for what we're looking at, but don't penetrate the second gate where the gravel road starts. Peel off before becoming engaged, and use the bikes to get into the woods. We know Billings has a diplomatic security team there and I don't want any shooting. Give me an assessment and we'll follow up.

"Knuckles and Jennifer, we'll park on the outside road, then enter slowly. I'll have out a US flag, and we'll sort it from there. Beemer guys pull security while we check it out."

I got an up, and we rolled. Eight minutes later, we were tucked into a turnout, waiting on the motorcycles to report.

When they did, I found out they'd rolled right up to the second gate, ignoring my orders. Obviously, they'd already sorted it out.

Brett came on, saying, "Bring it in, Pike. It's a mess."

"Roger that. What did you tell them?"

"I said we're Department of Homeland Security. Stick with that for now. They're too shell-shocked to ask for identification."

We came upon a disaster scene, meeting a guy in mirrored shades who was acting like he was calm and collected, but I could see right through that. He was shaken. We retreated to the house, and we learned the damage.

Two Arabs had somehow managed to kidnap the US secretary of state. The diplomatic security guys were giving us the information we needed, not hiding anything, which was surprising, because somebody was going to get annihilated for this goat fuck.

There were five dead in the house, all laid out neatly in the bedroom with sheets covering them. Four were diplomatic security, one was Haider al-Attiya. One other man was barely conscious, his arm a pretzel, with Brett providing him medical attention. Leslie, the assistant, gave us the best information. When she was done talking, I said, "Why did you guys release the Range Rover?"

The DSS man said, "Because the secretary of state demanded it. We'd already scrubbed it. There was no threat, and we sent a man with them."

I pointed to the bedroom and said, "One of those guys?"

"Yes."

"How did they get out?"

"They shot their way out. They came blazing to the gate and just started shooting. There isn't any cover out there. We couldn't return effective fire without harming Secretary Billings."

"And your cars? The up-armored vehicles?"

"They were parked at the cottage. When we got to them, we found them disabled."

Beating these guys up further was doing no good at all. I said, "How long ago? How much of a gap?"

"Less than twenty minutes."

So the slaying had occurred while we were on the road. Making me regret pulling over to the side and waiting on Blaine.

I said, "All right. We don't know what those guys are up to, but it's either murdering Billings or harming the peace talks. I need you to go through State and lock down that site. Call off the rest of today's activities and get them out of there."

"What are you going to do?"

I continued as if I hadn't heard him. "You got this scene. Call who you need to, at the State Department and the embassy, get anyone who needs medical care, but don't call the police. I don't need a bunch of gunslingers running amok with the SECSTATE's life in the balance. We'll take it from here for Secretary Billings."

He said, "Whoa, wait a minute, that's bullshit. Secretary Billings is my responsibility."

I appreciated the sentiment, but that wasn't going to happen. I wasn't taking a bunch of unknowns. "You've got your hands full here. It looks like you're one of the last men standing, and this is what we do. Someone needs to coordinate with the embassy, and it isn't going to be Leslie."

He nodded, accepting the information, then said, "I don't even know who you guys are."

"We're just another agency, but the other side of the coin. You protect defensively. We do so offensively. We've been tracking the Arabs."

He said, "So I guess we both fucked this up."

I took that in and then said, "Yeah, we did. We both trusted Billings's judgment."

★ **86** ★

Khalid saw a parking garage built into the side of a hill, an office building made of glass attached to it, and said, "Pull in there, get off the street."

Sabour made the turn, going underground into the darkness.

Things had happened so quickly that Khalid needed time to think. To determine his next course of action. The drive out of the cottage had been a blur of gunfire and fear, Sabour plowing through the men at the gate as Khalid fired out the window, Billings cowering in the front seat in abject terror.

He remembered only short glimpses, like the flash of a camera. The security man slamming into the car frame as the bullets stitched his chest, the brass from his MP7 ricocheting inside the car as they raced out, the look of shock on the men's faces at the gate.

Only one fired back, until someone screamed at him to stop, and then they were through, turning onto the main road hard enough to throw Khalid against the opposite seat. They'd crossed the Glomma River and entered the peninsula of Fredrikstad city, Sabour staying on Highway 110 until he swung through a traffic circle and began driving on surface streets.

Khalid had swiveled his head back and forth, but nobody seemed to be paying them any mind. Even so, when the vehicle disappeared into the underground garage, Khalid felt relief in the darkness. Sabour killed the engine without pulling into a spot.

He said, "What now?"

Khalid wiped the sweat from his brow and said, "We go to the peace meetings. We complete the mission."

Billings sat up and spoke for the first time. "Khalid. You cannot succeed. You didn't kill everyone, so they'll be coming. They will have shut down the meetings. Give yourself up."

Khalid cuffed him on the back of the head with the barrel of the weapon. "Shut up. You will take us to the meeting. Right now."

Billings cradled his head, saying, "Why? Why must you do this? What possible good will it do?"

"You will never understand. Take me to the meeting."

"No."

Khalid raised his weapon, jamming the barrel into Billings's mouth. "Killing you won't be harming the peace process, but it will be close enough."

He saw Billings's phone flash on his hip, the vibrating buzz filling the interior. Nobody moved. Khalid said, "Don't you dare answer that."

It finished, leaving them in silence. Khalid said, "I'm going to count to five. You nod when you want me to stop. If I reach five, I'm blowing the back of your head out."

Billings closed his eyes. Khalid said, "One," punctuating it by jabbing the barrel and tearing Billings's lip. "Two."

Billings nodded.

Khalid withdrew the barrel. "Good choice." He

handed his smartphone to Sabour and said, "Pull up Google Maps, then hand the phone to the secretary."

Billings said, "I'll take you there. I just said I would."

"No. You'll tag the spot on the map, then we'll drive there together."

Resigned, Billings took the phone. He marked a location and handed it back. Khalid said, "A museum? The talks are happening in a museum?"

"Yes. It's government controlled, and on a fortified island. You won't get in."

"We will with you." He leaned into the back and withdrew the hidden CZ 75, handing it to Sabour. "Switch seats. Billings drives now."

They did so and Khalid held up the phone. "If you deviate from the route, I'll kill you."

He saw a single headlight beam flash against the wall and said, "When this motorcycle passes, we go."

It took a moment before it registered that the motorcycle was coming down the exit ramp, on the opposite side of the garage from the entrance they'd used.

★ 87 ★

I studied the satellite image on the tablet, the rest of the team forming a circle around me in the van, all of us waiting on a complete triangulation from the Rock Star bird. If it proved correct, the vehicle was in a parking garage just off a street called St. Croix Gate in the heart of downtown Fredrikstad.

We'd left behind the snow-covered fields and copses of barren trees in the countryside for the stone and steel of the Norwegian town.

Initially, we knew only two things: The vehicle was a Range Rover, and it had taken a right onto Highway 110 headed toward the Glomma River. I'd loaded everyone up, but intended to learn much more than that fact.

We hadn't found Billings's cell phone in the house, so I was assuming it was still on his person. I'd first called Billings direct and had gotten nothing but voice mail. I'd then called Blaine, demanding he launch my bird and load Billings's cell phone markers into the electronic surveillance package in the nose. Believe it or not, initially I'd received pushback—because Secretary Billings was a United States citizen, and the Taskforce charter was forbidden from tracking AMCITS or otherwise interfering in their electronic communication unless they had been designated a global terrorist.

It was absolutely ridiculous. My first thought, given what Billings had done, was to push for a designation, but I knew that was going nowhere. The Oversight Council rapidly cleared up the idiocy, but I was going to make a pilot suffer over the delay.

The bird made one pass over the city and pinged on the phone downtown, with a circle of probable error of about seven hundred meters. We moved in that direction. By the time we'd gotten to the city center, he'd pinged a second time on a different trajectory and necked it down to the parking garage—but still with a hundred-meter circle of probable error. That could put Billings inside the office building next door, or in a patch of scrub across the street near the river, but I was planning against him being in the garage.

From the satellite photo, it had a separate entrance and exit, with the entrance on our street and the exit a block up to the north. Street view showed it to be at most two levels, and from the width, it wouldn't take a whole lot to search.

First, I wanted to isolate our target. Both the entrance and exit had drop bars, but they wouldn't stop my motorcycle posse. I decided to send them to the exit, basically having them come in the wrong way to prevent us from missing our target if they drove out while we came in. Then, Knuckles and I would enter normally while Jennifer would park her van near the entrance, sealing it off after we went down, protecting us from discovery.

I needed to collapse on the crisis site with overwhelming force, which would necessitate positively identifying the vehicle without arousing suspicion. A tough call, considering at least one of the men in the vehicle knew both

Knuckles and me by sight, and I wasn't sure whether Brett and Nick had also been compromised. I hoped the helmets they wore would camouflage our intent.

I gave out the orders and asked for questions. Nick said, "What do you want us to do if we see the vehicle and can assault? Call first or seize the initiative?"

I said, "Do what you think is right. The priority here is rescuing Secretary Billings. If you get down there and can do it, execute. If not, give me a call."

Brett said, "Rules of engagement?"

"Hostile force. Both Arabs are designated enemy combatants. Don't worry about imminent threat to you. If you get one in your sights and his back is turned, drop him. I don't care if you see a weapon or not."

Brett nodded and said, "Roger that."

My phone rang. It was the pilot. "Final pass complete. Do you have the data, or do I need to go around again?"

I looked at the tablet screen and the little green icon had shifted. About a millimeter. They were in the garage. I said, "I got it. You're cleared to depart."

I held up the tablet and said, "That's them. Let's roll."

We gave Brett and Nick time to circle the block, then Knuckles put the sedan in drive, inching forward, Jennifer behind us. My radio crackled, "Pike, Pike, this is Veep. We're entering now."

Knuckles took a ticket, and our drop bar opened. We stayed on the pressure pad, waiting. Nick called again. "Pike, we're in, and I can see the vehicle. Range Rover sitting in the middle, three heads inside."

We rolled forward, sliding into the darkness. We reached the bottom of the ramp, and the headlights of the motorcycles illuminated a late-model green Range Rover, three heads in silhouette. I recognized Billings in the driver's seat.

"All elements, all elements, Billings is driving. Hostiles are in passenger seats. Blood, Veep, lock down the front. We'll take the rear."

We're going to get the jump on them. I saw the bikes coming forward, still about fifty meters away, and I climbed into the back of the sedan, cracking open the left-side door, getting ready to leap out when Knuckles came abreast. Then the enemy decided to vote.

While we were still thirty meters away, the rear passenger door of the Rover opened, the window already down. A man crouched behind and began spraying rounds toward my men. I saw one of the bikes go down, the other goosing the throttle into the parked cars, the rider diving off into cover.

I leapt out, seeing the Range Rover jerk forward, spinning one motorcycle out of the way and racing up the exit ramp, shattering the drop bar at the top.

What the hell is Billings doing?

I rolled and swung up my weapon. The Arab dove into our row of cars, and I recognized him. It was the one I'd fought in the park, now on the loose with a weapon.

Knuckles dove out the passenger side of our car, into the parallel row across the garage. I said on the radio, "Target is on my side, my side."

I heard "This is Blood. Veep's hit."

I heard the Arab shuffling forward one car over, trying to escape. I leapt up on the hood and scanned the other side, expecting to see him crouched low. He was right in front of me, so close our barrels clanged together as he whirled to fire. I squeezed off two rounds just as he slapped my weapon aside, the bullets slicing into the car behind. I dove on top of him, ripping his MP7 out of his hands. We both rolled upright with only one of us holding a weapon. Me.

He leapt to his feet and I rose as well, barrel on his chest. I was a millisecond from squeezing the trigger when I heard Knuckles shout, "No! We now need his intel."

I realized he'd had him in his sights when I'd jumped onto the hood.

The Arab was standing with his arms raised, waiting on the bullet. I kept my weapon on him and said, "Get on your fucking knees." He just snarled at me.

I said, "You want a shot at the title, little man?"

And he charged right at me, spitting in rage. By all rights, I should have pulled the trigger, but I didn't. I dropped my weapon on its sling and he began throwing punches. I blocked every one, batting them away like he was a child, letting him get close and wrap his arms around me for a takedown. He tried locking his leg behind me, just like he'd done in the park, but there was an enormous difference between me being surprised and me being ready.

I sidestepped it, grabbed his hair, and head-butted him, slamming my forehead like a pile driver right above the nose. His arms turned to rubber, the fight completely gone. I kicked his legs out from under him and dropped him on his back, looking for Knuckles.

The entire episode, from the time the door of the Range Rover opened until I'd dropped him, had taken maybe forty-five seconds.

Knuckles reached me and said, "I can't believe you didn't pull the trigger."

"What? You just said we needed the intel, and you were right behind me. I was in no danger."

He shook his head, zip-tying the Arab's arms and legs, muttering, ". . . just embarrassed about that fight in the park."

Which was true.

I said, "Brett, give me a status."

"Veep's got an in-and-out of his right thigh and a nick in his bicep. Nothing life-threatening."

Knuckles finished searching the Arab, holding up a cell phone. On it was a map with a blinking blue marble. I recognized the site. The Fredrikstad Museum in Old Town.

Where the peace talks were being held.

★ 88 ★

Billings felt the bile rise in his throat, as if he'd had too much to drink and wouldn't be able to hold it in. But he kept driving, mainly because of the barrel in his gut. After all that had occurred, he was on autopilot.

The man to his right seemed to have no fear whatsoever, and Billings had no idea what he intended to do once he arrived at the peace talks. Run inside with a pistol, shooting like he was a madman in Paris? Shout obscenities at the moon? The guy was crazy. One thing was sure: He was absolutely calm. Almost serene. Whatever he had planned, it wasn't spur-of-the-moment.

Even though the old town and the museum were right on the banks of the Glomma, a stone's throw away from the parking garage, they'd had to retrace their steps, going back up the 110 to the large traffic circle miles away, then turn right, basically making a box to get into the ancient fort, as there was only one road that a vehicle could traverse.

The town was literally a defensive encampment from ages ago, with an actual moat that slashed out in a zigzag pattern around the village, which, due to restoration and upkeep, looked much like it had eons ago. And it was the reason the location had been chosen. A single choke point to defend against threats.

Throughout the drive, Billings had thought about his options, telling himself to fight. Wrestle for the pistol, or jump out, letting the man shoot at him as he ran away. In the end, he simply couldn't bring himself to do so. His rational mind said there were better options. There were armed men at the talks. Security guards even on the main road. There was no way the Arab would be able to penetrate anywhere dangerous. As soon as Billings got the chance, he'd raise the alarm and they'd take the man down.

In retrospect, his biggest mistake had been flooring the accelerator in the garage. He had no idea what had happened there. One minute, they were discussing moving to the peace talks, the next minute, Khalid was blazing away at two motorcycles to his front. It was insane. When the man in the passenger seat had screamed at him to go, he'd reacted out of instinct, wanting to get away from the gunfire, but he now wondered if they hadn't been police trying to help him.

Did he now look like he was complicit in whatever these evildoers had planned?

The Arab said, "Slow down. Checkpoint ahead."

In the words, Billings realized how much he had been duped. Haider had said the man spoke no English, but that too was a lie.

He looked forward and saw the spit of land that stretched over the moat, lined with trees. In front was a chicane of three concrete blocks, and two men standing near a warming barrel, bundled up in the cold, weapons slung.

He thought, *This is it. This is when it ends.*

Sabour said, "If you get us through this, you will live."

Billings felt the sweat break out on his head. He pulled forward and rolled down his window. The first guard began running a mirror under the frame of the truck and the next one said, "May I see your registration, please?"

Billings looked shocked at the question. He had no idea what to say. No idea who the vehicle was registered to. Sabour dug through the glove box with his left hand, his right hidden. He held out the registration.

The security guard said, "Sir, are you all right?"

Billings wiped his upper lip and said, "I'm fine. Just fine."

Reading the registration, he asked, "What is your name?"

Billings started to answer, when the pistol went off right in front of his face, the bullet snapping the guard's head back and the sound exploding in Billings's ears. Billings screamed, and the Arab rotated, shooting the second guard through the passenger window. The guard whirled, then fell to the ground and started crawling away, scrambling for his rifle on his back, clearly not mortally wounded. Sabour leapt out, stalked over to him, put the barrel against the back of his head, and pulled the trigger.

Even with the events of the last few hours, the act of violence shocked Billings.

Sabour returned to the vehicle and said, "Get in the passenger seat."

Billings obeyed, and Sabour came around, entering the driver's seat. He locked the doors, then switched on the parental controls, preventing Billings from opening his side.

He reached underneath his seat, pulling out a metal

case the size of a cigarette package. He flipped up a cover, and flicked a switch from off to on.

Billings said, "What is that thing?"

"Your ticket to paradise."

The Arab put the vehicle in drive and crossed the moat.

★ 89 ★

I handed the phone back to Knuckles, saying, "Check those bikes out. See if they still run." I clicked my radio and said, "Blood, Blood, this is Pike. You've got exfil. Get the hostile and Veep out of here. Koko, you copy?"

She said, "Coming down."

Brett said, "No issues. I got Veep stabilized one row over. Where's the hostile?"

"Right next to the sedan. I can't stay here with him. We need to move."

"Roger all. What'll I tell Showboat? Where are you headed?"

"To find a Range Rover."

I called Blaine on the phone, waiting for it to encrypt. I told him what had transpired, and that I'd need a cleanup crew at my location. I gave him the data in clinical terms, but then ended with what I thought was happening.

"I believe that vehicle is a VBIED. I think they intend to drive it right into the peace talks and set it off."

"You sure about that? I think this is something to do with Billings. A hostage thing. Why on earth would they set off a car bomb at the peace talks? They're from Qatar."

"I don't *know*. Middle East agendas are impossible to sort out. Why does ISIS behead members of al Qaida? Why does the Taliban fight ISIS? It's not worth finding a motive. That's what I think's happening."

"Do you have any proof?"

"No. No smoking gun, but we got a guy here you can put the screws to."

"That'll take too long. If you're right, we need to get moving. We called, but they wouldn't shut down the talks based on the actions at the cottage. All they did was put up a checkpoint outside the moat. You can still get through without any special identification—they aren't stopping tourist traffic—but they'll flag anyone strange."

"Get the word out about the vehicle. Tell 'em it's a Range Rover."

"I will, but it won't happen quickly. Especially if they're inbound."

"I've looked at the map and I can beat them there. They'll have to go far out of their way to get to the village in that vehicle. Thank God Norway actually chose a fortified one for the talks. I've got a couple of bikes that will probably make it on the footpaths. I get across the bridge, and we're cutting straight through the fields. There's a single path on the river. If we can use that, we'll go straight to the museum, giving them our intel personally."

"What about Billings?"

"Sir, he was driving the damn vehicle. If he'd have sat here in the garage, he'd be free and we'd be looking at victory. He's the one who hauled ass out of here. My concern now is the peace talks and the innocents there. Once I get them onboard, I'll look at pulling his ass out of the fire."

I heard nothing. I said, "Sir?"

"Okay. Okay, that makes sense. Just stick with the 'saving innocents' and drop the 'he's a jackass' if this goes bad."

I saw Nick being loaded and said, "I'll call when I can."

Jennifer came over to me and said, "We're ready to go. You need a hand?"

"No. Brett's not taking a hostile and a WIA by himself. He's going to need some help. This is just a Paul Revere ride to warn the locals that the bad guys are coming."

She squinted her eyes at me, sensing there was more. I said, "Get out of here before someone wants to know what the loud noises were down here."

She pecked me on the lips and said, "Don't do anything stupid."

"Do I ever?"

She got in the van and pulled away. Knuckles said, "Both bikes will function. One's banged up pretty good, but all he did was ding the engine cage and gas tank."

"Let's go."

He propped his bike up and said, "We doing something stupid?"

"More than likely."

We crossed the bridge across the Glomma and I immediately began looking for our own create-on-the-fly off-ramp. I found it a quarter mile in, when I saw a makeshift footpath snaking down through the snow, the chain-link fencing cut away by pedestrians looking for a way to get to the river without walking two miles and turning around. I pointed and Knuckles flicked his head, telling me to go.

I stopped the bike and threaded it through the chain link, pushing with my feet, seeing the drop down the slope. It was a little hairy, especially in the snow. People in cars were staring at me like I was about to perform a stunt, which I suppose I was. I didn't look like a touring rider, that's for sure. I had the bike, but no jacket, boots, or helmet. One man honked the horn, and Knuckles waved, waiting on me.

I said, "Maybe we should look a little farther on, where it's not as steep."

Knuckles grinned and said, "Maybe you should do a little more mobility training." I saw his head swivel, and I followed his gaze. From our height we could see the entire town and the moat surrounding it. Out in the distance, there was a single vehicle coming down the small ribbon of road that led to the tourist town.

It was our Range Rover.

If I'd had a helmet, I would have slammed the visor down with authority, then skidded down the slope in wild abandon. I opted just for the skidding, riding the back brake and letting gravity take its toll. I hit the bottom and waited for Knuckles to catch up. When he did, I said, "We need to hit it. They'll be inside the perimeter of the town in seconds. We get in, you cut north. I'll head to the museum. You track him, let me know how much time I have."

"Got it. Let's go."

The town was really nothing more than a simple grid, with about as many buildings as would be expected from a fifteenth-century construction. It wasn't large at all, and standing on any one road, a person would be able to clearly see the far perimeter. Which meant, once he was inside, we had very little time.

I hit the gas, throwing out the snowy mud before hitting the pavement, then went as fast as I dared on the asphalt. We raced to the river, hitting a dock and a small footpath. I went left, now restricted from gunning the engine. The footpath widened and I opened the throttle. We were past the moat.

Ahead of me, I saw a small cluster of people selling wares in what looked like an artists' colony. A bunch of painters and pottery builders. I couldn't get through them on the bike. I slowed and dismounted, saying, "Please let me through."

They gave me a startled look, since this definitely wasn't a motorcycle track. One man stood up and waved his hands, an older hippie-looking guy speaking Norwegian. I pushed the bike forward and reached a parallel street that dead-ended against a small picket fence. I glanced up and saw the Range Rover pass a street. A brief glimpse, but I saw it. The VBIED was on the island.

I threw myself over the saddle, saying on the radio, "They're in." Then goosed the engine, shouting, "Get the fuck out of the way!"

I let the clutch out and went ripping through the tables and stalls, not really caring what I hit. I saw plaster and canvas flying left and right, people screaming and diving, and then I was through. The footpath turned to asphalt and I increased speed. I passed the sally port on the river side of the town and flicked a hand out, telling Knuckles to take it.

I heard his bike's whine disappear. I continued on. The museum was the farthest building on the south end of the town, and I'd seen the Range Rover entering from the center. They were going to beat me.

I shifted gears, the bike now almost out of control. The end of the town appeared, the asphalt turning to dirt again. I hammered the brakes, twisted the wheel, and slid into the turn. Ahead of me, at the east end of the road, was the Range Rover, the old garrison wall of the museum the only protection for the men inside. Between us was the cul-de-sac entrance to the courtyard of the museum.

I saw a large group of people milling around a bunch of town cars and SUVs, a platoon of earpiece-wearing security interspersed among them, completely oblivious to the threat bearing down.

This is it. I thought through my options. Reach the men? Shout at them to run? Drive forward, guns blazing like a movie?

Or just sit. Because I was too late.

I saw Knuckles turn the corner behind the Range Rover, still going strong.

Shit.

I gunned the engine and popped the clutch, racing straight at the grille in an insane game of chicken. I caught only a snippet when I passed the open cul-de-sac, a brief glimpse of men scrambling and reaching for weapons, then I was past. We closed together until I could see Billings's horrified face and the steely eyes of the Arab driving, and I laid the bike down, sending it straight into the front of the Rover.

I bounced on the ground, skipping on the asphalt, and the Arab jerked the wheel, avoiding the bike and careening up onto the old grass fortifications on the other side of the road. The Range Rover fought for traction on the grade, eventually failing.

It groaned for a minute, two wheels off the ground, then flipped, sliding to a stop on the passenger side,

Knuckles right behind it. He leapt off his bike, running to the passenger side to kill the Arab.

He still thinks Billings is driving.

I knew different. I screamed at him, and he reversed. I saw the Arab frantically searching the floor. He raised something up, and Knuckles took the shot, one, two, three, four. Straight through the windshield.

The man slumped over.

Knuckles remained still. I slowly stood, hearing the men starting to react from behind the walls of the old museum. I felt a wicked pain in my left leg, but I could walk. I heard someone shout from inside the vehicle.

I shuffled forward, reaching Knuckles. Inside, Billings was moaning like he was in labor, and I thought it pretty fitting. He'd given birth to the biggest fuckup I'd ever been involved in. Knuckles said, "You okay?"

"I don't know. Too early. Let the adrenaline wear off."

Knuckles saw movement and snapped his head to the windshield. He shouted, "No, sir, no, no, no, remain still." I turned around and saw Billings trying to climb out, over the top of the dead man, his foot kicking the detonator the Arab had held.

Knuckles screamed, "Don't fucking move! Stop what you're doing!"

I grabbed Knuckles and bodily threw him over the old berm, diving after him. We hit the ground behind an abutment that had been protecting soldiers for more than five hundred years, and the vehicle went off, an enormous, earth-shattering explosion.

The sky rained metal, the thumps and dings crashing among the trees, the smoke and heat from the explosion flowing over us. I could hear nothing, the overblast still punching through me. After a second or two, Knuckles groaned and rolled over. I did the same, then grabbed his shoulder and said, "You okay?"

He shook his head, looked at me and said, "That didn't work like we wanted."

I flopped back down and said, "Bullshit. I'm still breathing."

Lying on the couch, nursing my wounds, I heard the bell ring and said, "Jenn! Can you get that?"

She came out and saw me flopped like a beached walrus. She said, "How long are you going to milk this? It's been three weeks."

I said, "I didn't see *you* getting blown up."

She said, "Guess you're still just mostly dead. Should I look through your clothes for loose change?"

I smiled at the Miracle Max reference and said, "As you wish."

She rolled her eyes and said, "Car bomb goes off, and I never hear the end of it."

"Hey, I haven't been milking it. I've been doing my fair share around here."

She reached the door and said, "Really? That's what you call last night? Your fair share?"

I squinted at her, because certain things really did still hurt, but she ignored me, answering the door. I saw Kylie Hale, Kurt's niece, along with someone on crutches behind her. I knew who it was. I finally rose. "Veep. Come on in."

Kylie came in before him, speaking in a stern voice. "Seriously? You expect a warm welcome? You recruit him and then get him shot?"

I said nothing, simply holding out my arms, and she let me wrap her up. When I realized she wasn't going to kick my nuts, I said, "No, no. Come on. I didn't *get* him shot. He walked in front of a bullet."

She leaned back and said, "I'm talking to my uncle about this. Don't think I won't."

I shook Nick's hand and said, "Talk all you want. From what I hear, he's been cleared by the Oversight Council for future operations."

She said, "Against my wishes."

I looked at Nick and said, "Well, I heard his father threw his hat in the ring for president. So you should expect a little bit out of the son."

I saw him flush. He said, "Pike, about that garage thing. I don't think Brett told you after everything was done. He saw the door open. He pulled on the guy and I was still moving. I blocked his shot. I mean—"

I cut him off. "Jesus, you are one glutton for punishment. Are you seriously saying you deserved to be shot? Nobody, no matter what, *ever* says that shit. When Brett shows up, I expect for you to say *he* got *you* shot because he didn't trust his aim enough to pull the trigger."

Nick looked over my shoulder and said, "Speak of the devil."

Brett came in, walking right into Jennifer. He hugged her and said, "Mighty nice digs. Didn't expect this from Pike."

She said, "What on earth does Pike have to do with our place?"

He laughed, knowing it was true. I said, "Well, nobody else in here is dealing with the mice invasion. She keeps trying to catch them, and that's failed."

The conversation was loose and fun, but it was a thin veneer for why we were together. A brittle layer that everyone was afraid of cracking, but it had to happen sooner or later. That was the point.

Knuckles walked in, waving a bottle of Jameson Whiskey. I said, "What the hell is that? We drink Bacardi."

He hugged me, then Jennifer, and said, "We drink what Guy drinks."

And the brittle layer was cracked.

I said, "Yeah. Yeah, you're right. Just waiting on one. But serve them up."

The end state of the mission wasn't exactly textbook, but Guy George had been right all along. If anyone had listened to him to begin with, the rest of the sloppy mess wouldn't have occurred. The Taskforce had, as I'd thought, declined to do our usual memorial for fallen members. I didn't blame them, since Guy's actions had, in fact, jeopardized everything we stood for, but I'd be damned if he wasn't getting one. I'd planned my own.

I'd wanted to do it in DC, at our traditional haunt like we always did, right after his burial in Arlington, but Kurt had said it was poking a sore. Make no mistake, he sympathized, but he had more on his plate with the death of the secretary of state than I could ever comprehend. He didn't tell me no, but I got the message. I planned it for my own house, in Charleston, South Carolina, with only the team.

Well, the team and one other.

We'd managed to escape Norway intact, but it was a close-run thing. The chaos of the exploding Range Rover helped, of course, but the rental agreements on the motorcycles had hurt. Knuckles and I had escaped by traversing a footpath on the other side of the berm, never engaging any of the security or the follow-on police forces, leaving the bikes where they lay.

The fallout, irrespective of Billings's death, was as

messy as I'd ever seen, and we'd been cut off from all operations for the near term while the might of the US government went into damage control. So far, they'd managed to explain away a lot of things with innuendo and bullshit. The attack on the cottage had helped, but that too was hampered by blabbermouths.

I didn't pay attention, because I thought the entire mission was a disaster from the get-go. For the first time ever, I let the Oversight Council sort it out. They made the mess. They could clean it up.

Knuckles poured the shots, and the doorbell rang again. The final invitee.

I opened the door and saw Carly standing with her arms crossed, looking over the balcony. I said, "You made it. I hoped you would."

She turned around and smiled. "I wouldn't miss it. Thank you for the invite."

I said, "Thank Jennifer. For me, it was only returning the favor."

She came inside and said, "Trust me, that'll never happen again."

After the garage hit, Jennifer and Brett had transferred Khalid to Taskforce control. Our data from the thumb drive, coupled with his interrogation, had buried the QIA official known as Sharif al-Attiya. He was a bad, bad man. Well, he was a respected member of the Qatar government, but once we introduced his transgressions into our liaison system through the CIA, the government immediately considered him a bad, bad man. Like those fucks weren't doing the same all the time anyway.

CIA had taken the ball at that point, tracking Sharif to Istanbul, Turkey. They'd asked for his transfer back to Qatar, and the Turkish intelligence guys had balked, asking for Qatar to formally request him. Of course, the Qatar government wasn't going to officially request his arrest, as the information that he'd been complicit in killing the secretary of state would be explosive. And so we'd been called in. Well, more precisely, a rendition flight had been, along with some coordination with unsavory Turkish characters.

Carly had asked, and been given permission, to run the repatriation, and because of Taskforce involvement, she'd requested me to be included as an "observer."

It was really not a high-speed thing, but it was satisfying. We'd flown to Istanbul with a bunch of CIA black-clad Ninjas, none who would say a word. We exited the aircraft, drove to a hangar, and met some unknown Turkish thugs. In the trunk of a car, they had Sharif, wearing zip ties and a hood. We took him, put him on the plane, and landed in Doha, Qatar.

When we'd removed the hood, he saw the man we were turning him over to, and we walked away, hearing him screaming his innocence. Nobody said a word when the screams were cut off by a slap. It wasn't our business. We were just the delivery people.

Twenty minutes later, we were back in the air.

We'd landed in Washington, DC, and I'd said goodbye to the Ninjas. They still hadn't said a word. Even given that, it had been enjoyable.

I kissed Carly on the cheek and handed her a glass of whiskey. She took it, and I turned to the room. "Everyone's now here. For Guy."

They all said, "For Guy."

I raised the glass and said, "May he rest in peace."

Carly started to respond in the same, but was drowned out with "Peace is an illusion. May he continue to fight."

She looked at me, then Jennifer, who was drinking her whiskey. I said, "Just tradition."

She downed her own glass and said, "I think he'd like that."

I said, "Lord knows Guy's said it enough."

Jennifer came over, her eyes wet because she was a softy for this sort of thing.

Carly said, "Kurt called me today. Out of the blue. Somehow, he knew I was in the United States."

With mock surprise, I said, "Who would have told him that?"

"He wants to talk to me. And I think I know what it's about."

I caught movement out of the corner of my eye, on the counter. A flash of brown. I said, "Not tonight. I don't want to do business tonight. This is for Guy. Jennifer, go take her and show her girl things. She'd rather talk to you."

Jennifer smiled and said, "Actually, I'd love to. I'm sick of being the only woman in the room."

Carly asked, "You're really always the only female?"

"Well, there's this crazy lesbian assassin we sometimes work with, but I'm not sure she counts."

Carly had no idea what to make of that. I said, "Jennifer's just aggravated because she likes me more than her."

Jennifer rolled her eyes and said, "Wow. How do you get through the door with a head that big?" She shouted, "Kylie! Let's go to the porch. Leave the testosterone zone."

They went through the door and I turned, seeing the bane of my existence, that damn mouse, chewing on a beer cap, of all things. Brett was laughing at a joke, and I waved my hand, quieting the room. I slowly opened the drawer. I pulled out the meat tenderizer and inched forward, solely focused on my prey.

I didn't hear Knuckles tap on the sliding glass door, getting Jennifer's attention. Didn't see his grin.

A red Solo cup slapped into the side of my head. I heard "Pike! Don't you dare."

ACKNOWLEDGMENTS

The Taskforce was created out of whole cloth, completely made up by me for my novels, but I used my experiences to do so, tapping into what I knew of the world in which I'd lived. The organization is nothing more than a fantasy we wished existed whenever we ran into the inertia of US bureaucracy, but inside, we realized why such inertia exists, and it's precisely to prevent any one individual from misusing a dangerous asset. America has had a love/hate relationship with special operations throughout its history, resulting in many units being disbanded or rendered toothless the minute the threat was gone because the cure was believed to be worse than the disease. It is only in modern times that special operations have flourished, but it has come with a price. The crux of repeated covert action in a democracy is that a nation can go only so far before its actions begin to erode the very ideals the unit was designed to protect, which is precisely why we have such robust oversight in US Code. The Taskforce has no such constraints, and I've threaded the potential for its abuse throughout my books. This time, I decided to explore it as a main theme.

We've all seen movies with the one guy out for justice, clearly harmed by some evil cabal of the US government running amok—and enjoyed it when he took apart that evil. But we also like watching the lone hero bucking the system, fighting the timidity and inherent roadblocks in our government to save the day from a deadly terrorist attack because the buffoons in charge didn't understand the threat. Those two themes are prevalent, from Jason Bourne to John McClane in *Die Hard*. The truth is much more nuanced but not necessarily far removed. When I was in the military, in combat and elsewhere, I read and heard many opinions about "restrictive rules of engagement," and that if the military would "just be let loose" we'd get the job done. This sentiment has appeared from histories written about Vietnam to the current fights in Iraq and Afghanistan, but such thoughts—when translated into action—do have repercussions.

I always have a few Operators read my book before it goes to my editor just to make sure I've not crossed any lines I shouldn't, but in this case, that wasn't the problem. I knew I'd written what I wanted when an Operator told me, "I don't like this book. I don't like Guy. We would never do that."

He's right . . . to a point. We *haven't* done that, and nobody I've ever served with or known in my time in the military ever *would* do that. But then again, we don't have the Taskforce, either. A unit completely unconstrained. The theme was worth exploring.

I now had a plot without a concrete tie to any enemy. I could go anywhere with that theme, and so my wife suggested where that might be. The only time I had for book research happened to fall on my daughter's spring break. After all the time I've missed during my daughter's life, there was no way I was researching this book by myself. I asked her where we should go, and she said, "Greece. With our daughter."

On the one hand, my daughter—with the exception of a trip to the Cayman Islands (in case you wonder where the Castle idea came from, it's because we stayed there)—had never been outside the United States, so I thought it was a good idea just to provide her some exposure to the greater world. On the other hand, Greece? What the hell could I do with that?

I dug in with research, and the more I read, the more I realized the role the Greek peninsula plays in providing a crossroads vis-à-vis terrorism. I brought the *shahid* into the plot from a refugee ship, seeing that as a potential threat-stream but not realizing how big a mess the refugee crisis would become after I finished the book. The back-and-forth of Greece's debt problems is a real thing, and Qatar's investments and machinations with Islamic radicalism are as well, both providing ample grist for the mill. All that remained was to check it out in person.

I'm indebted to a tour guide who would prefer to remain nameless. She took my family on a tour of the Parthenon and every other tourist trap in Athens, and then, because I asked, she took me into the largest Alpha Bank in the city, getting me access to the areas I needed to see with her use of the Greek language. She was petrified about lying for me, and I probably would have done better on my own with the ham-handed way she got us into the secure areas, but I was committed at that point. In the end, I got what I needed, and I'm pretty sure she turned me in to the authorities afterward, but since I didn't actually rob anything, it worked out. I can't thank her enough.

To a friend stationed at the US Embassy in Athens, thanks for getting me in to see it. As promised, I didn't write anything that would cause a security issue. Thanks for dinner and the ride in your sweet, up-armored BMW.

My daughter thinks I'm James Bond now. Which, of course, I didn't correct.

The rest of the research I'm taking credit for. I ran my family to death, and I'm sure my daughter, when asked about Greece, will say, "We sure have a lot of pictures of alleys, Internet cafés, and seedy nightclubs. And I thought we were going to sink on a ferry run from Crete to Athens." Although she *did* locate every facility I needed to research on my paper map, using Google Translate from Greek websites. Each night I'd build my research for the following day and hand her a list. She'd turn the Greek into English, and off we went, preventing me from wasting time.

I always like to offer my meager abilities for charity, and in this case it was a little special. My wife was selected to chair a charity event benefiting the homeless in Charleston a year ago, complete with an auction. When she learned she'd been appointed, she said, "Don't dare give up a character for charity. Next year is mine." And so it was. Guy George is a real person, and by his name, many homeless people in Charleston now have food and clothes.

Guy George's brother is somewhat real as well. The idea for his demise came from my cousin, a Special Forces soldier doing a tour in Afghanistan and tracking the new threat of ISIS. Luckily, in real life the roles were reversed. Nobody on his team was harmed, but the ISIS cell ceased to exist.

I mention my wife, but now I'd like to recognize her for real. I left the Army in 2010, and her role in keeping our family together while I served is nothing short of remarkable. Since then, she's quit her profession and has taken over responsibility for my entire career. She runs the website, posts on Facebook, manages Twitter, coordinates and travels with me on book research trips, brainstorms book tour locations with my publicist, coordinates with the marketing team at Dutton, and generally runs my entire life. I write two books a year now, which squeezes out every bit of available time. Make no mistake, if it weren't for her, there is no way on earth I could even begin to do so. Oh, and she's hot.

As always, a shout-out to my uncompromising agent, John Talbot, and the entire Dutton publishing team. When I'm traveling on a security contract and pass through an airport in "not sure why there's an airport here" land, I'll see a book of mine, and I know why that book is there. It's because of the dedication and perseverance of the Dutton team. I'm always surprised when it happens, but I shouldn't be, given the effort they put in on my behalf. I'm still humbled you took a chance on me.

★ 1 ★

One day in September 2001

Dexter Trippler didn't set out to murder anyone. Nobody in his position would. As an up-and-coming small businessman, killing another human being would definitely be counterproductive to his goals. All he was doing was trying to ensure the growth of his company.

But he killed nonetheless.

Representing the position of president, CEO, CFO, and every other position on his firm's board—which is to say it was barely large enough to be called a "firm"—today was the day when he hoped to finally break out. To catch the whale of a contract that would allow him to quit groveling for scraps at the military industrial complex's table and start throwing out scraps of his own.

The owner of a small aircraft maintenance firm called Icarus Solutions—a name Dexter thought incredibly clever—he had struggled to survive for years, barely earning enough to pay the rent for his hangar at the Sarasota airport. He had lived hand to mouth for so long he was no longer sure what the opposite would be, his privileged upbringing a thing of the past. The pressure had destroyed his marriage—although that had probably been preordained with his choice of a bride, who was used to the better things in life. He cursed the misfortune that arrived time and time again, convinced it wasn't his abilities but unseen forces conspiring to drive him into the grave.

That all changed the day he met the prince.

Seven months earlier, an aircraft from Saudi Arabia had landed in Sarasota, Florida, and a pompous delegation had exited, running through a spring shower to a caravan of limousines. They'd raced out of the airport without talking to anyone, and then one of the pilots had approached his hangar. An Aussie or Kiwi from his accent, Dexter could tell he was upset, even if he tried not to show it. It turned out the aircraft had a maintenance issue, and nobody within the Sarasota Manatee Airport Authority was willing to help him in the timeline required. The pilot said the "prince" would be in the area for only about four hours, and he wouldn't be pleased if his plane wasn't airworthy when he returned.

Dexter had agreed to help, and one thing led to another, until a crown prince of the house of al-Saud was personally thanking him. The entourage then left in the same flurry in which it had arrived, and Dexter found himself standing next to the one Saudi Arabian who'd remained behind. His name was Tariq bin Abdul-Aziz, and he was the reason for the prince's visit. The son of an incredibly influential Saudi financier, he lived in Sarasota and wanted to learn to fly.

Strangely enough, they'd bonded through that mutual love of aviation, with Tariq showing up for coffee each morning just to watch the airplanes come and go. Somewhere in the conversations, Dexter had mentioned how he had failed to secure a single government contract in the entire time he'd been in business, and that Icarus

Solutions was on its last legs. Tariq had smiled knowingly, telling Dexter he didn't understand how such things worked, taking the time to explain in detail the slimy underbelly of government deal-making.

And now Dexter was committed. Driving up to the access control point for Tariq's neighborhood, he wondered if he'd made a mistake. Didn't matter, because it was too late to do anything about it now. He gave his name and identification to the guard manning the gate. The guard looked at it, compared it to a board in the shack, then handed him a pass. Dexter put it on the dash, then drove his Honda Civic through the gates of Tariq's posh neighborhood, hoping the darkness would hide the dents and gouges on the Civic's battered frame.

Ogling the ostentatious McMansions that lined the road, most garishly illuminated with lighting that should be reserved for the Vegas strip, he felt giddy and more than a little scared.

Either the prince had come through, or he hadn't. If he had, Dexter would build a McMansion of his own, perhaps in this same neighborhood. If he hadn't, well, Dexter was finished. His entire business—not to mention every other asset he owned—would be forfeited for the two million dollars he'd borrowed to make the "donation."

At least he'd never have to pay another blood cent to his shrew of an ex-wife.

Small consolations.

Two blocks from Tariq bin Abdul-Aziz's house, he unconsciously slowed, not wanting to hear the decision. Reflecting on what had brought him to this point. Without even realizing it, he drove past the house, seeing one of the four garage doors open, an SUV with the rear hatch raised in front of it, the lights on inside.

He backed up and swung into the driveway, his head-lights sweeping across someone with a suitcase. He squinted and saw it was Tariq.

He parked and got out, now considerably worried. "Tariq, hey, what's up?"

Startled, Tariq whirled around, then grinned sheep-ishly. "Dexter, you scared the shit out of me." No sooner had the curse word slipped from his mouth before he was glancing around, looking for his wife.

A small man with an olive complexion and a pencil-thin black mustache, Tariq had initially surprised Dexter with his Western habits, but Dexter had learned he'd spent the majority of his life outside of Saudi Arabia, hav-ing first attended boarding school in England before col-lege in America. His wife, on the other hand, was devoutly religious and didn't take kindly to his Western affections.

When she didn't appear, he loaded the suitcase into the rear of the SUV. Dexter noticed it was crammed to the windows with all manner of items, increasing his alarm.

He said, "What's all this? What's happening?"

Tariq smiled, saying, "I received some wonderful news. I made it into a prestigious graduate program in my home country, but I have to be there the day after tomorrow. We're flying home."

Dexter saw Tariq's wife coming toward them from in-side the garage, carrying a baby and wearing a black abaya, her head covered in a colorful hijab.

Confused, Dexter said, "You're all leaving? For good?"

"Yes. We have tickets for tonight, but I hope to come back in a year or two."

"What about the house? Your cars? The furniture?"

"It's my father's house, actually, and he will deal with it. It's nothing."

Finally, Dexter asked the question that mattered the most: "What about me?"

He saw confusion flit across Tariq's face and realized that two million dollars to this man was the same as a five-dollar bill to Dexter. Something that didn't really matter.

Dexter said, "We had a deal, right? I created the shell company and provided the required 'donation.' I know it's already been withdrawn. Don't tell me you guys screwed me over two million dollars. It's nothing to you, but everything to me."

Dexter finally saw recognition. Tariq said, "Yes, yes, I'm sorry. I've been so preoccupied with packing I forgot." He placed another suitcase in the back, then turned around, formally straightening up and extending his right hand. Dexter hesitantly took it, waiting.

Tariq said, "Congratulations. After fierce competition and extensive vetting, you beat out thirteen other international companies." He winked, then said, "Based on my father's recommendation, the royal family has selected you for the maintenance contract."

And like that, all the fear was washed away. Once a beggar of scraps, Dexter was now a player. The owner of a multimillion-dollar contract that would guarantee his rise.

Dazed, he started to reply when Tariq said, "I'm happy for you, my friend, but we're late for our flight. I'm sorry, but I have to go."

He reached into the SUV and retrieved a briefcase. He pulled out a folder and said, "All of your contacts are in there. Remember, you can't mention either my father or me. Just contact the people in there and they will do the rest."

Dexter nodded dumbly. Tariq hugged him, kissing both of his cheeks, then climbed into the driver's seat.

He checked to ensure his wife and baby were settled, then gave Dexter a two-finger salute before driving away.

Dexter turned to watch him go, slowly winding in a circle. The car's taillights receded around a corner, and Dexter was left reflecting on his new fortune. He gripped the folder hard enough to bend it, thinking one thought: *Need a new shell company.*

He drove his old Civic out of the land of milk and honey, pulling out his cell phone as he did so. He clicked on the speed dial for a contact labeled CHIP SAVOY.

There was no way he would let his money-grubbing ex-wife know about his newfound largess, and to keep that from happening, he needed Chip.

A fraternity brother from college, Chip had done much, much better than Dexter up until now. Currently a hedge-fund manager on Wall Street, Chip had been the one to walk him through the initial establishment of the shell company in the Bahamas for the Saudis, and also the one who had fronted the "donation" inside that shell company.

They had been as close as brothers in school, and whenever they were together, the present income disparity between the two men disappeared. Chip treated Dexter like he always had—as his own blood—but Dexter knew that at the end of the day, money mattered. Chip was smart and had done the research on the contract. When he'd seen the companies vying for it—all of them the biggest names in the industry—he'd realized the potential for massive profits, given Dexter's light footprint. He'd fronted Dexter the means for success because he expected a return. And Dexter had no illusion that if it had gone south, his "brother" would have taken everything he owned.

But that was water under the proverbial bridge, because it had worked. Now all Dexter needed to do was protect his investment.

The phone rang and rang, then went to voice mail. He left a message, fantasizing about the Playboy Bunny Chip was probably sleeping with at that very moment.

He turned onto Highway 41, going home, and was hit with a logjam of cars. Traffic was always a pain, but not at nine o'clock at night. And then he remembered: The president was visiting Sarasota, doing some good-deal thing at a local elementary school the next day. He'd arrived thirty minutes ago, and his security team had jammed up every major artery.

Dexter muttered in aggravation, then settled in to wait, his twenty-minute drive to a beer now drawn out to at least an hour.

★ 2 ★

Chip Savoy exited the subway, fighting his way through the great unwashed mass of people also striving to leave. One man bumped into him, spilling Chip's morning coffee and eliciting some choice words.

The daily morning commute was becoming very trying, but it was the price he would have to pay if he wanted to live in Greenwich, Connecticut, instead of Manhattan. The city had been cool and new when he was scraping by for a living, but that had been years ago. He hadn't had to scrape for anything in a long time, and he had eventually decided it would be prudent to move to the upscale landscape of Greenwich. Nothing makes money like more money, and acting rich was half the battle.

Fine suits, fine dining, and fine cars—all a show for his clients. Well, mostly a show. There was no denying he enjoyed it, with the exception of the commute.

He'd taken to leaving his house earlier and earlier in an effort to beat the rush, but as far as he could tell, the rush started sometime around five in the morning, and there was no way he was getting up in the dead of night to arrive at work hours before any other executive. He had appearances to keep up, after all.

He reached the street and entered the flow of people

swirling about, all headed purposefully somewhere, moving faster and faster, as if the time spent on the sidewalk was dangerous. He stopped, glancing into a cloudless blue sky, taking a moment to simply savor the day. Once inside the office, he knew this simple pleasure of doing nothing but breathing would be overshadowed by the dog-eat-dog world of making money.

Eventually, he crossed the street and entered his building's plaza, showing his badge to the security man and walking through a small turnstile. After a short wait, he walked into the elevator and rode to the ninety-fifth floor, with others getting off before him, stealing glances at him as they left. The higher one went, the more money was spent on the space, and he was going very high.

The company he worked for had the entire floor, and the elevator spilled right into the middle of it. He exited, seeing the young guns already at work, slaving away in a cubicle farm that stretched throughout the office, all striving to reach Chip's level.

In the not-too-distant past, Chip had been one of them. Now, he had an office. Not a corner one, to be sure, but at least one with a view of Manhattan. The corner office would come soon enough.

He said a few pleasantries as he went through, leaving the cube farm behind to his coveted space away from the chaos. He passed by his secretary's desk—she wouldn't be in for another hour—and unlocked his office. He swung open the door, and the reams of folders sitting on his desk gave him a spasm of regret. It was like a continual gushing of paper and electrons, all of them deals staggering in their monotony, with little inspiration and certainly no joy.

Was this how his life was to end? Working day after day cloistered in an office, slaving to make a profit for a company that didn't even know his name?

Lately, he had taken to fantasizing about doing something else. Something in the outdoors, where the money didn't matter. Maybe something in Alaska or . . . Borneo. Someplace that would allow him to flex his muscles instead of his ability to read numbers. A place he had always wanted to be but never had the courage to attempt.

In exactly one hour and forty-six minutes, in the brief second before his life was extinguished, he would dearly wish he'd made that choice.

He sat down to work, pulling the first folder to him. When his personal phone began buzzing, he realized he'd lost track of time in the mind-numbing tedium of his chosen career. He glanced at his ridiculously ostentatious Hublot Chronograph and saw it was 8:45 in the morning. Too early for a business call from one of the partners.

He recognized the number and relaxed, punching the answer button and saying, "Dexter, tell me the good news."

"How do you know it's good?"

"Because if it were bad, you'd wait until I had to track you down."

He heard laughter on the other end, then, "Yeah, it's good. I got the contract. I have all the POCs and I've already talked to one. It's real. I'm in."

Chip stood, gazing out at the Manhattan skyline. "I'm glad to hear it, bud. Last thing I wanted to do was answer for a two-mil loss. When do you leave?"

"I haven't figured that out yet. Hey, Chip, the reason I'm calling is I want to set up my own shell company in the Bahamas. With that law office in Panama like we did with the Saudis."

"Mossack Fonseca? Why? You doing something illegal?"

"I thought you said it was perfectly legal."

Chip laughed and said, "It is, but it's never used that way. It's used to hide assets from taxes."

"Well, that's exactly what I want to do, except hide it from that bitch of an ex-wife."

Chip saw a speck in the distance, growing larger. He put up a hand to shield his eyes and said, "Ahhh . . . I see. Yeah, I can set that up. Actually, it'll work for taxes, too."

He paused, watching the speck grow impossibly large in the span of a second. He managed to get out "Holy shit," before a Boeing 767, last known as American Airlines Flight 11, slammed into the side of the North Tower, tearing through the heart of the building with the force of an avalanche and bringing with it 350,000 pounds of steel and jet fuel that incinerated all in its path.

Sitting in the den of his house, Dexter heard Chip shout, then silence. He said, "Chip? Chip, you still there?" He got nothing.

He redialed the phone, but Chip's line went straight to voice mail. He stood up and went to his Rolodex in his makeshift office, digging through until he found Chip's landline. It was no better. He went back into the den, thinking about whom he could call next, when he saw a breaking news story on his television.

He sat down heavily, not believing the grainy image of an airplane smashing into the World Trade Center.

He remained glued to the television the rest of the day, numb to the carnage. He spent hours on the phone with other fraternity brothers, trying to confirm what he already knew in his heart. Initially, like many, he felt outrage and anger. It wasn't until later that he would feel fear, when he saw a picture of Mohamed Atta, the ringleader of the hijackers.

A man he'd once seen at Tariq Abdul-Aziz's house.

★ 3 ★

I wiped the sweat from my eyes, the oppressive Charleston humidity making it feel like I was breathing water, even at seven in the morning. I waited for Jennifer to arrive, keeping track of her time and eyeing the eight-foot wood wall in front of me.

This was it. The cutline for winning the bet, and Jennifer knew it. I could smoke her on flat runs, swimming, and everything else, but I would be lucky to beat her on an obstacle course—especially after she modified each one to suit her strengths. But I had some leveling of my own planned.

She ran up, sprinting the last hundred meters, looked at her time, then put her hands on her hips, breathing deeply. She said, "You want to do double or nothing? Before we go?"

Standing there in her Nike shorts, ponytail askew, after losing all three of the first legs of the triad, it was a pretty bold pronouncement. She had a lot to lose.

I said, "What's the 'double,' since we aren't talking money?"

She'd apparently been thinking about it, because she

said without hesitation, "You clean the cat box and do the dishes for a solid month. No bitching about how you cooked or that the cat hates you. You just do it."

A pretty strict bet. We shared the duties in our house—which meant I let her do them when she couldn't stand the filth building up—but if I lost, I'd be on her timeline. Which meant I'd actually have to clean.

On the other hand, if I won, I'd get . . . well, something more.

Choices, choices.

Two weeks before we'd started talking about the differences in physical abilities between men and women, a conversation borne from the fact that women were now allowed into all combat positions in the military. I was against it for some select specialties, and—of course—she was for it all the way. One thing led to another, and we'd made a bet. A race, so to speak, with winner take all. To make it fair, we'd debated the rules and the course. We'd already completed 90 percent of the events, and I'd won handily on most—the swim being the only one that was pretty much a draw. But now we had the obstacle course on the grounds of the Citadel, the military college of South Carolina.

As obstacle courses go, it wasn't that big a deal—the usual log-walk-rope-drop chain of events—but after surveying the thing, Jennifer had made a modification for every single obstacle. For one, we couldn't just climb the rope, touch the top, and come down. We had to climb the rope, get on top of the beam holding it, and traverse to the far side.

I knew why. She was a damn monkey, and she knew that while I could win on pure strength, I couldn't match her climbing skills. I'd agreed because I knew I'd be so far ahead on points when we reached the obstacle course, I'd be able to coast.

Only I wasn't that far ahead. Not nearly as far ahead in our agreed point structure as I thought I would be. She'd proven to be in better shape than I expected—especially on the mental side. The ruck march should have crushed her mentally, but she finished the damn thing only eighteen minutes behind me, slogging over the Ravenel Bridge on willpower alone, the sixty-pound ruck looking like a giant tick on her back, making me wish I'd run the entire twelve miles instead of keeping Jennifer in sight, toying with her. I *really* wished I hadn't agreed to the point spread on the obstacle course. Because I was in danger of losing.

But there's no way I would admit that.

I said, "Okay. You're on. But if I win, I get twice as much."

She scowled and said, "I can't believe you think that's appropriate. I was assuming I'd just clean for a month."

I grinned. "You're sure you'll win. What's the risk?"

Still not agreeing, she kicked the body armor I'd managed to scrounge from a buddy at a National Guard armory near our office in Mount Pleasant. She said, "This is a handicap that I shouldn't have to wear. We don't do big army."

"No, we don't, but it's a handicap for every single male on the battlefield. You want to prove your point, put it on."

She did so, now wearing about thirty pounds of ceramic plates ensconced in a vest that would alter her ability to navigate the obstacles. I put on my own armor, looked at my watch, and said, "Ready?"

She nodded, staring at the wall so intensely it was almost comical. I said, "Five, four, three, two, one."

On the utterance of, "Whuu—" she took off, hitting the eight-foot wall in front of us and leaping over. I shouted, "Hey!" but she wasn't stopping. I sprinted to the wall, getting over it and seeing her on the obstacle called the "belly buster."

Basically, all you had to do was leap up onto a fat horizontal tree trunk about four feet off the ground, then jump out and catch another, higher, pole—usually by slamming into it with your belly while your arms draped over the top, hence the name—and pull yourself over. Simple. Except Jennifer had dictated that you had to go over the top pole, then back around, then fling yourself to the lower pole again. If you couldn't maintain your balance, you started over.

I saw her leap, then swing her body in a circle around the log, like some Neanderthal gymnast on bars. She made it completely around, but her armor caught on something, threatening to cause her to fall. She clamped on with her legs just as I leapt up on the belly buster next to her. I swung my arms once, then launched myself into the air for the high log. I slammed into it, got around about half as gracefully as she had, and saw her fling herself back to the lower log. I did the same, smiling that I'd caught her. If she was slowed down by the armor on this obstacle, it would even it up for me the rest of the way because it would hamper her on every other one.

She balanced on the lower log, then leapt back to the high one, scrambling to get over it and on with the course. I hit the lower log, windmilled my arms, and fell off.

Shit.

By the time I was through it, she was already on the ropes, two obstacles ahead of me, climbing like a demented spider monkey even with the armor on. She scrambled to the top of the frame holding the ropes, then began *running* down the four-by-four to the far side. No way would I be able to match that.

The course was two miles long, and I'd have to pray that the armor wore her out. I lost sight of her in the trees and just focused on my own technique, racing through obstacle after obstacle. Eventually, shouting penetrated the haze of my concentration.

To my right, some guy in uniform was yelling and waving his arms around. I caught a flash of Jennifer ahead of me. I ignored him, picking up the pace. I had only about a quarter of a mile to catch her before the end of the course, and the way we'd dictated the rules, every second was going to cost me dearly in points. Maybe weighing this part so heavily wasn't such a bright idea after all.

I saw Jennifer scrambling up the second rope obstacle—this one was supposed to be a simple swing across a mud pit, but like an idiot, I'd agreed to Jennifer's monkey modifications.

She got halfway up when she, too, heard the shouting. I saw her look at the man as I cleared the one obstacle between us. She climbed back down, then swung herself across the mud to the grass on the far side. I leapt up, grabbed the rope, and started climbing. She said, "Pike, there's someone shouting at us."

I reached the top and said, "So?"

I got on top of the beam just as the man reached Jennifer, screaming about what the hell we were doing here. He pointed up at me and said, "Get down from there."

I said, "Okay," and tight-ropewalked to the far side, arms out for balance. I hung from the beam, then dropped. I saw him with his hands on his hips, glaring at me, Jennifer looking like a toddler in trouble next to him.

And I knew I was going to win. Jennifer had an innate moral streak that would prevent her from not following the man's instructions. She would try to calm him and explain that we had permission to be here—which we did.

I, on the other hand, would finish the course. I saw both of their mouths drop open when I took off at a sprint toward the final obstacles, then heard Jennifer shout, "Pike! Get your ass back here!"

If I were smart, I really would have. But I had a bet to win.

By the time I'd finished the course and circled back through the woods, she was in a fine fury, glowering at me as I walked up with a "What did I do?" look on my face.

The man said, "She says you have permission from the Marine Corps to use this."

The Marine Corps ROTC department at the Citadel managed the O course. They'd actually built it, using their funds, but it was on Citadel property, so it was always a little push and shove over who actually had the right to grant permission to use it.

I said, "Yeah, Gunny told me it wouldn't be an issue, with it being Sunday morning and all."

"Well, he didn't clear it with the grounds department. There are releases, legal issues, a whole host of things—especially with the way you were doing the obstacles. We have an SOP for this thing, and you were way outside of it. I'm within my rights to call the police on you for trespassing."

I raised my hands and said, "Okay, okay, we're done anyway. Won't happen again. Sorry for the trouble."

Mollified, he said, "And I'm going to talk to the Gunny about this."

I rolled my eyes and said, "Fine. Can we go now?"

He nodded his head, and I began to walk to the start, Jennifer right behind me. When we were out of earshot, she punched my back and hissed, "I thought you said you had permission for this?"

"I did."

"No, you didn't. I've never been so embarrassed. And you kept going, leaving me there to try to explain. I don't even know what a 'Gunny' is."

I laughed and said, "So, is this about being embarrassed by that groundskeeper, or losing the bet?"

That really set her off. "Losing? Losing! If I hadn't stopped, he would have called the police. We'd be in the back of a squad car right now."

We reached the parking lot where I'd pre-staged a vehicle, and in a pious tone, I said, "Always remember the mission. Mission comes first. I finished the O course ahead of you, which means I won every event. Which means I'm the winner."

She became apoplectic, her mouth opening and closing without a sound coming out.

I said, "And I'm holding you to the double-or-nothing. I think you can pay the first installment when we get home."

Livid, she spit out, "I'll do *no such thing*. You are *disqualified* for cheating."

I laughed and said, "Calm down, little Jedi. You're going to blow a blood vessel in your head."

She took off her armor and got into the car without another word, slamming the door. I did the same, getting behind the wheel. Having had my fun and wanting to smooth things over, I said, "We'll call this one a draw due to outside interference."

She muttered, "Because you knew I was going to beat your ass."

Before I could get out a smart-aleck reply, my phone rang with a special tone. The one telling me it was a secure call. Meaning we might have some business.

I looked at Jennifer and saw the same little thrill I was

feeling, the earlier fight lost to history. No matter what I thought about the physical abilities of the fairer sex, there was no denying that mentally—at least for those like Jennifer—females were solid in a gunfight. I'd seen that numerous times firsthand. She wouldn't admit it, but she lived for the missions just like I did.

I put the car in drive and tossed her my phone, saying, "You can do the honors."

Driving back to our row house on East Bay I got only her side of the conversation, but from what I heard, we were headed out pretty quickly. She hung up and laid the phone down. I said, "Well?"

"Well, it looks like that Panama Papers scare has surfaced again. Kurt wants us in DC today. He's got us tickets on a flight in a couple of hours."

"I thought they'd scrubbed that data and we were in the clear."

"Yeah, they did, but apparently there's an 'Agent Zero' out there who's got another load he's going to release."

★ 4 ★

Dexter Trippler glanced at the time once again, then went back to his computer screen, searching a news story, willing it to have additional information. He'd been doing the same motion every thirty seconds for the past ten minutes.

Where the hell is he?

He scanned the story for the hundredth time, and it didn't get any less explosive. The International Consortium of Investigative Journalists—a collection of networked reporters who spanned the globe—was preparing to release a second data dump of the so-called Panama Papers.

The first leak had occurred in the spring of last year, and it was the largest illegal data dump in history, encompassing terabytes of information, so much so that one could stack WikiLeaks, Snowden, Target Inc., and every other leak together, and the Panama Papers would far eclipse them.

The target was a Panamanian law firm called Mossack Fonseca that specialized in off-shore shell companies. Completely legal on the surface, its main focus was hiding wealth from authorities, as the intricacies and subterfuge of the shell companies was almost impossible to penetrate—unless some insider calling himself Agent Zero decided to leak the information.

None of this would have mattered a whit to Dexter, except Mossack Fonseca was the same company that he'd used with the Saudis more than a decade before. When the first leak had occurred, he had lived in terror for a month, consumed with the fear that his association with Tariq and his father would be outed—along with Dexter's long-held suspicions that they had a hand in 9/11.

It had not. Even given the enormous scope of the leak, Dexter's shell company had remained ensconced inside Mossack Fonseca's digital fortress, protecting him from discovery. But now there was supposedly another leak on the way, and Dexter had much, much more to lose than he had a decade ago.

Although he'd never spoken to Tariq again—afraid of finding out his darkest fear and convinced that any communication would be monitored by federal authorities—he had taken the contract in Saudi Arabia, and it had proven lucrative.

He learned that having a contract begat more contracts, and he began to expand his business, branching out from simple aviation services to full-spectrum military industrialist titan. He had defense contracts encompassing everything from providing interpreters to SOCOM in Uganda to electronic perimeter security at a US consulate in Mali.

In short, he was now a player, and with that power came a duty to prevent this new leak from bringing everything down. He'd worked too long and hard, developing influence both in the halls of Congress and the halls of the Pentagon, and in the ensuing years he'd learned to play hardball better than most. It was why he was successful.

He leaned forward and punched an intercom button, saying, "Janice, has Johan called you about being late?"

Before she could answer, he caught a movement at the door, then recognized his head of security, Johan van Rensburg.

Dexter said, "Where the hell have you been?"

Speaking with a light Afrikaans accent, Johan said, "I just got in. I was delayed at JFK and had to spend the night."

"I thought you were coming in two days ago."

"Couldn't get out of Jordan. You told me to make sure the work was done before I came home."

Dexter's latest venture was a contract from Jordan's King Abdullah II Special Operations Training Center, providing armorer support to the various courses run there, with an eye toward increasing beyond that into the security realm itself.

Created jointly between the United States and Jordan in 2009, KASOTC was the only Special Operations training facility of its kind in the Middle East, with ranges and mock-ups that rivaled anything in Europe or the United States, and it was used by multiple countries on an invitation basis. Run solely by ex-operators from various countries, one could just as easily run across a Brit formerly in the SAS as an American from US Army Special Forces. It was where Dexter had initially met Johan, and had convinced him to leave his current contract as a CQB instructor with KASOTC and come work for Icarus Solutions as the head of Dexter's fledgling security division.

A former member of South Africa's famed Reconnaissance Commandos—the Recces—he'd left the military after the turmoil in his country in the early nineties. He'd bounced around from job to job, most on the African continent at various hot spots. He'd fought with Executive Outcomes in Sierra Leone, Sandline International in Liberia, and, most recently, at the behest of the Nigerian government against Boko Haram. He'd eventually tired of getting shot at and decided to go the route of training instead of operations, landing the job at KASOTC. Dexter wasn't privy to most of his past, but he was capable, no doubt, a fact that was belied by his ascetic appearance.

Unlike the Hollywood portrayal of SOF supermen, Johan wasn't a bulked-up Arnold Schwarzenegger, but more wiry, with ropes of muscle clinging closely to his frame and what looked like a permanent tan baked into his skin. Dexter didn't know all he'd done, but he'd heard enough from rumors, and he knew the scars on Johan's body hadn't come from playing rugby.

Johan said, "What's the fire? Why'd you call me back?"

Dexter pointed to a seat and said, "I've got an issue. Something that could cause significant problems with Icarus."

Johan sat down and said, "Okay."

Dexter toyed with a paperweight biplane, realizing he was treading on ground that he didn't want to plow. Afraid of what would come out. Dexter was a manager of aviation assets—things that flew. He had no experience in the real world of war, only the machines that dealt the death. He worked in the "defense industry," and, while that could possibly get him on TV as an expert, he knew he had no real claim to such a title. All of his employees were support—mechanics, logisticians, armorers, and the like. He had no real "security" experience at the sharp end of the spear. Johan was the only man he knew who could prevent the leak, but in so doing, Dexter would be placing significant trust in him. Giving him knowledge that could be used against him in the future.

There was also the problem of Johan's willingness to execute. He was a hard man, no doubt, but he'd shown a perverse sense of honor. There was no telling where he would side on this. He was ruthless to a fault, but only for things he deemed worthy. Dexter wasn't sure job security would measure up. Johan was a cynical killer on the surface, but underneath, he believed. He would not do anything against his personal code of conduct. And that code was written in stone.

Then Dexter remembered a conversation he'd had with the South African when he'd initially hired him: The man hated traitors, and considered organizations like WikiLeaks as enablers for the theft of national secrets. On top of that, he absolutely despised the press for perceived transgressions against South Africa, and that had continued on into his mercenary days. One night, after a few beers and a single question by Dexter, Johan had become apoplectic, ranting like a madman. To the point that Dexter had felt fear. The Panama Papers bore none of those taints, but it was similar in technique. All he had to do was spin it the right way.

Johan said, "Well?"

Dexter formulated his words but couldn't look him in the eyes. Johan always had a way of peeling back the soul, like he was mentally flaying you, and it was unsettling. Dexter was sure he'd falter if he locked eyes with the man.

He continued playing with the paperweight airplane, saying, "Do you remember the Panama Papers last year?"

★ 5 ★

Johan said, "Yeah. Some fuck stole a bunch of propri-etary information and gave it to journalists. What about it?"

"I told you about how this company was founded. About the first contract in KSA. You remember that?"

"Yes."

"Well, it was predicated—and I'm not proud of this—on a bribe to a certain Saudi contact. I did it, and now I'm where I am. *You* are where you are. No more run-ning and gunning. A nice job with a hefty salary."

"What was the bribe for?"

Dexter shifted the conversation, saying, "I used a shell company from that law firm in Panama. The first leak—before I hired you—was huge, but I wasn't in it."

Dexter pointed at the computer screen and said, "There's a second leak coming, and there's a good chance I'll be in it. If that happens, at best, I'll be crushed for the relationship by the prima donna politicians all look-ing for a score, and worst, arrested for illegal contract negotiations and insider trading."

He paused, wanting to see if Johan was on board, risking a glance across the desk. He couldn't tell one way or the other. The man's face was stoic, his shaggy blond hair partially covering his eyes. Dexter sagged back in his chair and said, "If that leak goes, I'm out of a company. And you're out of a job."

Johan leaned forward, brushing his hair aside and giving Dexter his full, uncomfortable attention. He said, "What's that got to do with me? What do you want me to do?"

Dexter said, "Well . . . I know who the reporter is that's going to meet the leaker, a sorry sack of shit like Snowden and Manning. I was hoping you'd meet the leaker instead. Convince him it wasn't in his best interests."

Johan picked an M&M from a bowl on the desk, popped it into his mouth, and said, "I could do that, I suppose. One less waste of flesh walking the earth, but it's not without risk."

"I understand. I'm prepared to pay you a great deal. This bribe I did can't see the light of day. Ever. It was nothing on the grand scheme of things, but it's everything to us."

Johan popped another M&M and said, "You keep saying that, but I've worked this side of the fence for a while. Bribes happen all the time, and you have leverage with the American establishment. Maybe it's better to let it out and fight it on the publicity front. My way is dirty."

"No. That won't work."

Johan straightened and said, "Why? You have the ear of sitting senators and half the generals in the Pentagon. Unless there's something more. What was the bribe for? Who got it?"

"It's not the bribe. It's the fact that it's Saudi Arabia. Ten years ago, that would be nothing. Now, with the Islamophobia rampant in the United States, I'll be crucified, no pun intended. I can't count on support from the

Pentagon or Congress. Especially after the administration released those classified pages from the Congressional inquiry into 9/11. The ones dealing with Saudi complicity in the attacks."

"Okay. Once again, what do you want me to do?"

"Interdict this 'Agent Zero.' Get his data, and destroy it."

Johan considered the mission, then said, "You want him dead. Is that it?"

Dexter hadn't thought about that, the question startling him.

Johan said, "Let's face it, if I meet him as the journalist, and I get his information, and it doesn't get exposed, he's just going to try again."

Dexter said, "Yes. I see your point. I suppose you couldn't just convince him?"

Johan barked a sharp laugh and said, "I could for the five minutes we were together, but once he's gone—and safe—he'll reconsider. He understands the risks. He's made powerful enemies with his release, which means he has courage."

Dexter nodded, knowing what he'd said was true. The Panama Papers had exposed corruption from the highest levels of foreign governments to the biggest bosses of organized crime. Whoever Agent Zero was, there were plenty of people who wanted him dead. Which made the decision easier. With that many enemies, nobody would connect a lone defense contractor to the action.

Dexter said, "I don't want the information out. Period. You do what you think is best. You'll be well rewarded."

He withdrew an envelope and laid it on the desk, saying, "This is the information on the reporter who's going to meet him. Don't ask me how I got it. Just understand that it cost a significant amount of influence and money.

You talk to him, find the meeting site, then assume his place."

Johan took the envelope and opened it. He glanced at the first page and said, "International Consortium of Investigative Journalists. Washington DC."

"Yes. I'll pay for the airfare and hotels, of course. And a handsome bonus when it's done. I'd like you to leave tomorrow."

"What about the journalist?"

"What do you mean?"

"Well, I can't just ask him for the source and expect him to gladly give it to me. And once I leave, he'll contact this Agent Asshole and tell him to flee."

Dexter instinctively knew where the question was headed, but didn't want to face the decision. Johan saved him from the problem.

He stood and said, "Don't worry about it. I fucking hate reporters. All a bunch of lying shitheads with rainbows and noble causes. They destroyed my country, then destroyed my employment in Africa, first with Executive Outcomes, then every other company I worked for. Now, they're trying to destroy me again."

He pocketed the envelope and said, "I'll do him for free."

FROM *NEW YORK TIMES* BESTSELLING AUTHOR

BRAD TAYLOR

The thrilling series featuring **PIKE LOGAN**
and the extralegal counterterrorist unit
known as the Taskforce

ONE ROUGH MAN
ALL NECESSARY FORCE
ENEMY OF MINE
THE WIDOW'S STRIKE
THE POLARIS PROTOCOL
DAYS OF RAGE
NO FORTUNATE SON
THE INSIDER THREAT
THE FORGOTTEN SOLDIER
GHOSTS OF WAR

And make sure to look for
RING OF FIRE
in hardcover.

"[Brad Taylor] is spot-on."—VINCE FLYNN

BRADTAYLORBOOKS.COM
 BRADTAYLORBOOKS